CRUISE SHIP CRIME I

CRUISE SHIP LAUNDRY WARS

STUART ST PAUL

Version 13th Dec 2020
Copyright © 2020 Stuart St Paul
All rights reserved.
DORIS VISITS BOOKS
Northwood, England.

ISBN-13: 9781727772739

Fast paced crime novels set during a cruise
(that you might be on).

Disastrous COVID-19 Cruise Romance
The cruise crime book series
C.S.C.I.
CRUISE SHIP CRIME INVESTIGATORS

(Season 1 – Building an Agency)

Cruise Ship Heist	Book 1	Paperback Kindle	ISBN: 9781798236024 ASIN: B07P93DDTV
Cruise Ship Serial Killer	Book 2	Paperback Kindle	ISBN: 9781548952839 ASIN: B07XV5S32J
Cruise Ship Laundry Wars	Book 3	Paperback Kindle	ISBN: 9781727772739 ASIN: B086VMRXXM
Cruise Ship Art Theft	Book 4	Paperback Kindle	**ISBN:** 9798630583253 ASIN: B08KGS6XTH

Disastrous Covid-19 Cruise Romance
　　　　　　　　　　　　Book 5　　Paperback　**ISBN:** 9798656058223
　　　　　　　　　　　　　　　　　　Kindle　　　ASIN:B08Q3FJ8LQ

Read Any Book
They can all be read as stand-alone stories, but the growth of the agency and character development are appreciated by reading in order or going back to see how the story got where it is. Enjoy.

For quizzers and new cruisers or those who always wondered, our compendium of terms is out.

ABC of Cruising:　　　Paperback　　**ISBN:** 9798577831660
　　　　　　　　　　　　Kindle　　　　ASIN: B08Q7S8D1K

ALL BOOKS AVAILABLE ON AMAZON

Most ships are totally multicultural, with a wide mix of nationalities and various languages as well as varied versions of English spoken below decks. These books reflect that.

This is totally a work of fiction. Any references to ships, locations and characters are invented. They may take from reality to create and give the book an authentic sense of cruising, albeit a side of cruising often never seen by the guest. All names, references, characters (Except for our dear friend, comedy magician, Manuel Martinez, with his permission), ships and incidents are all a product of the author's wild imagination.

Some ships don't have a laundry.
Some have one on every deck.
But they are objects, they don't war. People war.

There are wars in the laundry as cruisers know, some nasty tricks, but the story is far more serious than the title suggests – it is in both the guest Laundry and the huge ship's laundry.

CSCI can have no idea how big this problem is, they cannot even imagine. They do smell trouble; they only deal with big trouble. But not even Interpol were ready for this. Expect the unexpected.

In this novel, Cruise Ship Crime Detectives employ their first female investigators.

This, the third book in the series follows

CRUISE SHIP HEIST
CRUISE SHIP SERIAL MURDERS

It is not necessary to have read the previous book

1 WRONG ANSWER

Everything is bright white in the blistering early morning sun, except for the cell phone resting on Kieron's short-sleeved white-cotton, open-collared shirt. His hair is short growing back over a scarred injured skull and his dark tan helps him look very well. His otherwise fit athletic frame is stretched out on his white rocking chair though his serene peace and quiet has been broken by the call. His feet reach to the white rails of the first-floor veranda around his beautiful bougainvillaea and bird song surrounded house.

"No!" Kieron says.

"Great!" comes through the speaker.

"Not great. That's no," Kieron insists with the charm of a romantic fifties-era movie star in his British army officer accent. His unwillingness to work might be because he is still recuperating in the Caribbean island of Bequia. Hunter has had to deal with the pressures of mainland Miami and may think his partner has unwound too much. They are on the same time zone but not the same page.

"I'll pick you up from the airport," Hunter persists through the phone.

"No. You're not listening," Kieron says, but the caller has hung up.

Curious at the demand, he draws his feet back and stands slowly, cell in hand. The sudden rise makes him dizzy and he steps forward to keep his balance. He drops his cell phone into the top pocket of his shirt and takes a moment. Holding the door frame, he gains his composure, then ever the soldier he brushes his tailored white shorts straight.

Back in Miami, Hunter stands silhouetted at a large window looking down at a busy America; coaches parking, tourists de-bussing and jockeying for their luggage. He is nodding his head and speaking into his cell to his friend who has deliberately long gone.

"Great!"

He spins his cell phone annoyingly like an executive toy as he turns. Behind him is a wall covered in seafaring memorabilia from the company's previous cruise ships, ships that no longer sail with the company. From all over the world there are framed pictures and plaques commemorating first ports of call.

"He's excited. Can't wait. It's an unusual job for us."

He sits at the dark polished wood conference table that looks amiss in the otherwise typical plush modern office meeting room. Opposite him are two unwavering young executives in expensive, well-cut suits. Their name badges say, Chet Dean, and Bjorn Ironside, 'Three Kings Executives', an essential uniform accessory used on ships and continued on land. They ooze ambition and determination. Having them on a promotion ladder below must keep all above on their toes. Taking notes is a female Assistant Executive, her name, Diana Mond. Her badge is far from straight, and the cut of her black trouser suit and cheap heavy shoes show no ambition other than to finish the day. She is bored and finding it hard to stay awake even though the day has yet to start.

In the middle of a long table is an untouched water jug with half-melted ice like an egg timer speeding towards the end of the meeting. The early morning low sun bursting through the window has no guilt in hurrying it along. This is a place of pressure. Even the palms in the corners of the room fail to foster a relaxing environment, they bend to the light, trying to escape.

Hunter no longer has the energy to jump around after ever-younger seemingly soulless management. His days of leaping out of a plane into an ocean to solve crimes on cruise ships could be over. These executives seem too young, too junior but, but maybe he is getting older. However, Hunter is willing to humour the aspirations of these two youths because he has his own plan, a plan that suits him and will suit Kieron. It could mean he is looking retirement in the eye just as his buddy Kieron seems to be doing in the Caribbean. He just needs to get it straight before he reveals it. The cruise job, simple but very well paid, is not what he is excited about. It is where it takes them. It could be their final job. His military training still ensures he surreptitiously takes photo-shots of both executives in between spinning his smartphone.

"The deal is both of you," Chet insists.

Hunter is pulled up by that remark but keeps his poker face as he looks from Chet to Bjorn,

"This needs a couple onboard acting like guests," Chet says.

"Sure, Kieron and a female agent. I'll work as point man in the office."

Both the executives change expression.

"Why can't two men be a couple?" Bjorn says. He is the more serious one of the two.

"No. No. That won't work," Hunter is quick to repel. He thinks carefully before his next answer dates him, but he is beaten to the space.

"Gender is a continuum from heterosexual to homosexual. No need for rigidity, or to fit in, or stay anywhere on such a scale. You can both be non-binary," Bjorn suggests.

"My wife's pregnant. I like my position on the scale."

"Act," Chet suggests.

Hunter and Commander Kieron Philips were both serious special forces operatives. They may have been able to imitate any character behind the lines, but them as a couple on a cruise ship would stretch believability. If not for themselves, for the very traditional guest cruisers aboard. If these guys don't know their market, then this job is not for them. They worry him, not because the younger generation is far less judgmental, but their ambition is blind.

"We fought a lot of people far senior to ourselves to bring in outside help," Bjorn insists.

"You're using us to try and prove something?"

"To solve and suppress something efficiently," Chet says.

There is no doubt these two have a point to prove, it is beginning to seem more about them than the mission. Hunter slips his phone into record.

"Money transfer upfront."

"Deal memo done!" Chet says sliding a paper across the table.

Normally when staring at someone Hunter would focus on their top lip, not the eyes. It allows for a greater peripheral vision of the whole-body movement. These guys are not going to pull a gun, but it is the figure he threw at them in jest he is looking at, and he can see both his and Kieron's name.

Chet and Bjorn may both be many years his junior, but their determination is in no doubt. Hunter takes the deal memo and stands,

"I'll get back to you."

"We've signed off. It's functioned," Bjorn states. "Di, send all details of sailing and flights to Lisbon across to their office."

"We'll work something out. The ice cubes have melted," Hunter says rising.

"The ship sails tomorrow," Bjorn says without a smile.

Hunter walks away from the lavish cruise headquarters on Dodge Island, the purpose-built cruise island. There are huge cruise ships all along the dock. Everywhere people hustle with enough luggage to be moving to a new house. It is a world he knows very well having done years on mega floating hotels after leaving the military. That combination of talents might make him special on a ship, but understanding millennials is not his area of expertise. He chases a cab. If he went to the cabstand he would be standing in line with tourists and he doesn't have time. Sitting inside he studies the deal memo over and over, and the schedule which is the problem. Chocolate bars are being thrown in the laundry dryers on formal evenings on each of the Three King ships. He calls Kieron once again.

Kieron Philips walks out of his stylishly decorated washroom into an even more lavish bedroom. It looks like no one has ever lived there. Even his ruffled bed appears deliberately dressed for a magazine photoshoot, other than the small spills of blood on the pillow. He collects his Beechfield Straw Trilby hat from the wooden clothes stand and answers the phone again.

"Caribbean office," he smirks.

"OK. I'm laughing."

"Let's compare. Where are you sitting?" Kieron asks, slipping his mobile back into his top pocket so he can use both hands to steady himself but communicate.

"I'm relaxing. In a deck chair," Hunter answers.

"You have those in America?"

Hunter's cab pulls up in the disused, boarded-up commercial square of units. The less attractive side of Miami. He walks to the only sign of life, the two units in the top corner, past their CSCI unit with the unbranded jet-black glass windows, to the steely retro diner, 'Wild Mary's'. He turns back to look at the empty car park.

"We invented deck chairs! I'm outside the office, baking in the Florida sun."

Kieron's position in peace and luxury feels far more inviting. He stands at the top of the stairs by a large open window, white hand-crocheted net-curtains blow in the soft sea wind. Kieron smells the Bougainvillea outside.

"Your sweet smell of diesel, how I miss it," Kieron mocks via his shirt pocket. He carefully takes the first step down. "So, someone's been murdered on a ship and you can't cope without me?"

"No, there's been a few chocolate bars thrown in tumble dryers. I thought you could work your way off the subs' bench slowly," he hears.

Kieron pulls up at the remark, slips, and falters at the top of the stairs. He catches himself before a fall, but the fall that nearly killed him on his last job flashes through his head. He sits on the step.

2 WHAT CAN YOU SMELL?

Wild Mary's diner is a wash of red and cream seats trimmed with polished chrome. Hunter scrubs in and dons an apron, a cook's hat. He relieves Macey, a very pretty girl who looks totally out of place at the griddle. She is obviously an artist, not only is her pink corduroy coverall fashion with paint spills, her hair is up in a bun with brushes pushed in at various angles. She no doubt knows where each one is, whether a fan, angle, or mop brush. Macey is one of three black students who work there part-time, finishing their studies at the local college. The other two are smartly dressed and don't mind the small talk with the customers as they serve. Macey has her own style.

Hunter places his phone on the counter so he can continue to persuade Kieron Philips who he can hear still refusing from his perfect little island. He puts on an apron and starts to clean the griddle. It must be cleaned after the breakfast rush and no one likes that job.

"Be honest, you're sitting looking at an empty car park, surrounded by boarded-up commercial plots," Kieron is heard to mock over the phone.

"You couldn't be more wrong," Hunter says.

"Someone else moved in?"

"Can we back the truck up? The reason I called you, 'partner', was to ask when you're coming back? We've got cruise guests causing wars in the laundries on the MS Magi Myrrh. You'll have it solved in a day or two."

"You were serious?" is Kieron Philips's short, stunned answer and Hunter feels he, at last, has his partner's curiosity and can reveal his yet to be completed plan.

"Hello, Hunter!"

"Pivet, Hunter." *(Russian for hello)*

The two women's shouted greetings comes through Hunter's phone. The second was Russian or from another Baltic state where language has a stern tone. He is not pleased that Kieron is not alone.

"Ah, Georgie, Bedi! A happy trio out there in the sun," Hunter responds.

The sun blasts through every window in Bequia. Georgie and Bedriška sit at their breakfast bar in a showroom-like kitchen reading. Both are fit, slim stunning women and are now part of the conversation with Hunter. Kieron adjusts his Trilby hat and points to the door suggesting they leave. Without bothering to close or lock a window or a door the three stride outside into the idyllic grounds. They pass a couple of gardeners who they acknowledge.

"Help yourself to anything in the kitchen. Please." Georgie says.

"That mean the big American fridge freezer, boss?"

"I told you no," Kieron says. His answer could be aimed at the gardeners or his partner, but it is for Hunter in Miami.

Georgie closes the outside gate behind her and quicksteps across the empty clifftop road to catch the other two. She links Kieron's arm and smiles. He is now walking well.

"Sounds like you're having too good a time. But I need you to come back, today," Hunter relays.

"I can't see any reason to ever leave here," Kieron says, entering a footpath that cuts between endless colourful buds and the most fragrant smells. Bedriška powers ahead setting the pace.

"OK. How about getting our sixteen-million dollars back? And if Georgie's still in earshot, ask her."

Bedriška stops sharply and turns charging them with an inquisitive glare. Georgie shakes her head 'not to worry' and waves her to carry on walking, but Bedriška stays close enough to hear every word. She has never been told of that money and it shows. She doesn't look pleased.

"I'm listening," Kieron says.

The Miami diner's old bell above the door on a sprung metal circle, rings. In walks Jenny-E the journalist from TV station WBX25. Her cameraman, Dennis, in tow with his handheld rig that he places on a table.

"Are you in the diner? Doing the cooking, big boy?" Kieron is heard shouting from the phone which Jenny-E makes a move for.

She is beaten to it by Hunter who cancels speaker and puts it to his ear.

"Our favourite journalist has just walked in."

"I suppose that means you can't talk?"

"Got it," Hunter says just to Kieron, pulling one of six knives from a block. They are unusual one-piece steel knives with a double-edged blade which cause him to give them a moment's more attention than normal. He lays the knife down.

"I'm filling in for Wild Mary and the not so wild Stan, who, if you remember we sent on a cruise after we solved the murder mystery," Hunter continues to chop onions, turning back to Jenny-E, his sharp knife unintentionally points towards her. "I'll be with you in a minute," he says to her.

Jenny gives him a dismissive look; they both know she is not technically a customer though she will place an order. Placing an order is the rule for a cruise news story at Wild Mary's, which acts as the press office for the Investigators next door. Croc, another student who works there, holds a menu ready for her attention. Hunter excuses himself and moves away along the counter.

"I need you on this, I can't do it."

"Because you're playing chef, you can't do a job for C.S.C.I?" only Hunter hears.

"You like the name now?"

"It has a ring to it, Crime Ship Cruise Investigators," Kieron is heard to say.

"Cruise Ship Crime Investigators, but you know that. I need a husband and wife team," Hunter says, digging the knife tip down into the chopping board next to a pile of onions. It wobbles with a harmonic.

Hunter is easily heard by all three in Bequia who have a whole beach to themselves. The silence of the picturesque island is underpinned by the sea lapping softly against a few anchored pastel blue boats. Georgie walks bare feet in the water, her white pants finishing just below the knee and her beach shoes in one hand. She pulls Kieron into the sea and he stumbles as he pulls his shoes off and steps into the warm water. She holds him up, arm in arm laughing. Bedriška is not laughing. She has got as close as she can to them without her Ralph Lauren white Sayer pumps getting wet.

"You want me to take Georgie? She's not an investigator and she's got a job. Not that you'd think it," Kieron says, giving her a funny look.

Georgie steps away and splashes at him playfully,

"I work every day when I'm at sea. I deserve my weeks off the ship!"

Kieron is a little unstable as the water splashes so Bedi pulls him out onto the sand, links his arm and they begin to crab up towards a beach bar. Georgie runs behind them.

"I'll have to call Prisha Nah," they hear Hunter suggest on the phone.

"She would have to leave her job on ship to join you. Can't you and Elaine do it?" Kieron asks.

"No. She ain't an investigator, plus, she's twenty-five weeks pregnant. You can't cruise after twenty-four weeks. Not allowed on any ship."

"Is it still too early to say congratulations?" Georgie asks grabbing Kieron's other arm and leaning to speak to the phone in his shirt pocket. "I'm jealous."

Georgie looks across at Bedriška and mouths 'I want a baby'. Bedi is still not smiling.

"Thanks, Georgie. Scans and first tests are done, all good. One visit tomorrow to meet the ante-natal team. Elaine's well," they all hear.

"Congratulations," all three shout, slightly out of synchronisation with Bedi last.

"You got a party going on?" the pocket asks.

"No, we're walking to Jack's Bar on the beach, and we're the only three here for breakfast," Georgie explains.

"Tell me about money," Bedriška says. It sounds like it is an order.

"It's not about money, the Magi Myrrh is the wrong ship," Kieron says.

3 SHOW ME THE MONEY

In Wild Mary's Diner Jenny tries to grab Hunter's phone but he swings it away, so she shouts.

"Hi, Kieron. Hope you're feeling better. Can I get post-accident pictures to do a follow-up story?"

Settling back, she notices Macey painting at her easel at the end of the counter. Giving the painting more attention, she notices a NASA-like control room of three or four decades ago.

"Not your usual diner offering?"

Macey points at the black door in the corner, "Man cave."

Hunter takes the opportunity to slip away to finish his private conversation on the phone. "Buddy?"

Just a few steps up from the sand, Jack's Bar is a stylish alfresco beach restaurant with a Caribbean feel. The internal logistics have a similar commercial feel to the Miami diner that Hunter is taking care of, tall stools near the bar and dining set away but the similarity ends there. The Bequia chairs are heavy black-wood with arms and the tables have deep red cloth napkins and stylish silver cutlery. It is a little more upmarket than downtown Miami and a cool sea breeze of fresh clean air blows through. Flowers hang down from overhead arches and a single flower is on each table. It is made to feel tropical but the outlook to the sea is its real premium, enhanced by creole music.

Shaded from the blazing sun, the three take the table farthest from the bar. Kieron won't touch juice from a carton or a jar, but he knows that at Jack's it is freshly squeezed. He places his cell phone on the table and as they are the only customers, he leaves it on 'speaker'.

"Why d'you need Prisha?" he asks Hunter back in Miami.

"The contract is for a couple on the Myrrh, one cabin allocated to solve the laundry problem. It's great cover and the perfect opportunity. Prisha knows how we work, she knows the ships, and more importantly the office and paperwork."

"She supports her whole family in India on her cruise wage. She can't risk that for a few days' work."

"We're talking sixteen-million dollars. She won't need to work again."

"Our sixteen-million is not on that ship."

"I have a plan."

"Then you do it."

"I can't, I have ante-natal classes. This needs a couple, simple job."

"We might never see that money. Don't risk Prisha."

"We don't have a female agent," Hunter says via the phone.

"I am agent," Bedriška snaps.

"You're a hairdresser," Hunter blasts down the open phone, getting impatient.

"If you here, you would be on floor begging for life," Bedriška swiftly grabs the phone and drills into it. "I am KGB; you take me, I get pretty boy here to fly, I get your money."

"You'll have to share Kieron's room," Georgie says.

"No problem, he slept with you. Now, my time. I make it fair."

Georgie stands abruptly, shocked and pissed off. Kieron remains silent for a moment as he looks from Bedriška to Georgie before taking the phone back and placing it on the table. Restoring calm, he is inquisitive.

"How does a simple war in the laundry room on the wrong ship get our money back?"

"Yes, explain?" Bedriška asks.

"Yes?" Georgie angrily adds.

Kieron looks at the two stunning women, even at war they are very much a couple. Their relationship has teased him since Bedi arrived. His attraction to Georgie has been relegated to a friendship despite them owning two houses together on the island. They were purchased from a couple of stray millions from the heist that went wrong. He needs to make friends with Bedi, and this reveal of even more money has not helped.

"The two ships will berth together later in the cruise," Hunter explains via the phone.

"Then I am agent," Bedriška says.

"It is not going to happen," Kieron insists.

"Why?"

"Because I'm not well enough!"

4 SWAP PARTNERS

"Problem?" Jenny asks as she swivels on her red stool at the counter of the Miami diner. She sees the drama in every move and since Hunter pocketed his phone he is in deep thought. He tosses green tomatoes, eggs and grits for Jenny and Dennis's breakfast wondering if there is a human story in what he is doing.

"You have the knack for that, does Elaine have you cooking while she's pregnant?" Jenny-E asks.

She will find a story anywhere and knows the buttons to press. She has become a great friend of Wild Mary's, always orders food, and passes by when there is no need. She has helped Izzy who is a journalism student with her ear much closer to the street than hers. Izzy, like the others have effectively finished college but the chance of getting into writing or journalism is small. If she did get a chance at a local paper, she could see either the work or the wage impressing her. She has finished wiping the tables and is waiting for an invite to join them, but Jenny needs her story first, she needs to know what to keep and what to give to Izzy. Maybe a story on Hunter at home, that he and Elaine are soon to be parents might be one for Izzy even if it doesn't sell.

"Seems a few ships are having problems?" she uses to provoke a conversation.

"That right?" is all Hunter will offer in return.

Jenny knows more. She has clearly had a tip-off.

"Chocolate bars in tumble dryers and fights over laundry machines," she fishes.

"Really? Not all ships have customer laundry rooms, must be a good ship."

"That's protective! You have been employed."

Hunter turns equally inquisitive. Why has she been tipped off on something so trivial? He may have been a little protective, but half the investigator's job is to say the right thing and feed positive information to be spread. Now he is in a poker game with Jenny.

"I'm dealing with cruise crime here, employed as a chef?" he asks, placing their plated breakfasts on the counter then pouring them coffee.

"What is this job? You guys don't get called to stop cruise guests fighting in the laundry?"

Hunter leans over the counter as she and Dennis start to eat.

"Correct. We don't do guest problems; ship's staff do that."

"So, it's not a guest problem?"

"Enjoy your breakfast. You're always welcome, Jenny. If you hear of a job we should chase, there could be a commission."

Jenny looks over to Macey who might be painting them. Izzy is next to her.

"What's happening next door, girls?" Jenny asks.

"Maybe that should be a Sunday magazine special in one of your print titles, with one of Macey's images on the cover and me supplying the copy?" Izzy suggests.

"The man-cave is worth a special?" Jenny digs.

Izzy looks to Hunter for instruction. Hunter grins.

"Eat. Enjoy. Then you can do the tour."

Hunter finds some privacy and calls his wife.

"Elaine. Good news, we got the contract confirmed. But if Kieron doesn't come back, I've gotta fly to Lisbon. That'll mean me missing ante-natal induction tomorrow."

The tranquillity in Bequia's famous Jack's Bar has been fractured by Hunter's call. It has driven a wedge between the two women.

"Why you not tell me about millions of dollars?" Bedriška asks Georgie. Her speech always sounds like a command and a response is demanded. She snatches Kieron's phone without asking.

"Hey!" he says firmly.

She types into his phone and then slides it back into the centre of the table.

"Seriously, you 'ave big money?" she demands.

"No, we have two houses, I told you, two houses. I didn't tell you about money we didn't have," Georgie explains.

"Where is money? I get it!" Bedriška demands.

"It's not that simple," Kieron says.

Bedi's phone beeps. She reads it and types back.

"Who's that?" Georgie asks.

"Man who thinks I get money. I accept job."

"What job?" Kieron asks.

"Catch chocolate cruiser idiot. Then bring millions home."

"You won't get the millions," he says. "Wrong ship."

Bedriška reads from her phone. She now has more information than the other two.

"Hunter think laundry wars, easy to solve. Ships meet in Barcelona," Bedriška smiles.

"Did you ask about terms of employment, the fee?" Kieron probes.

"I know fee, sixteen-million dollars. For that, I share cabin with old fashioned English army commander."

"Old fashioned?" Kieron objects.

"You and Kieron? What do I do?" Georgie asks.

"You go back to work soon," Bedi says.

"So do you. You manage the spa on a ship."

"No, I have new job for Hunter."

Her phone beeps again, she reads.

"What? What are you typing?" Kieron asks as she replies.

"Name, address, nationality, passport information so he book tickets."

"No!" Kieron and Georgie wage.

"Kieron was couple with you," Bedriška says to annoy Georgie. "Now, we are couple."

"Am I supposed to accept you sharing a cabin with him?" Georgie asks, jealously.

"You sleep with him!"

"I apologised."

Their breakfast arrives. Fresh fruit and a small selection of newly baked breads with three boiled eggs. The two waiters smile and leave them. Bedriška goes for food, the other two are still stunned.

"So, it OK for you to have sex with him but not me?" she fires at Georgie.

"I didn't say that. But yes."

"How about me, don't I get a say in this?" Kieron asks.

"No." Both women say together.

"You eat. You need much strength. I will be testing you hard," Bedi continues.

Georgie stands sharply.

"Sit down, I joke. I know he recovering. I be gentle." Bedi is enjoying the tease. Her phone goes again, "We fly late afternoon," she reveals, reading.

"What?" says Kieron, totally against the turnaround he is being asked to make.

"Where to?" Georgie asks.

"Lisbon; meet MS Magi Myrrh. It has problem with guests. Not only problem that ship have, it is old."

"We don't do problems with guests, the on-board staff do that," Kieron states.

"Hunter say, ship dock alongside your old ship five days later. One with money. I will like new job," Bedi reads. "Barcelona. I might go shopping there when I have money."

"And you think if you move the money to your new ship, what? What is the point of it being on a different ship?" Georgie pushes. "You've still got to get it off any ship."

"Yes. But you get money for house here. We get money Bedriška go shop. He not reveal plan, maybe we get all. Maybe we drive it to Italy."

"What good is that, a trunk full of money in Italy? We want it here, clean," Kieron computes.

"Yes. I retire here," Bedriška says.

"But Kieron wants his share in Syria," Georgie reminds him.

"Syria? Not promising investment," Bedriška says as her phone beeps again. What was to be a very relaxing breakfast has taken a complete turn.

"We have local flight at four o'clock from main island." She looks at her watch. "Just few hours to get married."

Georgie throws a glass of water over her.

"That was joke," Bedi says, calmly looking up at her.

"Our romantic holiday here is ruined!" Georgie says.

"I'm not sure I'm ready for this war. Either war," Kieron says, in a sobering tone. "It's a long-distance flight and I'm still getting nose bleeds and dizzy spells, to say the least."

5 OPS CENTRE

"Tell Dwight to fire the screens up, we got press guests," Hunter says.

Croc wanders through the black cupboard door with Cruise Ship Crime Investigators painted on it. Jenny-E watches him vanish through the C.S. Lewis-like conduit to the offices next door which she desperately wants to see. Hunter takes the journalist's empty breakfast plates for washing.

"You're not a bad cook, Witowski," she says, still focussing on the magic door.

"Family's from the mid-west where they ran a diner."

"Really? I tried researching you. Never found that."

"Bet you didn't find much at all."

"I got zero. So, I made my own model of you."

"Huh."

"Polish name," she offers.

"No points for getting that right."

"Families arrived in the US around 1880?"

"Wouldn't know, wasn't there."

"Mainly in the clothing trade or medicine."

"Medicine? Never heard that. They were smallholders; Grandma never had a produce outlet, it became a café, then Dad made it a diner. Not sure you've a story there."

"You never know."

"I know," Hunter says, rounding the counter and leading her and Dennis, the cameraman towards the magical door.

"Izzy, throw the lock and join us."

Izzy jumps up and the 'closed for five minutes' board is up before Hunter can draw another breath. He lets her pass first. Macey is already in.

"We're one big family here, I like that. Wild Mary and Stan are away on their first cruise as a treat for the excellent work they did on what the press called, the Cruise Ship Serial Killer."

"When do we get to go?" Izzy asks.

"Can we film?" Jenny asks, she and Hunter ignoring Izzy's question.

"Sure. We're not on a case. Just building and testing equipment," Hunter offers.

"And the rest of your past?"

"Like a Russian Doll, an organisation within an organisation, within an organisation," he says.

"Within the CIA?"

"I know ships back to front and cruising up and down," Hunter says, knowing he is on camera albeit always in the dark as he shows them the room full of giant screens.

Croc is standing in the middle of the room, lit by the blue electronic hue. He is pleased with himself, but he is passed by another black who approaches in a powered chair. He has an even bigger smile.

"He's not telling you his old CIA stories, is he?"

The chair brakes sharply in front of Jenny and he holds up a huge fist to bump. One that is powerful and used to manual work, giving away that he has not been in that chair for long.

"Dwight. Dwight Ritter."

"That's a boxer's fist, Dwight," she says, fishing.

"Huh."

Jenny walks past the technology inspecting it, knowing she is on camera and this will be part of her clip. Izzy watches from the back wall.

"This is no back-street detective agency," she presents turning to camera. "These are world class specialist investigators who look after the multi-billion-dollar cruise ship industry and their millions of passengers."

"Cruise Ship Crime Investigators have the technical ability to match any country's top crime agency and can almost instantly track and trace anyone and anything," Croc adds.

Jenny takes her cue and walks up to him.

"And who are you?"

"It's classified," he replies.

"What do you mean it's classified?"

"I mean, they haven't told me yet!" Croc announces, laughing at his own joke as he so often does.

"Croc's head of our IT network. He built all this, and Dwight knows how to run it and get into any system in the world. Someone acts-up on ship, Dwight pulls all the clues into a massive spider," Hunter explains.

"So why did it take you so long to catch the Pacific Ocean Serial Killer?" she asks.

"Amusing way of looking at it. After a high altitude drop into the ocean from a plane, at night, it took us less than eight days to find one of the smartest serial killers ever."

Jenny walks back to Hunter.

"What makes you say smartest?"

"A woman, very rare for a serial killer," Hunter delivers. "After we managed our way around six days of false clues. When we had her in our sights, she fled the first chance she got."

"You let her go?"

"Off the ship? Damn right. We knew exactly how she escaped and where she was," Dwight adds.

"So, what's the case you're on now? Is it the disruptions reported on the Three Kings ships chat sites over the last week?"

"We don't do small stuff. We wait here until someone calls us, and Jenny-E, when someone does, you'll be the first to know."

Jenny liked the name check, she waves the camera down, they have their piece.

"I'll use all that. But I know you're lying. Rumours might be of small disruptions, but there's a dead body or something, somewhere. Or I wouldn't have been tipped off."

"Two little birds?" Hunter asks.

She nods.

"We turned them down, job too small. They're using you. They're dangerously ambitious and looking for a career-boosting photo op with us. But I reckon the press coverage will do us no harm."

6 THE MAIN ISLAND'S SECRET

The transfer to St Vincent, where there is a commercial airport is less than half an hour in a good boat, but it is a journey you don't leave until the last minute. Kieron has not been on that island since he escaped with a huge amount of cash with Georgie, where he met a nun who lamented the harsh reality of raising funds and he saw in her eyes that she cared, and he could trust her. His agent on Bequia sent the nun a laundered donation albeit anonymously and wrapped up in press release. The philanthropic action fitted Kieron's wish to help children as he had done as a soldier in Syria. However, it was also to excuse the vast sum of money seen in Sylvie's Bequia bank. She was a lot more than just their realtor, but even she couldn't stop an over-enthusiastic staff member posting a picture on social media putting himself, the bank and much else at risk. Accidents like that can cause huge problems. Kieron spent much of his special operations career undercover, engineering governments' spin-out of such situations. He helped the nun's causes but requested a proportion of the donation she received was sent to help children in Syria. He knows she fulfilled that strange request as part of the church's outreach programme. He learnt that their team managed magnificent work far more efficiently than he could ever have done alone. She may well have connected the surprise donation to their strange but brief conversation, but it is unlikely she would be able to pick his face out in a crowd.

They approach St Vincent and their small speed boat rounds the huge cruise ship berthed there and docks by a market area where a waiting taxi will take them to the airport. Kieron throws his holdall into the trunk as a local vendor approaches asking him if he wishes to buy Tri Tri fish. He looks down at her huge water-less bucket pilled full of the tiny dead white bait-like fish no bigger than shrimps. He thanks her but excuses himself to look back at Bedriška kissing Georgie goodbye. It is never an easy sight for him.

"We catch 'em only when the moon is right," the vendor persists.

Kieron turns to her,

"Right for what?"

"Tri Tri swim in."

He hands her a twenty-dollar Eastern Caribbean note.

"I'm flying out, or I would love to have tried them."

She scuttles away and he turns back to the uncomfortable vision of his two female housemates. It won't be easy for Georgie to watch him and Bedi leave. She will have to take the boat home alone.

In the taxi Kieron checks his watch. Being early he requests a detour into town and up the hill to the Gothic Cathedral which is also a school. He gets out and walks through the stone arches. The church was originally built to service the slaves and those who brought them into the colonies back in the seventeen-hundreds. Bedriška also gets out but to study him. She is curious about this man who her partner bought a house with during a dalliance. Two houses! And now there is talk of millions.

"Dull. Church should be grand, ornate," she says. "This is grey, like child detective witchcraft films."

Kieron goes to the giant thermometer painted on the noticeboard. It shows how much money has been raised and by what date. It is a warming sight to see it nearly replete and so many goals achieved. The updated line has a date by it which grabs his attention. Bedriška notices too, the date is the same date they purchased their Bequia house.

"You and Georgie?"

"Yes," he answers slowly.

"I approve."

"And I thank you," is the voice of an older lady behind them.

Bedi turns and looks at the nun, but it is Kieron she is talking to. He was not expecting this moment and it takes him a while to turn. He eventually offers her his hand. She takes it and kisses it. He was not expecting to be revealed or rewarded.

"Thank you for your generosity to the children in Syria," he says to her. "My daughter's family relayed your excellent work back to me."

"The work of our church is wherever children are in need and there are emergencies all over the world."

Her hand goes up to distressing pictures of children in Africa and Yemen that sit above the red line on the noticeboard. They show a far wider problem than the one that had distressed Kieron when deployed in the Middle East.

"You may have seen the problem in Syria and your eyes allowed your heart to be touched by emotion but look beyond your eyes. We try to help."

"I've also seen so much money wasted by aid organisations it hurts. I tried to help, but as an individual…"

"It is too hard and heart-breaking. Together we might manage the success you seek. As long as your donations are not the illicit gains of crime."

"Do I look like a criminal, sister?"

"What do they look like?"

"Not me, I can assure you; I was a serving soldier. If we can find any money, we'll try and persuade it to be given to your cause."

"We will," Bedriška says bluntly. "Children of Chechnya need help. They get recruited to fight and be suicide bombers. Young. Ten or eleven."

The nun nods as she studies Bedriška then Kieron again offering them a smile,

"We try, that is all we can do. Chechnya may be a step too far in the current unrest, but we have missions there."

"Missionaries sell religion," Bedi says, being bluntly political.

"Not all, but I understand your comment. I try and do what is right," the nun says.

Kieron nods. It is his moment to walk away having re-made an important connection with an angel he thought he would never meet again.

"Please!" she says, calling him back and holding out a white handkerchief.

Kieron takes it realising his nose must be bleeding again. The muscles on his face tighten revealing his concern.

"It is the heat. You must drink water," she says. "And see a doctor."

Kieron studies the cloth square embroidered with a wavy path to a cross, before wiping his face to reveal a little blood.

"I'll bring it back. Laundered."

"Follow the path and go safely, I will pray that you are watched over."

Getting back in the taxi Bedriška addresses Kieron, "Will you be OK?"

"I tried to tell you I had a problem."

"If you die, I will do the job myself. How much money do I give the old nun?"

"She'll only ask for what she needs."

7 THE BLOODED PATH AHEAD

The taxi speeds the five miles out of the small town of Kingston but unlike Bedriška, Kieron does not see much of the Island. He sits looking at the wavy pathway marked with blood. He tried so hard but helped very few children in the past. The main one was the girl he smuggled from war torn Syria whose family had all been killed. The one who now calls him dad. Despite his lack of belief in the sister's God, he knows she is the path to aid children in need.

"The money is hidden in a trunk," he says totally out of the blue.

"Millions?"

"Yeah. The trunk was supposed to be for the transportation of theatrical costumes and stage props. It should be in the entertainment storage area. We labelled it, crime evidence."

Bedi looks at the driver then leans into Kieron, putting a finger up to his lips. But Kieron is on a mission, driven by self-imposed guilt.

"Getting the trunk off the ship may be possible, but getting it through customs won't be easy," he whispers to her.

"What is C.S.C.I?"

"The company you agreed to work for, Cruise Ship Crime Investigators."

"I see British irony; money hidden in crime investigation trunk. Very funny," she whispers into his ear.

"If I don't make it," he says.

"I will. Do not worry."

"Be careful."

Bedriška stops him, "I am not stupid."

She looks out of the window. How everything can change in so few hours. But she knows that. She knows life can change.

"I text Hunter while you sleep."
"I didn't sleep."
"You did. I demand medical in Miami."

Kieron is not sure he wants to know if something is wrong. He was happy on the beach in Bequia. His little bleeds told him when he had been in the sun too much or when he had overdone it. He now faces the first of two long flights, a three-and-a-half-hour hop to Miami. It will be a test to his health and his new partnership with the mysterious Bedriška.

Kieron gathers enough courage to test his nose again. No blood, so he raises his head to look at the blue modern structure of Argyle airport where they are jockeying to park. The driver is quick to unload the two small bags and be off to find a new fare. Kieron cannot find the same enthusiasm and is much slower to collect his bag and catch Bedi.

The last time Kieron was at an airport with a tall good-looking woman was the beginning of his very first cruise experience. Then, a Latina beauty who was the calm before the unexpected heist on his first cruise ship. The trip where he stole the love of Georgie while Bedi was absent if only for two weeks leave. He managed to stir feelings in Georgie that she never thought she could have for a man. Will this jilted Russian partner have his back? Not that he will need her cover to deal with chocolate bars in the laundry. The money is the problem. He watches her; will she make it into America if she is ex-KGB? Flying into

Miami will put her in front of a hugely different United States immigration to the one that cruisers see.

Kieron wakes as the wheels hit the tarmac and his chin bounces on his chest. Bedriška leans over and pinches his nose with a tissue. He takes over squeezing it to his face and checks his shirt for blood.
"We go now," Bedriška says.
"The plane's still taxiing."
"We go."
She is up first to take his and her hand luggage. He stands but can't find his balance. The flight attendant takes his hands and leads him down the plane before anyone else can stand. He is keen to get off, the opposite of just three months earlier when he was last to leave. Then he sat at the back with an eye on all. The door opens to reveal a medical team waiting with a gurney. He knows this is because of his condition, the one he hopes he doesn't have. He holds the blood-red tissue to his face which he realises smells of ketchup as he is wheeled away. Bedriška is a player, not that he ever doubted her ability. He might not be bleeding but he does have a problem and he hates it. He hates not knowing what it is.

Immigration is also amazingly swift and the medics speed him away from airside to a waiting private ambulance right outside the doors.
"I feel fine."
"You ever get through American airport so fast?"
"No."
"So, don't argue."
Kieron lays wondering if the charade was for his health or for her to fast-track immigration.

8 SHE'S GONE

After a no-news day in Florida, Jenny-E returns to record a news piece to camera outside the blackened windows of CSCI, finishing by Wild Mary's Diner. She ends with a joke, a humorous style of reporting she often lacks. Maybe she is promoting the diner in return for the story she knows exists. Dennis, the cameraman, starts to pack away but she lingers and looks in through the window.

Wild Mary's has got busier with late afternoon orders, and Hunter is cooking again. He has found cooking allows him to think. Croc is standing at the counter nearby as if waiting for an order, but that is not the case, he wants Hunter to go next door. There appears a sense of urgency as the chef hat comes off, despite them having customers. Hunter follows Croc into the next room and Jenny's interest is ignited.

Jenny slips into the diner causing the bell to ring on the door. Izzy looks across from the table she is serving.

"Can I use the restroom?"

"Sure. But you gotta place an order."

Placing an order has become a pointed joke amongst friends. The restrooms are next to the cupboard that is the secret black connecting door. With a glance back to ensure Izzy is busy and Macey is not looking, Jenny takes the black door. She stands just inside the unlit air-lock-like cupboard structure that the double doors form. She watches Croc lead Hunter to Dwight at the far screen that she can't see. Jenny needs to hear. She dares to take a step into the shadows of the room and listen.

"All this technology and we don't have an intercom between here and the kitchen," Hunter says.

"I'll get it sorted," Croc offers.

"Should we ask Wild Mary before intruding that far?"

Hunter knows Mary is a force to cross.

"She never asked if she could hammer down your wall," Croc laughs.

"OK. We say it's so the restaurant can call for extra help," he adds.

"I needed to get you before you left for the airport," Dwight interrupts.

"Sorry, food orders went wild after we got rid of Jenny. People sense reporters," Hunter says.

'Nice,' Jenny thinks, 'not that you can sense one now'. She dares another half step nearer and stands statuesque in the dark listening to every word.

"This so-called crime we're solving," Dwight insists.

"What you got?" Hunter asks.

Jenny's eyes raise, she has confirmation. They are solving a crime and his partner is flying in, also on the job.

"Our three ships, romantically known as the three kings, are all for sale."

"For sale?"

"If ships are female, why is they kings and not queens?" Croc asks.

The two men turn to him but ignore the daft question.

"However, within five minutes, I'd found nearly thirty cruise ships for sale, all still at sea," Dwight continues.

"Wow. Our three ships are for sale. That stinks!" Croc adds as if he is one of the team.

Both Dwight and Hunter look at him and he falls silent realising he is there to listen.

"Stinks is right. I found long chat threads moaning about the smell of waste on all our three ships. Do cruise ships smell?" Dwight asks.

"No, smells get solved super-fast. If that's a recurring problem, then that stinks."

"The stink stinks. I like it," Croc laughs but stops instantly.

"You learning 'bout this industry?" Hunter asks Croc.

"Learning it stinks boss? Staying up every night in bed reading those brochures wondering which stinky ship I might get posted to."

"Good luck with that," Hunter adds.

Dwight isn't finished. He has several pages open on his screen.

"So, they employed us because of laundry wars. Chocolate bars in the dryer. Some turn into fights and two guests have been handed to local police at the next port. Bags off, everything."

"Not unusual, ships are fast to react and don't want those cruisers back. There's a list of never-again-cruisers."

"Who walks the plank?" Croc jokes, drifting into a pirate mimic.

"I'm sure the local police don't want them either," Dwight says, ignoring Croc.

"They're normally extradited under guard of the national airline of their passport," Hunter explains.

"Extradited? Under guard? That sounds costly," Dwight says, not knowing how the industry works and he needs to know everything.

"There is no actual guard. They're taken to the airport and held in a small area away from the public and shops, escorted to the plane, then under the care of the plane until they land. They then get escorted off the plane by the native police who do the immigration."

"Sounds like fast-track to me," Croc offers.

"They may be booked, certainly a recorded warning," Hunter adds, aiming it at Croc's jovial approach.

"Still don't seem much of a punishment," Croc defends.

"Lost their holiday, embarrassing flight home. It's ugly," Hunter insists.

"So, here's the interesting bit," Dwight re-starts.

"I was boring you?" Hunter says.

"Hey, I love learning about cruising and how these lucky people travel. Last time I travelled it was an e-vac home to an army hospital. Never did see the duty free."

Hunter holds up his fist as an offer of respect and they bump. Dwight now has the stage uninterrupted.

"This might not be related, yet, but four years ago on the sister ship"

"See they's all women, but we got the Three Kings."

"On a sister ship, MS Magi Frankincense, two British pensioners were arrested in Lisbon for being drug mules."

Hunter stands straight thinking.

"What was the stash?" Croc asks.

"Millions of dollars' worth of cocaine," Dwight responds.

"But that must have been on a ship repositioning from the Caribbean to the Med. It could only happen once a year, at the end of the Caribbean season. These recurring problems don't feel related."

"But it doesn't look like the pensioners got extradited."

"They got vanished?" Croc asks.

Hunter looks at his watch again, "Are you thinking revenge?"

Dwight dips his head, "All I got."

"Get all three ship's itineraries and any information on that couple."

Croc sits down at another screen and starts to look.

"Not you," Hunter says.

Croc looks round, guilty.

"How about you hang around outside cruise HQ on Dodge and wait for Chet and Bjorn to leave work."

Hunter points at two pictures he took with his smartphone across the table in the office earlier that morning.

"And what?"

"Follow them, note where they go, build a profile."

Jenny has more than overstayed her welcome and turns hearing movement behind her. She looks out of the door to check Izzy's position, hearing the two men closing behind her. She closes the door behind, then, without looking back, opens the second door to the diner producing a shaft of light. She accelerates away.

9 MEDICAL TEST

Flashing blue lights cut through the evening sky then change to flashing lights through the windscreen. Kieron never really considered he might be ill, but the journey has been too much and his eyes are heavy. He does not wake again until he is looking up at squares of light whizzing by on a corridor ceiling. Nothing else looks quite like a hospital ceiling, a sight he is only too familiar with. He ponders how he arrived here when just hours ago he was looking at blue skies, smelling tropical flowers, and thinking of going sea-fishing. He is lifted from the wheeled gurney onto the bed of a huge circular machine and knows he is going to be scanned again. He might as well sleep again, but he knows that won't happen. The noise is deafening as he is moved in jerking motions. Life has turned from bliss to torture. He hears gunfire, screams, explosions and sees bright flames and muzzle flashes; it is always deafening, and it never goes away. How much more can ever be wrong with your head than memories of war? They can't scan for those.

When his eyes open, he sees Hunter talking to a doctor. X-rays of his head are on a vast light box behind them. He feels naked, just a medical gown and he wonders how he was undressed? Who did this to him? Where did he lose the minutes? He knows the scans Hunter and a good looking young female doctor are looking at must be his.

"I hope you're not sharing my medical records with him," Kieron says. "When was I undressed?"

Hunter and the doctor turn. Kieron blinks and a wider view opens to him. Bedriška is there too, can he trust her? He stole Georgie for two weeks.

"Tell him doc," Hunter says.

Kieron is trying to focus on the pictures of his head on the screens, the area he knows he smashed when he was thrown off the stairs. He used every muscle in his body to ensure his head did not hit the steel, but it was not enough. He knows where the bleeds had been before. He would like to get closer, but he is restrained to the bed.

The doctor walks forward filling his frame of vision.

"There's nothing horribly wrong with you. You need rest after what was a major accident, but you know that."

"Like a cruise, relax, have everything done for you," Hunter offers.

"That sounds perfect," the doctor replies.

Kieron struggles to talk, no one knows the truth.

"What he's not telling you is, we work on the ships," Kieron says, sitting up checking his watch. It is 2030hrs and he is not sure whether the day has flown by or he has lost a day.

"Oh," she says thinking.

"Doc, he's just partnering Bedriška here. She'll do all the heavy lifting," Hunter offers.

"I do all work. Even sex, he stay underneath," she offers, which is too much information because there is no hint of humour in her delivery.

"You can sleep on the plane," Hunter says.

"Doctor?" Kieron asks.

"The French team did a fantastic job patching you up after your fall. But there'll be many small vessels still damaged for a while and they might get excited," the doctor explains, looking at Bedi.

"I excite people," she says.

"Get dressed buddy. You didn't tap-out. Not yet," Hunter says, opening the door.

He leads Kieron towards the door, but Kieron is engaged by the pictures on the screens. He can't recognise the damaged areas and thinks he must have healed extremely fast. Hunter indicates the dressing room across the corridor.

"Your clothes are on a peg."

Bedi stands looking at Hunter.

"What?" he asks.

"Plan?"

"In short, it's simple. The ship with the money on, sails from the Mediterranean to the Middle East then stays in the southern hemisphere. No chance of getting the money. MS Magi Myrrh berths alongside it three times before it goes. After the summer the Myrrh comes back to Miami where we can get the money off into a bonded warehouse. All you have to do is see the trunk moved onto your ship."

Hunter turns away sure his presence is no longer required dressing Kieron. Bedi will help. But she turns back to Hunter and watches him.

The doctor takes off her white coat revealing a nurse's uniform. She hangs the white coat on side of the monitoring cubicle,

"Think I'd make a good doctor, was I convincing?"

"I wouldn't trust you painting my house. Get out of here," Hunter says.

Bedriška watches through a crack in the door as Hunter knocks and goes into an office.

"Hi, doctor, I've told him. No flying." Bedi hears Hunter say.

Behind her, Kieron is changed ready to leave the cubicle.

"You two want to go down and get coffee, I'll settle the bill," Hunter offers.

Bedi leads Kieron out.

Croc is alone outside a club on Ocean Drive. He knows his two marks have gone inside the pastel green and pink three-storey building, three windows wide, the same as almost every other building on the street. He hears a wild open-top tour bus drive by where a brother is working hard on the commentary. He listens, then he flips his phone to call in.

"Macey would love it up here, it's all art deco along Ocean Drive. You know the machine meets Jetsons stuff. The two have gone into a club."

"Go in, see who they meet, try and listen," Dwight says.

"I only got eighty dollars left after the cab, Dwight. It might not even buy a drink here."

"It will."

Croc has never been in a club this rich and he is only in denim and a polo shirt. It does not look like the required dress code, but he can only get turned away and it wouldn't be the first time it has happened.

As expected, he is stopped at the door.

"No soliciting in here." The large villainous bouncer says at the door.

"I'm meeting someone," Croc says palming him a twenty.

"And no selling drugs."

"I'm clean bro."

Hunter leads Bedriška and Kieron from the hospital out to Elaine waiting nearby in a bright red drop-top.

"How did you like my doctor?" she asks Kieron as he kisses her on both cheeks to greet her.

"So, you had me checked over by Obstetrics?" he says feeling better.

"And it's official, you're not pregnant," Hunter says, as he slips into the front seat next to Elaine and the car pulls away.

"I guess I'll have to consider that too now. How do you avoid pregnancy?" Bedriška bluntly asks Elaine. Then remembering Elaine is pregnant. "I guess you not right person for advice."

10 AN ENGLISHMAN'S CASTLE

Within fifteen minutes they are pulling into the drive of Elaine and Hunter Witowski's detached property on Coral Gables, the premium address in Miami, Florida. Their car headlights show the manicured properties. As they curve into the drive Bedriška is impressed.

"Very nice," she taunts, her tone now intent on the millions she is hearing so much about.

"It's all mortgage," Elaine says.

"So, we must get job right?"

"It would be nice," Hunter says.

Bedi's long legs easily hurdle the side of the drop-top car. She nods approvingly before seeing Elaine circle to the trunk and pull out bags of shopping. Bedi moves sharply to take them from her because Hunter is helping Kieron.

"Thank you."

"Spasibo."

"Spasibo?" Elaine asks.

"Russian for thank you."

The interior of the house requires modification. It is not a patch on the house she has with Georgie and Kieron on Bequia.

Elaine starts to split packages.

"You need supper before you head to the airport. I've done that flight to Lisbon a few times. The night flight especially; food's not always great."

Hunter has gone to a table where several papers are laid out.

"Why are we not doing this at our new modern offices?" Kieron mocks.

"I thought it more important you started to feel like a married couple and Elaine offered supper."

Hunter focusses their attention to the ship's deck plans he has spread on the dining table. "Disruption caused by chocolate bars which are put into laundry room dryers on formal nights is what it says on our deal memo."

"We have a contract? How about payment?" Kieron asks.

"Working on it. I was told there is a routine. First formal night they hit the guest's laundry on these two decks. Second formal night on these two decks. Plus, a similar problem on these two other ships and on the last cruise."

"Two decks two people following orders to the letter. An active couple on each cruise ship paid to disrupt," Kieron offers.

"Sounds like they're professionals," Elaine says, daring to join in.

"No," the other three say almost together.

Elaine stands upright as if having been scolded.

"Professional not follow same routine," Bedriška says, almost apologetically. "And if experienced, you not take stupid job."

"I agree," Kieron adds. "This is a low rent operation, so why are we on it?"

"Because we are being paid," Hunter offers.

"Because we recover millions from other ship," Bedriška offers.

"Look, assume there will be a couple on your cruise, just tell us their details, let us report it," Hunter explains.

"Too simple. We will get idiots first night," Bedi says.

"But local crew could do that," Hunter offers. "We have to find who's pulling their strings."

"We beat information from them," Bedi adds.

"You find them, me and Dwight will do the rest. You fly to, and cruise from Lisbon. Your ship leaves tomorrow, the second ship rotates a day after you, the third at the weekend. Lisbon is the staging point. You're on an overnight flight, arriving in the morning."

"What when we find them?" she asks, gnarling her jaw. "We give them to local security?"

Kieron and Bedi look up for advice.

"No. Ship security has to play nice. You're guests, so if we need you to, you can have a row before they're arrested," Hunter explains. "We want to know who they're working for."

"Good, torture is allowed," Bedi states. There is no question in her tone.

"You have two formal nights before Barcelona, then it's all about our money," Hunter reminds them.

They turn and see Kieron sitting down in the armchair.

"You OK, buddy?" Hunter asks.

"Why didn't you go if it is that easy and quick?"

"We start ante-natal induction tomorrow. I wanted to be with Elaine."

"And that couldn't be moved?"

"No."

"I've known you three months. We met because you played out a major lie, even if it was to save your wife."

"You were the first one who I told the truth too."

"Only after the ship was wrapped up in a major heist and my daughter was kidnapped."

"Well, you got me as a partner now."

Elaine feels awkward; she was kidnapped and held in Madeira. Her life was threatened to make Hunter compliant. He was forced to be disloyal to his own cruise company, and then Kieron in a major heist. This time Elaine is not in danger, it is selfish.

The air pressure in the room has swiftly fallen leaving a void for a stormy encounter.

"Let's eat," Elaine announces to defuse the situation.

They all drift back into the kitchen except Kieron, he has tried to stand but is dizzy. He needs that moment again to get his balance. Bedriška watches him and then, uninvited, collects him, taking his arm for the first few steps before he commands his independence. When she is no longer required, she addresses Hunter.

"I want his full medical record to carry," Bedriška demands.

Hunter looks at her sternly, "Good idea."

"Before I step on plane."

Hunter goes into his briefcase and produces a file.

"Take this, it is my copy. You'll have a PDF of tonight's medical before you land in the morning."

Hunter is nodding in agreement as she now holds Commander Kieron Philip's medical jacket. She closes into the personal space of the tall well-built United States ex-Special Forces man. There is not a dip in her focus. She matches him in height and what she lacks in body weight she has in her ability to intimidate. She has no fear.

"Not phoney one from phoney doctor. You don't ever do that to me."

Kieron studies her command in an unexpected show of loyalty to him, "And we want a good plan for transferring the money," he adds.

"Working on it."

"Not good enough," Bedriška says leaning right into him, threateningly. Elaine is shocked, she has never seen her husband threatened. He did not flinch or move a muscle and she is not sure she liked what she saw.

11 FLIGHT TO THE UNKNOWN

Kieron and Bedriška sit in economy class of the night flight. They study the holiday cruise brochure under their individual reading-lights as most of the plane sleeps. Kieron has a particular interest in the deck plan, inking crew, and guest routes to and from the passenger laundry areas. The deck plan is the slice of the ship which reveals in detail the passenger areas and the features. It does not detail the areas behind the doors labelled 'crew only'. Kieron is fairly new to cruise ships, though his entry to the industry was a baptism of fire. His first ship was a money and drugs heist out of Panama. He did not know Hunter's wife Elaine was being held at gunpoint so a Latina drug princess onboard ship could get exactly what she wanted. Hunter had no option but to entertain the South American's demands, but in compromising the ship he could never stay employed by the cruise company. He had totally abused his position as head of security, albeit for a reason. The two of them were bound together in that heist. Their first true mission as partners was a serial killer on board another ship. Had they not been contracted within weeks of them starting Cruise Ship Crime Investigators, their company may have gone nowhere. Now CSCI is being called to a guest disturbance which might show there is a market for them in the fast-growing industry.

"Something feels very wrong," Kieron announces.

Bedi turns to him, she has been on many ships and though she never strayed far from managing the beauty spa she understands the way a cruise ship works.

"It stinks," is her flat reply. "Cruise companies not waste money on this shit."

"Were you KGB?"

"That not problem. Trust your partner, this not feel right."

"You're not just a beautician."

"I am department manager. I know tight ship budget. They not employ us for a laundry war."

"I agree, but…" Kieron starts.

"So, if we know stupid, the company who employ us know stupid, your partner know stupid."

"Employers always know."

"And never tell truth."

"You were KGB," Kieron insists, studying her for any facial twitches. "I'd hate to play you at poker."

"I no play poker."

"You don't like card games?"

"I get banned," she says, without any emotion.

"For winning?"

"Killing opponent, but he was cheat."

Kieron gets nothing from her face. He has no idea if that was the truth or she is playing a game with him.

"I know one thing about you," he says.

"You know nothing about me," she is fast to rebuke.

"I know you need to smile and act wife-like on the ship," he says.

"This is my wife-like romantic look even though I don't care about you. I care someone is playing poker with us."

"You think Hunter knows?"

"Is he stupid?" she asks.

"No."

"Then he know. He know they have bigger problem."

Kieron looks down at the brochure and turns the page to the lifestyle pictures used to advertise the cruise,

"Then he must think we will solve it before Barcelona, and this is all about getting the money off the other ship."

"If I get sixteen million, I retire. Work ends. Fuck ship."

"Why chocolate laundry wars?"

"Waste of chocolate."

"You like chocolate?"

"No. I hate."

Both sit silently making mental lists as they leaf through the brochure. Their attention to detail reflects how similar they are. Bedi reaches up and presses the call button for an attendant. A smart male cabin steward strides down the gangway on cue.

"I want wi-fi. Please," she smiles falsely and then brushes Kieron's arm.

"Which value?" he asks her.

"Which value should we get love?" she asks a very stunned Kieron, but before he can speak, she looks back at the attendant. "Full journey. My husband pay."

The attendant scurries away.

"I think we might need to work on the relationship," Kieron offers.

Bedriška looks him straight in the face. As the attended approaches, without warning she collects him under the chin with her hand and pretends to kiss him. The attendant waits with a credit card machine and an envelope. With the kiss satiated, Bedi takes the envelope, opens it, and uses the code. She is on-line before Kieron has finished paying.

"Can I get you anything else, would your wife like to see the duty free?"

Bedi looks up offended.

"You want to know what I want, ask me, not him," she says, waving the attendant away. "He thinks I am Russian bride; you think I am KGB." She turns back to her phone without the need for a reply.

"Let's hope we're both right," Kieron offers.

Bedi turns to him, once again emotionless.

"Think we should practice kissing proper kissing?" he asks.

"No," she says, and returns to her research.

"You might also find a sense of humour."

"Go to sleep."

Kieron leans on her arm but she shakes him off.

"Three ships all same size, same class. 'Three Kings' class. Under two thousand guests."

"OK."

"But cruise operator have fourteen ships. Why problem just on these three ships?"

"Good musing. Now stay in your wife character," Kieron jokes, laying his head back against her.

Kieron wakes as the wheels bounce on the tarmac of Lisbon airport. It is a bright day and he knows the rush to the ship starts as soon as they unbuckle seat belts. He baulks at a tissue tucked into his collar but as he pulls it away, he notices it is bloodstained.

"I don't like wipe nose, even if I am good wife."

On any other ship, they would be joining as crew and there would be a driver waiting, holding up their names before taking them to a taxi. On this occasion, they are holidaying guests rounded up and corralled into a group with cruisers. Kieron walks towards the coach he is directed to, Bedi watches from behind and sees him veer to the left. She catches him up, links arms correcting his line and she hangs on like a newly-wed resting her head on his shoulder as they walk.

"How am I doing?" she asks.

"Good."

"How you doing?"

"Good. I hope."

12 ALL LIES AND JEST

Back in the plush meeting room on Dodge, the artificial island in downtown Miami which is cruise-centric, Hunter sits with just Chet and Bjorn. Both wear suits, the ice in the jug is melting fast, and Hunter is frustrated that he is getting no more information.

"You tipped the press off," Hunter accuses, changing tact. "You know what? I need a purchase order to ensure we get paid, and the fee on the deal memo is just the first payment, due right now," Hunter demands.

"You have a binding deal memo," Bjorn replies.

"Not good enough. I don't get paid on deal memos. I want a purchase order stating that payment is due and then a bank transfer, preferably today. You need to call your executive assistant in to fix it up?"

"I'll run it through the process personally," Chet says.

Bjorn stands and Chet is one beat behind him, signalling the meeting is over. Hunter stays sitting.

"I know you boys are keen to go run that purchase order through as the very next thing you do, but ain't there more to this? My team are about to board your ship and they don't have much to work with."

"We got this agreed because incident numbers showed a trend that allowed us to action a limited investigation," Chet reveals.

"CSCI don't do limited," Hunter explains.

"We hope not," Bjorn adds.

"You get us paid, we'll kick the can and get you numbers you never expected." Hunter stands. "Or maybe you do."

They don't take his offer to deny the very deliberate remark.

"You were supposed to be on the ship," Bjorn hits him with.

"Trust me, the woman on board with Kieron would frighten anyone."

"That's not the point, the contract says the two of you."

"You got two of us, as per contract. I'm here riding point and researching. He's in the field. Or were you looking for a photo opportunity of us together? Fee gets bigger, the more kicking we do."

"Names, numbers and any trends," Chet says.

He gives them a knowing smile and then he follows the invitation to leave.

Following his early-morning meeting on Dodge island, Hunter enters the dark operations room where Dwight is glued to a screen.

"That your money suit, boss?" Dwight asks, his head fixed at the data on the screen he is researching.

"My only suit but those boys sure got a few. They got a few moves too. They know incident types and numbers."

"Trends," Dwight offers, deeply engaged in the text on the screen.

"Yeah, they like that word, except they said, 'any trends'."

"You think the ships are failing to report all problems and incidents?"

"Unlikely. Unless there's stuff they don't know," Hunter muses.

"Or stuff they don't think would go on these graduates' spreadsheets," Dwight explains.

"I demanded the first payment."
"First?"
"The number on the memo. First payment."
"That's what you got for the whole Pacific murders job?"
"They never batted an eye-lid."
That makes Dwight turn from the screen,
"Sweet."
"Is it? Ain't it confirmation of bigger trouble? They filled the purchase order in themselves, no secretary or executive assistant today to see the purchase order. Plus, I started the meeting floating your idea of the pension-age drug-traffickers."

Dwight tilts his head; Hunter knows he must share more.

"They didn't think it was old guys revenge, they used the word revenge."

"Oh no," Dwight says. "I checked on the oldies too. They might want but they weren't extradited and they ain't free. Very harshly dealt with. The old man was seventy–two when he went down. He had form, trafficking hash up and down Norway. They gave him twelve years in high security, a place called Monsanto. Constructed in 1863 as a fort, it was converted to a military prison and now it's a hardcore high-security prison despite being in a nice part of Lisbon. He ain't getting out of there."

"That's a serious slap. Could he pull off a revenge from inside? Where's his wife?" Hunter asks.

"In the Tires Women's Prison, she got seven years."
"Woo."
"Big sentences. I'd want revenge, but I do it."
"Maybe it's not the individual trafficker, Dwight, but the whole operation that was closed down. I didn't

think they'd have us eating off the kids' menu with chocolate bars, but I wasn't expecting to be dealing with a T-bone," Hunter says, still thinking. "It can't be drugs on ships. Wrong time of the year; back then the old folks were caught sailing in from the Caribbean."

"What if there's a huge stash of cash hidden onboard?" Dwight adds.

"And they have to take it off bit by bit like our stash of one-hundred-dollar bills?"

"If the chocolate is a game to get people thrown off, with money. That's worrying."

"Very. We've put Kieron out there," Hunter agrees.

"Bedriška's with him, she's one hard nut."

"You're telling me. She frightened the pants off Elaine."

"They've boarded. It's lunchtime in Lisbon. She's demanding a doctor's report you promised her. Says you sent a fake."

"She knew that when she left for Lisbon, so she must have seen symptoms that worry her."

"Says he's dizzy, loses orientation, walks veering to the left."

"Tell Bedriška thanks for the 'best diagnosis of Kieron's condition to date'. Keep it coming and I'll talk with the physician."

"You think she's gonna swallow that?" Dwight asks.

"Medical advice was not to fly. That's all I hid."

"She'll want to see the proper doctor's report."

"No, she won't, she knows we could forge anything. Tell her, the advice line (not to fly) I covered up. Was at the bottom, look again. Make a thing of us being surprised she never noticed."

"We don't mention the drug cartel?" Dwight asks.

"No, not even to Elaine. I can't worry Elaine, she's pregnant."

"You live in one of the safest parts of Miami, she's fine."

"They took her once before."

Hunter looks at him as he waits for the phone to connect his call, then his attention is his mobile.

"Doc. It's Hunter Witowski. You wanted any observations on Commander Kieron Philips."

13 HUMANE

In the Miami diner, Croc is behind the counter grilling while Macey and Izzy serve. There are about ten customers in from the breakfast session. The bell above the door rings and Jenny walks in and to the counter,

"So, you're an agent now?"

"Yeah, licensed to grill; don't understand the fuss Stan makes about cooking the same old stuff," Croc laughs.

"I saw you at the Ocean Drive club."

Jenny walks away, to Izzy. Today she is mixing things up.

"What's new Izzy?"

"You know, Jenny, if there was a story, I'd be writing it between wiping tables."

"I did the story this morning and you missed it. But I'd like you to do a human piece. On Hunter and Elaine. Keep them separate. Two stories as a series. Interview Hunter's wife, get the female angle."

Jenny goes back to the counter and presses the new 'office' buzzer intercom on the diner counter which neither looks retro or tech like the screens next door.

"Yoh, canteen, speak to me." Dwight is heard to say.

"You are going to need a different line when Mary comes back. It's Jenny. Tell Hunter I'm back with a question about three ships, all for sale, drug smuggling, and sewage smell."

Izzy upturns a coffee mug and slides it to Jenny who pours her own.

"Seriously, Jenny. Is news that slow? One of three ideas?"

In the dark operations room, Hunter and Dwight are shocked to hear her knowledge. Hunter puts his finger to his lips, then types, 'she bugged us?' They both start to search the room for a bug, but there is nothing obvious. Hunter leaves Dwight to continue checking the route Jenny walked when she was shown the room. Dwight pulls a torch for a detailed look and checks the back of the screens and under every surface.

"I'm sure one of us would have seen her leave something, we need cameras in here," he says to himself.

"Where does the smell come from on a cruise ship?" Jenny asks as Hunter takes the stool next to her. "And don't suggest Reporters. I found complaints about smells on the chat site and no mention of reporters."

Hunter looks at her long and hard before replying.

"Lot of chat sites out there."

"Guess I got the smelly one. Sewage?"

"Ships use a closed suction system down to the treatment plant right in the bottom of the ship's hull. It can't leak. Each Passenger produces nearly eight pounds of waste each day, but that's not a problem. When the pipes get blocked, they must be opened so an engineer can rod and flush. That smells."

"Is that why those old ships are for sale?" Jenny asks.

"All ships have similar waste systems."

"But old ships have old systems," she bites.

"That work as well as the day they were installed. There are over forty cruise ships for sale. Which ones do you mean?"

"Clever," she smiles. "You know which ships I mean."

"I'm not a mind reader. Is this you tipping me off there's a potential job?"

"Let's both cut the bull and follow the smell," she says.

"You have the nose for it?"

Jenny nods, agreeing with him.

"Deliberately blocked sewage systems?" she says.

Hunter swings around on his chair. "New cruisers flush things they get away with at home. Doesn't work on a ship," Hunter explains.

"So, what's forbidden?"

"I'm sure there's a list, but cleaning wipes are worst. That is whether they claim to be flushable or not. They block the Miami Dade sewage system and that is much wider. Nice parallel you could draw."

"And you've not been employed?"

Hunter shakes his head slowly and has that screwed up inquisitive look,

"We don't do sewage problems, not for Miami Dade nor ships."

"Old drug smugglers?" she tries, hoping he will accuse her of listening in to him because it would confirm the story.

"Wrong time of the year, that would be the end of the Caribbean season. Is this a bad tip-off from your two little birds."

"It could be Di, their executive assistant, she loves to pass on a story."

"But you're guessing," he says.

"Where's your partner? His daughter, Auli'i, thinks he's on a ship and that he's not well." Jenny says, revealing that she has been digging as well as listening.

"He's taking a break. Recuperating, I hope."

Jenny tries to look straight through him for detail,

"What's worrying you?" she asks.

"I'd rather you didn't do a piece on me or Elaine, nor mention her being kidnapped in Madeira. You've done that, its old news. She's pregnant now, it'll only cause stress."

Jenny lets that digest for a moment.

"Not only don't I believe you, I know you've lied to me. So, I owe you no favours. Nothing. Elaine's not out of bounds unless you give me something," she says.

Hunter pauses for a long moment, but it is only to suppress and control his anger,

"Last guys who held my wife hostage are all dead."

14 STAY FOCUSED

A corridor on a ship is like any hotel except it is narrower and the suitcases are left outside the cabin when delivered. A corridor with cases at every door is a sight unique to cruise ships. Bedi follows Kieron along to their room. She is concerned that he is using the walls to steady himself. That might be normal if the ship was in rocky seas, but it is berthed in Jardim de Tabaco Quay, Lisbon, on a change-over day. The agents check the doors for cabin numbers, then enter, throwing their bags onto the bed then stand back. Both had packed everything in a hand luggage but what they are looking at is the embarrassment of a double bed.

"Which side?" Kieron asks.

"You use sofa."

"I'm not sofa surfing, I'm not well. But you go ahead."

"No. I take this side," she says referring to the side of the bed nearest the door of the cabin.

Kieron circles round to the other side, and a large French window. He opens it and steps out to check access to their balcony. There is no doubt that he could climb side to side, drop down to the balcony below, or even climb up assuming it was not a force ten gale. He turns back,

"Look, if you want me to take the couch," he says, feeling guilty.

"No. We are adults. I not attracted to you."

"Thanks," Kieron says, looking at his case. "I'm sure the cabin steward can separate it into singles."

"Cabin too small. We manage. Now, two hours before final on-board. We go to Lisbon?" Bedriška asks, but there is little question to it.

When cruisers get onto the ship for the first time, they normally stay onboard. There are a host of reasons but the foremost is the desire to look around. They may never have seen the ship before, and they walk around in absolute amazement at the wealth of areas and activities. Or, it might have been a year since their last holiday, and they are looking for changes to the ship. However, fear is a big one. Fear is always a controlling factor. Guests might not wish to risk a trip into town with just two hours to sail-away, but crew members are different. Crew are used to half days or less in port because they often work mornings and by the time they are released from work, two hours is all they have. The suggestion from Bedi is not a strange one. Lisbon is also a great city and not too spread out, whereas many change-over ports fail to offer much interest. In Lisbon, the ships dock adjacent to the city and the walk into the main square is no more than minutes. Strangely, the shuttle bus often takes much longer because of the contrived route it takes. Bedriška is familiar with Lisbon. From the balcony, Kieron can see her point. He checks his watch and has 15.30hrs.

"You are not too tired?" she asks.

"I'm good. Unless you think we should be in the laundry?"

"No, we go."

"I guess there'll be no one in the laundry," Kieron says, collecting his cruise card and heading to the cabin door.

"Laundry busy, but no point today. Formal nights best for trouble."

Holding hands, they waltz back to disembark at the computer station set up next to reception. There is little on any ship that would surprise either of them, and that might be their downfall, but few would be looking at that detail. Few except Paul Lopkey, a juggling magician who is square on to them. He is embarking and gives out a large cry,

"Oh no!" he jokes and turns to leave the ship.

Philips knows he has been made and some of the boarding guests have seen the give-away, as have some staff waiting to leave. Lopkey turns back to address him.

"Don't tell me," he says, wanting to guess something or think of a funny remark.

Kieron can't let that remark come out. He knows he must tell his own story to the assembled audience, or he will be revealed.

"Look, love, it's the magician," Kieron says to Bedi and she knows there is a play being made. He then turns back to Paul, raising her ringed finger which boasts the under-cover story of a wedding.

"We got married."

Kieron gets right up to him, his mouth to Lopkey's ear as he hugs him, "say nothing, we're under-cover."

Lopkey was on both my last two ships, the Heist leaving Panama and then he took a bullet in the Pacific. Lopkey has every right to be concerned.

"I said I would never work on the same ship as you again," he offers as a powerful whisper.

Bedi kisses him and holds the hug longer; he is no doubt having the life squeezed from him. Kieron must interest the crowd of embarking cruisers.

"He was the singer on the ship when we met," he says, putting his arm around both Lopkey and Bedi.

"Hold me up, I feel dizzy," Kieron whispers to her past Lopkey, and Lopkey thinks he must hold him up too.

"Magician, comedy magician," Lopkey corrects to the crowd.

"You don't sing?" Kieron asks.

"No," Lopkey says, confused.

"Are you doing the same act?"

"Yes," Lopkey replies.

"Oh," Kieron says.

"Oh," Bedi copies.

"We'll give it a miss this time."

Kieron turns and is dragged out by Bedi, Paul Lopkey is left confounded. They wait to get off, next to half a dozen crew members all watching a steady flow of excited embarking guests. The officer in whites at the bottom stops the line and waves them down the gangway. Kieron offers the other waiting crew to go first, but they are solemn-faced and don't move. Bedi pushes him on, she swipes her cruise card, he swipes his.

"We go first, we guests," she says.

He gives them the slightest of looks not to be rude. However, he sees that they and their cases are not in a hurry to disembark. It must be crew change-over day as well as guests. He loses his balance on the gangway and catches the rail.

Away from the ship, they are guided to a dockside security building. Local police ensure all incoming luggage goes through an X-ray machine via a conveyor belt and people go through a walking X-ray. As neither of them are carrying anything other than their mobile phones and cruise cards, leaving is a formality.

"That usual? Security is normally done on ship," Kieron says, as they leave the building.

"Police always here in Lisbon."

Kieron looks back at queue from security and up the gangway waiting to enter the ship. They are free to visit the city.

In the sun, Bedi and Kieron walk along beside the dock towards the square, still hand in hand. His other hand speed dials,

"Hunter. I've been made. The cabaret act Paul Lopkey who got shot by Ruby and shared a hospital room with us in Tahiti, saw me as he boarded the ship. He made a big fuss which we covered."

"I'll call him. Carry on as normal."

"But not normal," Bedi says, into Kieron's phone.

"No, Bedi, you're right. Kieron, your doctor didn't want you to fly, but he was being over cautious, he didn't know how tough you are," Hunter says.

"He seemed OK about it when I saw him," Kieron says.

"That not doctor. Hunter put white coat on nurse," Bedi says into the phone.

"I needed you to fly. With proper symptoms, we now have an actual diagnosis."

"Symptoms, what symptoms?"

"Bedi ratted you out," Hunter says getting his own back. "You have Benign Paroxysmal Positional Vertigo or BPPV."

"Is it bad?"

"Not at all. You get dizzy, off-balance and walk like you're drunk."

"Ok, that fits?"

"It's to do with crystals in the inner ear, your previous fall dislodged them. Well, not the fall, hitting the deck. In short, they're in the wrong place."

"Does that mean surgery?"

"No, weird physio."

"How weird?"

"Best to start it in bed with Bedriška."

"OK. If that's an order," Kieron says.

"What physio? I not nurse."

"Keep focused on something as you wave your head, side to side. I just texted you the exercises."

"And this stupid job?" Bedi asks.

"Kieron, your new partner is very pushy," Hunter says, via the phone as they approach the square.

"Sounds like she's honest and she's got my back," Kieron adds.

Bedi sees his loyalty and acknowledges it as they both wait for a real reply about the job they have flown halfway around the world for. Silence is the interview technique that demands the other person speak.

"The company just paid a mega huge sum in advance. I'll send you the receipt, you won't believe it."

"I believe nothing," Bedi interjects. "There is more than laundry, we not stupid."

"Neither is Lopkey, the magician you're about to talk to. None of us is stupid," Kieron says.

"Only you," Bedi fires at him. "You too focussed on money."

"Like his stage act, what we are being sold by the cruise company is to deflect us from what they don't want us to see," Kieron says.

"What is it they not want you to see?" Bedi asks.

"We are looking for the catch. Just keep your eyes open because we genuinely don't know if there is something deeper," Hunter says.

"Yeah, and try and focus while waving our heads about," Kieron says, then he hangs up abruptly. He and Bedi turn into the large Commercial Square, "is anyone telling us the truth?"

"That statue of Joseph the first; true. He love opera and women; true," Bedi says, as they walk past the huge statue of a man riding a horse on a high plinth and through a huge arch. "It commemorates the rebuilding of city after earthquake; political excuse for building big selfie."

"How do you know?"

"Many times; I ship monitor on walking tour. Follow me. We go to castle."

"Why?"

"Because we cruisers, cruisers see castles and churches," Bedi says grabbing his hand and pulling him.

15 TRAM 28

Bedi continues to drag Kieron through the busy Lisbon crowds, as she runs to catch a tram, forgetting he might have a problem. He jumps on it behind her and stands squeezed between people in the tracked rail vehicle. He genuinely laughs, maybe for the first time in a while.

"Why you laugh?"

"Because I can't fall over."

"Sorry. I forget. In St Vincent, I never notice problem."

"In Bequia, I would just sleep in the sun when I felt nauseous."

"Tell me, honest, you OK?"

"Sure, the run did me good. My head was shaking from side to side as I focused on the number 28 of the tram. Where does it go?"

"Famous tram."

"Why?" he asks, still in good spirits.

"Go to top."

"Longest tram ride in Europe," an old lady tells them.

Bedi nods, which is her way of thanking the local; and she replies, trying to be nice. Her tone, however, is from the Baltic, not the Mediterranean.

"No time for longest ride, most is rubbish."

The lady decides not to engage with them anymore. Kieron lifts his watch to check the time. 1550hrs.

"Don't worry. We have time. I was trying to be funny," Bedi says.

"Oh."

The old woman gives Kieron a strange look that obviously suggests he rethink his choice of friends. The tram climbs the hill and turns corners only just missing the edges of buildings and other vehicles.

"You see church. Eusébio, footballer, buried there," Bedi says.

"And that's the attraction?" Kieron asks turning to the local lady for further details.

"Church of Santa Engrácia is Portuguese National Pantheon. Every famous person buried there," the lady replies, bluntly.

At the top, the narrow twisting road gives way to a busy square where many get off. They leave the tram and Kieron is dragged to a smaller statue than the one down in Commercial Square. Bedriška stops, seemingly very amused. For her, it is an unusual show of emotion.

"Statue of St Vincent, patron saint of all your houses and millions. We make selfie. Send to Georgie."

As Bedi tries to frame him and her with the statue, he ponders through his smile.

"Our millions, if we can ever get them off the ship, but trust me it's not going to be easy."

Kieron follows her over to a viewing area at the edge of the paved piazza overlooking the city and the dock below where their ship sits next to two others.

"What a fantastic view," Kieron says.

"Old city, busy port. Why we here?" she asks. "Just to be cruisers."

"I was told to rest and exercise in bed with you."

"I not nurse."

"Then be my wife."

An old lady hears him and thinks she has witnessed a marriage proposal. Excited, she stands looking at Bedi expecting an answer. Bedi feels her presence and wonders why they have an audience.

"What?" she asks the lady.

"He just asked you to be his wife, what is your answer? It is so romantic here." The lady pulls her friend over and their audience doubles.

"Romance!" her friend says.

"I try," Kieron says, joining the two women and putting Bedi on the spot by dropping to his knee. He looks up at her. "Will you?"

Bedi leans forward, pulls Kieron up by tightly grabbing his head each side and she kisses him with power. The two women applaud.

The couple separate, Kieron needs air.

"Tonight, I fuck him," Bedi says proudly.

The two women stop applauding and walk away embarrassed.

"Your romance needs work," Kieron says.

They are both stopped by Bedriška's phone bleeping. She reads for so long that Kieron walks back to the wall and looks from their high vantage position. He studies the port and the row of ships.

"The security was different," Kieron offers.

He is ignored; she is still reading. As inquisitive as he might be, he has to wait for her to return.

"More intrigue?" he asks.

"No. Your exercises. Look at ship, keep eyes on ship, turn head ninety degrees that way, then this, then faster. And faster."

Kieron does as he is asked until he feels nauseous.

"Good start," she says.

He leans against the wall to take a moment and notices a young girl next to him who had seen him and is now copying. She waves her head from side to side and says, "America, Europe, America, Europe."

Kieron laughs but remains bent over to the floor due to his nausea. She too bends over and laughs.

"Australia," she says.

Kieron laughs back at her.

"Good game, it over," Bedi says, dragging him away. "Exercises not for you to play with children. Need to get very violent for dislodge crystals."

"Great. Shake my head about and never take my eyes off a key focus. Like watching a magician?"

"Magician?" she asks.

Kieron waves his right hand and she watches it.

"You're looking here," he says as his left-hand tries to take her phone from her pocket. She grabs his hand hard and has him in a lock.

"...while the magician performs the real trick with his other hand."

"I hope he better than you."

"Lopkey is good."

"Not as good as me," she says letting him go.

He rubs his wrist and has an epiphany.

"The chocolate in the laundry and the fights are smoke and mirrors to distract us. Now can I have an ice-cream, darling?"

"No, you want me to look at ice-cream seller, I not distracted."

Kieron looks up the hill. Bedi gives him his phone back that she just took,

"I hope you not amateur," she says.

She drags Kieron along with disregard to his dizziness and confusion. They rush up past the castle wall, through a large arch gate, turn right and she drags him into a café called 28. It is a period diner based on an old tram, yellow and brown. The seats, the handrails and the lighting are all from trams. Pictures depicting the history of the tram are on every wall.

"Don't look at ice cream, look at custard tarts."

"Tarts?" he asks.

"Yes. Real reason I get off ship; Custard tart in Lisbon incredibly special."

16 QUEEN OF TARTS

Kieron silently gorges on the small, flaky pastry tart full of yellow custard sprinkled with nutmeg. Bedi watches him.

"That's wonderful," he says, still brushing crumbs from his mouth. "I had lost a lot of my taste since the fall, but that just brought it all back."

"You cruiser now, you eat as you want."

"We need to take some back," he says.

"No. Pastry go soft. They get rubbish."

"We'd never get them through that special security anyway," Kieron says to her, raising his arm to catch the eye of the waiter. "Can I get two more of these please"

"I no want more," Bedi says.

"They're both for me, I can taste again!"

"A local tart and you take eye off job."

"It happens," he says.

"That was humour."

"Very good."

The waiter brings the two tarts along with a couple of fridge magnets and a small model tram. He has an interesting recital on the history of the importance of the tram in Lisbon, which is built on seven steep hills. He guides their attention from the pictures on the wall to the seats all being original tram seats. His performance is aimed at upselling, which only serves to delay Kieron's deployment of the tarts, so he buys a fridge magnet. The waiter's showmanship instantly ends as suspected and Kieron can re-focus on his sugary tarts.

"What is special about any of these ports?" he asks her.

Bedriška thinks hard then looks at Kieron for a clue because he has started a train of thought. She has no other option than to recite the list of ports to see if he reveals anything.

"Lisbon, Cadiz, Malaga, Barcelona, Ajaccio, Naples."

"Which is pizza," he says, excitedly.

She ignores his stupidity.

"Sarande, Dubrovnik, Zadar and Venice."

"What is special about any of those ports, what are we not seeing?" he asks.

Bedi is genuinely lost and struggling, she eventually offers a lame observation.

"Maybe Corsica. Pronounce ay-ya-cho wrong, locals upset, might put chocolate in washing," she says, detailing the syllables in the pronunciation, which for her takes concentration.

"No, way offbeat," he says.

Bedriška doesn't like to give up but shakes her head. Holding up his last custard tart and twisting it to tease him. He starts to recite his own almost syllable-detailed, almost sung prose, which he must think about.

"The Queen of Hearts, she made some tarts. The Knave of Hearts, he stole those tarts. The King of Hearts called for the tarts and beat the knave full sore."

"Not good song. We leave now," Bedi says, encouraging him to leave.

Kieron scoffs the tart full score and picks up his phone, speed dialling. He checks his watch. Bedi taps it, she is insistent as they have a tram journey down the hill before a short run to catch their ship.

"Hunter, if you're with Elaine, go to a different room," Kieron says, and he waits.

Bedriška is concerned but impatient.

"Don't sing child song," Bedriška advises waging her finger from side to side. "He will worry about your brain injury."

She pays the bill and encourages him to leave. They swiftly walk down from the castle.

"OK, so aside from wonderful tarts in Lisbon, and the unusually very secure security portside. What if the pretty stupid play on the ships was aimed at us, CSCI, not the shipping operator. What if it was aimed at getting us on board?"

Holding his hand, Bedi leads Kieron down through the old castle gate. The sea is way below.

"I'm listening," Hunter says, laying his phone down next to Dwight in the darkness of the ops room. "Like Ruby, wanting a job with us at CSCI and killing to make her point? If that was her goal, and we'll never know."

Bedriška's face changes into one of serious curiosity. Her arm wraps around his shoulder so she does not miss a clue.

"What if it's about the sixteen-million-dollars we have in a trunk, and the Queen of Tarts," he pauses.

Bedriška wags her finger again.

"No sing," she whispers.

"Our Latina wants her money back. What if all this is to have us lift the trunk in Barcelona?"

"She could have rung," Hunter jests.

"Except she should be in prison," Kieron says, suggestively.

17 JINGOISTIC

The ship slowly passes under another of Lisbon's notorious landmarks, the huge suspension bridge; Ponte 25 de Abril, named after the Portuguese Carnation Revolution of 1974. The sight, like the Golden Gate Bridge in San Francisco, means they are leaving Lisbon behind.

Kieron and Bedi stand on the Sun Deck looking down at the entertainment staff who are wearing multi flag shirts and dancing around the swimming pool on Lido Deck. They are leading the entertainment for the enthusiastic new guests. The sail away party is in full swing and most are waving a small plastic flag which they might keep for the whole of their cruise if not beyond. Bedi has one for Sweden and is equally excited.

"You don't mind waving someone else's flag then?" Kieron asks her.

Bedriška looks at the flag,

"Sweden? Deposed Russian royals sent to die in Finland and Sweden. I loved my country. But it cheated me. It cheated me bad." Bedi turns to Kieron, profoundly serious. "I love Georgie, but she cheated me."

"Sorry I asked."

"We start violent exercise back in room," she says with some anger.

"Yes Queen," he says.

She has him thinking. "Who is this Tart Queen?"

"A drug lord's wife from Columbia who was trying to escape to Madeira."

"With sixteen million dollars?"

"Now she is in prison."

"You hope."

"Which is why you are a better wife than Prisha would have been."

"Who is Prisha?"

"She worked in the ship's office, more intellectual than muscle."

"I not stupid."

Bedi drags him away roughly. If the very flat sea is not a good excuse each time his step falters, the busy open bar might be. No one will take any notice. Only new cruisers are likely to feel any swell or those who have problems with their Otoconia, the calcium carbonate crystals in their inner ear.

Kieron is not sure if it was the run to the ship, or the Russian taskmaster asking him to whip his head from side to side, but he lays flat on the bed exhausted.

"That is what I'm supposed to do? I feel worse."

"Gaze stabilisation, I check on internet, perhaps Hunter lying again."

"I don't think he lies about that kind of stuff."

"What stuff does he lie about?"

"He lied to save his wife. I would lie to save mine."

"I am flattered."

"Not you."

"Spasibo."

"Thank you, I know, I will be fluent in Russian by the end."

"It also mean, forgive me."

"Actually, I'd lie to save you or Georgie and definitely my daughter Auli'i."

"I hear daughter is beautiful. But you adopt. I would like child with Georgie. We adopt," Bedi says, opening her case and pulling out a four-way extension lead.

"Good packing," Kieron says to change the subject.

"Never unpacked case. Switchable extension block is cruise essential."

"Switchable?"

"Chargers easy switch off when out of cabin."

"Efficient, I would expect nothing less," Kieron says as he slowly sits up. "I said, I would lie to save you and Georgie."

"Should I get emotional?"

"No, Bedi. No emotion is expected from a psychopath," Kieron says having to lie down dizzy again. "How often do I have to do these exercises?"

"Build up to five-minute session. Need three or four times a day."

"You are a psychopath! You just made me do ten minutes."

"Hunter says you tough to fly, I say you tough for advanced class."

"I feel like crazy," he says, watching her remove underwear from her case.

"Not for you."

"How long does this dizziness last?"

"Until I dress."

"No, this madness?"

"48 hours, maybe more. I think that bullshit."

"You do, do you?" Kieron says, trying to sit up. "I'll be OK by the end of Cadiz?"

"Bad feeling is first reaction. Treatment can last weeks. But not you!" she says.

"You don't agree?"

"No. If purpose is dislodge crystals to drop down. We do extreme class, work hard. I get them to drop."

"Did you specialise in torture?" he asks watching her pull out a small whip from her case.

"That stay in case."

18 UP ALL NIGHT

Although it is the middle of the day in Miami, it is dark in the operations room. It is sparsely lit by standby neon lights, none of the screens are active. The outside door opens followed by a struggle to hold it back, a shaft of daylight bursts across the darkened window behind the screens and vanishes as the door closes. Wheels whir up the ramp and Dwight's chair, headlights on, rounds into control area. He fires up the row of table lamps and sees Hunter at a desk,

"You look like shit."

"I feel it, I've been here most of the night."

"Wait 'til the baby comes, it gets worse."

"How would you know?"

"I had a wife and a new baby, they left when I came home damaged."

"That hurts, sorry. That would keep me up all night."

"It did."

"You're welcome to share duties when ours is born, uncle."

"You know what? I'd be more than proud to."

"But it's not the baby that worries me."

"Getting paid?" Dwight asks.

"Money's in the bank. It's the job that worries me."

"You wanna tell uncle?" Dwight encourages.

"Who's been messing in my kitchen?" Is the large bellowing voice of Wild Mary reaching them from next door.

"I said, whose been messing in my kitchen," beams through the intercom she has found. "Hello! If I come in and get you, it going to get messy in there."

Hunter shakes his head and walks slowly through the adjoining doors. Dwight follows, purely for spectator fun. He has never met Wild Mary.

"Cool it, Mary, there's one coffee mug and the griddle's cooked one burger," Hunter admits.

"Sounds like he's primed it ready to go," Dwight says.

"And who are you?" she shouts. "Customers come in that door. What you ordering?"

"Dwight works for CSCI."

"OK, what's he ordering?" she insists. "And you clean my griddle."

They both approach the counter.

"So, what had you up all night?" Dwight dares to ask Hunter, ignoring Mary.

"I tell you what had him here all night. He ain't allowed to make this mess at his house," Mary fires.

"I wasn't talking to you, Mary," Dwight says firmly.

The room goes silent for a long moment, broken by the raucous laughter from by the door. Stan has one foot in and a little of his head is just inside but now he dare not enter further as he senses a dangerous cyclone. The circular metal ring on the bell above the door is stretched to its limit on the brink of firing back and ringing the bell.

"Think me going to turn me around and have me another day off," Stan says, not capable of stopping himself from laughing.

"That's Stan," Hunter tells Dwight.

"Nice to meet you, Stan," Dwight starts. "I was asking Hunter what had kept him up all night."

Mary pulls a steel handled knife from the kitchen's knife block. Stan is still laughing.

"You going to go out and try that entry again, Stan?" she directs at her husband.

"You know?" he starts, but chokes.

"No, I don't, Stan," she interrupts.

"You know, I think I'm just dandy right here by the door."

"So, Hunter, what kept you up all night?" Dwight asks, again ignoring Wild Mary.

Stan is crippled with laughter. The bell above the door rings as he loses control. He steps forward to keep his balance.

"It's like he don't see you, Mary! You's a ghost."

"Kieron's phone call. He could be right about the Columbian drug dealers," Hunter admits.

"Them Columbians come anywhere near me and they're dead," Mary says, firmly.

Stan lets the door close behind him as he almost dances in, buckled up with laughter,

"Dead, she said. Dead they be," Stan sings.

"Stan, she's not met them. I don't think she's grasped the severity of the situation. They're killers," Hunter offers.

"You tell Colombo, I sleep well in my bed," Mary offers, her hand moving to the knife block.

"Yeah, nothing wakes Mary, nothing!" Stan laughs, having to sit.

"Last time you had anything worth waking me for, Stan, we were on Canaveral pier at the Space Coast Fair!"

"OK," Hunter says, turning back to his office.

Dwight spins around after him,

"Yeah, we'll be back after the B-movie's done," Dwight says, heading for the magic door.

A knife whizzes just over his head and embeds itself hard into the woodwork in front of them, right under the title Cruise Ship Crime Investigators. Hunter looks at the silver metal blade quivering at its abrupt stop and realises the special features of the well-balanced knives are not solely to chop onions. He and Dwight turn back and see her draw another knife from the block; looking like she has done it many times. Stan now falls off his chair with laughter.

"Mary, if this gets nasty there'll be a lot more of them than you have knives in that block," Hunter shares respectfully because he has been up against the mob.

Mary leans behind the grill and opens one of the spotless shiny stainless-steel overhead doors revealing a collection of knife sets. Hunter and Dwight are both focussed on the ornate armoury.

"I got me a lot to chop!" Mary says.

Ring. The bell above the door goes again. Croc enters. He stops concern that Stan is on the floor. He doesn't know he is crippled with laughter,

"You need the EMS?"

"All of them will if someone don't start ordering breakfast. What kind of ship you been running while I'm gone?"

"I'll have two eggs over easy," Dwight says.

"That's better, and?" Mary asks, looking at Dwight firmly to let him know he has not finished.

"Grits?" Dwight asks.

"Tomatoes," Mary says.

"Yeah, some nice ripe tomatoes be just fine, Mary."

"Oh, dear," Croc says.

Stan is laughing again,

"Oh, Dear," Stan chokes.

Dwight looks at Hunter who is shaking his head and might explain, but Mary has the floor.

"Sliced?" he asks.

"You mean green tomatoes," Mary adds.

"Green?" Dwight questions in disgust.

"Fried green tomatoes," she finishes.

"OK eggs and fried green tomatoes."

"You're welcome, whatever your name is," Mary says.

"I'm Dwight."

"It wasn't a question," Mary starts. "Now Stan, you get your ass up here and cook before that old act of mine starts up again."

"Act?" Croc asks.

"Didn't you know we had an act?" she asks.

Croc shakes his head as he helps Stan up.

"You should hear the whole story someday, son," Stan says.

"How long did it last?" Dwight asks, innocently.

"One night," Stan howls, falling back down laughing again and needing Croc's help to find any composure.

"Ain't a long story then?" Croc says.

Croc sets him on his way, and he shuffles up to the grill.

"Let me explain, guys" Stan starts. "Me is the eye candy of the show. Body ripped, six pack, pumping muscles all covered in oil. Can even do a little dance routine."

"And Mary threw the knives?" Hunter asks, looking at her in fear as she holds three knives in a fan.

Stan opens his shirt and reveals a huge scar at the top of his chest. Everyone's gaze moves from Stan to Mary, standing at the end of the grill holding a tragedy of knives in her hands.

"Ouch! Looks like that hurt," Croc says.

"Hurt her more. I sued her big ass!"

Croc is confused.

"Yeah. Union paid me out enough money to retire and buy this diner, but d'you think I could get rid of her?"

Hunter sits down next to Dwight.

"Who are these Columbians?" Mary asks.

"Didn't you read the Cruise Heist book I gave you?"

"I was enjoying it, Croc stole it."

"Croc?" Hunter shouts.

"Izzy took it," he shouts.

"Let me explain," Hunter says. "But spoiler alert because Kieron thinks the Latina drug princess wants her millions back."

"Sixteen million?" Wild Mary asks. "Damn right she does. What woman wouldn't want it back."

"Well, technically she stole it."

"Don't make a damn difference."

"Kieron thinks all this disruption was designed to get us on a ship. A ship following our old ship with the money on. We leapfrog around the Mediterranean, port after port until we're tempted to lift the trunk. Then they take it from us. I'm worried they'll take Elaine again and I dare not warn her."

"What?" Mary asks.

They all look at Mary.

"I never heard so much poppy-cock. If you worried about Elaine, why you here making my grill dirty? And if fancy-woman want you to get her sixteen million, why not put you on the right ship?"

19 AT SEA

Mid-afternoon in the diner, things have cooled down now everyone knows each other. Dwight is in front of a screen in the ops room. Hunter stands on one side of him and on the other side Mary leans on the desk. They form an audience for Kieron who is full screen on a video call from his cabin on board ship on the Mediterranean Sea. He is dressed for dinner; white shirt, bow tie, black dinner jacket.

"Very basic disruption tactics. Bedi had the same on the deck she was observing," he explains. "The target guest had a large bundle of ironing to do, but they were waiting, working slowly and occasionally throwing in a word or two to inflame things. They wait until it kicks off, crazy people arguing about who had the next dryer. When the winner starts loading their clothes, the mark collects their ironing and excuses themselves. Arms full of clothes, they pass the open dryer. Unseen, they toss a chocolate bar in the dryer. Because it could have been any of the angry mob in the room, I guess it was well done."

"What was the outcome?" Hunter asks.

"We both followed the marks so no idea what happened later when the disaster was discovered. The disruption couple are in cabin G237. Never came out until they were dressed for dinner."

"Kieron; just want to say you're looking smart. I like a man who dresses for dinner," Wild Mary interrupts.

"Thanks, Mary. Missing you all."

"And the FGT?" Dwight asks.

Now everyone looks at Dwight. They have no idea.

"Fried Green Tomatoes, surely you miss them?"

Wild Mary gives Dwight a firm look, which encourages him to get on with the report.

"Your Latina is still in prison in Lisbon. The Tires Womans' Prison which is the same as the elderly smuggler from the UK," Dwight states.

"That connection doesn't make me feel any easier, she could still have her Figaro here on board," Kieron says.

"Can I see the dress?" Mary asks.

Kieron turns his head away from the camera and Bedi appears standing at the back of the room.

"Figaro? You lost me," Hunter says.

"The Latina has a paid handyman. It's a song from the opera in the theatre tonight, tomorrow we're in Seville," Kieron insists.

"Listen, while you have her money she can't pay no handyman? You big that Latina's part up too much," Mary states.

"Very funny. Just like Rosina, the character in the opera, who is far too often given more than was in the original writing," Kieron explains.

"See, she been bigged up too," Mary says. "Love your dress Bedriška, wish I had that figure."

"Need hard work, Mary."

Mary turns from the screen, insulted. The others avoid any form of comment or facial expression.

"Gonna have to bring me up to speed on that, Kieron," Hunter suggests.

"The opera, the Barber of Seville, Figaro. Rosina the young ward of the grumpy Bartolo."

"Has Bedi been shaking your head about too much?" he asks, suggesting he is not making sense.

"No, that's all good. I hate to tempt fate, but no nose bleeds and I feel more orientated. Thinking straight."

"But singing rhymes, I shake him other way now," Bedi says, from the back of the cabin.

"I agree, the Latina could be running a team from prison. I've been granted access to see both women so I'm flying to Lisbon," Hunter says.

Mary is distracted by Croc entering the operation room,

"Croc, you get them hands I'm paying for back working next door."

"Jenny's back looking for a story," he replies.

"You tell her it's all based around an opera because they're in Seville, and Wild Mary will be straight out to explain," Hunter says.

"She says Di Mond has told her that both Chet and Bjorn have been let go from the cruise company."

"Di Mond? What kind of silly-ass name is that?" Mary asks.

She gets no answer as the room is stunned to silence. Though none of this makes sense to Mary, she is looking at each of the others knowing something's gone wrong. Croc leaves.

"You look after that boy, he's special. Very special."

"Like a father, Mary. Like a father."

"Good coz that boy never had one. He no idea what a father is, so you be better than that. You can teach him about all that opera, coz the only opera he know does a talk show on TV."

"You know what I think?" Dwight asks.

They all look at Dwight, including Kieron via the worldwide web.

"Truth is, y'all, you've seen more than you know and you ain't doing proper reports. Let's go back to basics. Try drafting a report of everything you've seen on the ship. Everything from the moment you got on to your concert tonight. Who is where, who is on the door, who stopped, who looked?" Dwight concludes.

"I've was doing this job in the military, for a long time," Kieron says.

"Then you know how to do it properly."

"Dwight. Are we even on this job if our employers are gone?"

"We got paid," Hunter interjects.

"They got popped for a reason. You guys report back everything, let me examine those reports in a way you can't," Dwight says like he is going to war.

"Firm, but fair," Hunter adds. "I'll call Di Mond after lunch and find out what went on."

"Yeah. What he said. Follow them chocolate bars, treat Croc like yer son, and pay my bill if you been paid," Mary says, then leaves.

20 CADIZ

Late evening in Miami, but overnight on the ship, Dwight sent a dossier on the couple in G237 with a reminder Kieron needs to report more often.

During the serial killer investigation on the last ship, Dwight worked at the land office and formulated variations of several software packages. He wrote code to see details in dimensions that can only be done in layers on a screen. It allows him to isolate every detail of a profile or a report and connect dots. It can turn innocent observations into key evidence that may have been otherwise overlooked. It requires eyes-on-the-ground evidence gathering followed by accurate inputting of acquired information at the operations centre.

In his communication to the ship, Dwight revealed the two marks are on the excursion to Seville in the morning, but that he dares not add Bedi and Kieron to that excursion for fear of breaking their cover. It is up to them to get themselves on the tour.

Gwen and Bert Randolph, from Pudsey, appear to do anything from promotion work to being TV extras but are often secret shoppers, people who are employed to shop to catch staff out who are thought to be stealing from the company. There are other sides to the job: they can also buy products to get them to chart, a very grey area of any industry's marketing. It is probably this route that finds them on the ship, acting the lead role they never had on screen. Dwight lives on detail, and there is a lot more than Kieron or Bedi might need.

As soon as they wake, they have a problem. They are running late to get on the early excursion from the ship. Kieron speed reads. Bedi throws her phone down and drags the duvet around her and goes to the washroom and closet. She may have been naked in bed all last night but being seen naked is somehow different.

"They are like El Cid," Kieron says, dressing fast.

"They kill?"

"Secret shoppers? No, they switch loyalties easily for money."

"And free cruise," she shouts. "Dwight should wake us earlier."

"Dwight is demanding more reports from us again," Kieron says, entering the small moulded plastic shower and toilet space. She is on the toilet. He is at the sink cleaning his teeth.

"Hey!" she says.

"We're married."

After a rush to wake themselves and having no time for breakfast, they enter the busy night club. With the lights on, curtains open and bars locked closed, it is more like a conference room. The red love seats are full of guests. The room is the staging post for over two hundred people, possibly four coach loads. They wait with their cameras, umbrellas, and sun hats for news of their tour coach being ready. On the small dance floor is a table with two tour staff checking names and giving out a round yellow sticker with the number twelve on. One for each person on the tour.

"They missed a trick here, they could be selling drinks," Kieron says.

"All staff working at breakfast," Bedriška says, then she approaches the desk and asks if they can be added as late joiners, only to be told that it is sold out. She lingers, helpless for a moment realising she needs to rise over the inconvenience of only having guest status. She rudely puts her small bag on the table and asks again.

"Are you sure?"

"You can go to the excursion office and see what they can do," the busy staff member relays, concentrating on explaining the waiting procedure to joining guests with tickets as she hands them a sticker each.

With no special powers on board this ship, but two stolen yellow stickers, Bedi walks to the exit and scans the room for Kieron who has gone AWOL.

Kieron returns, wraps his arm around her waist and guides her away,

"We're on expenses," he says, showing her two yellow stickers as they walk out of sight.

"Yes," she replies, also producing two stickers. "Taxi?"

"Taxi," he agrees.

"They want we follow chocolate bar criminals."

"...and write reports."

".. they have to pay," she concludes, as they head to the gangway by reception.

Cadiz port is part of the small city, which is said to have over two hundred watchtowers for looking out on either of the two stretches of sea it lays between. It is a city for spying. The port service road has coaches and taxis, just beyond is a railway station which has regular trains to Seville. They see the coaches all with a large number twelve on and a card saying, 'Andalusian Countryside and the Sites of Seville'. Paul Lopkey is by a coach, holding a clipboard.

"What's he doing?" Kieron asks Bedi.

"Any staff can be company representative on coach. Get excursion free," she explains.

"Is that our chance?"

"No. No-fuss here."

They wait for the groups of guests to appear so they can target the precise coach their marks, Gwen and Albert, take. Bedi is super-efficient, writing down all four coach colours and registration plates. Then they choose a taxi.

"I can do full-day tour," the taxi driver offers.

"One way to Seville. My wife doesn't like coaches but we're on the yellow tour," Kieron says, sticking the yellow sticker on his shirt.

"OK we follow," the driver agrees.

Bedi and Kieron make themselves comfortable for the hour and a half journey as they pull away from the dock after the coach. He is typing into his phone.

"This is Landward Gate, the only land gate into Cadiz, built in the 18th Century," the driver says on autopilot.

Kieron pauses and looks up and sees the coach go through the huge brick-built arched gate.

"You ever see the movie, El Cid, with Charlton Heston?" Kieron asks Bedi,

"No," she says.

"With Sophia Loren?"

"Still no. Was he good murdering mercenary?"

"He defended Christian Spain against the Moors."

"Then film wrong. Even his name from Moors, old Arabic El Sayyid. He fights against Christians, he fights anyone. He was real prostitute," she says harshly, with even less tone. "Just like us, just like secret shoppers."

Kieron is taken aback by her stern remarks. Maybe he will never get used to them, but that felt angry.

"I hope our shoppers aren't going to slaughter the rest of their group," Kieron adds.

"No."

"Are you religious?"

"No."

"It's easy to be an atheist until the shooting starts," Kieron says.

"What?"

"Just something a chaplain said to me when I was lying in a field hospital."

"Good place for him to recruit," she says.

"Yeah, but a high turnover of members."

Kieron continues to type.

"What you type?" she asks.

"My report. Miami will be asleep now, so I am going to ping them both everything, keep waking them up." "Good idea. Absolutely, anything we did and saw yesterday," Bedriška says, preparing her phone. "I send them selfie with St Vincent. Tell of two women watch because you propose marriage."

21 WHOSE KITCHEN?

"Who's been messin' in my kitchen again?"

Dwight is in his chair extracting data from the reports sent over by Kieron and Bedriška. He likes data, it speaks to him. Sometimes it shouts at him, but this shout is from Mary, and she's wild. His head turns slowly to the dark space between him and the connecting door. He flicks on the table lights which until now he had not needed. Mary stands, angry, and looking at him, the only person in the room.

"It ain't your kitchen. One, you don't do the cooking, and two, Stan tells us he bought the diner," Dwight says.

His brevity comes from a different place from where Kieron and Hunter had to find theirs. He was once a fighting soldier, but his daring now comes from knowing he can't be knocked down any further. He loves being an analyst and knows he is making a difference. He loves being a team member, and now he has joined CSCI he has a family, but Mary is not seeing him that way yet. Mary is giving him an unforgiving look. For once, she is so taken aback by his remark that she can't speak.

"Mary, tell me what's been moved. What was eaten? All the clues, every single one, and I'll build a profile of the messer," he says, very straight face.

"You think that's funny?"

"You never knocked or said excuse me? I was working. I might have just had a thought on how to catch a killer and you blew it straight out of my head."

"Someone gonna get their ass murdered in here before long."

"That might be true, but it won't be today, and it won't be me."

Stan chokes with laughter at the door. He has been listening to at least some of the conversation. Mary turns sharply.

"You get and clean that grill."

"Can I order what I had yesterday, please, Stan?"

"You sure can, Dwight, I'll buzz you when it's good and done."

"Thank you, Stan."

"You have a wife at home? Has to deal with that cocky mouth?"

"No Mary, my wife left when I got these new wheels. I'll buzz you when I have something on your messer."

Mary takes a moment.

"Serial messer," she adds.

Finishing his breakfast, his motorised chair at the table near the counter, Dwight pats his mouth with the serviette, then reaches for the coffee.

"Stan, can't help noticing there were no green tomatoes this morning."

"Don't get much past you detective boys, but you ain't getting your money back," Stan says.

"Someone be paying Mary, somewhere, somehow, but it ain't me."

"You be paying somehow, someway, sometime," Stan says.

"Then I'm paying in skill. My boss paying in dollars."

"We all prisoners of our own experience, Mr Dwight, all prisoners."

"Where is she, Stan?"

"She left to steam-off at the grocers. See, she likes the huge green tomatoes. She don't want them ripe. But them suppliers say someone down the line goes and ripens them red now before they get here. Mary, she just want to take green ones out dat chain."

Dwight freezes instantly, his face sunk deep into an unmoving gaze. Stan looks and wonders if anyone is still at home.

"Now I seen that look. On the pier there was one of them hypnotist acts, he made people look like that. Never seen it done with talk of tomatoes," Stan says filling Dwight's coffee mug. But Dwight is not taking any notice; he remains fixed in another world. Stan walks back around the counter, his eyes not leaving Dwight. He loads two clean plates and hits the small service bell. Nothing from Dwight. Izzy attends the counter and Stan nudges her to look towards Dwight.

"He turned to stone, just like Lot's wife," Stan says.

"Genesis 19.26," Izzy says, holding a plate in each hand, her gaze fixed on Dwight.

"Like so much of the Bible, misquoted and misunderstood. Lot turned to salt. I need to turn to stone like Atlas, the Titan who fought the gods of Olympus because I think we might be up against some real nasty mothers," Dwight says without moving any other muscles on his face than those that operate his mouth.

Izzy walks away to deliver her plates as Hunter passes her without the usual greeting. He is zombie-like, thoughtful as he walks in, and sits opposite Dwight. He slides a sheet of paper over.

"Set me up, Stan," he says without looking at him, his focus on Dwight. The two men look at each other with great concern.

"We out of green tomatoes, Hunter."

"Good, Stan. That's good," Hunter replies still looking at Dwight.

"You giving me a list, right?" Dwight asks without looking, his emotion dark.

"Yeah."

Dwight gives the faintest of nods, his lips hard pursed in anger.

"I think I know what's on it," Dwight says in a soft fierce voice. He has been dreading a smell he has been sniffing in this job. He senses Hunter's cold anger confirms his dread.

Elbow on the table Hunter raises an angry, clenched fist. Eventually, with the slightest of movements, it is offered to Dwight who eventually connects with it. This is no fist-bump greeting, this is a meeting of strength and hatred. This is a power bump they may have used before a battle.

Stan slides a plate of food under Hunter's nose,

"Looks like you too wound-up to eat, boy."

"Oh, I'm gonna eat, Stan. I'm gonna need all I got and more."

Wild Mary enters and sees Stan with Dwight and Hunter and she charges over towards them. Stan is quick to cut her off. He shakes his head 'no' to silence her as he drags her away.

"Them boys are ready to kill someone," he says, quietly.

"I'm ready to kill someone."

"No. I just see something in their eyes that I ain't seen since my pa got back from Vietnam. I'm telling you, Mary. One time you gotta listen to Stan. What's going on at that table needs to leave this room and never come back."

22 HAUNTING HISTORY

Kieron and Bedi watch Gwen and Bert through the cascading water. They are on the other side of the Vicente Traver fountain in Seville and have hung back, although the group they are with have moved away. It looks like a simple disruption to make the group late.

"Best way to hide is to be in plain sight, but what are they hiding from?" Kieron asks her.

"They just bait. Small fish."

"For us to catch the bigger fish?"

"To keep us from big fish. I make new report."

Seeing the group start to make quite a gap they circle round behind their two marks catching them by surprise,

"We've lost the group," Kieron announces to Albert.

Albert looks around; he knows where they are. Looking forward they see the group they must catch them up.

Kieron has used a similar move a few times, just playing stupid. Well trained operatives would be on to them, but these two are amateurs.

The stooges' efforts to be last or slow the tour down is also upstaged by a lady in an extended-width wheelchair. It is not motorised and needs to be pushed and her much smaller husband looks like he might not make the full day without help. Paul Lopkey has already had to help with the chair on inclines.

Kieron missed much of the explanation of the huge half-circle Plaza de España which runs around a moat with four bridges representing the four ancient kingdoms of Spain. He turns and gives it one last look, annoyed that he cannot stay and explore, or relax and take a rowboat out. Whilst the plaza is very much a work of modern history, being built in 1928 for the Ibero-American Exposition of 1929, he is taken by the scale of the work.

"Russia Red Square far more impressive, and it real," Bedriška says to Gwen and Albert who are lingering with Kieron at the back. Kieron accelerates to catch her up.

"You're missing the point. This is an effort to reflect elements of Renaissance and Moorish styles."

Bedriška stops and turns.

"You mean like Disneyland? Epcot?"

"No."

"Yes," she insists. "I understand tourism. Go to St. Petersburg. I show you, we do same. Phoney re-build of St Catherine's Palace, not even gold," she turns and goes again.

"But if we didn't rebuild these places, show off the glory, our culture and history would be lost. How much of Russia she has ever seen? Eh? Eh?" he asks Albert and Gwen befriending them.

It is a good question. He doesn't know her well enough to know the answer. They certainly don't.

Kieron sees Paul Lopkey struggling with the chair at the busy Avenue de El Cid so he steps in to take a turn. Until then Paul had not noticed either of them with his group. Paul looks at their yellow circle stickers, but he knows that neither of them left his coach.

"You can't follow our tour, you have to stay with your own group," Lopkey says.

"This is our group," Kieron says, defiantly pushing the woman across the road. "Ask the two at the back."

"No," Paul says looking around, now conscious of the two at the rear. Paul then rushes after Kieron who has pushed the chair on.

"You want me to help or not?" Kieron says stopping mid traffic.

"No, stay with your own group."

Bedriška leans in.

"In Russia, follow wrong tour, KGB shoot you."

"Exactly," Paul jokes.

"If guide wrong, he get shot," she says.

"Exactly!" Kieron states, pushing again.

"But..." Paul is lost.

"Here, you don't have KGB. Except me. I am only one with gun. We follow, you don't get shot," she says, without the hint of a joke.

"But I do get shot, that's the problem," he loudly whispers at her, catching her and pulling his tee-shirt aside to show the wound.

She lifts her tee-shirt and shows two old gunshot wounds,

"You want play silly game of snap?"

The group catch the local guide up at the horseman on the raised stone plinth. Kieron takes a breath.

"You know I'm not a well man," he says to the woman in the chair who ignores him.

"This very impressive statue of Rodrigo Díaz de Vivar - 'El Cid'," the tour guide shouts above the traffic noise even though he has a microphone and a small loudspeaker strapped to his chest. He looks up in awe. "What do you think?"

The statue is surrounded by tourists, not just the yellow sticker group. Pictures are taken from every angle and Bedi notices that the marked couple are hanging back, avoiding the cameras.

A portly American tourist turns and addresses 'our guide'. His voice needs no amplification,

"Not a bad copy, but it ain't the best. Great American Artist, Anna Huntington. My favourite of hers is Don Quixote, saw that in the Murrells down in South Carolina. Sad, full of emotion. You see that one?"

"She donated this to the city in 1929," the local guide adds.

"It ain't the original though. Just saying."

"Thank you, sir. Follow me," the guide shouts to our group, "watch the road."

"You should see the version of this in Lincoln park!" the American shouts after them, in his way, trying to be helpful. It has however taken some of the wind out of the guide's performance.

Bedi and Kieron follow last, not hanging back because of Gwen and Bert Randolph, but because of the chair.

"You see, more copies, more cheats," Bedi says.

Kieron thinks but stalls, he does not know what to say. She appears to be anti the tourism industry she used to work in.

"Baltic churches, same. Each one has bone or blood for tourists, you will see," she says. "Poor bloody saints, bodies smashed up, bits sold everywhere."

An eerie sound hits them before they have entered the Jardin de Murillo. The towering Christopher Columbus monument, replete with ship midway up cannot be missed as a meeting point. At the base is a busker bowing an electric cello. He is playing the distinguishable, haunting theme from the television show 'Game of Thrones' to a digital backing track. Seville may be steeped in old history, but it is this modern history that causes the performance of the local guide to peak.

"Sometimes the real world is not as spectacular as depicted on television, but here that is not the case. Welcome to Dorne, the southernmost of the Seven Kingdoms where the colours are far better than any ultra-ultra HD screen. Since 'Game of Thrones', visitors to Seville have more than doubled. It was filmed in four locations of the Alcazar; the

Ambassadors' Hall, Mercury's Pool, the Baths of Maria Padilla, and here in the gardens. Any fans?"

Kieron's phone goes and he turns away to answer it. He signals to Bedriška to take the wheelchair.

"I not push wheelchair," she says, dismissing the possibility out of hand.

Kieron signals for Albert to take over as he is the next nearest to the chair at the back from the group. He has no option other than to help.

Kieron walks away with his phone. Bedi watches Kieron whose face changes to concern as he nods and takes directions. She becomes so anxious she too ignores tales of modern invention for television and walks to Kieron.

He ends the call and looks up to her. She knows there has just been a major game-changer.

"Trouble?" she asks, knowingly.

"Yeah," Kieron says, still computing information that has knocked him sideways.

"Hey! Someone gonna help me?" the woman in the chair shouts.

Gwen and Bert have vanished.

23 HISTORY REPEATING

Bedriška may be impatient but she knows Kieron needs a moment of thought before he explains. Neither is listening to the woman in the chair who wants to be pushed nearer to the local guide to hear him explain the history of the older area. She stands up and her huge frame waddles forward with difficulty, then her husband arrives and pushes the chair behind her.

"The royal palace dates back to 913 when the region was controlled by the Moors. From a history of the Al Mahad Muslims who built their sacred Giralda with an internal sloping spiral path to the top, so the Muezzin could ride up on a donkey five times a day for the call to prayer. They had square coins, they ruled from fortified towers, burning Jews and Christians alive."

He stops for a moment then adds, "men are capable of killing each other to defend a religious doctrine that they scarcely understand."

It goes over the guests' heads as they wait for the commentary to continue. Kieron fills the gap,

"All murderers are punished unless they kill in large numbers and to the sound of trumpets."

The guide looks to Kieron with half a smile; for once his line has been understood. Kieron's public and military schooling meant he knew the words of the French Enlightenment writer, historian, and philosopher, Voltaire. The Guide powers on, not knowing Kieron's head is now full of the same hatred.

"They were then over-thrown by Christians. Bells were installed in the tower to call for their prayers in the converted cathedral. The Spanish Inquisition followed, many Muslims and Jews were slaughtered. But, the cathedral might be most famous for housing the remains of Christopher Columbus, who we now admit was history's most iconic slave catcher. Seville, Cordoba and Cadiz were the three largest slave markets in Spain in the 1500s. The soil here is rich with Christian, Muslim, Jewish and African blood."

For the first time, Kieron realises that the tour guide is mixed race. Maybe Muslim, maybe Arabic or a mix of all the blood below his feet. The guide and Kieron lock eyes again in a synergy of mutual respect. The guide's political digs have bounced over the heads of the rest of his holidaymakers, but he sees Kieron understands the hurt and pain.

Bedriška waits respectively quiet. She still has no idea what has happened, but it feels like someone has died. Someone close to him.

"Time to talk," she says.

"All Hunter asked was, what did I think of the girls waiting to leave the ship when we went out to visit Lisbon? What were their expressions?"

Bedriška's face rarely changes, but she is looking serious as she computes.

"You know what makes more money than the international drug trade?" he asks her.

"Mr Columbus did," she answers.

"And there was us digging at Dwight for getting us to report everything."

"Who pick up on this?" she demands.

"I think both Hunter and Dwight did, which makes it even more annoying. We missed it. We were wasting our time watching the Milky Bar kid."

"Who?"

"It's a television thing. Chocolate bars. It never was about chocolate."

Kieron and Bedi ignore their marks; the report will just be a repeat of itself now and it is useless. They also ignore the man resting with a beer after having pushed his wife. Like many of the group, they sit outside tapas bars in a cobbled Moorish courtyard surrounded by flower dressed houses. Kieron is looking at the fridge magnet of Christopher Columbus. He plays at distracting with his left hand while his right-hand returns to grab his large beer. They are both in the process of thinking through the new problem that is before them.

Lopkey shouts from the corner of the small beautiful square.

"Coach is here!"

Kieron necks his beer and looks at the bill. He hands the waitress two twenty Euro notes,

"Can I get two bottles to go?"

He waits for his beers watching the others leave. He sees Albert slouching in a chair with no sign of leaving.

"No rush, we in taxi," Bedriška reminds him.

"No. We're on the coach."

He takes his beers and they go.

Lopkey stands by the coach door counting guests back in. Kieron and Bedi are last and make his full complement, but he knows they don't belong,

"Not your coach."

"We swapped with two others who wanted to be with their friends."

Paul hesitates.

"We thought of you as our friend, so we said yes," Kieron says a little more bluntly than normal. Paul ticks all his guests back, writes the time and gets in. The coach door closes behind him.

Way up in the square, Albert has a chair with a view of his transport. Kieron can see the annoying idiot's wry smile as he lifts his half-drunk beer, confident the coach will wait for them. He is late, the coach is late. If it hits rush hour traffic it would make the ship late. The coach pulls away.

Albert puts his beer down and runs. Gwen is confused; she hadn't been watching.

"It's going!" he shouts back to her.

She shakes her head, confident.

"There are four coaches, we just find one of the others."

Kieron can only imagine what they are saying, their plan having been foiled in their failure to delay the ship. Their coach is now in a convoy behind the other three. He is wondering if Albert is a major problem, how does the jigsaw fit together?

24 I-CHECKIT, WE-CHECKIT

The coaches' race through the scenic Andalusian countryside to make their strict return time in Cadiz. Ships must pay huge fines if they overstay their parking at the port. If they miss their allotted sail-out time with the local pilot on board, in a busy port other ships will have been allocated leaving slots immediately afterwards. Not being able to jump into one of those being five minutes late could put them back an hour or more.

Sitting in the last pair of seats before the rear steps down to the side door, Kieron finishes a long phone call only to start reading a long text which Bedi is already well into reading on her mobile, but she stops.

"I feel sick," she says, nuzzling into him.

Kieron is sure it is not a romantic gesture but more so they can whisper privately without those around them listening.

"We stood next to girls waiting to leave the ship. They were scared. We never realised."

Kieron considers, "We're still guessing, it's only a theory."

"No. Not theory. True."

"Consider, each of three ships terminating up to six girls, at each major Mediterranean tourist port," Kieron tests.

"Company know this not about chocolate. They know," Bedi is angry. "Now, I see faces wait at gangway with cases."

"No. Stop. You're imagining too much now. Getting too involved. This is a job."

Bedriška turns her head and looks up at him hard.

"Don't judge me. Woman are humans, not job. Columbus sold humans, not slaves. Nothing changed. Man still evil."

"Let's hope we're wrong, we don't have crew movement details for any other ships or ports," Kieron says hopefully.

"I don't like this job. I don't want this job."

Kieron takes a moment and looks down at her. He cannot see her face, or her eyes, not that she ever gives anything away. This is the first time he has felt her show emotion.

"They need us, Bedi. Now. They need us now."

She slowly looks up at him.

"You not understand. We not sent for women. We sent to get problem off ship. No one cares. Trust me. No one cares."

Kieron must let that sink in, not just what she said but why she said it. He surmises Bedriška must have been down this road before. Bad exposure in a past case could make her unstable. It could make her a liability. He needs to ask Georgie what she knows about Bedi's past life. His head is full of questions,

"Five ports buying, that's thirty-plus crew leave each cruise, each ship?" he computes. His shock compounds as he realises that could be as many as ninety women every two weeks, he realises this is a serious trade

"There will be pimp on ship. Big chief. Men at each port. Sex smuggling, evil big business, well organised. Serious. I can't do this."

"I can. I need your help to make sense of this."

"Ship go in circle. Pick women up from one port, drop them at another port," Bedi explains.

"Why a ship? Why not cut the ship out of the equation. Just take the women straight from the agent into the trade?" Kieron asks.

"Interpol. They make people trafficking hard. But, new control to cruise ships. Only tested on big ships. These three small old ships not yet on i-checkit scheme Interpol runs for passenger movement."

"Then we'll close it down," Kieron says softly. He pulls her in close and cuddles her.

"You will try."

"Welcome to CSCI, it's what we do," he says.

Kieron reads his smartphone.

"Gwen and Albert are small crimes, forget them."

"We did. They're back in Seville."

Kieron takes the top off a beer and hands it to her.

"I will kill these men," she whispers to him.

"That's better. It's not quite what we've been asked to do, well, not yet. But that's better."

His phone rings again.

"You know what we need?" he hears Hunter ask.

"What is that partner?"

"Prisha, working undercover. A girl in the crew."

Bedriška's head tilts up to watch Kieron deal with Hunter.

"She's got kids, Hunter. She's not trained. They'll kill her, or sell her and we'll never see her again," Kieron worries.

"Five of those girls were from the laundry. We need eyes in there, she's perfect. I'm gonna fly out soon as."

"Soon as what?" Kieron asks.

"Soon as I get Prisha on a plane."

"No," Bedriška says, having heard the phone which is as close to her ear as it is to Kieron's. "Get me and Kieron below decks. I spot these people." Bedriška looks disturbed; she has a tight killer's jaw.

"Get us below decks. Have them put on a full tour."

"Not sure I can, the two guys who employed us have been suspended," Hunter reveals.

25 THE LIST

Hunter bangs on the door of an apartment but there is no answer.

"It's Hunter Witowski, open the door before I take it off the hinges."

Croc stands behind him wondering if he means it, but the door is slowly opened. Behind it is a frightened-looking Chet in a onesie,

"How did you get past the concierge?" he asks.

"Don't ask stupid questions," Hunter says, pushing his way in and looking around. Croc follows him, closes the door, and stands by it.

A shy looking Bjorn comes out of another room in a matching onesie.

"Put the coffee on Bjorn. No more ice cube timing-out a meeting to save your ass," Hunter snarls.

Bjorn goes to the kitchenette, Hunter follows watching his every move, looking everywhere.

"Nice apartment boys."

"We might not be here much longer."

"Live fast, die fast. This is a big boys' game and I'm not sure you even knew you were playing it."

Bjorn pours his coffee and he sits at the breakfast bar.

"Would be a shame for you boys to lose this," Hunter says sipping his coffee, watching them, and playing the silence routine. If he doesn't speak, they will. But they give him nothing, they are just number crunchers and responders at junior management level.

"So, what about our second payment?" Hunter asks like a mafia boss come to collect the rent. Neither was expecting that.

"We're not in the office, at the moment," Bjorn explains.

"Slight hitch," Chet says.

"So, I pull my people out now?"

"I'd rather you didn't," he says, slowing down replies.

Hunter pushes feeling the hesitation. "Why? Not your problem. You don't work there anymore."

There is a silence. Hunter wonders if they know what is going on at sea. He needs to stir them up further.

"You enjoyed this Miami for a while. Now you need to change states. Find another profession? Hunter suggests. "You got the sharp clothes or are they rented?"

"They're ours, luckily we're the same size," Bjorn says.

"We swap, it makes us look like we each have twice as many suits," Chet says, but he is biding time.

"That's smarter than I had you down for."

"We played a move at work. We each had an annual budget. We used both, almost total, to book your company," Chet says.

"And it's gone, we stop work?" Hunter challenges.

"Technically there was nothing wrong in what we did, it was just unconventional," Bjorn admits.

It is the first time they have revealed any of what is really going on.

"Stuck your neck right out, and backed it up with laundry wars and decks smells recurring on a spreadsheet?"

Hunter's eyes dig into them for more, but they give him nothing.

"Maybe you can get your job back? I solved your little problem. You're right, chocolate bars in the laundry, we have the names of the players. That'll do. Where do I send it, to Di?" Hunter asks.

Both guys look like they've lost. He pushes them by going for the door. They chase after him.

"It never led you anywhere else?" Chet asks at the door.

"Where was it supposed to lead? Chet. What did you want me to find?"

"Honestly, Mr Witowski, we don't know. All we knew was that guests and staff were seriously not happy."

"Why?" Hunter asks Chet, then turns to Bjorn, "What? You had a gut feeling?" Hunter drills.

"Yes," admits Bjorn.

"You didn't tell me staff were unhappy."

"No, that seemed obvious and on all three of our ships. No other ships on the fleet," Bjorn says.

"And you were thinking, solve this, become a hero. Get promoted. Larger budget, larger apartment. More nights out."

The two guys start to nod.

"Sit down there, get your devices out. Or pen and paper."

They do as they're told and go over to the coffee table. Hunter goes into the kitchen and pours himself another coffee.

"Someone wants to be the president of America, what do they have to do?"

"Get elected," Chet answers.

"Then we got two presidents of America," Hunter says as he sits down in front of them.

"Well, the current one has to go first," Chet says.

"So who has to go for you guys to get promoted?"

Chet and Bjorn look at each other wary.

"Does this mean you're going to get rid of someone. For us?" Bjorn asks.

"Now you're being stupid."

The two young men relax.

"You don't have that kind of money."

Chet stands up, annoyed. "Where's this going?"

"No," Bjorn says fearfully.

Hunter smiles, he is not surprised by the answer.

"No? You guys were expecting me to find something big, to get you promoted?"

"Our turnover of staff was much higher than other managers. We had no idea what we were doing wrong."

"Here's what I want, and I don't care how you get it. Within the hour, I want a list of everyone who works at cruise HQ. Even people you've never met. Then I want notes against their names. Dolphins fan, gambler, dates hookers, cycles to work, put it all down. I want a list of every crew member who left a ship, where and when. I want to know where the new ones joined. Names. In and out. And be warned, someone in your company does not want you to find that information. Don't answer that door."

"Is that meant to frighten us?" Bjorn says.

"Only if you want to stay alive."

"I'm sure I can still log in, tons of executives work from home," Chet says.

"Log in once, get the information, get out."

Both the young men nod.

"Important. I want you to organise a below decks tour tomorrow. Repeat it until our team are on one. Everywhere below decks," Hunter demands.

"That might not be so easy," Bjorn says.

"No one gets promoted for doing easy jobs. You understand my list?"

They nod.

"I'm gonna leave my man Croc with you. He wants to get in when you log in. He'll do some stuff then leave. And I don't want him coming back to my office in one of those."

"Onesie." Croc says. "It's a onesie."

Hunter gives him a strange look and refrains from asking whether he has one.

26 OPERATION LAUNDRY

Macey, the art student sits at her easel painting. She's caught a wonderful profile of a worried Dwight lit by the blue haze of the large screen he works at. She has used the echoes of screens along the bench to reflect his image as a haunting reminder of the hunger technology has. Macey is a talented undiscovered painter and she does not flinch when Hunter enters the control room, not until he stands blocking her vision. Croc appears from his resting place behind the screens wearing a onesie.

"You spent the night?"

"No way! I got it as a joke."

"Joke over, put some clothes on."

"No, he looks great," Macey says.

"Feels good."

Hunter gives him a suspicious look. Croc backs off, not wishing to overstep his mark and grateful for being used as an agent able to learn how Dwight operates. Macey has no such self-reproach. She folds the sheet over and sits waiting for inspiration.

"You want the good news or the bad news?" Dwight says without moving his gaze from the screen.

"There's good news?" Hunter asks, walking to the far screen, studying. With so many screens in play, it is obvious Dwight is routing something out.

"Croc set up a phantom executive on the system. I have the ship arranging an immediate below decks tour. They wanted the names of our operatives, but I refused to give them."

"Tour to include laundry, biggest turnover of staff," Croc adds.

"But they were suspicious. Not sure we'll pass for cruise HQ again," Dwight says.

Croc is shaking his head, confident, "I could probably get our phantom on the payroll."

"No."

"I'll get the crew movement next," Croc says, as a devoted member of the team.

"Di Mond rang. Cruise HQ asked you to go in, someone may be on to us in their system," Dwight warns.

"I doubt that," Croc says confidently.

"It'll be about the contract and our fee," Hunter says as he parades back down the screens and stops at Croc. He takes a moment with him.

"You learning?"

"Too much."

Hunter is spoiling Macey's eye line once again just as she'd raised a brush. She puts it down and gives up; the operation has got in the way of another masterpiece.

"Prisha's on three months leave, they think she'll be back home in India seeing her family," Dwight says. "But she's not picking up."

Hunter slides his mobile from his rear denim pocket, hits the passkeys and hands it to Croc,

"Ring her from this, see if she takes a call from me."

Hunter sits next to Dwight.

"Assuming the ships are transporting women," Dwight starts.

Hunter shakes his head, he hates this. "Human trafficking has to be the worst."

Macey pulls a wider brush from her bun of hair, fills it with paint and flicks it over a new sheet. Strokes up and down. An abstract image of women screaming, arms in the air, quickly forms. She tilts her head and listens. Dwight turns to Hunter and in the top right-hand side of the canvas she outlines his head looking down on the women.

"Interpol is all over sex trafficking, but I can't find a reference to them working on cruise ships," Dwight explains.

"Are Interpol actually being successful or just pushing making the traders move?"

"We need them as long term allies," Dwight suggests.

Hunter thinks for a moment,

"OK. Interpol solve crimes. We work with the cruise companies to get the crime off their ships. Make sure they know we ain't stepping on their toes, and we're different. But we don't talk to them yet."

"You think cruise HQ knew any of this when they hired us?" Dwight asks.

"I'm not sure they even knew they hired us," Croc chirps in.

"Walk me through everything you have Dwight," Hunter says.

Dwight slides along to a screen showing a map, mostly sea, with lines joining port to port.

"It's a fourteen-day cruise, Lisbon to Venice, then fourteen days back using different ports."

"Currently leaving Cadiz. Malaga next," Hunter says, finding the ports quickly on the map.

"Delivering anything is simple, you pick up from point 'A' and deliver to point 'B'. We know Lisbon's a delivery port; we missed that handover. The next port is Malaga, I guess that'll be another delivery port. Guessing. Barcelona is delivery, Ajaccio I don't see as either one or the other; not big enough to have a significant sex trade. Naples, maybe a delivery port. But then the ships stop at Sarande in Albania. That feels like a collection port," Dwight shows.

"Zoom in on Albania?" Hunter asks.

The map widens and it shows the bordering countries.

"Wow. There's a minefield. Macedonia, Serbia, even across to Bulgaria."

"Albania is not without severe poverty and organised crime. It's a tier-two country."

"Meaning?" asks Hunter.

"Countries whose governments do not comply with minimum standards set for dealing with sex trafficking. It also borders Montenegro, which has been given tier level two plus a WL code. The ships stop there on the way back so that might be the collection."

Hunter looks at him, "WL?"

"Watch List," Dwight answers. "It might mean making efforts but failing to bring numbers down. But, also sounds like government PR. My guess is that Albania's a gas station."

"We need to see the actual crew flow on and off the ship," Hunter shouts.

"On it next, boss," Croc says with Hunter's phone still to his ear, still waiting for Prisha to answer.

"And get the list of local shipping agents they used, Croc."

"Then we tell Interpol?" Dwight asks.

"No. We still don't have a crime. We only have our suspicions."

Croc is behind Macey pulling his onesie off and trying to use the phone. He is looking at the cauldron of screaming women.

"Wow!" Croc says. "I've seen girls working the streets, but never thought of them sold like this."

"Would you mind undressing somewhere else?" Macey demands.

"Never is there a worse job than seeing humans taken from their families, abused and sold to slavery," Hunter says.

"You're telling a black man?" Dwight offers.

"I'm respectfully reminding everyone it still goes on and the people who do it have no regard for human life. They will kill at the drop of a hat."

Croc's onesie comes off and his Wild Mary baseball cap drops on the floor.

"I got Prisha, boss."

27 INDIA

It is late evening in Mumbai and the rush hour shows no sign of slowing down. Ten-thirty in Miami is eight-thirty here in Mumbai. Crowds swarm towards the amazing Victorian gothic Chhatrapati Shivaji station. Prisha walks against the flow, holding her smartphone to her ear, a book under her arm, guiding her two children across a road in and out of the noisy cars, trucks, tuk-tuks and motorcycles. The little ones have been brought up in this chaotic world of horns and noise and are far more used to crossing than their mother who spends nine months of the year away on a cruise ship. The youngest, her daughter, is carrying a three-tier, silver tiffin.

"Let me think Mr Hunter, you are ringing me, so there must be a problem. You must need something."

"I miss you."

"Mr Henkel sent me his book, he needed nothing from me."

"Sigmund, what did he send?"

"First Steps in Applied Criminal Psychology. I love it. I want to go back to university and study this science."

"I need you here first."

"When?"

"Now."

"But I am on leave, in Mumbai with my children, my brother and my parents."

"I don't have any control over criminals' timetables, Prisha."

All three are safely across the major road and weave in and out of people on the sidewalk, leading into the back streets. The children run on ahead. They know the way.

"It is not possible, Mr Hunter."

"You're special, Prisha, we need you."

"So you must need an Indian girl who understands ships, understands what you do," Prisha says, trying to figure out what is going on. "Where are you?"

"I'm in Miami?"

"Are you safe there?"

"Of course I'm safe."

The signal cuts out and Prisha is left with no one on the line. She speeds up, a skip in her step to catch her children who she can no longer see, but she knows they are around the corner. She loves visiting Bukka, her brother who owns a small repair shop mending the huge American style double-door fridge-freezers. He set up the business with the money he got from the shipping company when he was hurt in a lifeboat accident. It was dropped into the sea with him in it. He should not have been in the lifeboat, but crew often feel encouraged to ignore the regulations and cut corners, making lifeboats the second most dangerous place on any ship, second only to the watertight doors.

His new industry is thriving, and as she arrives a giant re-furbished fridge-freezer is being lifted onto poles set between two pedal-bicycles. When it is done the two children applaud.

"Bukka, this doesn't look like it will work," Prisha says.

Ignoring her remark, he limps back into his shop, taking the tiffin from his young niece.

"You are my little dabbawalla," he says to the young girl. Then he turns to Prisha, "look sister, what do you see?"

"I see a man working too late into the night," she argues.

"No different from the hours I worked on a ship. Look again."

Broken appliances fill his shop. She shakes her head.

"This business is a success; it could be huge. Everyone wants an American style fridge-freezer and we have an endless supply," he smiles.

"Are they stolen?"

"No sister. In Europe, they refuse to mend them. They just throw them away."

"Why?" she asks.

"They do it to save the planet."

Prisha shakes her head again, this time confused.

"How can it be ecological to throw this away?"

"The new eco gas they use is inflammable, so first-world repairmen are not allowed to mend or re-gas them. They send them to me. I have four containers full of more at the docks and nowhere to put them. Even more coming. I need to expand, I need you to organise my office, my orders and the incoming shipments," he says.

Her phone rings again and she turns away to answer it as a bullock with a cart pulls up outside ready to collect a fridge-freezer.

"Hunter, what do you need because it can't be a data wrangler; you could find that skill anywhere," Prisha asks.

"I need you to join a ship as a crew member, in the laundry."

"You want me to join the laundry?"

"You are going to work in a laundry? I need you here!" Her brother says, as he opens his tiffin with her children who sit to share his food outside his shop.

"Don't go away mummy," the girl says.

Hunter has heard everything; although the ambient noise of the city is still high it is not the din of the local train or the terminus building like when he tried before.

"It's where we think the problem is. A week, two weeks tops," he pleads.

"Do you ever wonder what I need, what anyone else needs?" she asks.

"Prisha. I'm just explaining the offer."

"I have come home to see my children, to help my brother, he needs to expand. He needs larger premises."

"What does he need, an investor, a partner?"

"Yes, and yes. My life has changed now since working with you. I want to go back to university."

"What if I could help you make all of that happen?" Hunter says.

28 NAKED UNTRUTH

Bedriška wakes nuzzled in the arch of Kieron's axilla, just as she had rested there on the coach returning from Seville yesterday. It is not about sex, they share a bed, they share warmth and they share a problem.

"How long you been awake?" No matter how she tries to soften it, it is still a demand.

"An hour maybe."

"You should have woken me," she says, getting up and going to the washroom. She is beyond taking the duvet or bothering to cover her.

Kieron may have been awake for an hour, but he will now have to wait his turn in the washroom. They share a room like a married couple or best friends, but there is a clear pecking order to facilities.

"Is it too early for Miami?" she shouts from the shower. The shower curtain is pulled but the door is not closed.

"Maybe not, but they've been silent. Hunter has to go back into cruise HQ before the office opens."

"And he was up late last night pestering Prisha the moment she woke? I hope she says no to him."

"He wants to find their man inside the ship; we can't do that from above deck," Kieron states entering the washroom.

"Please. This is private," she says.

"We've slept together all night."

"Now we awake."

Lunch was planned to be as casual as waking up had been, in the served dining room with a glass of wine. Kieron was an officer and he still likes his luxuries when they can be afforded. But on the walk, there is an announcement of a below-the-decks' tour, and immediately they divert to reception to join the queue. Of all the people there, they are the only two who must be on the tour, the only two it has been arranged for; but still, they must remain undercover. They have no 'golden ticket'.

Hunter is sitting in a meeting room on Dodge Island opposite two older cruise executives, wondering if they all come in twos. One is a very tall, fair-haired Scandinavian type, Marty Kaye and the other an American, Frank Pincer. The cruise industry has an incredible mix of employees from classic seafaring countries as well as experts in business. The water jug is brought in by Di Mond who worked with the missing Chet and Bjorn, is now the only constant element for the three ships.

"Excuse me," Hunter says lifting the jug. "Could we have one without ice. I find it so distracting, reminds me of the melting ice caps."

He hands the jug back to her and turns away to eat a pastry from the breakfast platter. Eventually, he offers the two executives a spreadsheet they have never seen.

"Got this late last night from the press who have been chasing us every step of the way. We were looking at guests, they are looking at staff. Why d'you think you're losing staff?"

"We use these three ships to train inexperienced staff and then we move them around the brand. It's mainly newer staff who leave, not those who've been loyal to us, and us to them for many, many years," Frank explains.

Hunter stays quiet. He is still waiting for more information.

"Entry grades are the hardest to keep. Not everyone takes to working in a ship. We compete with hotels which is why they leave at busy ports such as Barcelona and Malaga. We're their free ticket to Europe's millions of hotels," Frank adds confirming information that is on the chart.

"Is that your area, Frank?"

"Not directly Mr Witowski. But I'm happy to help you or explain that to the press."

"Thanks, Frank. Can I get a full work-up on each of the staff you've lost in the last month? Where they joined, which cruise agent hired them?" Hunter asks, studying their faces. "Now, about a second stage payment?"

"The two executives you were dealing with have been released. They should have made it clear the payment you have had was to be and is the full and final payment," Marty says.

"So, you've just come in on this mess?"

They both nod.

"How would you like CSCI to wrap this up and tell the press what we've done?"

"What exactly is it you've done?" Marty asks.

"Connected the dots," Hunter says. "And, the more we look, the more dots we find. Look, how about we both tread water for a day while Di Mond runs you up to speed. Our guys are having a ball on-board your ships."

"Ships?"

"Agents on all Three Kings, as fully paid up guests."

"We're glad they're enjoying themselves. There is an internal investigation as to how such a large fee was paid to your company. I'm sure you can understand it seems a ridiculous sum to investigate guest laundries, which should be an internal matter."

"That makes us both investigators," Hunter says shaking hands with each of them then heading for the door. He turns, "One more thing."

"Actually. I'm away for a few days from tomorrow. Call Dwight Ritter if you need something."

Hunter leaves them unsure whether they will comply to his request. It was obvious they were the ones in the room who knew the least.

29 BELOW DECKS

From the main dining room, Bedriška and Kieron follow the tour through a galley and out into the lounge bar it also serves. They are led down the crew stairs to deck five and the medical centre. The guests take the unusual route through the 'Crew Only' door down a corridor of cabins and then out to the main walkway of the ship, i95.

Both Bedriška and Kieron feel a sense of coming home, both having worked on ships before. They are then led to the laundry area. The hostess addresses the tour.

"For those of you who have never been down here before, take out your cameras, take out your phones because this is going to get pretty exciting," she starts. "Meet Micky."

Bedi lifts her phone to record everything.

Micky, the head of the laundry takes over. His English is not as good, but his enthusiasm makes up for it. He explains that he has about twenty to twenty-five staff working twenty-four hours a day in three shifts. As he introduces the few of his team on the front line, they seem happy, but it is obvious that their English is not as good as the staff that the guests meet. The first row of five washing machines take the napkins and tablecloths from the dining area. These are all turned around in three hours. Each machine can take 125Kg.

"How much training is needed to work here, or is this somewhere untrained staff start when joining a ship?" Kieron asks. He studies Micky.

"I get all untrained staff. Anyone can work washing machine; I train them, they go to other jobs. Always training."

Leaving these machines, they enter an open factory area starting with nine washers dedicated to guests and officers. These are next to a huge cage at the bottom of a chute that drops from all the decks as high as deck sixteen.

"They start here," Micky adds.

Kieron remembers the last ship he was on where the chute did not drop directly into the laundry and carts of linen had to be wheeled along i95. The first dead body from the serial killer laid for hours undetected in one of those carts. He was now seeing this area from a different angle.

"All this washing must be labour intensive," Kieron says, fishing for staffing plans.

"There's more. I also have a dry-cleaning machine for stains and special items," Micky smiles, "If you have a stain or a problem, send it to me and I will deal with it personally."

That was not the road Kieron was trying to take his questioning, but he has time and is hoping someone else in the group pipes up. He and Bedriška exchange looks, they both feel that this is not their man. This is a man dedicated to the beauty of clothes, and a man who has been on this ship for years. Micky engages in what must be his party trick. He has a shirt set up on a steam machine and at the press of a button, it is blown full of steam. A guest jumps back as if she has seen a ghost and the rest laugh. There is not a crease in the shirt. He switches the machine to blow air and the shirt billows even larger, arms out as it dries.

"Staff with no training can't work that surely?" Kieron laughs.

"It just a button. Easy." Micky says modestly still not giving them anything.

"Now, come, we go to the flat iron area," Micky says leading them on.

Kieron begins to take pictures like all the other guests, but he is ensuring he has the faces of the few staff on duty.

"Go," Kieron says to Bedi.

She rushes off to have her picture taken with the staff who giggle and pose. Job done.

Micky is by the finished items, hanging on rails. He prides himself in the care taken to get the wonderful evening dresses looking fantastic, whether sequined or chiffon, light or heavy with pleats.

"These will be delivered to guest rooms within hours, ready for them to wear tonight. Formal night, big night."

Kieron holds back, taking wide pictures of the flat iron area with the rows and rows of domestic washing machines stacked high behind them. He has noticed a big man, like a shadow, almost following them.

"Bedi, want your picture taken with a big hunk?" he whispers.

She turns and sees the man who is lifting huge piles of laundry and staying away from the tour.

"Yes, I am in love," she says powering straight up to him. She feels the muscles on his arms. "This I like, Micky! I need him in my laundry."

The man is caught, his picture taken, he has no chance to think or fade away.

"No, he is mine," Micky says suggestively.

Bedriška is back on the tour with Kieron as they reach the Jensen towel folding machine. Oona is there, Kieron has noted her lapel badge and knows Bedi will have her face on camera.

"Each machine here folds two hundred towels an hour," Oona explains as she feeds the machine herself in what looks like it should be a two-person operation.

The party of guests are impressed with Oona's power.

"Two hundred towels; means they have to hit at least three towels into the machine every minute without fail."

"That is like a workout, you must be fit." A member of the touring party suggests.

'At last', Kieron thinks, 'I thought I was working solo'.

Oona stops feeding the folder and shows her muscles.

"And in her, we might have our below decks muscle," Kieron whispers to Bedi.

Kieron turns back and waits his turn as the guests ask Oona questions. His turn arrives.

"Do you have a high turn-over of staff here?" Kieron asks.

"Always. Some not strong enough to survive" Oona says.

Micky pulls the tour away and turns to him, "I am always training, sir, always training new staff. It is part of my job."

30 GOODNIGHT CHILDREN

In Miami, lunch at Wild Mary's Diner is in full swing. Next door, Dwight is by himself, boxing data.

"Don't like it when it goes this quiet," he mumbles to himself.

At sea in Europe, it is evening. Bedriška and Kieron are dressing, rather sombrely for a formal night, hungry from not eating all day.

"We need Prisha below deck, but I don't like," Bedriška says, lining her eye with a black make-up pencil.

In India, it is nearly midnight and it has been a long day for Prisha. She is spending a last night with her family, all up extremely late because she leaves again tomorrow. She is excited by her hyperactive children but exhausted from her day in Mumbai city. She daydreams between playing with them, her head trying to catch up with the speed at which things have taken effect today.

"Brother, it is only hours since you and your lawyer negotiated a major property deal."

"I did not even have a lawyer yesterday. I need your skills sister. Mama, you should have seen her, a phone in each hand arranging funds from Miami."

Her children both pretend they are on the phone, saying hello to imaginary business friends in Miami.

"You need two phones, children. With the other phone, your mother was negotiating with the property agent on price."

They all raise two hands with phones, one to each ear. A new game.

"Then, I had to use my acting skills mama-jee."

"I did not know you were an actress."

"Neither did I! But I had to pretend not to speak English."

"But you can speak English, Prisha, we gave you an education."

"I know, I thank you Mama-jee. But I had to meet with a shipping crew agent in Mumbai and pretend I had none."

"Surely they want you to speak English?"

"She got a job in the laundry," her brother says, "when she could stay here and run our business expansion."

"It was me taking this job that got you the new land."

She cannot tell her family she has joined an investigators agency, that would worry them. She acted to tell the agent of her hotel experience in the laundry area, cleverly refusing the first two ships offered because she said the huge size frightened her. Over ten years ago they did frighten her. Today, she convinced the employment agent that maybe one day in the future, when he felt she was used to the industry, she would try a mega-ship but today she pointed at the picture of a smaller ship.

"The laundry pays that much money? I should come, I can wash. I will go and see this agent."

"No mama. You do not need to see an agent. I will explain all when I come back," she says kissing her mother, then her children.

Each day the crew employment agency does place new crews. He is paid for each head he sends to be safely employed. This is a perfectly legal trade in humans. Employment agencies and head-hunters exist all over the world. It might appear simple to find staff for a glamourous job at sea, but it is not that easy to find people who will leave home to work a nine-month shift before taking leave. She now has an enviable new job as an investigator. She sends her first reports back to Hunter saying that the crew-agent did his job well; he accurately told the story of work at sea, and at no time tried to sell her anything underhand. Prisha feels for the girls being sold into sex-slavery and challenges herself asking if she had done enough. Reporting is a key part of a field agent's job and she wonders if he needed more, maybe the man's description, or a written image of his office. However, she knows they would ask if they needed more.

She reflects on how she had walked down past the Taj Hotel earlier in the day. She remembers hearing the news of the people killed and held and hostage there and fearing for her relatives. She realises how lucky she is. Life is hard and strange. Poor people were all around her on the streets with rich tourists just away to her right at the huge Gate of India taking pictures. She stood staring at the sea beyond, daydreaming about being rich.

Waking from her daydream, she kisses the children again. They wave her away for being sloppy. They understand little of tomorrow. She will fly to Madrid, then travel to Barcelona. An entire day of flying, then more travel at the other end. Tonight, she will once again put her children to bed not knowing how big they will have grown by the next time she sees them.

"You are acting like you are not coming home," her wise mother says, studying her.

"Mama-jee, I promise I will come home."

31 GOODNIGHT CAPTAIN

Bedriška has the figure to showcase a long dress; she could easily be a model. However, that would not be her first choice of profession. Kieron is wearing a plain dinner suit, though he is far more comfortable in his ceremonial dress uniform with the awards he has earned. However, sporting a row of medals might be an unknown embarrassment, he is sure that Bedi has her own medals she could brandish, though she chooses not to expose anything about herself. Today was the closest he got to knowing anything about her and he understands more why Georgie is attracted to her. All he knows is that she has worked in some form of enforcement and she doesn't like the sex trade.

They stand second in a small queue in the atrium, arm in arm. Photography has set up their camera. The lights are in black photography umbrellas on stands either side for a formal picture against the backdrop of the ship's wonderful classic atrium. Guests are grouped everywhere for a Captain's cocktail party, nursing their free drink. One drink is always free but Bedi has bagged two already and is yet to join the party. It is their turn; they pose as the perfect couple and no one could argue with that. The photographer is ready.

"Smile."

"No. Stop," she says, breaking pose. "I need champagne glass. Here!" she signals to a waiter.

There is nothing to dislike about her, she is direct but funny and polite. She gets a pair of fluted glasses, one each, smiles and folds into Kieron. Maybe he has tamed the beast. The flash goes again, and again. She feels Kieron recoil like he has been hit. He doesn't show it but she is holding him. She knows why Kieron has broken the pose. She gulps her drink and puts her glass down as she thanks the photographer while holding onto her beau tightly. They retreat out of the back of the temporary arch the in-house photography team have built. Kieron needs help walking, something has happened. The next couple step in behind them as Kieron laughs it off but he needs to hold on to something.

"Breathe," she orders.

Bedi takes his drink, downs it, placing it with a waiter and uncharacteristically not taking a refill which implies she is taking this seriously. Kieron holds the rail overlooking the grand sweeping steps that snake down two floors. The atrium is packed with elegantly dressed guests and flashes are going off everywhere. All he can see is flashes inside his head.

"How bad?" she questions knowing the camera has triggered something.

"Let's move away from the edge."

With arms linked she leads him away knowing two things have affected him; the flashes and the height. She must report this.

"I'm good. It was just a moment."

"You need more exercises tonight."

"You getting rough in bed is always welcome," he jests.

Bedriška releases his arm. The comment was unacceptable but proves he has got his shit together again. A waiter approaches with a smile shown by all the staff, a smile that sets the tone for the guests. If only the guests' teeth were as good. They both take a drink from the tray offered. The ship does not need to sail at speed because there is no swell this evening. It will be fun if Kieron can last. Paul Lopkey is on later in the theatre, so they intend to eat and then see him.

"Empty stomach," he says.

Her silence is probing.

"I meant, add 'empty stomach' to your report. I ate nothing all day."

"You react to flashes."

"Do you think Gwen and Albert made the ship?" Kieron asks changing the subject.

Holding him close and smiling in a newlywed's clinch, she whispers, "I don't think. Their names were called. Ship does not wait. Easy they join next port."

"If they let them back on."

"They will. It happens many times. But they not happy."

"They were troublesome diversions from the sex trade before they were unhappy," he suggests.

Bedriška is close so no one else can hear their conversation. Kieron notices her lips are perfectly outlined, her cheeks chiselled with artistry, and her eyes are a work of a craftswoman. It shows that she spent years working in the spa.

"They follow orders," she whispers. "What are Gwen and Albert to sex trade?"

Kieron kisses her. Just a lingering peck. He doesn't know why he had no control; she was just too close. She was in a zone that only lovers inhabit. Bedi takes a moment to pull back, then looks at him confused. She must play his wife; it was an act, right? She smiles nicely while putting him in his place.

"Not allowed. Please answer my question."

"Nothing. They are not related."

"Wrong."

Kieron feels drawn to her again.

"Stop," she says. "Think with brain. Not other man part."

Kieron shakes his head just a little, he stumbles again.

"Three ships, all problem, all sex trade?" she says to focus him.

"Maybe."

"Gwen and Albert are involved," she insists softly, powerfully.

"So, we're missing something. Can I kiss you again?"

"No."

32 GOODNIGHT MIAMI

The working day draws to a close at last in Miami and Hunter feels like an exhausted engineer working both time zones and with a baby due. He has got his team onto a ship-tour to see the laundry, got his girl in India joining the ship's crew. Bjorn has acquired details of crew movement, but the pressure is still on as he has solved little and has invested heavily. Time is running out for him. Though Elaine does not know yet, tomorrow morning he must board a flight to Spain. There is much to do on the case before thinking about lifting money from their old ship. He also needs to do some rough accounts because he invested more than their huge fee in Prisha's bother's new refrigeration business. If he and his team fail to recover the trunk with sixteen million dollars from a neighbouring ship, he will have the new job of convincing his partner that bringing him back for this contract was a wise investment. That is apart from ensuring his domestic life is taken care of, and to fulfil his promise to get Prisha an education.

He walks through to the diner knowing he is about to be confronted with both of those.

Hunter sits with Elaine. Mary joins them at the table. His mind flicks from the conversation about the forthcoming baby when Sigmund walks in. The cycle clips, tweed jacket, bow tie, beard and short scholar's haircut instantly give him away. Sigmund Henkel was helpful on the serial killer job, but he never saw or met him.

"Sigmund!" Hunter says, standing. "I've been desperate to meet you."

Sigmund changes his fumbling direction to the table, but Hunter collects him and steers him away.

"They're talking babies, we'll catch up with them later."

As they enter the darkroom, Sigmund re-acquaints himself with Dwight. The both worked on the Serial Killer contract in the Miami, Dodge Island office of the previous cruise company.

"I wanted to meet you Sigmund. Even though this job is not a criminal mind thing," Hunter teases, to break up their reunion.

"No criminals in a crime?" he asks.

"No, not that kind of crime."

"But it is a crime? What is it?"

"I wasn't bringing you in to help. I wanted to meet you before I flew out. Dinner to say thank-you is well overdue and you should see this."

"I'm even more interested. In what crime is it that the criminal does not have a mind?"

"Dwight, I'll let you explain. Then come through to eat."

Hunter turns and leaves them together walking past Croc who has slipped in to listen and watch. Every day he feels more like he is one of the team. Hunter sees him lingering.

"Croc, first rule of any business. Don't be shy. Get in there and introduce yourself."

"As the burger guy, or the IT specialist?"

"Just say hi, I'm one of the team."

Hunter leaves him and breathes a sigh of relief as he walks back to the table.

Mary grabs his attention first, "When you gonna clear your expense account here?"

"Do you want a part investment in Mumbai?"

"No."

"Then not tonight."

"When?"

"It's in the post."

Wild Mary looks past him to where Croc is in the doorway watching Hunter like a hawk.

"Croc's burning a hole in your back. You need to do a little investing there."

Hunter turns, "Croc!"

Croc comes in and sits next to Mary.

"So, where d'you want your career to go?" Hunter asks him.

"Why d'you ask?" Croc asks. No one has ever asked him that.

"Just fixing things up before I go. We've never had a chance to talk much. Macey wants her pictures sold, Izzy has a journalism dream. Prisha wants college university, but you never ask for anything."

"Never had anyone to ask," he says.

Mary tilts her head as if that was an insult, but she knows that it is not personal, there is a deep sadness in the boy.

"You must have a dream," Hunter drills.

"Dunno, all I'm good at is hacking, and when I do that I get into trouble."

"Hacking?" Hunter smiles.

"Yeah. What I've been doing for you, getting into systems."

"You're not in trouble. You work for us now. Sad thing is, you can't tell anyone. You tell no one what we do, what you do. And you only hack what we ask you to. OK?"

Croc nods fast, impressed.

"Ummm... What about your career here?" Mary asks.

"What? Flipping burgers?" Croc asks.

"And what's wrong with flipping burgers?"

"Nothing," Croc cares.

Dwight wheels up to their table and spins to a stop. He has got very used to driving up to the diner tables. Hunter slides over so Sigmund can join them,

"Sigmund, this is Wild Mary, and my wife Elaine. We are expecting our first baby."

"Congratulations."

"Thank-you," Elaine beams. "I just wish Hunter was home more."

"I like the diner being attached to the workplace, I think it leads to a good aesthetic," Sigmund says.

"The diner is a workplace, it is 'the' workplace," Wild Mary insists.

"I hear that your food's pretty damn good, Mary," Sigmund says.

"You right there Sigmund, that's why it's always full of kids with good taste and know they can study here."

"Elaine. Maybe this could be your second home too?" Sigmund offers.

"Sigmund. This is a second college for the kids. Mary loves them all. You should pass by more often, make it your second home. I wanted to help Prisha, expand the education she got in Mumbai. How would I go about that?" he asks as he slides his phone to Dwight to read the message he has left open.

"That book you sent her got her all fired-up," Hunter finishes, to distract Sigmund.

"Hmmm," Sigmund grins. "There is no such thing as a free lunch."

"Yeah. I was just explaining that to Hunter he should settle the account," Mary bullies in.

Sigmund chuckles, he likes the mix of people at the table. "Sadly, apart from books, there is not much I can do for her, even if she were here. The entry requirements for our courses at the university are extremely high."

Hunter nods, having heard the reply but not taken it in. Sigmund knows he was slung a huge question, but whatever was on the phone was bigger.

"But she can learn here where I am interested in your work. What was on your phone?" Sigmund asks. He is challenging a deal he has offered

Hunter nods to Dwight. Dwight slides the phone to Sigmund.

"Do we all get to read it?" Mary asks.

"No. How much do I owe you?" Hunter asks her.

Wild Mary just waves her hand down, like it doesn't matter, "I'll just add interest 'till you ready, and add Elaine and Sigmund to the account."

Sigmund sliding the phone back to Hunter, "Intriguing."

"Real intriguing," Mary says to mock.

"How are the crimes above deck connected to the crimes below deck?" Sigmund questions, as if he has just been invited to the party.

"That's why we're sending Prisha in undercover, below decks," Hunter reveals.

"That's very unwise," Sigmund warns.

"Part of the education, you can ask her how it's going when she gets back," Hunter offers.

33 GOOD MORNING INDIA

Prisha is cooking breakfast for her children before they wake. The small apartment is quiet with just her brother and mama awake. The mood is down, no one likes her leaving. The family all live together and always miss Prisha though they depend on her salary.

"Thank you, sister. I understand the sacrifice," Bukka says.

"Do you Bukka? One day she must come home, one day before her children leave home as adults," her mother says.

Both children enter, immaculate in their school uniforms. Prisha adjusts the clothes.

"On the ship, our uniform has to be perfect."

"Which ship are you on, Mummy?"

"I am on a small ship.

"A small ship?" they both say in surprise and some disappointment.

"Yes."

"But you are an officer on a very big ship," her son says. Size is important to them. They are proud that their mother works on huge ships.

"I am going there to help them solve a problem. They need my big ship experience. Then I should be home again."

Both children smile, proud. They have a story to tell in school. She kisses them.

"How tall will you be when I get home?" Prisha asks.

"I won't grow," her daughter says.

"I will be this tall," her son says his hand reaching as high as it can go.

"I will take you to the airport," Bukka says.

"No brother. You have much work to do now. You need more staff; staff to move containers, to equip the office."

Bukka shakes his head,

"This will be your job. This will be your company when you come home. You will be chief operating officer."

The children laugh.

"No." Prisha says, "Little Bukka junior and miss Buki will be your officers. We are building a family business."

Her son protests, "But I want to go to sea, mummy."

"We are building the best refrigeration business in India so you never have to go to sea, so you can stay with your family."

Bukka junior contemplates. Then his face lights up.

"We will mend all the refrigerators of all the ships that come to India."

Mama-jee turns her wise head to recognise his clever idea. Bukka sits with a serious face nodding, his head moving sideways.

"This is true wisdom, sister. Bukka junior will run our 'cruise ship refrigeration division'. I will teach him."

Prisha smiles.

"And me," Buki says.

"Sister, you may have to continue with the ships until you have ensured our business."

"But you are not ready, Bukka. You sit here while others work. I need you to plan and build and be ready because there are a lot of ships, and a lot of American style fridge freezers."

"Are baap re." *(Hindi for OMG)*

"Bukka!" Mama-jee scolds.
"Oh my God." Bukka junior sings thinking it funny.
"Oh my God." Buki sings and dances too.
"Stop. First, we have much demanding work," Prisha says, but already she can imagine the expansion.

34 GOOD MORNING PHOENICIANS

Malaga is a busy city with a major airport for holidaymakers visiting the whole coastline, from Costa del Sol to Costa Tropical. The small busy port was originally built by the Phoenicians around 1000 B.C. An eastern extension of the natural harbour serves as a cruise port, mainly the smaller cruise ships. Some of these ships use the combination of port and airport to make it a 'homeport', where guests change-over and the ship begins the rotation all over again. These smaller cruise vessels can get to some of the interesting, more boutique ports along the Mediterranean. They also have interesting routes, some travel to the nearby African shores and stop at the likes of Tangiers and Casablanca as well as staying in the Mediterranean. As ports go, Malaga could be central to a cycle of human trade, routes where girls could be picked up and dropped off, moved from poverty to promised riches. That trade is only of concern to CSCI as it affects The Three King Ships they have been contracted to protect. Hunter and his team need to stay focused on their three ships which run a popular route with tourists and seemingly a perfectly eclectic mix of ports for traffickers. Malaga must be a delivery port, a port where Kieron expects women to be leaving with high hopes only to be sold. He and Bedi sit in prime position watching guests and crew walk from the ship's secure perimeter on the dock. It is late morning and there have been no women leaving with bags escorted by someone who looks like they might be pimping them.

Bedriška knows the port well. Like in many ports the returning visitors will know all the popular tourist attractions. Almost always, the historic ports are protected by a castle looming high on the hill, this one is complete with amphitheatre from the Roman period. The city below has a major shopping centre and a giant Millennium wheel.

"They have Picasso museum here," she says.

"Yeah?" Kieron autoreplies, studying the local map and tourist flyers he was given as he left the ship.

"His work is madness," She offers.

"Yeah. Good job he didn't do this map."

"I like he see madness in face of rich buyers who pretend they like his candour."

"His candour? Your English is improving."

"But he deliberate mad, you think?" she asks.

"He was a talented artist," Kieron says.

"Why?"

Kieron just wags his head, lost.

"They have early works here," she offers. "Not mad. These are quite different, incredibly detailed, before he saw mad buyers. Then he make angry work to reflect buyer's face."

"That's your theory?"

"You look. Every artist enjoy mad buyer, and that is what their work says. I find mad buyer."

Kieron looks at her. She is focussed on the people leaving the ship.

"Picasso was born here," he says.

"Was he?"

"Museo Picasso Malaga. Says here, two-hundred and eighty-five works donated by his family," he says.

"Mad people with money make crazy market in any trade."

Bedi stands up; she has seen something. She smiles at Kieron. He looks and sees three young women with their bags walking towards the dock gates with the head of the laundry, Micky, who they met on the tour.

"I wouldn't have guessed he was involved," Kieron says.

Bedi's poker-face has let her down, it is obvious she is angry and shocked.

"We need to know their story," she says. "Everyone has story. Story tells of madness and mad buyers."

The women are led down the long stretch of modern white arches between street vendors. They cross the road, cross Promenade Pablo Ruiz Picasso and head into the botanical gardens that run the length of the bay. The botanical area offers shade from the sun and peace from the traffic.

Like a couple of tourists, Bedi and Kieron wander carrying local literature. His smartphone recording elements of the Spanish port. However, they are following their mark and most of the photographs are of them and the handover.

Micky, the head of the laundry shakes hands with a much harsher looking bald man. He takes no money but hands over the girls who, for the first time look worried by this unexpected move. They look to Micky for an explanation. Micky ignores them, there is no goodbye. It is like a switch has gone off in his body and he no longer knows them. He turns and marches away and Bedi turns to follow him back in the direction of the dock gates. Kieron wonders if she might kill him before he gets back to the ship. He follows the thicker set, taller man who does not have the cruise crew smile. The girls are looking worried but two other men are flanking them now. This has become sinister and they're scared, but it is all too late. They are bundled into a black minivan, the men jump in, the door slides closed, and nothing can be seen through the darkened glass.

Kieron waves for Bedi to hurry and re-join him as he turns and stops a taxi.

"Follow that black van, don't lose him. But first, wait for my wife."

"I can't follow if I am waiting for your wife!"

Kieron turns and waves.

"Where you going?" the driver asks.

"Wherever that van goes."

"It is not possible if I can't see him," the driver states.

Kieron looks as the van accelerates away. He jumps in the taxi.

"Go!"

35 FREEWAY

The taxi pulls onto the freeway, still some distance behind the van.

"You want me to catch him?" the driver asks.

"No, just don't lose him," Kieron says leaning forward. His mobile phone goes.

"Sit back, take your call. I got your van."

Kieron sees the name Bedriška on the screen and answers.

"Hi. Is Micky back on the ship?"

"I lost him, but guess who is?" Bedi says into her phone.

"Gwen and Albert?" Kieron guesses.

"Yes."

"I'm on the freeway, going," he pauses as he looks for the position of the sun, "South. The road to Gibraltar," he says into his cell-phone.

Bedriška, standing in front of the ship, checks her watch. There are already guests heading back to the ship, though that could be those who wish to have lunch and a glass of wine onboard and not have to worry about rushing back.

"You would be at least twenty minutes behind. Stay at the ship. What time does it leave?"

Bedriška spins around and looks at the ship.

"Seventeen-thirty."

"I have four hours, if I'm not going to Gib', then I should have time to get back."

Bedriška starts to walk up the gangway, her cruise card out ready as she continues to speak on her phone.

"Do not engage," she stresses.

"Engage? A very military term," he suggests looking out the window. "Just passed the exit for Mijas. Speak later."

Kieron finishes the phone call.

"Mijas is very nice. Famous for donkey taxi," The driver says, showing he was listening.

"You still got that van?"

"Yes, it is towing me. On the way back I could show you Mijas."

"Why would I want to see donkeys?" Kieron asks then feels a little guilty for putting the place down. His phone bleeps. It is a text from Dwight. Hunter has left

Miami for Madrid then will meet him in Barcelona tomorrow, the port where they are supposed to go for the sixteen-million-dollar prize.

Kieron sits back and ponders how a KGB agent loses a mark following them back to the cruise ship. He wonders if she really lost him, or her anger got the better of her and Micky will never be seen again.

Bored, Kieron starts shaking his head about in the back of the cab. The driver watches him in his rearview mirror as he slows down and turns off the motorway.

"You OK?" he asks.

"Yeah fine. Where are we?"

Kieron checks his watch. It is three o'clock. The van is still in front, and they are entering a trendy, built-up city.

"The playground of Spain. Puerto Banús," the driver says. "Here you can hire any car, like Maserati or Lamborghini, just to drive around and show off. Money. Money. Money."

"Pretence of money!"

"Yes. Crazy."

"What else can you buy?"

"Anything. Absolutely anything."

The van weaves through some back streets and stops one block back from the seafront. They watch the women get manhandled from the van and straight into a girlie bar which infers every service you can think of. Kieron films it all on his phone. And presses send.

"I think I will drop you here and go back to Malaga," the driver says sheepishly.

Bedriška is standing on the lido deck watching the cruise port area below. On her smartphone, she watches the footage of the women being thrown into the bar. It makes her angry. She looks up with gritted teeth. She takes a moment then rings him.

"Kieron. Time to rush back. Job done."

"I've decided to stay. Tell them your husband is going to re-join in Barcelona."

"I can leave ship and join you."

"No, I'll get Hunter to divert here, after he lands in Madrid," he says.

"These men are killers."

"You know them?"

"Yes."

They lose connection. Bedi wishes she was there. Bedriška calls a waiter.

"Vodka."

"Double?"

"Triple."

"With what?"

"With smile."

36 PARTY TOWN

The seafront in Banús is premium; restaurants wrap around the point at each side of a harbour looking out to the few lit party yachts that break the darkness. Couples stroll by looking for a waterfront table for two, like the one Kieron has. Kieron Philips knows how to lace the palm of the maître'd when asking for a table for one. He orders a good wine and chooses a prawn garlic starter dish, then paprika fish of the day with olives and garlic. He doesn't rush as he knows Hunter landed in Madrid and caught his connecting flight to Malaga. He will have an hour in a taxi to Puerto Banús.

By the time he arrives a second bottle may have to be ordered, though Hunter is more of a beer drinker. A smart man approaches his table; he leans in just enough to be private, not too far as to impose.

"Can I suggest a lady to join you tonight," he says and smiles.

Kieron shakes his head dismissively, but the man knows not to leave too quickly. Kieron indicates the other chair, the man sits, Kieron pours him a small glass of wine.

"You have eaten, so, maybe a lady to join you for a drink, then go back to your hotel?"

"It is not something I had considered," Kieron adds fishing.

"There is such a wide choice, choose your skin colour, hair colour, order another bottle and she will be here to help you drink it."

"How long?"

"Twenty-minutes."

"What if I just want someone to talk to? No hotel. No sex."

"One-hundred euros and she will be happy to chat."

Kieron nods. The man stands.

"Forty euros now, sixty to the girl. Have you any preference?"

Kieron shakes his head wondering how he might engineer a girl from the ship, it is unlikely they are let out. He sees them as retained and working against their will, though he could be wrong.

"A non-smoker," Kieron says and shakes hands with the man, again seamlessly palming the forty euros.

Sitting again, he feels lonely. He lifts his mobile from the table and dials Georgie.

"Oh, you guys haven't forgotten me?" she says.

"Far from it."

"It is nice to hear from you; I've heard nothing from Bedi."

"It's the first we've stopped."

"Really, not a minute to ring me?"

"I miss you."

"You've got a cheek. You're living with my partner and you ring me for phone-romance."

"I'm sitting in a Spanish harbour and Bedi is on the ship sailing away from Malaga."

"You've left her alone?"

"She's a big girl."

"Did you have a row?"

"No, we've been getting on very well. She's a great agent."

"I'm not surprised."

"Why, what do you know about her?"

"It is for her to tell what she wants you to know."

"OK, but one thing. This may have turned into a sex trafficking problem and she seems affected by it."

"She will share what she wants to when she wants. You may learn more about her than me."

"Where are you?"

"Greece. We were in Rhodes today. It's a beautiful old walled city, but I feel I've seen it too many times now. It sounds lively where you are."

"Trust me, this was the quietest bar. I'm waiting for Hunter. He thinks he might make it by midnight. I hope this place stays open."

"It sounds like it will."

A young woman stops outside the restaurant and focusses on Kieron waiting for confirmation. Like a gentleman, he stands as she approaches.

"Hi. I'm Jessica."

"I have to go," he says into the phone.

"She doesn't sound like Hunter," are the last words Georgie says, and they are without humour.

"Research," he whispers and ends the call.

Kieron looks at the woman. "Jessica, please sit."

"Can we deal with the business first?" she asks.

Kieron slips three twenty euro notes under the purse she lays on the table, and she slips them inside.

"I have an hour before my friend joins me."

"I can have a friend join me."

"Not tonight. We're meeting other friends at the Electric."

The woman tilts her head, her thick flock of curled auburn hair flops forward.

"We can go somewhere much, much nicer," she suggests.

"Why, what is it like?" Kieron asks with a feared expression.

"The girls are not happy there, they are immigrants, not used to escorting. My friends are professionals, they have standards."

"If I have to stay tomorrow, then I'll take you up on the offer. But tonight is not my call, and I have to attend."

"What business are you in?" she asks.

"Dentist," he says as he watches her smile.

37 BURN MICKY

By midnight any ship is quiet in the guest areas and the MS Magi Myrrh is no exception. Bedi sits alone at the bar; she has probably drunk the best part of a bottle of vodka, but she is as still and thoughtful as she was at the beginning of the evening when she intended to go into dinner. Her slacks and colourful long top pass as evening wear but they are a cop-out really, she was not making an effort when she left the cabin. She has been alone all evening; none of the team rang her, and she didn't ring Georgie. The one thing on her mind is Micky, the bad apple on the ship, must answer to someone. What they have seen thus far cannot be all of it. There is always more.

A middle-aged officer with a boring hairstyle, dressed in white uniform and open-neck white shirt walks in and sits next to her. She ignores his introductory smile and looks at his gold lapel badge, the one all permanent staff must wear in public areas.

"Richard. How can I help you?"

He is hit by her frankness. The guests always have the advantage because they can see the staff member's name. Only the bar staff know the names of the guests from continually taking their cruise cards as payment for drinks.

"How do you pronounce Bedriška?" he asks.

"You did fine," she says. But Bedi is not concerned with his pronunciation, but by the fact that he knows her name, which means he has been called by bar staff. She glances again and see's he is the night security manager. She looks around the bar and realises she is the only one left which is why he has been called. They wish to close.

"Goodnight guys," she says to the waiters slipping off her stool and standing away from the bar. Base level biology claims five senses, but the body has many other ways of sensing. The most important is the one that ensures vital life processes. These are breathing and maintaining a regular heartbeat. These go on even when asleep or inebriated. Bedi is Russian, she was brought up drinking vodka, but she is out of practice. Her body systems are feeling the effects of alcohol more than they would have ten years ago. Her brain is telling her that. Her central nervous system is telling her that the alcohol has passed through the blood-brain barrier and is playing directly with the neurons. Here is where her training comes in, here is where she is taught to overcome torture and exposure, this is the time her brain is schooled to fight changes in behaviour. Now she fights for the simple solution of going to find her room. Her brain is realising that this man, with probably of years' service, is the night manager for a reason. He is a good loyal employee but not the brightest match in the box. If she says she needs just a minute, he will sit with her. He will also order her a coffee. His job is to solve problems. On this ship and he must have seen a lot of goings on. She has drunk herself into a perfect interview situation and now she needs to interrogate her subject gently.

"You know alcohol kills off your brain cells and they never come back," he smiles.

He has overstepped his position by saying something that could inflame a situation, but that just confirms Bedi's previous superfast assessment.

"We both know that not true," she says.

"I think it is," he argues through a smile.

"OK, one of us knows not true, and you not doctor."

"Oh," he says thinking.

"Google it, you have whole shift. Nothing happen on this ship," she leads.

"You'd be surprised," he starts.

Her coffee arrives, she thanks the waiter then turns to Richard, "Caffeine masks depressant effects of alcohol. You feel more alert. You can drink more; then it all gets worse. Water is better, but I am OK."

"Are you alone?"

"Tonight, yes. My stupid husband missed the ship. He fly to Barcelona."

"I saw that in the log," he says.

"I bet all excitement in log never actually happen at night."

"You'd be surprised," he says again.

"Second time you said. Only thing surprise me is number of crew this ship loses at every port. Women leave Lisbon. Women leave Malaga."

Bedi has dived straight in. She can't be bothered to sit up all night waiting to find out if this man knows anything. "And most from laundry; why?" she asks, seeing his jaw drop. He is on the ropes.

"It's demanding work," he tries.

"What? Putting linen in washers. Waiting for machine. I worked big hotels. Job not hard. People are hard. People make people leave. People in laundry causing problem. You think hard. No?"

She may have controlled her speech, but her behaviour is pushier, and she knows it. She is wondering if she will remember what he says in the morning. She goes to her phone and starts to record.

"What on earth makes you say that?" he asks.

"My husband in girlie bar, with stripper. She says she used to work on ship in laundry."

"I get why you're drinking."

"He get back in Barcelona. Excited because she tell him of secret girlie bar on ship."

"I've been here for ten years and never seen a girlie bar."

She leans in, "No, it is secret."

"There isn't one, but let's not tell him."

"He says ask for Micky. Big man on ship. Can you help me to my room please? I don't feel well."

"Yes, certainly. I'll just call a female officer to help."

He leaves and uses his radio.

Her cell-phone rings. It is Miami, still early evening there. She can't focus, but Dwight must have received the conversation and listened to it. He will now know that Micky has been burned. He can tell the team. He picks up.

"I hope you hear me; I am drunk?"

38 ELECTRIFIED

Hunter and Kieron wait in a short queue outside Elektrik Kitty. Hunter gets bleeped. He reads to Kieron from his cell,

"Dwight says Bedi's burned Micky. Suggests we blow his cover this end," Hunter reports.

"Micky? I thought she'd kill Micky, the pimp on the ship," Kieron explains.

"Hi, guys. Members club," the head doorman says.

Both can see he is weighing them up and membership is an excuse to say 'yes or no' at the door. They both have the stature to be a handful for the doorman and his team, and potential problems are weighed up outside. They might not get in.

"We come recommended," Kieron says.

Hunter finishes his text and is eyeing the cash booth next to the door which is security camera central.

"Who?" the doorman asks.

"A guy called ...." Kieron's memory falters.

"Micky. Off a cruise ship," Hunter reveals.

"We met him today, in Malaga. Our wives went shopping," Kieron adds.

"Spent a fortune, this is payback," Hunter smiles.

"Micky?" the doorman asks.

"Micky. Short Asian guy. Said he sent some new girls down today," Kieron says excitedly. He knows he may have gone too far, but he has assessed that he and Hunter would take the security staff easily.

'ID?" the doorman asks, pulling his camera phone out ready to make a record.

Hunter shows his, it says 'Owen Creed'. The doorman photographs it. Kieron takes longer. He only has his real ID and that is a day-one rookie error. He plays embarrassed, as if he can't find it.

"One's enough," the doorman nods, asking to look in Hunter's small bag. They are in.

'They should ask why he has a change of clothes', Kieron thinks, 'they are not too bright', but he can no longer suggest anyone is not up to scratch.

"We don't know a Micky, but come in, Owen," the doorman says, giving his female suited assistant the nod to swing the door open for them.

Inside the music is pumping loud; red and purple lights swing around the walls and ceiling. Some girls are on poles, others wander around disinterested, off-the-beat and in need of classes on how to use the pole. There is a sweet scent of cocktails in the air which is no doubt pumped out to encourage drinking.

"Micky's not a girl, right?" Hunter asks.

"No. He ran our laundry tour."

"Coz I think they're gonna check."

"So, we've got about ten minutes," Kieron suggests.

"Micky wasn't selling to the club then?"

"No. He took the women from the ship to a handover and they were brought here."

"I've not read that report."

"I haven't typed it up."

"Remember the golden rule," Hunter says.

"Yeah. Dead men can't send reports," Kieron says.

"I'll tell Dwight we're in here."

Kieron takes the last two steps to the bar. "Two beers."

"Thought you were a wine man?" Hunter raises an eyebrow.

"D'you think I'm risking the wine served here, after that fantastic bottle with my dinner? Sadly, a bad wine stays with you far longer than a good one."

Kieron slides the girl fifty euros and nods for her to keep the change. That will get them attention. They clink bottlenecks together.

The two men walk towards the centre of the club taking in every detail. The dance area is small, the booths around the edge are just large enough for a private dancer and most are in use. They study the internal doors that are also guarded, seemingly unnecessary. A fanfare starts and lights flash. The dancers step down from the stage.

"Hot wives dance," stings from the public address system and there is a mini stampede to the stage. These women are arguably better looking, better dressed but keener than the professionals that left.

As the crowd converge on the stage, the two drift away. They watch as two guests are let through a guarded internal door with one of the dancers. Then another goes through by himself but hands in a card or ticket to the doorman. The door is open just enough for them to see that they are walking down to a basement. Kieron catches a waitress.

"What's downstairs?"

"Anything you want. That's premium," she says moving away with her tray of drinks.

He catches her. "How do I go premium?" Kieron pursues.

"Pay at the bar, sir."

"Do they look as good as you, or are they the old hags they can't let upstairs?"

"No one's as good as me," she flirts.

Hunter steps in. "Seriously, have they been down there all season or are there any new girls down there?"

"We get new girls all the time. I saw new girls arrive today. You might be in luck or do you want to travel first class?"

The waitress is flirting with them, and will no doubt be back after she has despatched the drinks she carries. She can sense a sale.

"What good can we do by going downstairs?" Hunter asks Kieron.

"Sadly, none, and we have about five minutes left. I have her conversation recorded. I've got the doors on film. We're done here."

"Report sent, just in case?"

Kieron nods.

"We should concentrate on the 40 million in Barcelona. This is a job for Interpol."

"We should; girls held against their will is not our job," Kieron says.

The two men smile, standing firm.

"We have no plan for this."

"And no backup."

"But," Hunter muses.

"If they are being held?"

"If they are? We would obtain better evidence."

"And we don't need sixteen million."

"It might be handy," Hunter ends.

"Let's go," Kieron says.

Turning with perfect timing they meet the herd of approaching doormen head-on. The man they met at the door is at the front. Behind him, the female bouncer looking evil, as if she did more drama classes than front-line service. Then two other suited men who are no doubt locals.

"We spoke to Micky. He never told anyone about the club. Give me your smartphone you've been filming with," the doorman says.

"No," Kieron says.

The doorman looks from him to Hunter, then back to Kieron.

"We're leaving," Hunter says.

"No, you're not," the doorman says.

Hunter turns to Kieron, "Do you realise, we have never done this together?"

"I know. It's crazy, we've known each other for… how long? And we've never once," Kieron agrees.

Both men turn back to the doorman.

The woman in black steps forward, "We train in Krav Maga."

Kieron squints, "Is that near Malaga?"

"It is a deadly form of self-defence."

Hunter leaves it for Kieron to answer.

"I appreciate the warning. And it's a touch embarrassing for us because normally my wife would be here to deal with you. But she went handbag shopping. And she's deadly serious when she goes handbag shopping."

"Deadly," Hunter adds.

In rage, the woman's arm snaps out towards Kieron. His body swerves away as he catches her wrist, twists her arm in a circle and lifts it over the male doorman's neck engulfing him. It snaps sharply and pulls them both backwards off-balance to the floor, broken. The two agents walk between the other two doormen who are stunned by what they saw.

"Normally, I would have joined in," Hunter says.

"Next time. I didn't want you to have to put your bag down, Owen."

"She was using Krav Maga," Hunter says with even more sarcasm.

"I don't think so. Israelis never wear cheap suits."

At the exit, the two sidestep into the booth used by security. Conveniently for promotion, the camera on the stage is the one feeds the screen in the street. It is still presenting the hot wives, all with less clothes on than they started with. Hunter unclips the hard drives, one by one. He drops them into his bag. The systems all fail. A doorman rushes to stop them.

Kieron looks up, "You need to call an ambulance for your head of security. I already called the police. I think your female security officer just attempted to kill him."

The doorman goes inside.

Kieron texts Dwight a report and asking him to send in the local police to save women held in the basement as sex slaves.

39 DAY OFF

Residential areas in downtown Puerto Banus are quiet in the early hours of the morning and this one is perfect as they can spy no street cameras. The two men walk, one each side of the road, just inside the parked cars as if in a conflict zone looking for guerrillas. They are choosing a car that will be easy to steal and get them down the motorway, and a second similar car. Having made the choice. Hunter slides under the first and takes off the front and rear license plates with a screwdriver from his key ring. He moves to the second, removes the plates and replaces them with the plates from the first car. He has the door open in seconds, alarm disabled, and the ignition started. Its real plates are tossed onto the rear seat. Taking the road out of town, the early morning delivery traffic is just beginning to start, and as they reach the motorway it is alive.

"Where do you fancy going? We seem to have the day off," Hunter asks.

"I felt I missed out on seeing the donkeys in Mijas on the way down."

"Mijas for breakfast it is."

"A bar with internet, I've a lot of reports to send Dwight before I die," Kieron says lightly.

"A dead man can't send reports," Hunter adds.

"Correct."

Less than two hours later, Mijas is still not awake. They circle a mountain top road and park the car that they never want to see again. They walk up to the town, glancing over the waist-high white stone pillared wall at the incredible view smothered by the flat blue morning light. It is silent.

"They might suspect who we are by now," Kieron suggests.

"Maybe, but I'm not sure that matters; technically we're off the job."

"Oh. You didn't tell me that bit."

"No, well, the two execs who hired us were let go. They didn't have permission to spend that kind of money and they're being investigated."

"It was a lot of money," Kieron says.

"But now we have proof of a much more heinous crime."

"Sex crime," Kieron adds.

"A sex crime they won't want their ship associated with. They might still have a job, and we might still have a contract."

"This is way bigger than a chocolate bar job. It must be a new fee."

"I'll have Dwight discuss it with the new executives," Hunter says. "After he's released the evidence, informed Interpol, let the press know, and fully embarrassed the company so they need us."

"Miami won't be in their offices for another eight hours," Kieron says, checking his watch.

"Dwight and Croc never sleep," Hunter adds.

"Good. Because from this point on, it gets more dangerous," Kieron suggests.

"Sex traffickers put no value on life; not mine, not yours. Hopefully, we won't need Prisha to join the ship tomorrow."

"Maybe we can get her on our old ship in Barcelona."

"And she can carry the trunk off."

"Well this job is not about money now, even if we don't get paid. So Prisha can work on the other cash," Hunter says.

They arrive at the empty donkey stables. Opposite is an alfresco family café hogging the whole cliff top - up to a small church. The view they have enjoyed all the way up the hill is getting better as the sun breaks through the mist. An old man is wiping the morning damp from the tables and chairs.

"Can we get breakfast?" Hunter asks.

"Sit, please, sit," the owner insists, pulling chairs into position. "Few minutes, I bring you coffee and a menu. And Spanish news?" he asks.

They sit down, declining the local newspaper.

"Sigmund's back on our team," Hunter starts.

"Serial sex offenders, Sigmund?" Kieron asks.

"I did it to get Prisha on the team. That and investing in offices in Mumbai for her," Hunter gently breaches."

"Tell me about this private investment you personally made?"

"We had to invest."

"We?" Kieron asks.

Hunter nods as the menus are placed on the table and the noise of pressurised steam from a distant coffee machine announces business is open.

"I had to make a judgement call," Hunter explains.

"So we own an office in, where?"

"Mumbai. It's not an office for us, though I'm sure there's room."

"So, what is it we own?"

"It's more to do with refrigeration."

Kieron nods slowly.

"Repairs," Hunter adds.

"That was a gap in my investment portfolio. Not that I have an investment portfolio, or any money having been released from the army without a pension. You do remember that I have no money?"

"The fee covers it."

"Great."

"Only just, but I have a plan for getting the sixteen-million off the other ship," Hunter says.

"Tomorrow now involves us with Prisha again?"

"Yes."

"We are kind of busy, so I hope it's quick and easy. Do we just walk on your old ship and get them to crane the trunk off?" Keiron asks.

"That's pretty much the current plan, but I am open to other suggestions."

Two coffees are placed on the table. The man then stands waiting for an order.

"You have fried green tomatoes?" Kieron asks.

The owner looks puzzled, trying to translate that to something he might be able to offer.

"No," the owner adds hesitantly.

"Ok. I'll have everything you got then. Full breakfast. Whatever you recommend," Kieron says.

"Me too," Hunter says.

The owner nods and leaves them.

"We should go onboard ship with huge pockets," Hunter adds.

"We?"

"You, me, Bedi and Prisha."

"Pockets?"

"Worse scenario; we can't get the trunk off, we can walk away with what we can carry."

"That's what you got?"

"Worst scenario. A bucket load of cash!" Hunter enthuses.

"We're pack-donkeys?" Kieron asks.

"Some cash in all our pockets," Hunter nods in reply to Kieron. "Unless you got something else?"

Kieron looks across at first donkeys being lead down into the square and the stable,

"You know how this donkey thing started?" He starts.

Hunter shakes his head; he doesn't have a clue.

"Local farmers. They used donkeys to farm. Tourists asked to ride them. They made more in tips from donkey rides than farming."

"Donkey rides pay better than food production?"

"That's why we have a world food shortage."

"That simple?" Hunter asks.

"Often is that simple."

The owner returns with two plates of food.

"Good news, my wife find the most green tomatoes and she fry them."

"Wild!" Hunter says.

"Wild," laughs the owner walking away.

"So, we sell the ship the idea of donkey rides off the ship, from inside, down the gangway."

"How?" Hunter asks.

"We say local unions insist. We fill their side saddles with money in the ship, empty them off the ship, send them back," Kieron finishes and starts his breakfast.

"That won't work."

"OK, here's another one. Knock, knock."

"Knock, knock?" Hunter asks.

"No, you are supposed to say, 'who's there'?"

"Who's there?" Hunter asks.

"The donkey to collect a parcel."

"Lack of sleep does not agree with you," Hunter says to Kieron.

"And how much sleep had you missed when you bought a fridge shop in India?"

40 TAXI, BUS OR HIRE CAR?

The little tapas bar in Constitution Square overlooks a fountain built from marble, recovered from a landslide in 1894. The sound of running water against the backdrop of singing crickets is a lullaby. Falling asleep in the sun with a beer may be more for locals than tourists on a tight schedule, but neither of the investigators slept last night.

"I like Mr Croc," Ronaldo says, shaking them awake. He is the young son of the Spanish owner. Kieron comes around first because his hand is being tugged, but they both feel safe, relaxed and away from trouble.

"He said you would give me a hundred euros."

"Croc did?"

"Yes, he said I was very good."

"One hundred?"

Hunter wakes. He looks up at the sun, shakes his body out, picks up his bottle of beer and sees it is empty. He shows it to the landlord who rushes to get a new cold one.

Kieron is on the phone, "Croc? I patched into the kid's computer at this bar,"

"Already down-loading, it's fast internet there."

"Don't allow him to sign in or let him post while you're working. We want to stay under the radar," Kieron says.

Another round of delicious food pays in dividends because as Croc works, they talk with the family about bus times to the airport, and the owner's daughter offers to drive them. That is likely to be another hundred Euros, but they didn't wish to steal another car, or leave any trace hiring one. The buses would be the safest option but even they are often fitted with security cameras. Being invisible is not easy in a modern world, which could well be why the ship's crew have become such great portage for the smugglers. Being local is perfect.

The airport in Malaga is always terribly busy. If it wasn't for the retreat of the private lounge with a business section, a good day would have been ruined. Hunter is on a call with Dwight in a private cubicle. Kieron waits for him outside in the business centre where he takes two large envelopes that might come in handy if he has money he can post.

His boredom triggers him to call Bedi and share that they have at last gathered evidence, he hopes some is on the club's cameras. Maybe they can concentrate on their trunk and sixteen million. He ends the call with a harmless suggestion that she might call Georgie and the call instantly turns sour.

"You spoke with her? Why?" Bedi demands.

Kieron knows he has just made a stupid move. He holds his breath while seeking a way out, and then he breathes.

"We are going onto the other ship tomorrow; her old ship. Georgie told us where she thought the trunk was left. We need you to come with us. You'll need big pockets, maybe a small bag," Kieron says.

He waits to hear if his move has worked, or if he pulled out that dangerous Jenga log and the unstable stack is about to topple. Again, the pause seems endless.

"We keep what we can carry?" Bedi asks.

Bedi might be miles away on the ship but he can imagine her poker-face. She is a hard lady and he would hate to have to negotiate with her daily. The partnership she has with Georgie seems strange given how soft the Georgie he knows is.

"How on earth do you expect me to answer that," Kieron says, relieved to see Hunter approach.

"It's Bedi, I told her to wear pockets tomorrow. She wants to know if she keeps what she can carry."

Hunter takes the cell phone from Kieron and lifts it to his face.

"No." Hunter ends the call, and swings his small bag onto his shoulder,

"Gate's up. Let's go."

"Something bothering you?" Kieron asks, following Hunter out of the lounge.

"A lot's bothering me. This is one of those jobs you wish you'd never taken. I knew from the outset it was bad. I knew it was never about laundry wars; they happen on every ship."

"At least we got a big fee."

"That all went on our Mumbai Fridge Repair Company."

"All of it?" Kieron asks.

"It got us Prisha. Prisha gets us below decks to join those dots, that will get us the second payment."

"Which now isn't there."

"Probably never was, our two young executives have flown the nest," Hunter states.

"What, like popped out for a coffee?"

"No, vanished. Dwight and Croc can't find them and they've been trying since the kitchen tour; all day yesterday and all day today."

"They'll turn up," Keiron says with no confidence.

"One thing young Croc got right about this job."

"What?"

"It stinks," Hunter says.

The two men walk determinedly through the airport. At the gate, they show their boarding cards, passports and pass through in autopilot. They are both thinking hard. Kieron is first to break the silence,

"It's time to bring Interpol in to look after the women. Then we share all this information with our previous shipping company. We suggest we know what we're looking for and should give their ship berthed in a quick once over in Barcelona. Just in case they have the same problem."

"One step ahead of you there, Dwight's on it."

"You were one step ahead of me with the freezer deal too. But, did you bring the key to the trunk or is it still on the nail in our wall?"

Hunter holds the key up.

41 NIGHT TIME IN LAS RAMBLAS

At Barcelona airport terminal 2, the pair jump on the RENFE train. It goes directly into the centre where they get off at Passeig de Gràcia and change to the Greenline metro. It is just one stop to Plaça de Catalunya. They could walk, but Hunter knows his way around the metro, so it is easy. With no wait for luggage at arrivals, they do the journey in 35 minutes.

Catalunya Square is lively; people in Barcelona don't venture out to eat until around nine at night. Although the square sports familiar franchise names like 'The Hard Rock' and 'Kentucky Fried Chicken' it is also the start of Las Ramblas which is a long dietary paradise of a street.

"Watch your wallet. The world's best pick-pockets come here," Hunter tells Kieron as they weave in and out of tourists.

For Hunter to warn him they must be good. They need to find somewhere quiet to eat and discuss plans to search the other ship and leave with as much money as possible. They also need a place to stay for the night. Kieron has a pocket full of cash from Bequia where he has a bank account, both have slush funds in Florida, but this trip is bleeding money fast.

"Prisha. Where are you?" Hunter asks on his cell phone to her.

"Mr Hunter. I am undercover, I shouldn't reveal unless you have a password," she says.

Hunter smiles at hearing the cheek of her sweet Indian voice,

"The password is, 'dinner in Las Ramblas'."

"No. There is no agent near there this evening."

"Where?"

"I am not in the centre."

"Are you alone?"

"Yes, just me. No other Indian girl was silly enough to fly this far around the world for a job in the laundry."

"Grab a cab."

"To which end of Las Ramblas? It is a mile long."

The two men stride through the crowd, past endless human statues, and flower stalls.

"Will anyone miss her tonight?" Kieron asks.

"Roll call will be on the ship tomorrow. It sounds like she's the only one joining. They'll collect her at an agreed time. Until then she's on her own."

Kieron follows Hunter left off the main drag and into a busy square, Plaça Reial. Like everywhere else, the front-of-house managers work as hard as time-share salesmen to encourage trade. Whilst the seating outside in the square has its attraction, the Restaurante Italiano wins on privacy inside. A table between their bricked arches, walled with a wine collection has their name on it. Tonight, is about planning and getting Prisha on the same page for both operations.

Prisha enters shortly after a bottle of red wine has nicely aired and some huge grilled garlic prawns have been set out as a shared starter with bread and olive oil. Prisha is dressed simply but looks a million dollars. She has a natural beauty, flawless skin, and jet-black hair.

"She is a catch," Hunter says before she arrives at the table.

"And with her own fridge company I hear," Kieron says standing.

The waiter eases her chair in and pours her a glass of wine. She does not resist the alcohol as she would have before she joined the team on the last ship. Although she may have been in danger then, her first CSCI attachment, this is the first time she will be solo and deliberately thrown under the bus. Two buses.

42 NIGHT SHOPPING

They can afford to be light-hearted this evening as they won't be sending Prisha back to her hotel alone. Her small hotel is used by air and ship crew and has spare rooms. However, the three on the ground have no intention of retiring back to the hotel until Hunter's credit card has been abused in the late-night shops.

Eating and shopping in the busy cities of Europe are evening affairs. Between one and four o'clock in the afternoon, most shops will be closed for a staff break or *siesta*. The Catalonian government did vote to end the workday at 6pm, but that will never work here while there is trade outside.

Over wine and food, the team discuss plans, and Hunter shows them the stickers he had made in America before he left. 'Crime Investigation Equipment, Sterile - Do Not Open. Unload in Miami'

"That's a great idea, better than 'crime evidence' which is the way we left it labelled. No one would expect evidence to be left there that long. But, I'm not sure about the 'Unload in Miami'. Customs in Miami would surely seize that cash?"

"Correct, but this ship never goes to Miami. Not even on its world cruise."

In the well-lit fashion shops, Kieron finds found dark green pants with pockets everywhere. They will carry more cargo than their name implies, and they have a children's size that fits Prisha. The two stand in front of a mirror.

"You know what I'm thinking?" Kieron asks.

"No." Hunter snaps.

"I'm thinking, we all wear the same pants. A uniform," Kieron adds.

"No," Hunter repeats.

Kieron takes a pair from the shelf and throws them at him, "Onboard ship you wore a uniform without question."

The owner of the shop is determined to find matching shirts. His initial attempt, while Hunter is changing, both Prisha and Kieron agree immediately is too Gaudi. Gaudi is the extravagant colourful local artist whose name is now an adjective. The shirts have too much pattern and are too colourful. He finds a khaki shirt with a single breast pocket that almost completes the uniform.

"You know what else we need?" Kieron suggests to Prisha. She shakes her head and the owner waits in anticipation.

"A belt. A utility belt. With a water holder, utility tool, torch," Kieron says.

"No!" Is Hunter's shout from the dressing room, but the owner has left and Prisha is passing his shirt into the curtain draped dressing cubicle.

By the time Hunter comes out, Prisha has called Bedi on the ship to get her size. Commander Kieron Philips has threaded a belt with a water bottle holder on the hip. He is now adding a thin LED torch into what was a pen holder. He turns to Hunter who is almost matching them.

"What do you think?"

"We need a badge," Prisha says.

Kieron turns to the owner who was about to speak, "No. We'll get that designed."

"I was about to say that these pants are shorts too," the owner adds. "The legs zip off."

"Perfect," Hunter says.

"We'll take them."

Kieron has his phone out, sending video back,

"Dwight, you getting this?"

"Oh yeah. More than I'm getting favourable reaction from your new stone-cold corporate guys that run your three ships."

"Not my guys," Hunter shouts.

"They're not sucking-up the trafficking connection on the evidence you got. Say the girls could be going voluntarily."

"Do they want to pay us to get evidence?"

"That was not on the cards. I didn't hit it off with Frank and even Di is now blanking me," Dwight admits.

"Frank worries me; him and Marty are protecting something or someone, or maybe they are just old company men. Watch them," Hunter offers.

"They asked me where Bjorn and Chet have gone, seem to think they are our people."

"Avoid that hole."

"Croc has a theory. He thinks the night he was following Chet and Bjorn, they were following someone."

"Recheck his video and find out more about that club."

"Frank ain't gonna like hearing more about girls being run on his ship," Dwight adds.

"Tell him our fees double when they step on board. And they will," Hunter says, now wearing his new uniform."

"Don't forget us crew back home with that kit. I'll send all sizes through."

"Sounds like a mail order. I'll send you the supplier."

The shop owner looks really pleased with this order.

Back at the hotel, the team are wise enough to split and the two men go in first carrying all the bags. They notice one man idling in reception, so they make a fuss about the soccer game the receptionist is watching on TV.

Prisha arrives and they ignore her. She takes her key. In seeing her, the man leaves. Kieron follows him out at a safe distance. Hunter watches the male receptionist carefully to gauge whether he is in on it, if there is anything to be in on. Though Hunter was offered the elevator opposite, he takes the stairs, two steps at a time. Catching Prisha on the second floor he follows her to her room, which is searched before he hands her shopping over and leaves.

Hunter splits the shopping between his and Kieron's room and in both, he utilises the two drinking glasses from on the desk beside a bottle of water. He sets them one on top of the other just behind the door as he pulls it closed and leaves each room.

Back downstairs, the same receptionist is there watching the television.

"OK, Sir?" he asks.

"Sure. Going out for a smoke."

Hunter doesn't smoke, but it is as an excuse that needs no explaining. He stands in the street looking left and right. He has no clue where Kieron has gone so has to wait for his mobile to ring and it does

"Where are you?" he asks.

"He went into a club. You want to guess what it's called?" Kieron invites.

"Elektrik Kitty?"

43 HEAVY HEADS

Even though it is early, Hunter's first instincts are to walk to Prisha's room and check she is alright. As the door opens, a glass falls at her feet.

"Just checking," he says.

Her eyes squint, she holds her head and bends to pick up the glass alarm she triggered.

"See you at breakfast," he says. "No rush."

She nods still half asleep and feeling she had a drink last night.

"In uniform," he adds, as the door closes.

Breakfast is a buffet almost everywhere you stay. In his uniform, Kieron is waiting outside the dining room as Prisha and Hunter arrive.

"We should get breakfast on the ship," Kieron says.

"Good idea, but let's get a coffee," Hunter says.

"We don't know who's from the ship. Best no one sees Prisha in a CSCI uniform. Plus, Bedi's waiting," he says holding a bag with her uniform.

In the taxi, Kieron begins ripping local tourist magazines into quarters and fitting them into his cargo pockets.

"What do you think?"

"Good call," Hunter agrees.

Kieron opens the bag and passes them each a couple of tourist magazines. By the time they drive by the tall statue of Columbus pointing towards the new cruise berths and India beyond, their new flat-looking uniforms have bulked out pockets even if they don't look lived-in. Passeig Josep Carner crosses the major traffic circle at the bottom of Las Ramblas but they favour a port road. They head towards the bridge Pont de la Porta d'Europa which takes them across to the purpose-built cruise wharf. Their older ship which hopefully has the trunk full of money is berthed towards the far end which is Terminal C. Their first call is her smaller ship, berthed nearest the bridge at Cruise Terminal A where Bedriška waits. Hunter steps out and hands her the bag with her uniform. Bedriška looks him up and down disapprovingly.

"Seriously?"

"Two ships, two jobs, undercover here, but an investigation unit up there."

She walks off to the terminal building's washroom to redress. He turns and leans in to speak with the driver.

"Next, terminal C. Then we need you to wait with our bags, then take two of us back to the hotel."

The driver is keen for any paying fare. When Bedriška returns he opens the door for her and they get in.

"Terminal C."

The four uniformed CSCI operatives are given cruise cards in lanyards and are shown up the gangway at their old ship. They wait as those in front of them have their bags checked and X-rayed before entry is allowed. Many of the staff remember Hunter, some remember Commander Kieron Philips who can't hide from the superhero nickname he acquired on the Heist job when they acquired the money. Inside they are escorted to Hunter's old office. Jacob Augusto, Head of Security is the new name on the door.

"Mr Witowski. I have heard much about you and was told to expect you. But I must admit it was a surprise. I am sorry but we don't have as many murders as when you were here. I think we're crime-free."

"Your head office asked us to walk around. By ourselves. We know the way."

"Maybe you will share your findings with me before you leave?

"I'll do you that courtesy."

The four take the laundry first so as not to just make a major rush for the trunk. They are sure they are being watched. The whole of i95, the major crew highway is examined, if only to ensure that anyone watching them on camera will get bored and give up. It is familiar, as are the staff and it is easy to feel like home, but they need to get to the storage area on the deck below. Dropping down below the stage, they are alone and can search for their chest. As expected, it is tucked away at the back, luckily not within any camera view. Stacked on it are some other smaller boxes. They work well as a team to reveal it, and Hunter produces his key and tries to work the padlock, but his hands are too big. Prisha takes over, having the smallest hands and she pops it open. Hunter steps in and slowly lifts the lid, dreading what he is going to find in there. To his relief the money is intact. He steps back for them all to see.

"Circle around, lose the junk in your pockets and fill up."

He makes stacks of one hundred dollar bills ready to load pockets.

Kieron fills his pockets as fast as he is passed the bundles. Hunter stands and looks at him.

"The uniform is bad enough, but any more would look beyond ridiculous."

After each of them has left, Hunter fills his own pockets and closes the lid. The stickers are rolled over as official seals.

"Prisha. I need your small hands."

Prisha is back within seconds and the lock snapped closed.

"Great," he says. "Lifting."

Kieron slides the box in. Prisha and Hunter lift and wedge the boxes back above it.

"Only one problem with this plan," Kieron starts, sliding another box in to be lifted. "We have to walk off the ship with pockets full of money."

"Who'll stop us?" Hunter says.

"We've done it, this is a success," Prisha says.

"Kieron!" Bedriška shouts from the door of a small office in the storage area. He runs to join her, lying there are two drug users, out of their heads, lying on the floor, smiling.

Crack! Keiron is hit over the head and he goes down. Bedriška is grabbed from behind but her head goes up hitting the chin behind, she spins her elbow into the unsuspecting jaw and the assailant goes down. Hunter pulverises the second attacker. She rushes to Kieron on the floor, bleeding from his head. This was the last thing he needed just as he was getting well.

"Prisha, call it in," Hunter shouts also going to Kieron.

Prisha rushes to the house phone on the wall.

"Jacob. It is the CSCI team. Deck 2 storage, door 2C. We need back-up and medics."

"Man down. Drug users discovered, and hostiles," Hunter shouts over her.

44 PAYDAY

Jacob closes his office door behind them, the door that Hunter would have closed just six months earlier.

"My team are upstairs having breakfast. Kieron has been cleaned up. He'll be fine," Hunter reports.

"Is that what you were looking for? Drugs?"

Hunter shakes his head, no. "Log it as a local find. Take the credit. Let's both say you briefly welcomed us on board, told us it wasn't a good day to look around because you had your own sting going down. We agreed between us, we'd come back on board when berthed together in Naples. We had breakfast and left. You handled the drug bust. Just slip the arrest time."

Jacob thinks for a minute. It will look bad for him if Hunter came on board and found that straight away, taking all the credit.

"What were you here for?" he asks.

"If I tell you now, you'll go looking for it. The crew will know you're looking, and it'll vanish. Let me join my crew for breakfast and turn this into a social," Hunter suggests.

Jacob eventually nods, they shake hands and Hunter leaves knowing he will get a second try at his trunk.

Hunter has missed the grand cruise ship breakfast even though he rarely eats much. It is the massive selection and ability to choose. He takes a full breakfast; he is hungry but on the way to his team's table he is bombarded by old friends. Even crew who were not his friend when he worked here are glad to see him back. Eventually, he gets back to the table with a tray of food.

"Kieron isn't feeling good," Prisha says.

Bedi is looking at Hunter like it is his fault.

"How you doing?" Hunter asks him.

"OK. I'd rather it wasn't my head, but it wasn't the part of the skull previously damaged," Kieron explains with a large bandage stuck to his hair. "Luckily I heard the swooping sound and my arm went up."

"Too late," Bedi says.

Hunter eats and talks. "We're getting off, with no bags not even the keenest officer will stop us. In the taxi, we unload the money into the bag. I reckon we have five thousand in each pocket. Should be around a hundred-grand. Not a bad mornings work. Keep a couple each as spending money, there's no point draining the expense account. Bedi and Kieron, you change clothes in the washroom at the lockers at the cruise terminal, put the bag in a locker and get on board your ship. Prisha and I will take the taxi back to the hotel; she's not being picked up until one."

Kieron produces two brown envelopes, closed, sealed, postage stamps and addresses on. Not enough money in them to cause any attention.

"One is Auli'i's address in New York, the other is Sister Anna in St Vincent with a note on the back, for Chechnya. No company or title so they can deny it. I plan to leave them on reception for post."

Hunter looks at his watch, "Today's post will have gone."

"Even better. It'll get posted at the next port. A port which we go nowhere near."

Hunter thinks, looks at the seal and the postage.

"Spanish postage, is the next stop in Spain?"

"If it isn't, I won't leave it."

Bedi stands up. She has a hand under Kieron's arm to help lift him, not that he needs it,

"We go."

Back at the hotel, Prisha is at a small table in reception with two postcards of Barcelona and an envelope. She lingers, not knowing what to write.

"Not a real message, no details. Your family need to be able to deny any knowledge of where it came from," Hunter says, standing over her.

Prisha is shocked and embarrassed.

"I see everything, I know everything," he says. He pauses for a moment and adds. "I said you could keep some bills," he says encouraging her to carry on.

On the back of the first card, she writes, 'for the two girls'. She slips five one-hundred-dollar bills between the two postcards, then slips them into the envelope.

"Don't post it here," he advises.

Prisha slides that into her jacket and is excited.

"My daughters can go to school."

"We're a team."

"You are so kind."

"Moving money is such a problem. We'll do the same in Naples, but I don't think you'll be able to join us?"

"How will you manage without my small hands?"

"I'll think on it."

The receptionist walks over.

"Your taxi is here."

She looks at Hunter and hands over the rest of her money.

"My first repayment."

He smiles; she leaves. Hunter watches her go, then walks over to reception, takes an envelope and two postcards. He repeats the same trick she did. On his postcard, he writes. 'On account.' He is tempted to write more, but he refrains. He addresses it to Wild Mary's Diner.

Onboard, the ship guests move in and out. Some are back for lunch, some going into Barcelona late. In a lounge area to the side, two officers plus their head-of-security are there with the night manager. They are questioning Kieron.

"My wife was drunk. She's Russian. She gets drunk."

"She specifically told us you said there was a girlie club on this ship. To ask for Micky."

"I did? No. I missed the ship and was at a girlie bar called Micki's. And Micki is a girl by the way."

There is a long silence. Kieron volunteers nothing more. They know nothing.

Bedi stands on the lido deck looking over the edge. She can see Micky outside the secure perimeter gate. He has two girls with him, but she can't intervene. She hates him. She hates what he is doing but she must stay on the ship and protect Prisha. She has called Hunter and he is on his way to deal with off-ship matters.

The taxi pulls up with Prisha now in her civilian clothes. She gets out. Her small bag is slung over her shoulder and she plays the part of the timid Indian girl going to join her first ship very well.

Micky steps forward and introduces himself. He shakes hands, then puts his arm around her. But he is not bringing her towards the ship.

Bedi's blood runs cold. Something is wrong and her feet start to move. She watches helplessly as a black van pulls up. Micky helps the first two girls in.

"No," she shouts to them, but Micky turns, and her mouth is smothered.

Micky pushes Prisha in the van. He is then hit hard. He has been double crossed and is being bundled into te van. It pulls away fast.

Bedi dials on her phone as she runs for the midships staircase.

"Hunter. They've taken Prisha. Black van took Prisha, Micky and two girls."

"I saw it, I'm following."

Bedriška races each flight of stairs. She turns into reception where they're still interviewing Kieron.

"One down," she shouts at him.

Bedi is bleeped through security and runs down the gangway.

"Excuse me, there is an emergency. My wife."

Kieron turns and leaves the security team before they can stop him, he holds his card out. It bleeps under the infrared scanner and he is free to leave.

Kieron runs down the gangway and catches Bedriška at the Spanish port gate.

"They took Prisha before she entered the perimeter," she shares as they hail a taxi and leave.

Officers on the gangway watch. They understand nothing at the moment.

Inside the taxi, Bedi is on the phone to Hunter and directing the driver until she sees the black SUV van.

"There."

"I've got it, I've got it," the driver repeats.

"What happened?" Kieron asks as she sits back.

"Micky there with two girls. He wait for Prisha. When she arrive; black van arrive. They take everyone."

45 GOING WHERE?

Prisha lies on the floor of the bus. She twists her body around to look up at the two girls who sit on seats forward of her with men viciously guarding them. She was thrown in legs first so at least the guards can't kick her head. Micky is unconscious next to her and they have cable-tied his wrists. She is worried; she is part of a team, but she left Hunter in the Hotel and Kieron went onto the ship. How will they know where she is? Fear makes her blood run cold; they will kill her if they think she is an agent. But she is an agent and evidence gathering is what she does. She can call Dwight. She turns the cell to silent, starts a video call with the camera on Micky's face, then back on her miming shhh. She points it up, she gets the two girls and the man.

"Roger that," she hears Dwight whisper. "Leave it recording."

It hits her that she has at least five hundred dollars in her pocket. If the men find that they will know she is a plant. She looks at the blood from Micky's face and knows she will be smashed up then killed. She slips the letter out of her pocket and looks for somewhere to hide it. The van stops and in panic, she takes the two postcards and money out from the addressed envelope and pushes them into Micky's jacket pocket. The doors burst open and she is ripped from the van by the driver. Her camera is still secretly recording, and she drops the screwed-up envelope to the floor, she does not want them to know her family address. Prisha is brutally pinned to the side of the van while they get the others out and the driver rings a bell on a side door. She is near a corner and from the posters on the wall, it is a sex club. She fights to look around in the hope that someone is there. Where are they? She is thrown towards the side door of the club and she resists for an extra second to scan for her team, for anyone, for help.

Hunter steps from his taxi in time to see an unconscious man thrown down the stairs and the last man enter the club. He rushes to the side door, but it clicks closed just before he makes it. Stepping back and looking around, he can see the building has been made very secure. He dials Dwight to report, sending a picture of the club. Kieron and Bedi pull up in a taxi and get out, paying the driver with a hundred-dollar bill and asking him to wait, but as soon as they have turned away, he speeds off.

In the dark basement, few lights feature on a small dance area with poles and mirrors. The other two girls are looking concerned as reality sets in. Micky is thrown on the floor in front of them and he groans. Prisha is dragged up onto a chair and slapped, any confidence she had drains. The other two women are also slapped and the fuller-bodied one is pulled up and spun across the room to one of the men who rips her top off.
"Nice."

He puts his face in her chest and she screams. Fear fills Prisha and her two companions. Micky is pulled up onto the spare chair and punched hard. Water is thrown over his face to wake him.

"Double-dealing Micky. Thought you could play two games. Selling girls yourself? We can't have our supply dropping, we have orders to fill."

The man punches him. His blood splatters over Prisha's face. All the girls scream. The torturer leans over to the women.

"You behave, we look after you. You cheat, we beat you."

He turns back to Micky. "How much money are you making for yourself, Micky?"

"I only do what I told."

Crash. He is slapped to the floor. The man forages through his pockets. He finds the envelope that Prisha put there and she is dreading what is about to happen to him. She has caused it. The man opens it slowly, pulls out the money.

"Someone is paying you very well, Micky."

Micky is heaved up, so he is face to face with evil.

"I've never seen it before," Micky cries.

"It says, for the two girls!"

Thud, he is punched left, then right, and falls to the floor. Prisha feels every blow as the guilt hits her. She wants to defend him, but then she will be abused.

No one stops to look at the sex club during the day except the three CSCI agents and they find every door closed and locked tight. There are no windows and neither Kieron nor Hunter can see an easy way in but time is of the essence. Both men walk to the other side of the street to look at the front of the building. The souvenir shop next door is open, and it has an apartment above it with a roof garden. The only way is the hard way. They cross back over the street and enter the shop.

"Interpol Police," Hunter says to the young staff working in the shop. He flashes a page of his passport faster than he stampedes to the door at the back of the shop. Kieron stops to confuse them.

"Who is in the apartment?" he asks, then turns and heads for the rooms at the back of the shop.

"No one," the shop keeper says.

"Show me," Kieron demands.

They climb the stairs double time, power through the top room and out to the roof garden in seconds. Kieron offers his hands locked as a step. Hunter puts his foot in Kieron's hands, and he jumps as Kieron lifts. The American clambers onto the raked tiled roof and though there is nothing to hold on to, he swings himself around, digging his palms and toes into the rough surface. He swings a hand down to pull Kieron up. But Kieron can gain no purchase with his toes so quickly stretches to get his other hand into the old gutter. It breaks away.

"You will pay for the roof!" the shop owner screams at them.

"Go," Kieron orders and Hunter turns and runs up struggling to climb the gradient of the roof. With less than a dozen steps, he is across to the roof of the club. Settled safely, he takes a breath as he looks down to Bedi in the street for directions. She points further across and confirms when he is above the club. He starts to shed tiles.

"You pay," the shop owner shouts at Kieron. "I call police."

"We are the police. Now lift me."

Kieron bends the man over. He does not know why he accepts the order, but Kieron leaps up using his back as a springboard. He drops a few hundred dollars for the owner, then runs up to join Hunter.

The removed tiles are stacked, Hunter pulls the knife from his utility belt and cuts the roofing felt underneath.

"That uniforms come in handy," Kieron smirks.

They both look in. It is dark. No one sits in the dark, so Hunter takes the risk and drops down.

Taking the small LED torch from his belt, he scans. Nothing. Then light reflects from a dozen or more eyes and there are whimpers of fear. Women who live in a squalid section of the roof they have made home are frightened. Blankets lay on the floor, a small altar they have made to pray. The women look at Hunter in fear, wondering if they are 'friend or foe'.

"Clear," Hunter shouts up.

Kieron swings down and arcs his light around.

"Handy; that utility belt?"

He stops short when he too sees the frightened women.

"Police," is his instant response to ease their panic.

"Where are evil men?" Hunter asks.

A girl points to a door. Seeing it, they both move sideways and kick together. The door shatters and they crab down the stairs, sure those below have heard their entrance.

"Is there a gun in this belt?" Hunter asks.

"No. The torch is heavy enough to be a baton."

"It's smaller than my hand."

The next level is a corridor of cubicles with beds and a one-way mirror. At the end, they crab down the next set of stairs to the ground floor club level and find the side door to the street. Bedriška is outside waiting.

"Go down. Ask for a job. See if you can make the girls run back up," Hunter suggests to her.

Without question, she boldly takes the stairs down and uses her Russian to perfect effect. He English is always shit.

"I need job. You have job?"

"Where did you come from?"

"Ukraine. I sent down for job."

She walks straight to them, her hand trailing behind her waving the frightened women out. They need no further encouragement and run.

"I swam."

She instigates a fight.

Outside, Kieron hails a taxi. He ushers Prisha and the two other women in. Kieron holds one door open, torn between sending them or waiting as he can hear the rage of the men downstairs. The rage stops, then there is a single voice. He knows Bedi has finished the job. She runs up the stairs and out, diving into the taxi.

"Back to the hotel, get into Hunter's room," Keiron says slamming the door.

Bedi passes the driver a one-hundred-dollar bill and the car leaves.

The men, recovered from their scrap, burst out onto the street where Hunter fakes an argument with Kieron outside their door blocking it. The security men from the club try to push them aside but they have picked on the wrong two. They are mercilessly thrown down the stairs. Kieron is down after them.

The frightened imprisoned women from the loft reveal themselves from the upper stairs, taking the opportunity to escape. Hunter pulls a cab over, then a second to fill with the women. Two shots are heard from below.

"Go, go!" Hunter urges as he empties his pockets of handfuls of one hundred dollar bills and gives them to the women.

"That's all I have."

"Don't worry. I'm loaded," Kieron says coming up behind him.

Kieron and Hunter take the last taxi.

"Are they going to follow us," Hunter asks.

"They won't be doing anything."

The two men sit back silently catching their breath. They are running through what happened and what needs to happen next. There are likely to be more clubs than those in Puerto Banus and Barcelona, and the henchmen they have met so far will be from the lower ranks. A new gear will engage when they report up.

46 DEBRIEF

Prisha and the two women rest on the edge of the hotel bed. The small room is crowded but clean and safe. Bedi, Kieron and Hunter look at each other, computing the situation as if it was a military campaign.

"Will Micky try and go back to the ship?" Hunter asks.

"He might be dead," Prisha says, trying hard to recover.

"Good," a woman says with cutting vengeance.

"You two ladies can't go back. But Prisha, if Micky's not going back no one knows you. You are expected so you should join the ship," Hunter suggests. "We should solve this."

"I need to leave now. I might have missed it," she says looking at her watch. She stands and tosses Hunter her mobile phone.

"Evidence."

"We should go too," Kieron says standing.

Hunter agrees. Bedi and Kieron rush out after Prisha.

In the street, they wave down the first taxi. All three jump in together.

"Cruise dock. Terminal A," Bedi asks.

The driver checks his watch. He knows what time the ships leave, and he knows they are late.

"A hundred dollars if you get us on that ship," Kieron says. In the last few hours, they have been giving money away.

"You think Hunter is safe by himself?" Prisha asks.

"He always has Dwight, and you did well reporting back to him immediately."

"We need Interpol to close down all their clubs."

"We can act so much quicker than them. Let's get back on the ship, get a drink, then start what is going to be a long debrief," Kieron says.

"We save some women back there," Bedi says.

"I hope so," he says.

"We did," Prisha agrees.

"Nice work," he says, to them women.

"Interpol must save more," Bedi says.

In Miami, Croc can see Hunter sitting on a bed next to two frightened women. There's a large insert box saying 'recording' and another saying 'downloading'. Dwight's screen is clear of boxes.

In Barcelona, Hunter has connected Prisha's phone to the hotel internet and stuck it to the TV with chewed gum. Dwight is visible on the screen and they are tiny in a box on the screen. One of the women is telling her story when a knock on the door makes her jump.

"Room service."

Hunter swings the chair from the desk to the door and leans it so the back is under the handle. He has no weapon, so it is dangerous to open the door even a few inches. He has ordered sandwiches and sodas, but he has no idea how far the evil web spreads and how many hotels are fed by call-girls from this club.

Outside is a waiter. Hunter can see the tray of sandwiches, sodas, and his two beers.

"Leave it on the floor," he says taking the chit through the small opening and signing. He watches the waiter walk away then opens the door enough to get the tray in. He leaves the chair against the door. He cracks a beer and the two women drink but the sandwiches don't get touched.

"We were told of better money, better conditions and shorter hours if we took work in the city. They said we could live in Spain."

"Who told you this?" Dwight asks.

"Micky."

"There must have been someone else, who else?"

The girls think, then one speaks.

"I think there was an officer, higher rank than him. Micky feared him."

"What was his name?"

"I heard him say Lars once?" the other woman says softly. Her questioning tone reveals she is not confident about her answer.

"And where did you work?"

"I was waitress until I get in trouble."

The door crashes open. Before he can react, Hunter is shot. The chest hit spins him around, his head hits the wall and he drops to the bed. The two girls are pulled from the room screaming. Hunter tries to move; then he can hear nothing.

On the lido deck of the ship the sail away party is in full swing with the entertainment staff working hard, delivering their set-routine, and encouraging the guests to join in. Classic hits that everyone knows set to a German, beer-drinking Schlager beat. The crowd sing 'Sweet Caroline' but not sung in the way it was in the original hit. This is a full-on disco track. The sail away is always so much better when the weather is good, and today, leaving Barcelona, the sun is shining.

Bedi and Kieron are on the Sun Deck, above the main dancing around the pool. This is the first chance they have had to notice the sun all day. She has a large vodka and he has a beer. Convinced the last stage went as well as it could, they are in a muted celebratory mood. Looking down at the party, Bedi starts to sway her hips and they hit his. He bumps her hips back as they begin to relax.

"We make a good team, don't we?" Kieron says.

They laugh together for the first time in ages, possibly the first time ever. It is cut short as they hear his phone ring. Kieron answers and tries to listen over the music.

"Dwight in Miami. Man-down, Hunter's down."

With the phone to his ear, Kieron's instinct takes over. He backs out of the crowd and goes to the outer rail of the deck. He looks down to the sea and back to land. The ship is powering away and the land is becoming distant even if the high drop is manageable.

"Dwight, I could jump but," he hesitates.

Bedriška looks at him assuming the problem. She looks at the jump into the sea and the distance back.

"It's too far," she says.

"She's right, the swim would take hours. You need to have the ship release a lifeboat and take me back."

"What?" she demands.

"Hunter's down," he tells her listening to more information. "They took the two women."

Bedi necks her vodka, places her glass down and holds the rail.

"We can do it," she says ready to swim.

"No, wait. Hunter's on his way to hospital. The police are there and are raiding the club. Interpol are taking our brief seriously and working with Dwight. He will update us in five minutes with a status report on Hunter, but we need to stay here. Prisha could be in trouble; the key man is an officer. He might be named Lars. It's not about our money anymore."

47 LARS TANGO IN CORSICA

Having trotted down all the internal carpeted floors, Bedi and Kieron walk into the atrium to descend further to deck five. It is quiet as the shops cannot re-open until they reach tax-free waters. On every ship, there is a framed family-tree type chart of senior staff with names, job title and a picture. The Captain with key heads of department going down two ranks shows no Lars. The Head of House Keeping with his own chart shows no Lars. Bedi photographs both and sends them to Dwight as Kieron walks to the reception.

"Could you please connect me to Officer Lars."

"Do you have his full name, Sir?"

"No, just Lars."

"I don't know a Lars sir."

"Can you run a search, it's important."

The receptionist does run a search. Kieron is not sure she would share any information with him, but she might know how to deal with the request better when she discovers who the officer is.

"There is no officer with the name Lars on this ship, Sir."

Walking away, Kieron raises his phone,

"Dwight?" he asks as his call is answered.

"No, it's Croc. Dwight's on a call to either the cruise operator or Interpol, or both. You got the head of IT."

"Croc, Bedi just sent you the 'heads of department', but no Lars known on this ship. I need a full officer list."

"I got one, we've got everything," Croc says.

"Look for an officer called Lars, or anything like Lars."

"No officers called Lars. Nothing like it, Kieron," Croc says. "Grab a beer and let me do the digging. Nothing you can do there."

Bedi and Kieron stand in the centre of the atrium, the wooden dance floor unused, the cafe to the side noticeably quiet. They look up the huge ornate atrium, it looks totally different reaching up three decks. They are both searching for ideas.

"We call Prisha, she must help with Lars," Bedi suggests.

"She gave her phone to Hunter after she was abducted."

"I need more vodka," Bedi says. "Then, I go down to laundry and give her my cell."

"The vodka's not a clever idea. Giving her a phone certainly is."

"I go now."

Kieron has no time to disagree. She is through a 'crew door' before he can give it much thought.

Bedi marches down i95 and storms into the laundry which is working at full steam. Unlike a day ago when they took the tour and there were few staff, now there are many workers. Some look at her, but no one stops her. She sees no Micky but someone new must be in charge. She cannot make an obvious line to her undercover agent. She takes a parallel line to get her close. Prisha has noticed her.

"Please, what are you doing down here?" Oona, the imposing woman they met on the tour.

"Where my dress? Where my dress? I sent it days ago. Where my dress?" Bedriška shouts, still moving towards Prisha's area while looking at Oona. She keeps blasting the same demand asking one worker then the next. They all look puzzled. Oona approaches her.

"You are not allowed down here," the supervisor tries again.

"You not allowed to steal my dress!" Bedi fires at the supervisor, turning towards her on a circle that will take her past Prisha. She holds on the surfaces as if for stability as she travels, and when she gets near Prisha she leaves her cell phone. No explanation is necessary. Prisha cunningly claims it.

Bedriška whip-turns to face Oona.

"Micky was doing my dress personally. Where is he?"

"Micky is not here."

"Not here? Get him! Now!"

"He is on leave. What does your dress look like? I will personally find it," Oona says.

"Good. It is red. My dress red. To fit me, look at me. Look at my size," Bedi says marching towards the door, "My red dress! Leave at reception," she shouts. "Micky has my dress."

Bedi finds Kieron waiting by the crew door she took.

"Micky on leave, Prisha has my phone. Now I get vodka."

Bedi strides up the atrium stairs and all Kieron can do is follow. He is sure she won't be going back up to a rowdy pool bar so it must be one of the other seven bars inside the ship. She leads him into the Chart Room on deck seven. It is a standard name for a bar on a ship for classic lounges. This one is no exception, lots of wood and brass. It has a circular bar in the centre of a long thin lounge down one side of the ship which all guests pass as they walk along the promenade deck. Here guests are expected not to be rowdy but respect the silence of others. Bedi sits first and a waiter is with her in an instant.

"Large vodka and draught lager beer."

"Anything with the vodka?" the waiter asks.

"OK, another large vodka."

The waiter is confused.

"Two large vodkas and a beer, please," Kieron explains.

The waiter takes her cruise card and leaves. She notices Kieron's cautionary look.

"I do report tomorrow, in Corsica," she says. "Tomorrow I have time; nothing happen in Corsica."

Kieron answers the phone. His ring is on silent.

"Listening," he says softly.

"Hunter is doing fine, my guess is he'll discharge himself tomorrow and be on a plane to meet you in Naples, I'll call you again," Dwight says.

Kieron pockets the phone.

"Hunter's OK. He'll meet us in Naples," he shares with Bedi.

The drinks arrive and she necks the first, then the second. The waiter looks shocked.

"What? I am Russian."

The waiter looks at Kieron who sips his beer.

"English."

Bedi signs the chit and the waiter leaves.

"But for the wound, he could have come to Corsica," Kieron suggests.

"Nothing happens in Corsica."

"Keira Knightly had her honeymoon there."

"Did you go?" Bedi asks.

"No."

"She your friend?"

"No. We just have the same name. Kinda."

He drinks his beer looking out of the lounge window at the bouncing white water running away from the moving ship. The sun is dropping fast.

"What we do with money in Barcelona locker?" Bedi asks.

"Good question, the cash is a problem. But better on land than on a ship. We will move it to somewhere safer."

His phone goes again. Bedi moves across to sit next to him.

"Make room for my ass."

Kieron smiles. She squeezes in close to hear his call.

"You could be riding into a shit storm," Dwight says.

"How?" Bedi dares ask. "Corsica! It sleep!"

"It's your only stop in France and believe it or not, Interpol has an office there."

"On the beach?" she jokes.

"Seriously, the first female president of Interpol, and current boss, just happened to be director of the judicial police in Corsica back in the 1990s. She was a great policewoman."

"I like this woman."

"She wants in, they want to be involved."

"Is she sexy?"

"Just saying Corsica might not be easy unless you keep your heads down. They don't like other players and want you to back off."

"Do they know who we have on board?" Kieron asks.

"They're demanding to know, I'm blinding them with reports; which reminds me, yours are over-due," Dwight remind them.

"I was thinking of sitting on the beach tomorrow and writing it. It had sounded like a relaxing place," Kieron mocks.

"Well, Corsica has a fierce mafia history with connections in Russia and Africa," Dwight continues.

"With strong woman," Bedi stings.

"Yeah, Bedi, you're right. Many strong women, but not so nice. Here's another one. Marie-Jeanne Bozzretti was elected mayor in 2001."

"I love Corsica. Full of sexy female energy."

Bedi waves her cruise card high at a waiter.

"And forced to resign in 2002 amidst all kinds of allegations."

"Woman in power always victimised," Bedi says.

The waiter attends,

"Same."

"She was assassinated in 2011 while out shopping. Eight shots in the back. In her handbag, on the back of her shopping list were details of eight of the prostitutes she allegedly ran. Add in possible tax fraud claims and connections to night clubs. Just saying don't expect an easy ride there."

"So, we get a scooter to a small quiet beach," Kieron suggests, putting his arm around her. "Like a couple."

"It is our cover, don't get excited," Bedi says.

"I would like first draft reports tonight," Dwight says and hangs up.

48 COURSE YOU CAN

Hunter wakes from a very heavy sleep sucking rubber. He removes the oxygen mask and reminds himself of where he is. The hospital signs are in Spanish. Barcelona, he remembers. He looks at the drip into his body, he knows that is just fluid. It is never a good day to get shot because he has never drunk enough water. Yesterday was hot he remembers. Hot; just like a normal day in the desert. His mind wanders to the new generation carrying bespoke water bottles on the sides of backpacks in Las Ramblas, continually sipping. He wonders if they added a grain of Himalayan pink salt and a squeeze of lemon. No, they weren't in the desert, they weren't in Iraq or Syria? He wasn't in Las Ramblas yesterday, was he? He should be visiting hospital with his wife. They have a baby due. No, he looks down at the well-dressed chest wound. It is his right-hand side. He breathes hard to test it. His lungs feel fine it must have missed vitals.

"Why didn't they finish me off, how did they miss?" he murmurs. "Amateurs? If they were, I must be getting old and slow."

His head drops back into the pillow. He remembers the ships; working on cruise ship crime was supposed to be easy. Memories all flood back as he wakes fully. He mentally walks through the attack. He flinches as he remembers catching the bullet that spun him and he remembers being hit on the head. Using his shoulder, he pulls up the bed and raises his head again and feels the back of his head where there is an undressed bump.

"Snap, Philips. Snap," he says, looking for a nurse.

He checks the rest of his body; only one bullet wound.

"Not finishing me off, always a mistake. Why? They took the women. The women were more important than me. I need to speak to Dwight."

He stops talking to himself and running facts. They were not military or government level hit men, not even mafia hitmen. Lesson one in a conflict, not executing the double-tap will come back and bite you.

Hunter raises himself up and feels the finger-clip he has on. It detects oxygen levels and will ring the alarm as soon as it is removed. It is the medical version of *proof of life*. He drinks his whole glass of water whilst looking around. He sees his clothes hanging in a small open closet with a transparent plastic bag containing his phone. He tries to figure out the layout of the building so he can get out fast. Always know your escape route. In most cases, it is on the back of the door as the fire escape route. Even from a distance, he can read it. There is no point in escaping if you don't have an objective. First, report back.

"Nurse!" he shouts but his voice is hoarse.

He reaches to the bottom of the bed and pulls his medical record from the hanging pocket. He was admitted yesterday. Surgery to remove a bullet. In the 'next of kin box' is written the words Policia with an officer's contact name. They got that bit wrong; he thinks. He looks as far as he can see and there is no guard, he is not a suspect or under arrest. Dwight will have spoken to them so why is he not next of kin? Maybe because he is in Miami. He drops the records and lays back down.

He remembers the two girls being taken as he passed out, but he was on-line with Dwight; that must be how he got here. The policia will be after the abductors; the club should be closed down. Interpol should be involved too. They should have Micky if he is not dead.

Prisha, Bedi and Kieron will be safe on the ship. He looks at the clock; 1045hrs. Wow, how decadent. You should be out of bed soldier.

His partners will be in Corsica. That means he must be in Naples tomorrow morning. He looks at his clothes again. His uniform will have a bullet wound and bloodstains. He needs to revisit the shop and buy spares, but he has no money. His first objective has to be the funds. He needs funds to move about. He must move the money from the cruise terminal locker,

Dwight should have set up a bank or a safe deposit box. His eyes dart to the plastic bag, the locker key is there next to his phone, he can see it.

Hunter's brain, having covered the basics, starts to remember Lars; they must find him and flush the sex traffickers off the ship. He remembers the two young head office executives went missing. Dwight needs to report to Cruise HQ and get them newly instated. Then maybe they can go for more funds from the trunk on his old ship. He sees a nurse.

"Can I get dressed and go?"

They all have a smile meant to put the patient at ease. The same as cruise ship staff. She has a tray which she places at the end of the bed as she goes for his chart. He sees tablets in a paper cup and a syringe in a small pulp-tray, but he didn't see any serious medication in his notes.

"Just for the pain, then dressed and go," she replies collecting the tray and moving nearer, pulling a wheeled table in as she must have done a thousand times before.

"I don't really have any pain," he says thinking it makes no sense that he can go home afterwards.

She leans in for his arm.

Hunter snaps out and grabs her head, slamming it down into the bed. Taken by surprise she fights back, but silently. Hunter slips out of the bed; his finger clip comes off and an alarm starts. He knocks the tray away, kicks it further towards the door and rolls her over. A male nurse comes running to the door.

"Pare! Stop!" the male nurse shouts desperately.

But Hunter has the upper hand, he rips her white coat open, revealing a shoulder holster and weapon. He takes the gun and rolls her over pinning her down.

"Look at the syringe. What's the medication label say?" Hunter demands the male nurse do, as he holds the female nurse to the bed, gun at her head. Now he is in pain from his wound.

The male nurse collects the syringe and a small bottle. He starts to read, then accelerates, he draws the liquid and launches at Hunter. It is a two-man assassination team. Hunter pistol-whips him across the face. The syringe flies against the wall as he goes down. She spins out. She is no amateur; this has stepped up a notch. She twists her arms to release his grip, then kicks and punches to get free. Hunter shoots her in the thigh but that does not stop her. Standing on her bleeding leg, her other leg snaps up and out towards his head. He shoots her in the crotch. She buckles, but quickly follows up with a punch and second kick. He shoots her raised knee, then the standing knee and she goes down. He kicks out hard at the male nurse who is trying to stand and who reaches inside for his weapon. Hunter hits him hard across the head with the gun butt, then unclips his gun holster and rips it off his shoulder, but from the floor he grabs Hunter's leg. Hunter drops but manages to slide both guns away from them as he hits the floor. He collects the syringe, which he powers into the male nurse's neck. The nurse buckles. Hunter sees cable-ties in the nurse's inside pocket and he cable ties both of them to the bed. He keeps the spares. Hunter collects both guns and looks to double-tap them, but refrains.

"You are only alive because I might need the ammunition. The day has just started," he says hurriedly dressing and taking his things. One gun goes in the back of his pants. The shoulder holster is slung on and clipped quickly. The gun placed in it. He looks to add a white coat, but they are both too bloody. He searches for the two assailants cell phones. He takes both of their pictures and steps outside the glass partition of his single bed area. He checks every possible approach before moving.

Behind him, the assassins crash through the glass, charging him. Hunter pulls both guns and shoots them. The dividing wall falls and glass shatters into a million pieces.

"Good planning. Safety glass," he mumbles.

As he passes through the next set of doors, he sees the real hospital staff all cable tied to radiators, their mouths taped. He considers releasing them, but instead picks up a spare white coat and escapes fast.

"Any questions contact my next of kin, 'policia'," he says speeding up.

49 BEING WATCHED

The narrow beach below the busy road is quite crowded. Bedi is stretched out on her ship-issued beach towel, wearing sunglasses. She models a bikini very well and her exposed skin is fully creamed. Next to her, Kieron has his top off, but he is in shorts and socks. He is sitting, leant on his elbow reading his phone.

"We're on," he says, standing.

Bedi fails to move, even after he has his shirt back on. He sits back down to get her attention.

"A double assassin team tried to hit Hunter."

"Take your socks off."

"Bedi, did you hear?"

"Where?"

"Barcelona."

"Where are we?"

"Corsica."

"Sorry, cannot help."

"We need to..."

"What?" she barks. "We need to what? I have just got dis body very in cream."

"Very nice."

"So, why do I move? The ship does not leave until four-thirty."

"It's not a holiday."

"This is disguise."

"As what?"

"Tourist. Good looking tourist. I hope body not cause attention."

"Unlikely."

Bedi sits up, "Don't make me slap you. I see you look in cabin," Bedi lies back down. "It not Christmas. But, I go for walk."

"Why?"

"See cathedral behind us."

"You hate churches."

"But we watched by three men on wall behind us."

Prisha has a few me-time moments in her small crew cabin on the ship. The only reason it looks ample is that she brought little with her and she has it to herself at the moment. It is small, but it would berth two if the ship were not a few crew down. She dials the CSCI office.

"Dwight," she says, excited she has connected with the team.

"Prisha, you have Bedi's phone?"

"Yes. I'm on the ship. She is too but I have not seen her since she gave me this. I've been approached by one of the women in the laundry, Oona, who said that she is leaving soon to work in the city. It was definitely an early approach."

"Stay interested, don't agree to anything."

"I won't, don't worry. I saw where they go."

"We want to know who she reports to? She must have taken over from Micky so someone will be training her, watching her, but he'll be dangerous so don't push."

"I saw them in the club, beat Micky. If Interpol raided, he'll be glad he is in police custody."

"Look for any lead on an officer called Lars but assume he's extremely dangerous. And stay on the ship."

Hunter checks every which way he can as he walks over the bridge to the cruise wharf. Phone to ear, Croc answers,

"Hunter, you got shot, man!"

"Occupational hazard."

"Try living in Overtown,"

"Overtown?"

"Overtown, Miami. Your Longshore office might only be blocks from Dodge Island, but two blocks the other way, the real i95, you into the projects."

"Ghetto?" Hunter says, looking around to ensure he is not being followed as he turns into the terminal building.

"An area that's economically destitute, trust me it is, and it don't make sense with so much wealth by the sea. The lives in there matter."

"You live in Overtown?"

Hunter walks to the locker, his mind is racing, he half expects the money to be gone. He turns the key.

"Used to. I was adopted, Auntie died last week, it was her gig. Landlord turfed me out yesterday so I'm looking."

"Looking for what?"

"A home."

Hunter is caught by that remark as he unzips the bag and stares at the money. His rough assessment is at least one hundred thousand dollars.

"Last night I slept under the desk here. Hope that's OK?" Croc asks on the phone.

Hunter re-zips the bag and lifts it out.

"Sure, we should get a proper bed and facilities in the office for overnight stays and emergencies. Bed, food, microwave. I need you as a night watchman for a while."

"I got food next door," Croc smiles.

"Don't go messing Wild Mary's kitchen."

"I'm not crazy. Black kid in a diner after hours might get me popped by Five0. Hunter, you be careful not to get capped again. Them bullets ain't love letters."

"I need you to hack into two phones. The battery is almost done on one. What do you need?"

"You need a cell charger."

Kieron sits on his cruise ship beach towel on the Corsican beach. He is in long khaki shorts and has his shirt off. He notices how the crafted body he had for years is just beginning to slip over his waist band. But his sixth sense is still with him, he slips his sunglasses off and cleans them, while using them as a mirror.

Bedi is looking around the colourful classic Cathedral. Prisha is emptying linen from a huge machine in the laundry on ship. Hunter is in a Barcelona mobile phone shop with two new phones in boxes and he is choosing accessory cables. Croc is in a camping shop looking at fold-away beds.

Meanwhile, two men sit on the sea wall above the beach watching Kieron. A man stands outside the cathedral watching Bedi ponder inside. A man flanks Hunter in the station as he heads for a train. An officer stands with a female worker watching Prisha struggle with the bedsheets. Two youths in sneakers and hoodies watch Croc shopping.

Hunter steps on the local train to the airport and walks down from carriage to carriage. The whistle blows, doors start to slam, and an announcement is made. Hunter squeezes past a group of people, changes direction and gets off. The train starts to move, and his shadow is locked inside. Hunter walks quickly through the station checking he is no longer being followed and he takes the train to Madrid.

Bedi walks to the side chapel, exits the rear arched cathedral into the street and circles back to the front. Her stalker has gone inside, she has lost him. He heads for the confession box on the left where Bedi could be hiding. Bedi re-enters the Cathedral through the front door, is now behind him and accelerates keeping low, as she must have done so many times, both as a child escaping and a soldier on duty. She hits the man mercilessly and with perfect timing, taking him into the box. They struggle, fighting for grip. The man pulls a knife. Bedi smashes his hand into the wood, once, twice, and again but he won't drop it. The man resists a stranglehold, but she crashes his head against the side of the box shattering the partition. Bedi kicks his knee and the man drops trying to turn against the heavy knee in his back. Bedi grabs his chin and rips. The man falls lifeless, slumping over the small wooden bench ready to repent. Bedi searches his pockets for identification. He has no wallet, no card just a phone which Bedi pockets along with his knife.

"Forgive me, Father, if you look. But you never look when I need you."

She looks through the curtain and exits taking a direct line to leave the church, putting a hundred dollars in the collection box.

"That for children."

The confession box collapses. Bedi puts another two hundred dollars in the collection.

Outside, back in the harsh sunlight, she stands behind one of the small palms on the front terrace which is surrounded by parked scooters. She assesses her exposure to the other two hitmen, whichever way she crosses the road, and they are above Kieron. She calls him.

"You're being watched."

"I see them. But they're not shading me from sun," he says, looking at their reflection in his glasses.

"Leave it for me," she says. "I call Dwight to give him this cell number. Albanian language spoken in Barcelona club. That why I no get it. 'Shqip' not like any language. Be ready to move."

She ends the call with Kieron watching a small delivery truck pull up outside the piazza at the front of the restaurant next to the cathedral. Leaving the engine running, the driver opens the back and lifts out two large wooden trays of fresh bread rolls. He carries them up the steps and past tables shaded by large square umbrellas. He vanishes inside. Bedi moves quickly to take the truck, leaps in and guns the accelerator. It reverses with power straight across the road causing traffic to skid and break. She is fearless, ramming into the wall trapping one hitman's legs between the wall and the truck. Boxes bounce forward and the doors swing open. The other hitman falls off the wall onto the sand some five meters below. Kieron is straight on him and efficient puts him out.

Bedi leaves the truck and avoids the chaos around it. She goes back across the road towards the cathedral and takes a parked moped, stabs the key slot with her would be assailant's knife and twists. She speeds in direction of the ship; she skids at the opening for the beach waiting for Kieron. He rushes up the stone steps from the beach holding his rolled cruise ship beach towel as he pulls his shirt on. He straddles the scooter behind her, and they race away.

"Guy on sand?" She shouts back.

"Dead," he says.

The main area near the port is only around the point. The scooter turns left into the market square and parks. They stop at a vendor and buy tourist tee-shirts and hat. Bedi also buys a beach dress she knows will fit her. Then, arm in arm they walk past the waiting electric tourist train, cross the road at the zebra crossing and head back to the ship looking totally different.

"Safe?" Bedi asks him.
"It appears I might be," he says.
"First one try to kill me with a knife."
"In church?" Kieron asks in fun.
Bedi nods.
"Disgusting," he says.

Croc walks out of the camping shop excited but weighed down by the folded bed in a parcel and two other bags. He balances his phone into the nape of his neck as he multitasks.

"When it's downloaded, press hash 1 to open the phone on your desktop"

"Got it," Dwight tells him.

"That's an easy one then. Get his ID, open a shopping app or a taxi account; everything will be access free, cracked."

The two youths confront him, hoods up.

"Waz cracked? Zat where you get rich?"

"I'm shopping for someone."

"With their plastic?"

"My own plastic"

"You got money to share."

Croc hands over the few bills he has left.

"Dig deeper bro'," one of the hoodies demands.

"I'm clean," Croc insists.

They grab him, grab his phone.

"Call's over," they shout reaching for his phone. Croc resists, he is stabbed. Left bleeding out on the sidewalk.

50 PIZZA

The cruise guests are dressed for dinner, lights appear dimmer inside and outside it is dark. Night has fallen and the ship peacefully powers through calm seas. Bedi is in a simple but stunning long dress and Kieron in pants and a jacket. It is a casual night and that means a collared shirt and or jacket for dinner. They enter the dining room to be told there is a long wait for a table for two so reluctantly they agree to share. It is not that they are unsociable, it is the questions that might be asked and will have to be answered or avoided. To date, their cover story has never been tested. They are led to their table of six and they are the last to sit. After introductions and niceties, they are handed a menu each.

"You know what I fancy tonight?" Kieron says.

"What?"

"Pizza."

"Don't be silly, Naples tomorrow. You eat all pizza you want," she says leaning into him.

"We should sit on a table for six every night," he swoons.

"Why? You like it?"

He turns and looks at her smiling face, he leans and pecks her lips.

"I told you,"

"It's our cover," he says.

"No. It is order," Bedi says.

"OK. I'll try harder."

"Look at menu and behave."

Hunter strides from a taxi into the Pizza Village, a beachfront festival dedicated to pizza. The festive area stretches one kilometre, lighting up the coastline, with excitement and is full of local and foreign tourists. Whilst many are there to sell pizzas and make money, the competition is serious, and the long white judging tent intrigues him. Blue plastic barriers ensure the public is kept from the judges who sit on long benches. They are tasting pizzas and making notes. It looks like it will never end. He wonders how anyone can stay sane enough to judge one pizza against another with that volume.

Outside, the cooks are showmen. He watches dough being thrown and spun; it is hypnotic. His night is spoilt by the call from Dwight, a call he can hardly hear.

"Croc's in hospital, it's serious."

Croc was right. He, Kieron and Bedriška may all have spent time with their lives deliberately at risk, but the biggest risk to Croc is his home. Home is where you are supposed to feel safe but where knife crimes have become acceptable and the guilty are rarely punished. Hunter looks at his watch. There is nothing he can do, but his brief evening off is over. He knows that is not the last call he will get tonight.

He heads into a small back street cafe, where he studies Dwight's file on each of the nurses in the two-member assassin team that failed to kill him.

In the Miami operation room, Dwight has the same files across his screens, with their criminal records, family members and crimes they never got prosecuted for.

"The team that hit you are Spanish mafia. Raimon Russi and Dolores Lopez. Either the Spanish have an interest in our crime ring on the ship, and I see no connection to the clubs, or they took a paid contract to kill you from the ring who don't have their own capable people in Spain."

"I guess they never checked my file first," Hunter says on speaker.

"Not that they'd find much. Jenny-E's a damn good journalist and she found nothing."

"We know so little about anything," Dwight says. "This is all about phones. Croc has been teaching me how to crack mobiles. Kieron's hitman was Jean-Marc Bozzretti, from Southern Corsica, also local. I don't need to tell you, keep your head down. It's not worth overstepping. Stay focused on the ship's problem."

"Let them know it's full of danger," Hunter says.

"Then let's hand it all over to Interpol. Stay safe, just link chocolate bars to the women leaving the ships and come home," Dwight says.

"Hand what over? We've not proved the ships are involved in a crime. Is anyone with Croc?"

"He gets visitors; why?"

"He's family."

"You've got family back home? You're a civvie now; start acting like one. Let's hand this over."

"Is someone with Croc?"

"Mary's there."

"Police got the kids on CCTV outside the shop; they're two kids from his block. They'd noticed he'd got money."

"He's never going back to Overtown, Dwight. He can stay at the unit until I talk with Elaine."

"You're becoming way too human to survive out there."

"You think it's safer back home?"

"You want me to tell Kieron about Croc?" Dwight asks.

"No, I'll tell him when I see him. We all need to focus on Lars. Who is Lars? Who is running this? Send a report to Frank Pincer at Cruise HQ. Try and show the ship is being used for Human Trafficking."

"He knows, but he doesn't want to know."

"Then maybe we can get that trunk full of money off our other ship. Get it laundered to bit-coin and buy an apartment or two in Miami. Dwight, you go home now."

"No, we just got a proper bed here and I ordered pizza."

"With green tomatoes?"

"No."

51 BEHIND CLOSED DOORS

The glow of the television is just enough light the room. Everything is subdued. There is something about saving each other's lives, something about bonding which breaks barriers down. They lay in each other's strong arms, thinking. It is hard for either to switch off from the job, hard to ignore someone might be out to kill you, but together they feel safer. Their voices are softer, this is a different conversation from any they have had before. They are now baring their souls to each other.

"Will you go back to managing the beauty salons again?" he asks her.

"I think. One day."

"At least you don't get shot at."

"No one shoot me on this job."

"When were you shot? I've seen the scars."

Bedi nuzzles into him and pecks his arm.

They stay close, breathing close to her but he knows she has said no many times. Even though he finds her mix of characteristics incredibly attractive.

"What makes you so angry with the sex trade?" he digs.

Bedriška stiffens and there is distance between them again.

"I hate demand for sex that make slave."

"You mustn't be a prisoner of the past," he says.

"We are prisoners of our past. Our ship head for Pompeii, 'ave you been there?"

"No."

"History full of slaves. You know how many brothels in Pompeii?"

Kieron makes the slightest of moves with his head, with his eyes. He is there to listen to her. He cares about her and she can see it.

"More than thirty-five. Sex slave brothel called Lupanar; it mean wolf-den. Lupa is she-wolf. I was child she-wolf."

"You escaped."

"Yes. Each time ship stop in Naples I go stand in shit city of sin that tourist admire and I cry. I look at erotic carvings found in Lupanar. I hurt for children, for women, and for men who were slaves. In Naples, I walk back to ship, through modern city and watch it still happen every day."

"Still happening?"

"Naples is new Pompeii, out of control with sex. Governors suggest zone for legal prostitution. They don't need ships," she says.

Kieron softly kisses her head, a sign of friendship. There is no other implication.

"Not even Georgie ask me these questions."

"Georgie has never seen the dark side of the world we've seen."

"I hope she never see," Bedi says.

In the all-white private room in a wing of Miami hospital, Croc opens one eye, then another. Wild Mary stands and leans over him. She looks like an angel.

"What you doing trying to be one of them agents?" Mary shouts, breaking him out of the image.

He says nothing, he isn't strong enough to, but he knows he is not dead. He looks around. He has never been in a room like this. He closes his eyes from the radiance.

"Don't you close them eyes on me!"

He musters the energy to speak.

"I was shopping."

"Leave the shopping to me, you hear? I ordered you a proper bed and sofas for that unit. Damn camp bed, damn camp shop."

"And, a widescreen TV?"

"What? You got TV's all over the place."

"They're screens." Croc tries to sit up. "I've got work to do. They need me. Can I go now?"

"No!"

"But."

"None of them buts, what work you got to do?"

"Stuff Dwight can't do."

"Ain't nothing that big ass can't do."

"There's loads he can't do."

"And you can?"

"Damn right."

"That's my boy. You special and you tell them. Me get you one of them fancy laptops, and I'll make 'em pay. You work from here."

52 NAPLES

As soon as the ship is given customs clearance and guests can leave, Bedi and Kieron, both in their large pocket CSCI uniforms, take the gangway. Bedi has added a small backpack to her attire with a water bottle in the side. Hunter is waiting for them at the bottom, having already gained access into the secure customs perimeter for the two cruise ships. They walk the short distance to the neighbouring older ship, now only three in the team.

Standing at the top of the gangway, Jacob waits for them. He stops the downflow of guests to let them up. He greets them, shaking hands, and passes them the lanyards they need to be bleeped in by the computer. He has one left.

"Just three of us today," Hunter says.

Jacob gives him a look, knowing there is a story there. But he suspects there are a few stories. He leads them into the larger ship's much bigger atrium.

"We reported our drugs incident to Interpol, and it seems they're busy with your prostitution racket. I don't think I have that problem here given the way they described it."

"Nice of them to give away our operation."

"We've not had staff leaving at any port," Jacob says. "We are running with a small staff shortage."

"It's new. Those ships just got involved, we're on it super-fast. Interpol gets their information from us," Hunter says. "It's that hot."

"What's your brief?"

"Move it off our ships."

"They will go somewhere else," Jacob says.

"Exactly, which is why we're on your ship early. A favour to an old client," Hunter says as looks around the ship he was on for eight years. Jacob is sticking to him like glue.

"I'm hungry, I think I'll enjoy breakfast for once," Hunter says, "feels like being back home."

"I'll join you. I like to be seen in the buffet occasionally and I have carved out time today to walk around with you."

They walk in towards mid-station but Bedriška lags behind. This is one of the ships where she managed the spa for a few years. She also lived here with Georgie who was the Entertainment Manager. She also knows that the other two will be with him some time.

"My Witowski!" she calls forward. "Can I join you in half an hour. I don't want food."

Hunter looks to Jacob for approval, Jacob agrees. They go on without her, but Hunter stalls. If she is doing what he thinks she is doing, she will need the key. He walks to her.

"Bedi, we're not going to rush, you've got longer if you need it."

He touches her hip, discretely pushing the key into her belt. He joins the others who are holding the elevator. It starts empty but stops at floors collecting guests on the way up to the buffet.

Bedi exchanges the briefest of niceties with a crew member she recognises and then excuses herself and goes into the crew-only area and down two floors. She knows her way around this ship.

The boxes on the top of the trunk look like they have been moved. She photographs them before lifting them all off, then with her phone she photographs the seals and labels. She must get her hand down the gap to unlock the padlock. Last time Prisha did it. She can see it is not going to be easy. She tries it without the key first. The padlock is intact and locked, she needs to work the key down there. With a flat hand she holds the key between two fingers and slowly manoeuvres to the padlock of the trunk. Trying to feed it in, she drops the key.

The buffet is still busy despite the high number of guests off on trips. Many of the trips will have been to Herculaneum, the ruins of a town of about 5000 people. It stood in a narrow strip between Mount Vesuvius and the coast and was wiped out by the same eruption that hit and smothered Pompeii. Though less famous than Pompeii, it has in many respects more detail with near intact wooden furniture and almost legible papyrus scrolls. It is also a lot nearer the ship. Some guests may have ventured out on the train that stops at Pompeii and goes further to Sorrento. Some may have avoided the volcanic area because, while safe, the memories of the guests who died in New Zealand's White Island disaster. They may prefer a boat trip to Capri at the tip of the mainland visible from Sorrento. Some of the guests still onboard ship will be visiting the Pizza Festival, which is near the berth, but that does not get into full swing until later.

Hunter sits down with Jacob. Kieron is still finding fruit and nuts for a healthy breakfast.

"We didn't get to look at anything last time, so we'd like to start again. Bottom to top. We might see something that helps us," Hunter suggests.

"Like what?"

"Truth be told, we don't know. But things to watch for are unhappy staff. Or those with a drug or gambling problem."

"I guess it's great to have a heads up before it starts," Jacob says as Kieron sits down.

"They need to infiltrate and convince a member of staff to be a double agent. It could be someone who needs money."

"Debt and dependence, not easy to spot," Jacob admits. "No one saw your problem."

"No. But that'll get them in, and they're not nice people to owe money to. Expect the worst gangsters who will sacrifice any human life to control this person and build a trade. A character change is something to look for."

Bedi is laying on the floor, her belt off, trying to feed it under the trunk. It does not have enough substance to push through the gap. She hangs it down the front again, buckle down, and tries to swing it back and forth. She hears a forklift truck coming. Bleeping sound, then the flicking yellow. It gets close and stops.

"What you lost?" the driver shouts.

"Keys. Somehow, they go under here. Go figure."

He jumps off and looks under.

"It'll be quicker to lift it. Can you stand over there?"

The driver swivels the wheel and the truck spins round at the tower of boxes in front of it.

"We never touch these. It's theatre stuff."

"The back case is mine."

"What's in it?"

"Crime investigation equipment. Fingerprinting, blood sample tester. All kinds of stuff."

"Was that from last year?"

"Yeah. We were hoping the ship would get to pass Miami."

"Not this ship."

The forklift pulls the first tower back. Lifts the top trunk back. Then puts hers on top.

"How's that?"

Bedi nods, "Thanks."

The driver is flirty; sailors at sea don't get to see a wide variety of women. He pulls out his pen.

"You want to write down my number in case you need anything else?"

He takes her hand and writes on it. Bedi thinks twice, then realises that he might be useful. She waves him away. She has a job to do.

53 THE HIT LIST

Later, within the secure area of the port, Hunter, Kieron and Bedi sit in the corner of a basic European café where crew go to use free wi-fi. The signal is good until there are more than about fifty sitting around, then connection is so slow it is worth walking into town. It is very Italian; coffee and alcohol are available for breakfast. Both are drunk by the few local dockworkers at the bar.

Bedriška drops her overweight bag on the table. She passes bundles from her pockets to them under the table. They fill their pockets as Bedi watches the few workers over by the ship. The supervisors ensure a lengthy list of goods makes it on to the visiting ship in a brief time window. Tomatoes, milk, chicken, paper all vying to be next while waste is removed, and fuel-oil loaded.

"I empty bag into my pockets before walk on ship."

"They're looking for bottles of alcohol. That's not a large enough bundle to catch their attention," Hunter says.

Kieron gives him a questioning look, "Booze?"

"Not allowed their own booze. It gets confiscated on entry; returned at the end of the cruise."

"Then they have to drink it before they fly?" Kieron smiles.

"Goes in their hold luggage," Hunter explains, then he looks at the ship being loaded with supplies. "I was hoping to get the trunk off. But as this job's got more dangerous, it's in the safest place," Hunter reveals. "Tomorrow, Sarande, both ships tender guests to shore, so there is no chance of getting close to the money."

Bedi shows the name 'TJ' and his phone number written on her arm.

"What's that?" Kieron asks.

"Number of forklift driver on our old ship. He will move anything for me."

Hunter types the number into his phone.

"I said for me."

"I want it checked," Hunter replies, calling Dwight.

"He won't be awake yet, let alone at work," Kieron says.

"He's sleeping at the office while the mission's hot."

The phone is answered.

"You thought I was sleeping, didn't you?" Dwight says.

"I didn't, Kieron did," Hunter smiles.

"Well, Kieron was right. Do you know what time it is?"

"Time our ground support was awake. Now talk to me, then go fry yourself breakfast."

"Yes, sir."

"Three of us here. Prisha is on the ship."

"Don't let her get off. Not for anything. I've warned her," Dwight insists.

"Dwight. I was hit in Barcelona; they were hit in Corsica. What're your thoughts?" Hunter asks.

"Don't feel special. They have no idea who you are, you just got in the way of their operation. Both, hits were local mafia guys with long criminal rap sheets. Amateurs. Their people will now hound the traffickers for having lost people. Payback, local wars, who knows. Interpol wants them all now so, they should have forgotten about you. Let's hope they shut down, leave the ships and vanish."

There is a pause. Kieron decides to break the silence,

"Or?"

"They'll be very angry with us," Dwight explains.

"Make us look like Interpol agents," Bedi says.

"They'll kill Interpol agents and police," Dwight suggests.

"Good job you not here, I would break my wrist patting you on back," Bedi replies.

"Good job you're not here,' Dwight snaps back. "Any idiot can work out who looks after cruise ship crime and where to find me, alone, here in Miami."

There is a long silence as they recognise the danger their office is in.

"You want Croc's who dun it list?"

"Sure. You look after Croc, he's just a kid," Hunter says.

"Smart kid. OK; the two executives at Dodge Island, Miami. The assistant won't even take my calls now."

"As head of people trafficking? No. I didn't have them in my crosshairs; too weak," Hunter says.

"Elektrik City club owners. They could've booked Spanish hit squad if their own operation is small and short-staffed. Then Micky from the ship, if he lived."

"No, it's bigger than that," Kieron adds.

"Next, Gwen and Albert. Then Paul Lopkey, and then last..."

"Lars," Hunter drops in.

"A code name. Ain't a real officer on any of the ships, so I reckon it's a codename."

"Lars means god or king, one who is crowned. One of the three kings," Kieron says.

"Did you go to one of them fancy schools?" Dwight asks.

"I'm afraid I did."

"How is Croc?" Hunter asks.

"Wondered when you would ask. I visited him last night. He's fine, loves the private room. Wants to move in and live there but is more likely to break out sometime today. He's good at this you know."

"Now, I go to beach?" Bedi asks.

"I don't think you should leave the ship, it's too dangerous," Dwight says.

"Are you thinking I should join the ship and stay out of Naples?" Hunter asks.

"Yes, but I think join the next ship, the MS Magi Gold that berths tomorrow. I reserved you a room out of town for tonight," Dwight says.

"Is it nice?"

"Do you have your toothbrush?"

"I don't have a toothbrush but Bedi gave me a spending allowance."

"Can she post Mary some money to pay for the furnishings? She is doing our unit."

"Mary's furnishing?" Hunter asks.

"More like building a home for Croc."

"I'll send more money."

"There's a taxi outside, it's paid for. It's in the name of Jean-Marc Bozzretti," Dwight relays.

"Who's he?"

"The guy who tried to kill you in Corsica, I used his taxi account."

"Is that good idea?" Bedi questions and there is a moments silence.

"He's dead. If it is going to flush something out, you're prepared."

"Is the hotel booked in his name?" Hunter asks.

"No. The taxi is taking you to the wrong hotel, you have a walk through the city. I'll text you details."

"Whose name is that booked in."

"David Cornwall."

"Who's he?" Hunter asks.

"Seriously?" Kieron asks.

"Yes."

"The real name of greatest spy novelist that ever lived," Kieron explains.

"My life is book," Bedi says.

54 WASHED UP

Prisha looks wrecked. She opens the door of a large linen washer and steps back from it, exhausted. She pulls a cart under the door and using it as purchase, she finds super-human energy and dives headfirst into the machine. She has to use her whole-body weight to drag the sheets out because she has no strength left. She lets them fall into a small truck, then slides out after them. Straightening her back slowly, she goes to the shirt steamer and releases the pressure on a shirt that has been blown to perfection. She reaches for a hanger but drops to a chair and brushes her damp clammy hair off her face and looks at her watch. Oona approaches; Prisha looks up without the strength to smile.

"I'm done. That was all I had left."

"I need you to work a double shift."

Prisha is too tired to take in what that means; she stops.

"I need to sleep."

"I need sheets on guests' beds tonight. Take them to the folding machine."

"Who is with me there?" Prisha asks.

"No one. You're by yourself."

Prisha shakes her head in despair.

"I am short of staff, all the women all leave here for better jobs in the city," Oona says, leaning in to throw her a deliberately placed bone.

"I must have a lavatory break first."

"Straight back," Oona demands.

Prisha runs off, charges into the washroom and slams the door behind her. In the cubicle, she takes out her cell.

Hunter leaves the secure perimeter around the ships and walks down the sidewalk towards the taxi rank. There is a black people carrier waiting. He leans in the open window.

"Jean-Marc Bozzretti?" he asks, straight-faced.

The driver nods and Hunter gets in. The door automatically closes and locks. Hunter slides onto the middle row of seats. He automatically checks the space behind him, old habit. He exhales a little but notices the driver has not started the vehicle. In the rear-view mirror, he can see he is being eyed and checked against some detail held below. He eases himself forward a seat to be nearer the door. The driver snaps round, silenced handgun up. The shooters eye visible behind the sight. Hunter throws himself forward off the line of aim, grabbing the wrist of the driver and breaking it backwards. Turning the gun around, the first bullet goes straight through the windscreen. But although it punches a perfect hole, the safety glass stays intact. They struggle as the assailant's own finger is squeezed again and his head explodes. The windscreen is splattered red.

Hunter pulls out his personal cell-phone and photographs what is left of the driver's face. He leaves the driver's printed job sheet for Jean-Marc Bozzretti with a picture on that looks nothing like him. He pulls a cloth from the dash and uses it to lift the bottle of cleaning spray clean used to keep the interior smart. He sprays and he presses the door release button using the cloth to open the door. He sprays everywhere he has touched, wipes down the seat, the grip, and the internal door handle. He presses the button to close the door with the cloth, he wipes the exterior door handle and the bodywork where he leaned in to speak to the driver.

He rips the driver's phone from a dashboard mount and after a quick double-check that it is all washed clean, he turns and walks away.

With his head bowed, his hands continually cross his face. First, he brushes his hair with his fingers, then removes his jacket and lifts it forward. The thirty or so steps back down the road are completed in just seconds. Feeding into the middle of a group of ship guests, Hunter shows his pass to the security guard at the customs perimeter gate. This is where a flash of the magic cruise card allows entrance, and he has a day pass to the old ship, the detail of which is not fully checked. Ignoring the holidaymakers around him, head still down, he puts his jacket in a tray on the conveyor belt and walks through the X-ray arch. When his jacket is out, he turns sharp left back to the café.

The *kill or be killed* state of mind is not something anyone enters lightly. Not even an agent used to going underground, or staying above ground and becoming invisible. Certain chemical changes happen in the body way beyond just adrenalin that drive every move with a need for utmost care and supreme confidence. Having walked straight passed the café he enters the large metal fabricated supply warehouse and goes directly to the supervisor's office. Along the wall outside are coat racks and shelves full of everything he needs to go native. He dons a coat over his jacket, then a yellow high visibility jacket, safety helmet, headphones. He looks around and takes two clipboards from the office, then a reel of red and white striped plastic tape. He turns to leave knowing he has a choice of two ships, but he can't stay another night in Naples.

Now effectively invisible, Hunter weaves between forklift trucks lifting stacks of accessories bound for the ship. He watches the first exit the huge doors, piled with potatoes. It has two workers on it hitching a ride, sitting on the flatbed as it heads for his old ship. That has to be the second choice. Another truck of potatoes is ready and waved across to the other side of the large warehouse door. Two workers jump on and he moves swiftly to hitch a ride. He stands, holding on, his head buried in the bags of produce until it swings round and the two jump off to disconnect the flatbed from the forklift. He steps off, waits for his moment then walks straight into the ship, checking loaded produce being wheeled in through the watertight door. Hunter knows this routine, he has been a supervisor, before he was promoted to head of security. He knows how the loading officer splits incoming loads so that office, kitchen, hotel all get their turn to get their lot in and cleared away from the bay. A load has gone left, the next will have a different route. He diverts left as a new grand piano goes straight with all hands around it. Following the food produce route, he turns into the body of the ship. Clipboards and tape are placed down, then his hat, then his hi-vis and jacket are off and he is on the crew stairs as a guest. He is on his cell-phone immediately,

"Dwight, the taxi driver is down. He had a job sheet for Jean-Marc Bozzretti. I look nothing like him! I have his phone and I'm a stowaway on the Myrrh. What's Kieron's room number?"

He pushes a door which says, 'you are now entering a passenger area'.

Hunter knocks on a cabin door. Bedriška answers, Kieron stands at the far end of the room using the remote to flick through the television channels.

"Room service."

55 THE PLAN

The ship has sailed far enough from the Italian coast for the shops and duty-free to be opening. Bedi and Hunter pass by reception where she takes advantage of there being no queue. She puts six hundred dollars of their cash surplus onto her account. Tonight, is a casual night but Hunter's clothes will be inadequate for the lounge bars. Kieron could do with a little more apparel shopping, but his mind has not been on the dress code.

While Hunter looks at a jacket he would never wear back home, Bedi has found another dress she likes.

"We're supposed to be shopping for me," he says.

"You are big enough to choose your own clothes."

Everyone likes Bedriška's cheek, even though at times it is hard to know when she is being seriously demanding or offensive.

Hunter picks up a tracksuit to sleep in, and holding it he thinks out loud,

"Shall Keiron and I top-and-tail and you take the sofa?"

"No," she says deeply offended by his suggestion, "I sleep in bed. You take sofa."

Hunter is stopped in his place, but it is clear, that the subject is closed.

"That dress is too big for you."

"I know. They get my size," she says.

By the time they have left the shop the staff have made a good early sale.

"Maybe I need to put more money on my ship account," she says as they head for the elevator. He looks at reception and can see it now has a queue.

"Tomorrow. Not twice in one day."

Kieron and Hunter enjoy a pre-dinner drink sitting on stools in the lounge bar, 'North, South, East & West'. It is at the top of the mid staircase and connects to a speciality fish restaurant, Ocean 11. It may be a play on the film, but it is simply using what is on offer: food from the ocean and the deck it is on.

"Does Bedi always take this long to get ready?" Hunter asks.

"I've never noticed, we've always left the room together."

"She threw me out."

"You're not married to her like I am."

"My, you have got close," Hunter suggests, tipping his empty glass at Kieron as he has the cruise card.

"Same and a large vodka," Kieron asks the bartender slipping his card forward. Hunter's beer is served first, and as the vodka is put on the bar as Bedriška walks in.

"Did you want anything with your vodka?" Hunter asks.

Kieron offers a knowing smile. Bedi has drunk the vodka.

"Yes," she says, putting her glass on the bar.

Hunter is confused, but Kieron circles a finger which the barman understands is another large vodka.

"You're looking lovely," Keiron says to Bedi.

"You've gone soft," Hunter says, necking his small beer and queueing his glass for another refill.

"Just a tip, don't try to keep up with her."

In the speciality restaurant Ocean 11, the tables are set further apart than in the main restaurant and the service is more personal and attentive. Each of the three have grilled fish, with a bottle of white wine to share. Kieron chose it, noting that it was not on the menu downstairs. He appreciates that this is a good bottle of wine and that it has been almost left to him as Bedi is still drinking vodka and Hunter has another beer. Their table by the window looks out to sea. In the distance, the sun is setting fast over the horizon. As it sits on the line between the sky and sea, patterns rattle across the calm surface of the water, hustling for attention against the red and grey sky. All three watch, waiting for the magic moment they have seen many times. The sun vanishing is always special, the speed increases for the last drop and there is a small flash that appears as it tries to hang on. But, as always it finally sinks, and everything changes.

"It's a shame Prisha can't join us," Hunter says.

All three leave perfectly raided fish bones, and with the meal over they lock eyes to toast. The two men pick up their wine glasses and Bedi follows with her empty Vodka glass.

"Well done, not one mention of business over dinner. Cheers!"

"I like that game," Bedi says. "Let's play again."

"No. Dwight tells me eighteen new workers are expected to join tomorrow in Sarande. Fifteen are women, and their applications just tick the box, 'hotel experience'. None filled in any details," Hunter explains.

Bedriška stays quiet, she looks out the window at the dark sea and plays with her empty glass. She is not annoyed that they have started to talk shop, but that women are being used.

"What if we stop them getting on," Kieron suggests.

Bedi turns and looks to him, as wonderful as his intentions are, it is not a solution to the problem.

"If they don't show someone on the ship will be raging mad. That someone will be Lars," he explains.

"What happens to women?" Bedi asks. "They still get sold. Somewhere."

"Our contract with the cruise company is to stop a problem. It may start with chocolate in the laundry, but it has morphed to people trafficking in the ships laundry. They can't sack us now. The problem is to get it off the ships, all three ships," Hunter states.

"We don't have a contract at the moment," Kieron suggests.

"Then we save women, fuck ship," Bedi says.

"Agreed. Let them suffer the bad publicity, not us," Hunter says.

"Find Lars, we solve the threat to many women, and we might get paid though that doesn't concern me," Kieron confirms. But, as Dwight suggested, Lars could be in Miami.

"Sure, we all know it might lead back. Maybe that's why the kids hired us. Maybe they got burned internally. We don't have to give up," Hunter argues.

"No!" Bedi agrees. She holds her glass up. "Vodka."

"OK, to find Lars, we need to stop women from joining the ships. How do we do that?" Kieron asks.

"Even if I got ashore and managed to detour tomorrows group, it won't work on three different days," Hunter suggests.

"Even if we could do it for each ship, it would get exponentially more dangerous each time."

"For us or women?" Bedi asks, deliberately being cantankerous as she drinks the glass that has just been delivered.

"We can't save anyone if we're dead, and we've all cheated the hit teams on land so far. Is there an easy way to do this staying on the ship?" Hunter asks.

"Let's stop tomorrow's group. If they feel they've been rumbled, they might just close the operation down," Kieron pauses.

"Women must be safe; we get them jobs in Corfu. It is thirty minutes from Sarande in fast boat, ferry two hours," Bedi suggests.

"If this organisation thinks anyone in Greece is stealing their employees, they'll end them," Hunter says.

"They need to vanish, and the Albanians not notice. Three days running?" Kieron questions.

"It will end in blood bath," Bedi says.

"What if in Corfu they get off the fast boat, and get straight onto the ferry somewhere else? Dwight can go through the routes."

Bedi lifts her empty glass. The waiter can't walk between the bar and the table as quick as she drinks them.

56 A KIND OF MAGIC

Leaving Naples on the east coast of Italy means a sea day to Albania in the Ionian Sea. It is a relaxing day for guests who can enjoy the ship, but it might not be the most relaxing day for the CSCI agents. However, away from land, they won't be attacked by mafia hit squads.

Their day has a late start. Hunter is awake first. Sitting up on the sofa in his night tracksuit, he is studying his phone. Bedi and Kieron stir.

"With your new-found magnetism for staff, we need that romance at work contract we talked about," Hunter says, concerned.

"You have other woman?" she says directly to Kieron who is millimetres from her. "Oh yes, my woman, Georgie," she scolds, pushing him away. Rising she steals all the duvet which she wraps herself in. She walks to the washroom leaving Kieron uncovered. He pulls a pillow down to cover his embarrassment.

"Are you standing to attention, soldier?" Hunter asks.

"Be fair, hard not to," Kieron admits.

"I never notice," Bedi shouts back.

"I'm studying over-night messages. Dwight doesn't like our plan. He thinks it needs more thought," Hunter replays.

"It happens tomorrow. We have day to change or it stand." Bedi shouts from in the washroom. "Fast boat to Corfu. New boat anywhere, Italy, Greece. We have options."

"No, he doesn't see it or any of those suggestions helping the women," Hunter explains. "Corfu and

Albania are close, and the Albanians have a huge presence on the Greek island. He doesn't think the women will be safe anywhere, so we should think over our actions on a boat anywhere. More importantly, and he is right, we don't get who in Miami is pulling the strings."

"What is his idea?" Bedi demands standing just outside the washroom.

"He thinks we need to make the women vanish into thin air. We should have the magician on board, Manuel Martinez, come up with a better plan. Apparently, he's quite a player in the Magic Circle."

"They don't give secrets away," Kieron says.

The two men at a cabin door form quite a frightening unit. When the yet to be fully dressed Manuel Martinez opens his door, he is understandably daunted.

"Can we come in?" Kieron asks.

"No," Manuel says, confused, not knowing whether to be natural or in his stage persona.

"Wrong answer," Hunter says, and he leads Kieron in past the smaller shocked magician at the door.

"I hope you tip your cabin steward," Kieron says, looking around the room.

"You can't just burst in."

"Make us disappear then," Kieron says with a smile.

"When d'you get off?" Hunter asks.

"Venice, why? Who are you?"

"We need to do something, and you're the man to help us."

"Me? What're you talking about? What's it got to do with me?"

"You're a magician, one of the best. You can fix it," Kieron explains.

"Does the Captain know?"

"No, but he doesn't even know I'm on the ship," Hunter says.

"He knows I'm on the ship. Well, he knows someone's on the ship, he doesn't know it's me," Kieron deliberately confuses. "Paul Lopkey would have helped us."

"Lopkey?" Manuel asks, standing in the small corridor area still holding his door open. Hunter and Kieron fill his cabin, masking the unmade bed.

"So, you think you're invisible?" he asks them.

"And he's sleeping with an invisible woman," Hunter says.

Kieron turns to him, "Too much."

"Yeah, sorry. That might confuse you."

Manuel closes the door. They are going to stay.

On the lido deck, deck nine, the sunbeds are fully in use and there is a hosted aerobics class happening in the pool. Kieron is in his shorts and a thin T-shirt. He walks to the edge of the pool and watches the swimmers calmly stroke through the water behind the group of water dancers. He turns and looks at the clock on the bulkhead above the bar and grill. It is a classic old clock, seen on all ships above the pool. It is nearing midday and he impatiently looks around for Bedi. She had asked for more time, so he left her in the cabin bathroom. They agreed to meet near the pool snack bar, but he is not going to let her make him late. Another minute clicks by and he turns on his heels and leaves.

The meeting room is on the floor above the lido deck at the front of the ship, deck ten. It is in the Captain's quarters which are at the very front of the ship behind the bridge. Above there is the lounge bar on eleven that looks out to sea, which is one of Kieron's favourite places. He walks to the room with officer efficiency.

Already seated at the large central table in the small but comfortable dining room which doubles as a meeting room is an officer. Kieron leans across the table, the officer stands and shakes hands. He can see the officer's name badge on his open white shirt which sports his three-stripe epaulettes.

"James Morrison. Hotel Manager. I hope I am who you were expecting, and you're not lost."

"No. All good. Commander Kieron Philips, undercover. Not sure as which character yet."

The Captain enters perfectly on time and walks straight to him,

"Philips."

"Sir."

"Captain Martyn Fox."

He indicates that they should sit.

The door opens and Bedi walks in, in a white bikini covered by a chiffon kaftan. She carries a towel.

"I am in disguise," she announces.

"What as?" Kieron jokes.

"Tourist." Bedi goes to the Captain, "pleased to meet you, sir. My name, Bedriška. I come to say hello."

With the introductions complete the Captain states,

"Grim business you've uncovered. Not sure I like it on my ship,"

"It is on all three of the King Ships, Sir," Kieron adds. "We have agents on them all. I would rather only us in this room know anything at this time. Well, us and the team we need to engage."

"Meaning?"

"We need to borrow crew and lifeboats during tomorrow's tender service. We have a plan we would like to run by you."

57 NO REHEARSAL

Manuel Martinez, the comedy magician, is supposedly a successful immigrant from Cuba. He is really from South London and his flamboyant handlebar moustache and accent are just part of a grandiose act, but that is show business. Because he is a solo performer using no band and no large stage props, he can work in front of a curtain and is ideal to schedule the day before the show cast's biggest extravaganza. Stagehands began to build the set this morning and the show cast is rehearsing. As they finish, Manuel marches down the aisle of the stalls clapping. It grabs their attention.

"Bravo!"

Bedi, Hunter and Kieron walk behind him and Kieron also applauds. The cast look at Manuel because he is fun and most know of him or his act,

"OK, meeting in zee dressing room, go, hustle."

It could be a joke, but the entertainment manager and staff walk in from their offices under the stalls. The dancers leave the stage with no idea what is going on and rumours begin.

"Within half an hour another twenty people will know our plan," Hunter says.

"And by morning twenty more," Kieron says.

"I kill anyone who talk," Bedi says, climbing up the side stairs from the audience to the stage.

Manuel has simplified the CSI mission so much it is hard to imagine that it was ever any more complicated. In the morning, while guests are in Albania, the stage crew complete the build for the cast to perform the extravaganza. About four in the afternoon the cast will have a final show run-through on stage. That is, if they are safely back. But they have no idea what is to happen.

Kieron diverts to an area at the back of the dark stage behind the backcloth and looks down behind the tied storage flats near the stairs that lead down to dressing rooms and exit. He looks at the area where his daughter was previously rescued from on another ship. Hunter joins him and they both stare at the empty space. Manuel stands next to them confused. He has no idea that was where Kieron's daughter was trapped in the very trunk the money is now in. She was within seconds of suffocation before being cut out of the airtight trunk with a grinder. Both agents have the same thoughts and images of that cruise, images that brought them together as both faced near-death experiences.

"Is there something I should know about?" Manuel asks, totally confused.

Both men turn and look at him as if weighing him up.

"Not yet," Kieron says. "But maybe, if this works out, we might have something else for you."

"What?"

"We need to make a trunk disappear."

"Then reappear," Hunter finishes.

They enter the female dressing room and it falls silent. Six female dancers, two male dancers, two singers, and five entertainment staff are crowded inside

"Hi," Hunter says looking at each of them.

"We need your help," Kieron asks politely.

"You will help," Bedi demands in her Russian tone which defines the seriousness of the meeting.

"And we'd rather you didn't tell anyone," Kieron offers.

"Not back home, not on the ship," Hunter says.

"Tell no one," Bedi demands again in a very threatening tone.

"Is this a comedy act?" A male singer asks trying to lighten it.

"No. I am KGB. You will not talk," Bedi states.

They look to Manuel, mainly because he has been on the ships for years. Most of them aspire to have a solo act like his. They are expecting to see his smile, but he is unusually serious. The door opens and the CSCI team part for Captain Martyn Fox. The ensemble knows this is serious.

"I look forward to your show tonight, Manuel, as always and thank you for helping," the Captain says. He turns and addresses the cast. "And, I'm looking forward to your show tomorrow night. So, I want you all back on board, safe, after these three have finished with you."

The Captain delivers a business-like smile, "That is if you agree to help. And you're not obliged to."

"Here's the plan," Hunter announces, waiting until he has all their attention.

"I watch you good. You will be safe," Bedi says.

58 PROTECTION

"Mary, Albanians have been trying to buy into the Dolphins, and not that your food ain't good but there's a great Albanian chef making waves here in Miami," Dwight says to her.

"He ain't cooking green tomatoes like my Stan, bet you that."

"Just saying. Eyes and ears open."

Mary crosses the border from the operations room to her diner, when she sees Croc walking in uneasily, head bandaged and bruised. He is followed by a thick-set black guy with a bulky hooded jacket, and an old sports bag slung over one shoulder. They pass without a word.

"That stab in the chest affect your manners, boy?"

"That your ma?" the hood asks.

"In here I'm everyone's ma! And my eyes and ears are wide open!"

Croc has turned back and is trying to wave her away but though she is small in stature she is a huge stubborn presence.

"Dwight?" Croc calls asking for his help.

"Mary, I got this."

"He your pa?" the new guy asks.

Croc screws his face to show that was a ridiculous suggestion.

"Let's get down to it bro, the family tree ain't on display," Dwight says firmly.

The hooded guy steps around Croc towards the ops room and closes the suspicious Mary out behind the connecting door.

"This ain't no computer store is it?"

"No man, you don't wanna know what this is."

"Well connected, eh? Who to?"

Dwight fires up video pictures of the new guy on his screen. Despite his hood, low cameras he never saw have his face. Recognition software puts diamonds on his eyes, nose, cheekbone, points of his mouth, and chin. Up bounces his name, Big Dog and his criminal record before all the dots are placed.

"You'll put that down before I blow all these screens away."

"You know that ain't gonna work out for ya, Big Dog," Dwight says, spinning round. "We got guns focussed where the camera focuses."

"Why d'you want me?"

"We don't exist. Occasionally, we need firepower from another mother."

"Like I suck it up, not you?" the new guy asks wandering around.

"You don't look like a sponge, and if anything in that bag connects home to you, then you ain't as good as Croc here told me you were."

Big Dog likes the twisted compliment. He slaps hands with Croc and fist bumps hard. Dwight remembers the brief choreography and offers one last demanding bump. Dog recognises the strong ending and accepts.

"How you be in the chair bro'?"

"I took a stray one."

"In the hood?"

"Not your hood," Dwight says, offering enough of his past to connect with the guy."

"What's the spat?"

"Nothing that comes home."

"So, we good here; you ain't chasing family?"

"No man," Croc says to him. "I told you, no family."

"So, who these for? You ain't a player no more, I don't see no army, and your man Croc ain't a gunslinger?"

"Ghosts, all my boys are ghosts, all long dead."

"I got pieces. Long as you got the 'biscuits'," Big Dog says, opening his bag of guns and pulling out an Uzi.

Dwight takes the automatic gun.

"I might be able to find you a band of 'dead presidents'," he says, as in seconds he has broken the piece down into every component part. He checks the barrel, puts it back together and spins it up.

"OK, so you play, but being fast ain't part of the game," Big Dog says.

"I don't miss with toys. No one here misses. No one here goes down for pulling the trigger, you hear me."

"James Bond-like. License to drop."

Dwight looks up to him. He holds his hand out for another piece.

"Occasionally, we dress to impress, a little firepower apparel."

"Call Big Dog."

"Ain't the name on your rap-sheet."

Dwight takes a second, then a third gun and tosses him more hundred-dollar bills than required, "Leave the bag, take the day off, you sold out."

His hand goes out for a proper handshake which Big Dog acknowledges.

"Nice grip. You can get a lot done with a good smile and nice grip," Dwight says.

"You get more done with a gun," Dog says.

"Al Capone."

Big Dog stands puzzled at the reference.

"Capone said, 'you can get more done with a good handshake, a great smile, and a gun'," Dwight explains.

"I'd like to meet him."

"Not too soon. He only turns up at the finale."

Croc leads his colleague through the passage to where Mary is standing behind the counter. Croc is two steps into the diner; but Big Dog, lingers in the connecting doorway, looking around.

"You boys play nice in there?" she demands, fishing.

"Bitch, it ain't none of yours!"

Mary's hands are up like lightening. One knife swishes past his head into the woodwork, the second over his right shoulder. His right hand goes into his jacket and a third knife goes under his arm pinning his jacket to the wood behind him. He slips his arm out of the jacket and raises the gun at her.

"You're out of blades, mama."

Wild Mary flicks open the cabinet on the wall showing off her collection of throwing knives.

"Name's Wild Mary. First woman to turn a set of knives into an automatic weapon. Send me the bill for your jacket. That's if your bitch can't sew."

Dwight is right behind him in the chair.

"She likes to show off. You're welcome if you got good manners, just come in and order off the menu, say please and thank you, and she loves you."

"Might just pull in yer yard when I need a feed up. Guess the discount's good."

The usual door-bell rings as the Big Dog leaves and Dwight powers over to take Mary her three knives back.

"What if you'd have hit the kid?"

"Mary don't miss," she says.

"Thought you missed and put a hole in Stan's chest."

"Who said I missed?"

59 RESTLESS NIGHT

Because it is a sea day, it is a formal night. Kieron and Bedi look stunning striding into the theatre. As they find seats and sit, Bedi loops her arm in his and leans on him.

Hunter does not have a dinner suit so wanders backstage in his smart casual clothes acquired yesterday in the shop. He walks down the few steps and into the male dressing room. While it has some personal materials lying around from those who use it regularly, it is empty because Manuel is a one-man show. The magician stops working a set of balls around his fingers; a dexterity exercise. He looks up,

"I thought we were done."

"I could be visiting to wish you good luck."

"Why don't I think that's the slightest bit likely?"

"OK. I thought it best to catch you before you went on."

"Catch me before I go on and make me nervous?"

"Come on, you don't get nervous."

"I never used to."

"New problem."

"Hi Manuel," Manuel mimics Hunter, "got something I'd like to run by you, shall I do it before the show, or after, in the bar?"

"Tomorrow, big day in Sarande. Day after, Dubrovnik. Same gag but we won't be tendering, likely to be berthed alongside the other ship."

"Needs thought," Manuel says.

"Maybe you could give it some while you're on tonight?"

"My mind will be on nothing else."

Hunter turns to leave.

"Oh, and tomorrow. I have to remain in Albania, to meet our next target ship."

"Gotcha," Manuel says. "Just like me, two shows on this ship, two on the next, then two on the third."

In the background they hear the entertainment manager on stage introducing Manuel, he can hear his usual build-up.

"If you don't mind, I better go," Manuel says squeezing past him, his accent turning from south London to Cuban as he goes.

Hunter takes the back entrance from the stage, it leads through to level three, front crew stairs. He goes up one flight to the promenade deck, walks out and along a short distance before leaning over the rail and looking out to sea. He finds his phone and dials home. "Elaine, darling!" he starts.

No cabin is totally dark, because light from the hall creeps under the door. They are far from water tight. Bedi looks ethereal, lying asleep in bed. Hunter cannot sleep, he is texting Dwight in Miami.

'Still not heard from Prisha, we need her eyes and ears below decks when this goes down'.

'OK'.

'Am still not happy about being in Albania overnight until MS Magi Gold berths'.

'Roger that, DO NOT try and buy a gun'.

'I know'.

There is a gasp of air and a muted scream, then whimpering. Hunter looks up and it is Bedriška. She is having a very disturbing dream. He feels he should wake her. He stands over her about to intervene but Kieron waves him away. He has it, he is used to Bedi's nightmares. She turns and holds his arm.

Hunter lays back down on the sofa. He has been places and seen bad shit and done bad shit, but he found ways to deal with his dark memories. It looks like she still has a lot to deal with.

"Never seen that version of CBT," he whispers to Kieron, knowing Kieron has dealt with the same stuff. "If my therapist had laid naked, cuddling me I would have worried."

They may never have spoken too much about it, but it goes unsaid; Kieron will know the basics of how to help Bedi. Most is listening and being there and she will be in control of all that. However, Hunter lays watching the pair, not just concerned about Bedi, but knowing that Kieron doesn't have the space to be the real therapist she needs. He watches Kieron fall asleep with her and he feels both their pain. Now he understands her abrupt harshness and the drinking. She is one of them, damaged.

60 THE SWITCH

Today they are in Sarande, Albania. The waters are shallow, and it has no pier or berth for a cruise ship. Tender boats are almost always lifeboats, and they leave the ship from a platform mechanically slung down from the side. In rough seas transferring from ship to boat can be dangerous. In some ports, mainly in Greece, local unions insist local boats are used. Hunter and Kieron hope that will not be the case here. There are a variety of elements that can change the ship's own exercise, but thousands of guests and crew must be taken to land and then brought back at least once in a day. Today the sea is very calm and stepping from platform to boat is no more than stepping from a concrete dock to boat or train to platform. However, a slip can be fatal, and every care is taken to ensure that accidents do not happen.

The deck used for this disembarkation when at sea is deck five, between the medical centre and officer cabins. Either side of the ship will open but today they are using the side that looks towards to the horseshoe bay front line properties. All on the ship can be seen from the shore. The pressure on the lifeboat tenders early in the morning is high because coaches wait on land to take guests on excursions.

Kieron is on the bridge next to the Captain. They have both seen a small group of mainly women arrive on the jetty and their cruise cards have been requested from the ship.

"Game on," Kieron says into his phone to Dwight.

The officer corridor is normally empty this time of day, but it is filling up with the team of female hosts and dancers now working with CSCI. Dressed in plain civilian clothes, each carrying a small plastic bag or a cheap rucksack, they are no different from any tourist going ashore. The real guests wanting to use the tender are being held by an officer one floor up, which is very normal. He has sent the first twelve down. The disembarkation deck is never allowed to overcrowd for safety reasons. The dancers, hosts and first dozen guests mix as if all heading on a trip to the ruins of Butrint. That excursion is the first trip out. Also, with them are Bedriška and Hunter who aims to use Kieron's cruise card to get off. The two men do not look the same. As the cruise card is swiped the picture held on the security system is pulled up. Guards have a way of holding their hand in front of the reader until they are ready, the guard looks up and removes his hand. As Hunter is about to swipe his card, Bedi steals the guard's attention.

"Have you seen these ruins?" she asks.

"I've seen lots of ruins, but not these, ma'am," the security guard replies.

Hunter waits, the guard is not distracted enough.

"What? You must!" she insists. "Demand the day off. It is the largest collection of ruins in Albania. Occupied since the Stone Age."

Bedi pauses then as soon as Hunter's hand moves in she restarts the distraction pushing him forward,

"The ruins date back to 800BC, it has also been a Roman colony and a Byzantine city."

The guard cannot ignore her, and Hunter slips through. Her card is in the computer and her face now fills the screen.

"Have a nice day," he says to her then he contends with the rest of the queue.

The team of dancers hurriedly settle at the front of the lifeboat as indicated by Hunter. The next guests fill in behind them and the crew do not notice anything strange. Guests continue to be helped into the boat and begin to fill the bench seats as normal. When it is full, it pulls away from the ship and speeds towards Sarande. In the sea other lifeboats circle, some going around the ship, each waiting for their time to berth alongside the slung platform outside deck five. Everything appears normal.

The lifeboat approaches the small pier used for the tender operation. It could almost be considered a jetty as it is an extension of the land, concrete on rocks at the end of the beach area. With two cruise ships anchored in the bay, the ships have managed to adopt stations on opposite sides of the concrete structure.

The boat is pulled tight to the side and guests start to leave. Until later in the day the volume of returning guests will be small. Apart from two ship awnings, there are several umbrellas to shield guests from the sun, but there is no hiding from the hawkers selling taxies and tours. On the final approach, the CSCI agents see the group of new crew on shore waiting to be put on board.

Bedi faces Hunter, they are always parting but something feels final. Too final.

"You stay safe," she says turning his obvious concern back on him.

"Don't do more than you have to. Be on the next boat back."

They kiss both cheeks and he watches her leave with the crowd of guests. He stays on the boat worried that she is alone. He detects an instability which is always dangerous in the field.

On the Bridge an officer radios an order,
"Return with crew only, no guests, over."
"Roger that," they hear the boat driver say.
The officer, watched by both Kieron and the Captain, only knows what he is told as he is told it.

Pretending to find her hat, glasses and organise herself with a free local map of the town, Bedi watches the tender from another jetty umbrella.

At the awning, the officer opens the envelope and hands out lanyards with crew cruise cards attached for each of the new staff.

"Welcome aboard. Join the boat. You will be officially scanned onboard as you enter the ship," the officer in whites says. His smile is reassuring.

The land agent who delivered them steps back, having become redundant.

The dance team have not left; they are still inside the tender hiding low below the seats. From the pier, the lifeboat looks empty. The crew who run the boat now know something strange is going on but have no idea what. The new crew get on and their agent watches them settle into the boat. There are only six guests wanting a tender back to the ship and they are asked to wait. The agent watches the boat power towards the ship.

On the boat, the dancers are quick to execute the plan. They adopt a frightened woman wishing to become ship staff and demand their clothes are removed. They offer them a simple rehearsal tracksuit and tell them to dress. As rehearsed, the entertainers are firm and insistent. The dancers put on their partner's clothes which shocks the reluctant women as well as the boat crew who are not in on the plan. The new crew are further concerned when their cruise cards on lanyards are taken back, even more so when Hunter goes along with a bag demanding they drop their mobile phones in. He ties the lanyards and drops them in the bag too, there will be no record of them ever stepping on board and, they won't. By the time the boat berths alongside the MS Magi Myrrh, the new women are hiding under the seats fearful of Hunter. The dancers get out dressed as the new crew purely as a show for the gang's local wranglers who put them on the boat. The first dancer passes the bag to the officer on the platform who passes it inside to Kieron Philips. Captain Martyn Fox recognises Hunter from the meeting in the dressing room backstage and they exchange a knowing small wry smile.

"Good luck," the Captain offers.

Hunter tips a small salute.

All aboard, the entertainment team pass the medical centre which has been taped off and with a big sign saying under quarantine. They enter the crew-only officer's corridor and rush to their own rooms where they will shower and change into their own clothes. Their part in the plan is over.

The Captain instructs the security guard to work with Kieron as that lifeboat pulls away. Kieron offers his cruise card and it is swiped to confirm him on board. Each card from the bunch of lanyards is swiped on board. Kieron leaves with the bag of eighteen mobile phones, which if traced are on the ship for as long as Kieron keeps the batteries alive. The next boat pulls in with the six or so returning guests waiting to disembark.

Back on the jetty, the local agent has seen in the distance his group transfer to the ship, never suspecting it was the entertainment team in disguise. Bedi has got close enough to film him as he phones back confirmation.

His message, whilst in Albanian, is simple,

"They're on the ship."

He walks away satisfied. Bedi follows him, she needs the phone number he called, and she will get it.

Kieron reaches the lido deck to watch the lifeboat tender circle to the blind side of the other ship in the Ionian Sea. No one notices that the Magi Myrrh lifeboat with the new crew aboard docks at the platform of Hunter's old ship. Jacob is waiting and the new crew board the other ship. The circle of those with knowledge expands. The boat leaves dismissed to circle its own ship.

The new crew are taken along the storage deck, the one below i95. They are now safe on a new ship which had a staff shortage. Hunter shakes Jacob's hand and thanks him.

"I'm gonna change clothes, just in case," Hunter says.

"See you in my office?" Jacob says.

Hunter re-dresses so as not to look the same in case he was seen by anyone. His updated look is smarter, collared shirt with a buttoned top pocket and creased pants rather than jeans which he puts into a small bag.

He makes straight for the trunk full of money. It is not there. Hunter searches the storage bay which is where all the rarely used materials are stored. Eventually, he finds it, deeper in the back under two other trunks. It is safe but he won't get to it without help. He finds the number of TJ the forklift driver in his mobile and ponders how to lift our trunk from this ship. Eventually, he admits defeat and walks away. Today is not a cash day, there are bigger problems.

Guests fill the lifeboat tender and Jacob walks out onto the tender platform with Hunter to say goodbye,
"See you in Dubrovnik?"
"Don't think so, but you never know…"
Hunter sits down. The boat powers away, and as it turns there is the view of the shore. He calls Dwight.
"I'm on my way to the beach."
"Croc is hacking the phones of those women as we speak. He'll pinpoint last night's location. They must be using a staging hotel," Dwight says.
"Bedi should have found that and be on her way back to the ship."
"Nothing from her yet. You should get out of town until tomorrow! It's tiny, and they'll know each other. Someone'll give you up. Stay well out."
"Where?"
"Castle, monastery, anywhere. Be a tourist, get safe."
Hunter looks around at the boat stopping at the jetty. He was the last in; he needs to concentrate because he will need to be the first out.

61 SARANDE BY NIGHT

Getting into a taxi is a leap-of-faith for an agent in the middle of nowhere, especially after an attempt on his life in Naples and hits on his partners. Now in Albania, he knows this journey could be an ambush. Hunter may not be armed but he is sitting on full alert watching the driver's every move. He asks him to give him a tour of the local high spots. The town could be any in Greece or on these coastlines, but smaller and less inhabited. The further away from town and the further from civilisation, the more he realises how vulnerable he is in this terrain without a gun. The taxi turns away from the coast and heads up into the mountains. He is watching like a hawk. Even though he is sure this guy is no killer, desperation comes in all shapes and sizes. He considers his footwear: certainly not hiking boots and he has no water. The driver is wearing boots that look a similar size to his. This mountain track does not look like the road to a tourist attraction. The road to the Monastery is long, narrow, dusty and with little either side to suggest any importance. There certainly is no hotel to stay at or for respite. There are no signs, nothing to promote the town's featured attraction. Doubling back on themselves they descend. This seems an unlikely route; if the driver is not kosher, he may stop where the car could be surrounded. His only chance would be to drive the car.

"Can I sit in the front; I am getting a little travel sick?"

"Sure."

The driver pulls over and Hunter looks around. Almost nothing.

"I get unbelievably bad car sickness. The mountain. Up and down."

"Yes, yes, yes. I am OK. I drive. My wife, she get sick."

"Can I drive?"

The driver shakes his head. The request has made him very uneasy.

"My car," he says wearily like it is his only possession.

"I pay double."

"You go slow. You go where I say?"

"Sure."

The driver nods and they swap sides.

Hunter drives slowly through a small row of houses, hardly a town but it has a church. None of the houses would rate as tourist villas; they must be in a small village.

"Not exactly easy to find."

"For me, OK. Go straight."

Hunter gives way for a car coming up the hill in the other direction.

"OK, just go."

The driver seems less worried about his car. Hunter swerves around livestock and children. Following the man's hand signals and stops. The driver gets out and shows him the landscape and ruins around them.

"Is it good?"

"The monastery?" Hunter quizzes.

"Historic!" the driver enthuses.

"Yeah, it would be," Hunter says under his breath still concerned, not that he has anywhere else to be. He walks towards the ruins.

"It has story."

"Every ruin has a relevant story," Hunter jokes, though his tone might mean the words are lost in translation.

"Forty Christian sailors, they want to shelter from bad storm. They refuse to renounce their faith and had to go back down. They died in storm, become martyrs, monastery named Forty Saints."

"So many stories about people needing a room at night this side of the world," Hunter says quietly, knowing the driver would never get his dig.

"Eh?" the driver asks.

"I said there is a story of tourists with a baby going to a hotel in Slano, near Dubrovnik. The owner opened the door naked, all but a tie around his neck. He said they could go in if they were all naked."

"Really?" the driver asks excitedly.

"Hotel Slano, a nudist hotel and the owner does wear a tie. I made up the bit about the couple."

"You been?"

"No," Hunter says as they walk further into the ruins.

"Well. It's undoubtedly ruins, and I ain't gonna question the monastery bit."

"You need to pray? I wait here?"

Hunter looks at the driver, his instinct tells him this driver is safe.

"Good idea."

Hunter walks down between some of the rubble degraded walls. He has walked between ruined houses in many ruined cities, normally with a gun in hand and looking for signs of life and avoiding improvised unexploded bombs.

"You have time to go to Lekuresi Castle?" he hears from the driver behind.

"Is it near?"

"Very near. Once a city in grounds."

"A citadel?"

"Yes," the driver shouts.

In the dark operations room, Croc is well-lit by his screen, working at what is now his own desk. Dwight is leaning forward to the floor in his chair. It looks very overbalanced and is not going to work unless he is trying to do a forward roll.

"Do you know it's lunchtime in here?" Wild Mary says, standing in the dark doorway between the diner and the operations centre.

"Ah. OK. I'll buzz my order through in a minute," Dwight says, without rising for air.

"I was thinking more about me being busy and you having my staff."

"Oh."

She walks in and sees Dwight in his impossible position. She looks at Croc. "Is he OK?"

"Yeah," Croc says double busy with multiple screens.

"Did you hear what I said?" Mary fires at him.

Croc turns and looks up at her, "Do you need me to come in?"

"Or Macey?"

Croc looks around and sees her in the dark, sitting at her easel.

"I'm busy," Macey says before he speaks.

Mary looks at Izzy who is on Croc's new laptop.

"That Croc's new laptop?" she screams.

"It's good," Izzy says.

"Apparently," Croc says, standing up to get the others attention and see who can go next door.

"I'm busy writing copy," Izzy says.

"What for?" Mary asks.

"We're doing the web site."

"What, you writing a paragraph?" she taunts.

"A very important statement, Mary."

"If it takes you that long to write a paragraph you chose the wrong profession, girl."

"Macey's doing the image, she takes longer."

"Then you'll give it to me to code up?" Croc says. Izzy nods.

"That'll take me about an hour, or two."

An outside lines rings, it shows on all screens but Dwight has his head under his chair. Croc turns to Wild Mary. He holds up the five digits on his right hand, five minutes.

"Two minutes!" she demands and leaves.

"CSCI," Croc says, just as he has been told.

"Frank Prince here," bellows out on all speakers.

Dwight's head comes up with a smile,

"Hi, Frank. It's Dwight. Now you see the probs you guys have? Decided to run a new deal by us?"

"No Dwight. Looks like you're working for another company," Frank says.

"That right? Well, you sure ain't paying us."

"Today's 'Cruise Island Daily', article."

"Not read it."

Dwight waves to Croc to search on-line for the paper. As he finds the story, Frank relays the content.

"Statement from our main competitors bites home."

"We don't like biting, Frank, nearly as bad as being shot at," Dwight digs.

"While other cruise lines have been found to have ships used for Human Trafficking in the

Mediterranean, our ships have been given a clean bill of health by CSCI; Cruise Ship Crime Detectives."

"They've done well, Frank and a good name check for us. Lucky you never got named."

"We did; Interpol is currently investigating the MS Magi Myrrh, MS Magi Gold and Frankincense."

"That's not good Frank."

"No. We're talking to our legal department about suing."

"No, you're talking to me and I can't help you because we don't have a contract."

"You're right, you don't, Dwight."

Frank hangs up.

"I just put the story on your screen," Croc says.

"You better go help. Izzy! Macey! All of you, next door," Dwight demands.

Beer in a plastic glass, Kieron walks around the lido deck looking at each sunbed. He is searching for Bedriška as they had different duties during the switch. Over the ship's address system, he hears, "will Bedriška Philips please call or visit reception."

He knows what that means because he heard it for Gwen and Albert in Cadiz. The ship's computer system does not register her as being back on board. Something must have gone wrong with their plan, or, Bedi deliberately didn't get back on the ship. He dashes to a lift knowing she could well have gone rogue, her hatred for sex traffickers was an issue that if they were overmanned, may have taken her off the job because she was a risk to them and herself.

At the reception desk, complete with beer, Kieron shows his cruise card.

"You called my wife."

"Yes sir, our system does not have her registered as onboard."

"She must be."

"It's very rare for us to get it wrong, did you go off the ship today?"

"For a brief time, then I was the guest of your Captain, Martyn Cox, and had a private bridge tour."

The receptionist is taken back slightly but writes all that down verbatim. Kieron likes that, information clearly recorded to paper as it is received. It can all be checked later, even if her memory is questioned.

"And your wife, sir. Bedriška. Was she with you?"

"No. She went to the beach."

"And has she come back? Because we are waiting to sail, and I need to see her before I can log her onboard."

Kieron's blood chills. He knows she stayed on land to exorcise her nightmare. The big question is, what does he do? Rule one, report back and await orders, even if his urge is to get off the ship. He is torn; he wants to get off and ensure she is safe.

Just twenty minutes of a very peaceful drive along the coast, the taxi pulls up by a restaurant on a jetty. Again, Hunter can see no hotel, but they may rent a room.

"Just in time, sir," the driver says getting out of the car. "Boat trip every evening to mussel beds. Then eat the best seafood possible. None fresher."

Hunter follows him. The driver either knows the owner or he is witnessing a commission-based greeting. Whichever way, Hunter takes the trip with four couples and a beer. It travels out in the lake and there is an explanation of the farming and production of shellfish. The ruins were interesting, as was the monastery from 600 BC, but this is a far better attraction. With the sun dropping and another beer in the cool box Hunter relaxes. Rarely does he feel like he wants to ignore his phone.

They never see the sun in the CSCI operations room, it could be day or night. Croc now lives there so he has become someone with no time scale and decreasing vitamin D.

"Bro."

"Yes, Croc."

"All the mobiles line up with the details on the employment forms the new staff filled in. They've all been getting calls since being on the ship."

"From who?"

"I was just about to get to that, but between me waiting tables and cleaning the kitchen."

Dwight knows he is being played and ushers him to get on.

"I reckon a mid-town hotel block. I found it on a hotel booking site and it seems to be the cheapest in Sarande. Sending that to you now. I'm surprised I found it before Bedi."

"Send it to Hunter and tell him that's likely the place to avoid."

"He'll go straight there," Croc says.

"I know. It's like telling you to get some rest or take some air."

"Dwight, what I need is a week on one of them ships. Like an apprenticeship."

"Except we need you here and in good health. Go lay flat when you've done that."

Croc types away, then hits send. He stands and looks at Dwight struggling, still trying to bend under his chair to fit a gun.

"You OK bro'?"

"Slide under and hold this up while I cable it."

Crock lays on the floor and squeezes under the chair, holding the Uzi up. A phone rings loud on the screen and Dwight sits up.

"Kieron!"

"Dwight, Bedi's not on board!"

62 BEER AND MUSSELS

Hunter has a table to himself looking out over Buthrot's lake. The clean sea air has a heavy hint of lemons from the nearby trees. The mixed seafood was the freshest he had ever tasted and that includes a wonderful, never forgotten meal he once enjoyed in Key West. Fast wi-fi is something neither of the ruins afforded. They were not best equipped for tourists, though to commercialise them would have taken away some of the historic magic.

Reporting back to Dwight in bursts of recollection is stopped by an inbound message. Bedi never made the ship and it has sailed. Hunter looks up at the glow of Sarande, ten kilometres away down the SH81. He is at least twenty minutes away. The unreported nightmare he witnessed Bedi struggle through last night may be relevant. He starts to type his report of it. He ponders over mentioning the heavy drinking, but he knows these things cannot be ignored, and if she is a player she would expect to have to defend it. He calls a waiter to pay. His driver was left playing chess with some locals on the other side of the main building before it got dark. He agreed to cover any food costs, not drink. It was a firm message that he wanted a sober driver. He looks at the check and the amount the restaurant has charged is less than the tip in many establishments in America demand. He drops fifty dollars, far more than expected, and walks fast, phone to ear, waiting for Kieron to answer,

"OK, be straight, how fucked up is she?"

"No idea, but she was coping. I think I was helping."

"Did you bring the shit back to the surface?"

"No. The job did that. I think she spent time in the sex trade. Let me call Georgie. You've been sent the hotel they used in Sarande, she'll have followed them there, but don't steam in. She might just be working the case."

"I'm less than thirty minutes away, you have time to collate the facts before I storm it single-handed."

Hunter gets in the car. Behind them is the glow of Ksamil, but they are in pitch dark as soon as they leave the jetty area of the restaurant. He won't see anything until they get back to Sarande.

Kieron has returned to the Lido deck, where there are now just a few stragglers from the day's fun plus a few remaining early-birds dressed for the evening, there for a sun-downer that turned into two. He is at the rail looking out to the sparsely lit coast as he rings Georgie,

"Hi. How are you?"

"Are you supposed to ring me?" Georgie asks.

"Was Bedi harsh because I rang you before?"

"She wasn't happy, but then she often isn't happy."

"Has she said anything about our job?"

"Why? Kieron, tell me, why," she worries.

"Has she history with the sex trade; something that hurts her? She's gone off by herself and I want to know how angry she is."

"Get her back!"

"Will she have lost it and be after revenge?"

"Get her back!"

"We will. What's the story?"

"I don't know much, except some nights she has to wade through hell to make it out to the next day, nights when all I can do is hold her."

"That I know."

"You've been holding her at night?"

"Georgie. I've had to. She has nightmares. What happened? I need to know."

"She was a child sex worker in Russia. She killed someone and ran away. When she was arrested, they dropped charges, but in return she had to work for the KGB. Once again, she felt she was a slave. How bad it was, I don't know, I only get bits. I know she doesn't trust men."

"OK. That adds up."

"Is she in danger?"

"Hunter's there, he'll bring her back."

Kieron ends the call and feels not only a sense of guilt but a horrid pain because he can do nothing about it. He dials the number in his phone under Bedriška. Prisha answers which shocks him.

"Prisha. I forgot you had Bedi's mobile."

"So, you didn't want to talk to me?"

"No. I would normally leave agents alone with their handler. When they are under-cover I would not know when they can talk. Often you can't."

"I have a short break, I need it. I'm in my cabin, which I still have solo because my co-worker has not arrived."

"We know, we are squeezing them dry."

"Thanks. I am still doing double shifts which can't go on. Rumour here is that the eight new workers have been quarantined on arrival. We've got to wait for help. Oona says if I don't like it, get off in Venice."

"Good. That makes Venice a focus. Did you report it to Dwight so we can work it?"

"Of course. He wants me to question why the new staff are in quarantine. He suggests I say it is a lie."

"Be careful. Get someone else to fire your bullets."

"I am not silly, Kieron."

"Let me think about Venice. Stay safe."

He ends the call, then returns to the beer he has been carrying since before he went to the reception. He checks his watch, he looks at his phone and finds 'Bedi's new phone' but he calls Hunter,

"You there yet?"

"Just checked in. Not happy with my room."

There is a loud female scream, it goes on and on. There may be two women screaming.

"That doesn't sound good," Kieron says, and he continues to listen as Hunter reacts, leaving the call live and dropping his cell phone into his shirt breast pocket.

63 POLICE & VODKA

Hunter leaves his small washroom, picks up his small bag from the bed then is distracted by a noise from outside. He opens his room door and sees a thin naked woman is covered in blood down the far end of the hall, years of military training hold him back from rushing in. He steps forward and kicks the door opposite then retreats. The door opens opposite and his neighbouring guest comes out. He does wander along inquisitively. Hunter takes his cell out and rings Dwight. "Woman covered in blood down the hall," He drops the phone in his pocket. "Unlikely to have been attacked by Bedi, but I guess she might be at the centre of it."

He sees drops of blood on the off-white marble floor but drips also lead in the other direction towards the stairs. Hunter ensures he destroys it further as he traces the bloody trail the other way knocking on doors to wake guests. Looking down the stairs he sees Bedi. The sound of heavy footfall announces men starting to climb below her. The window by her would be too slow an escape.

"Bedi," he calls. "Up here."

She turns and runs up to his position.

"Fall in behind me."

He walks back towards his room. For her, it is back to the trouble, but she trusts him. Agents rarely question confident orders in times of conflict. She walks looking backwards on his tail. The footfall on the stairs echo closer. There is no furnishing in the old hotel to absorb the sound. He stops by his room.

"Shoes off. Shower," he says pointing into his room.

She slips her bloody shoes off and steps in leaving no blood on his floor. He pulls the door almost closed and walks forward to loiter behind guests as a bystander in the hallway. He collects his phone and raises it high to film. Two managers push through all the voyeurs. He follows their lead through the crowd as the third with his camera held high. Inside the incident room, another woman has slid down the wall in that room and sits holding a man who is a mess of blood. Dead.

A second man is dead on the bed as the phone comes down level to Hunter's mouth,

"He's from the jetty; he was supervising the new crew. Killed on the bed, his neck slit ear to ear. He's been rolled over and his penis has been cut away. That feels like a message from Bedi. She's safe showering."

Hunter looks at the naked woman in the hall covered in blood, whom the manager is harassing for details. It is not her blood. He films her, "That looks like the man's blood. Maybe she was underneath. She rolled him over to escape."

Hunter pans his camera to the bed again, "That's a stencil of her body-shape." Hunter pockets the phone.

"Rape," Hunter shouts to spread news. "She was being raped."

The manager finds it difficult to push people back.

"Interpol," he says and slips by to the blood-covered naked woman. She looks at him, she understands little English.

"Where are your clothes?" he asks her miming the same.

The woman points to a small case, he steps towards it, encouraging her to toss the body off her lap. He snatches two towels from the washroom and hands one to her. She starts to clean herself as he uses the other towel to open her small old case. He takes out trousers, tops, and a dress. More than is needed. He goes back to her keeping his towel and offers her some of the clothes with a kind smile. He mimes for her to cover herself and calm down. She dresses destroying the second crime scene. Hunter leaves with some clothes and the towel and joins the crowd.

"Call Interpol, call them," he shouts to the managers to confuse his use of the term earlier.

"He was strong, he had a knife, he ran down the stairs," he says pointing to distract people. "Blood on the floor."

The crowd look down moving and further destroying the location crime scene.

"It was woman," the screaming woman says to him.

"No, a man dressed as a woman," he corrects her. "A man dressed as woman. Man as woman, very strong. Strong man. Powerful man dressed as a woman." He covers. Seeds planted to confuse any investigation; he backs away from the crowd.

"You got that?" he asks his pocketed phone.

"Yes," Kieron starts. "I got Dwight on the line too."

"Yeah. I was about to go to lunch," Dwight says from Miami.

"I'll be quick."

Like all guests, he is corralled away by the manager. Leaving his shoes at the door. He tosses the woman's clothes on the bed and takes the plastic bag from the trash bin. The towel goes in as he goes to Bedi, in the shower fully clothed. The water splashes off her and red blood runs away. Red runs out of her hair, off her arms, from everywhere.

"Are you hurt?" he asks her, seeing her utility knife on the shower floor.

"Don't be silly," she says hitting him with a look that lets him know she feels insulted.

"That was a messy statement you left."

"It was needed."

"Dump those clothes in here," he says dropping the bag outside the shower. "Clothes on the bed."

Hunter walks across the room collects his shoes and puts a chair against the door. He concentrates on his phone again; Kieron is still there.

"Kieron, did you hear? She's safe. Two men down."

"I'll text Georgie. Bedi'll need a large vodka. Good luck," Kieron says.

"Thanks, report to Dwight, you don't need details, you can imagine. She's efficient," Hunter says.

Police sirens fill the air and blue flashing lights stripe the street as cars skid to a stop. Boots stampede into the hotel and up the stairs.

Blue lights flash through the windows and bounce off the walls. Bedi rings the bulk of red water from her clothes then drops them in the bag. She points to the two bloody mobiles on the side which he cleans and wraps in toilet paper then wipes down the surface.

"Cell phones have everything. No? Call to superiors and contacts on ship?" Bedi says.

"Job done," he replies knowing they already have all the cells from the new women earlier.

"No, it just start of job," Bedi says, still naked. She uses the portable shower head to wash everything down.

"We should go for a beer," he suggests.

"Get bottle vodka."

Hunter steps out of the room, slips shoes back on and stands in the hall.

"This is a brothel. I thought it was a hotel. Are we safe? How many murders?" he plants again. He wants Interpol called.

The police run by further destroying the crime scene and he asks them the same question.

"Brothel?"

The police force him back, everything is in Albanian.

"Let's go," Bedriška says from behind him. She is dressed, has the wrapped mobiles, his small luggage bag and the trash bag of wet clothes.

With the encouragement of the police officers, everyone is moved downstairs. Outside there is a growing, interested crowd of locals. Hunter cannot understand their questions.

"Brothel," he shouts. "They sell women."

Bedi crosses the road keeping her head down.

"Brothel. Rape. Five prostitutes murdered. Hacked to death?"

He leaves them translating the message he repeated, and all its variations are being relayed to others.

Bedi is in a convenience store with a bottle of vodka. She sorts through the wet clothes in the bag and finds her money. It is wet and blood stained. Hunter comes in.

"I'll pay," he says grabbing four cans of beer and baby wipes.

As police cars go the other way, he spreads the same hearsay in the taxi as they head to another hotel on the other side of town.

"People say that prostitutes were attacked in the brothel."

Now the story they invented is spreading as they getaway. They need to get back to the ship without a trace. They must disappear.

There is no plan to stay at the hotel or in Sarande. Another taxi takes them to the service station on the wrong side of a motorway. Keeping the wipes, Bedi throws the wet bag of clothes in the back of an open-back truck on a journey south. Hunter notices how she needs to be told nothing, she is a skilled operative. Bedi finishes what is left of the vodka and wipes the bottle while she waits for Hunter who is on the phone. He is watching her drop the wipes in a car park trash bin.

"You sure, just leave them switched-on and toss them in the woods?" Hunter asks as he walks close to her.

"Yeah. I'll clean the history and I'll switch them off," Croc instructs from Miami.

They stand at the edge of the motorway and in a gap in the night traffic they run across. They clear the central metal barrier and cross the other lane.

Hunter tosses both phones in the bushes.

"Still good?" he asks Croc on his cell-phone.

"I'm on them, where are you?"

"Walking away."

"I'll switch them off after I've got the data. Speak later," Croc signs off.

They continue through the lorry park and hitch a ride with the first driver they meet going to Dubrovnik. The sight of a one hundred dollar note seals an immediate deal. It is always easier in a truck, though a little slower.

"I was having a fantastic evening. Found a seafood place that overlooked a lake," Hunter says sarcastically.

"I had a good evening too," she says with a meaningful grin.

64 BLOODY HARD WORK

Croc is remotely busting into the two phones left in the bushes. He has done 18 phones in just over twelve hours. A list of numbers rolls down the left-hand side of his large screen, the second list of numbers roll down the right side. Buttons appear; Save Messages, Save Voice Messages. Croc clicks yes to all. Destroy Information, Destroy Sim Card. Croc clicks yes to all.

"This phone techy thing becoming a full-time job plus, plus, plus for me," Croc says spinning in his chair. "I'm gonna be salaried, right?"

"Well this office became your new home," Dwight says, turning to him. "You paying rent?"

"I got me a whole list of numbers to sort and trace. I gotta be getting some over-time."

Dwight leans back in his chair,

"I ain't the right paygrade to talk money, just keep proving yourself before they get back."

"Bedi is one crazy mother."

"I got me, two crazy mothers in the field. I'm like Charlie with angels."

"You need me out there on one of dem cruise ships as the third angel, there was always three," Izzy boasts.

"Poor Prisha is having to work more than 12 hours a day in a laundry," Dwight offers.

"Yeah, I don't do that," Izzy makes clear.

"The other little angel is running around town like Chucky on steroids covered in blood."

"Bedriška? Macey asks. "Never seen her but I got her fixed in my head,"

Dwight is out from the desk wheeling round in the space behind the screens which changes every time he looks. There are draft paintings hung on a string that hangs behind the row of screens, and in the corner above the desk where Izzy works, she has a large sign over it saying, 'Press and Promotion Department'. Macey has her easel in a space under a light.

"That her in the shower?" he asks looking at Macey's work.

"Washing off the blood," Macey replies.

"More blood," Dwight suggests.

Macey pulls a wider brush from the bun in her hair and paints more blood on the abstract woman in the shower. Dwight is watching carefully and when she looks at him, he shakes his head.

"More?" she asks

Dwight nods.

She pulls an even wider brush from her head and paints blood everywhere.

"That one goes nowhere near the web site," he says. "Them pictures, team. They're classified."

"Did someone really try and kill Bedi?" Izzy asks.

"I think people been trying to kill that girl for a long time, but she rips them apart," Dwight explains.

"Yaaaaas Kween," Izzy says.

"Oh Yeah, you girls should always cheer a home run," Jenny E says from the door. She didn't hear the part that matters. However, the room is now silent. "So, I have a story; just wanted to run it by you for a quote while I was passing."

"We goin' home now, Jenny," Dwight says

"Well, into Wild Mary's," Izzy says.

"No, I'm goin' home," Dwight says.

"Give me something," Jenny pleads.

"You been getting enough. That last article caused us all kinds of problems. Go and ask those two young executives who tipped you off at the start."

"I would but I can't find them, and their secretary won't take my calls."

"Jenny. Shame on you. She is an Executive Assistant."

"Well, she can't find them. Thinks it is my fault."

"Now there's a strange story," Dwight says, as he wheels up to her waiting to use the connecting door, she stands in. It hustles Jenny back. He watches her go out the door main door, spins around into the opening and claps his hands.

"Home. We're done because our team is asleep in Europe. Tomorrow we hit Kings Landing."

"That like Game of Thrones?" Macey asks.

"That where they're goin', but unlike Naples, there ain't no brothel in Kings Landing."

"There was, run by Littlefinger," Macey corrects him showing she was a fan of the series.

"You know what, Macey. I'll have the whole team check that out."

Dwight leaves.

"Goodnight Mary!" he says wheeling himself out of her door. The bell pings.

Back in the ops centre, the girls want to see the gory pictures only Croc has access to. They pressure him to show them, but he is adamant he can't. That makes them bully him more.

On the ship, Prisha finishes a shift and collapses on the nearest chair exhausted.

"Am I done, Oona? No triple shift?"

"Tomorrow you're training some new crew."

"New crew? I thought there was no new crew."

"Ship's crew who have been promoted up to the laundry," Oona says.

"How do you get promoted up to here?"

"You're in a lucky position, people want to work here. Here and the kitchen are jobs than can lead to promotion."

Another young female worker joins Prisha and helps her up.

"Promotion?" the other girl asks, but Prisha is in fast.

"What if we decided to leave this lucky position? Like you said, a city job in Venice. We want off the ship," she says beaming and linking arms with her girlfriend. Only Prisha knows they will never leave the ship. Oona thinks she has two girls to offer.

Hunter's camera moves down a line of blood on the wall to the woman cradling a dead man covered in blood. It pans to a second dead man covered in blood on the bed with a zoom to his slit neck. It is seen on all the screenns.

"She cut his dick off!" Izzy screams. "Oh My God, you can't paint that Macey."

She looks around and Macey is not there. She has passed out on the floor. Looking back, she sees the freeze-frame of the second woman half-naked, covered in blood and mouth open in a scream. Croc goes to help Macey.

"Sit up."

"I like the work here in Miami better," she says.

"Me too," says Croc.

"Dwight was right, I did need to paint more blood."

65 DUBROVNIK

As the truck enters Dubrovnik, the driver wakes Bedi and Hunter up. It is morning in Croatia but still night-time in Miami. The first thing they both do is check their smartphones. The driver probably thinks they are victims of a modern society addicted to social media, but they don't care, they have reports to read and to send. Each will detail last night because the same facts can be told two different ways and contrasting views can often lead somewhere. Dwight's notes are important because he is the point man at the Ops Centre. He is all-seeing and now trusted to come up with ideas on the next move and overall direction. However, Croc is still working through the Miami night on the blood-covered phones from Sarande. He has effectively become the night operations chief and is keen to use the solo shift to be taken seriously at CSCI. He has reported on his phone hacking work with some predictions and knows they will come back at some point; he must stay awake. Hunter sends a text saying call me, that he cannot speak, that he is with other people. It is nearly six in the morning in Europe. That means in Miami, everyone, including Croc should be asleep, and this is not urgent. Miami is five hours behind.

In the ops room, Croc has been waiting for such an opportunity. It is one o'clock in the morning and having a text while alone makes him the officer on duty and gives him the perfect chance to show he is ready for promotion. He lays his notes out in an easy to read fashion and has the tables of mobile phone numbers on his screens. He has made a third column of numbers; these are numbers the phones have rung and the location of those numbers. He has gone over everything in his head, not just because the cell phones are truly cracking the case and women will be saved, but because he wants a full-time job doing this. He rings Hunter.

"So, you can't talk, I got that, OK, here's the rundown. I have traced three mobile numbers called regularly. They must be on the three ships due to position. Yay! Well done Croc I hear you shout. I also have numbers going up the chain. I need time to find who owns them and dig a little deeper to find more about them. Most look to be Albanian, not an easy language. Of the two phones you got in Sarande, there's a difference. One, I think was owned by a local commander; he calls everywhere, up and down the chain. The other, just a worker; almost all calls are to the other phone. I'll do another report when I get more from them," Croc reports.

"Sorry, who is this?" Hunter says in a disguised voice, still sitting in the cab of the heavy truck, now on the by-pass road above the large Croatian city. It slows to pull into a service station.

Croc freezes with fear. Who has he rung? What has he given away? Did he push just one number incorrectly? Did he ring someone else by mistake? Frank Pincer? He can't breathe, he is so worried he has done something wrong.

"I'm kidding. Well done, son. Get some sleep now and start again later with a fresh head," Hunter orders in his normal voice and the call ends.

Croc breathes again. He is mentally and physically exhausted. He leans back on his chair waiting for life to come back into his body, but it doesn't, he drifts off, then shakes himself awake. The day is just beginning in Europe. He starts running on the spot, then realises he needs some air. Keys in his pocket he opens the door of the unit and sucks at the cool night air. He closes the door, leaving the unit for a walk. As he turns the corner, he is jumped by two guys in cycle helmets and glasses, that is all he sees. He turns and runs. One bicycle is fast away and cuts straight into him, the other is behind him and slides to block him off. He is trapped, squashed between them and he feels his knife wound begin to weep. Hands in his pocket, damn, no phone, he left without a phone. He tries another burst away, but he is sandwiched in and he has no strength.

"Croc. Don't run."

He hears his name, knows the voices but has no idea if they are friend or foe? Too many people from his neighbourhood know he has a job and money now. He is a target. He will never be able to leave the unit.

"Croc. It's us."

The voices are not from the street and he has not been beaten. 'Who the?' Croc thinks slowly, focussing on the expensive bicycles, the matching lycra, matching glasses and helmets. He realises it isn't gang colours and no one he knows would ride a prissy bike like these. Is he safe to raise his head? He does. It is Chet and Bjorn.

"Dudes. I tried the onesie, but I ain't ever gonna be seen in lycra. Where you been?" he demands firmly.

"In hiding, and we only dare come out after hours.

"Using our car park as your own velodrome?"

"We should never have started this," Chet says, looking around nervously all the time.

"I get that."

"Our lives are in danger?" Bjorn insists.

"I get that too; the body count is stacking."

"Who's died?" Chet panics.

"All our agents have been attacked by serious hitmen."

"Let's go," Bjorn says to Chet, worried.

"No, come inside," Croc suggests firmly like he was one of the agents.

Croc unlocks the blackened unit door and they wheel their bikes in. He locks the door behind them, grabs his phone from the desk and, unseen by the green office players, he flicks it to record. He follows their fascination with the screen corridor.

"How much do you guys know?" Bjorn asks, still worried.

"To be honest, not much. And what we do know, no one believes," Croc explains.

"No one?" Chet asks.

"Di Mond just passes us to Frank Pincer, and he certainly doesn't want to know."

"Frank is a waste of time. Anything you find, he'll hope goes away before he has to report it up. You've got to get higher," Bjorn says.

"Higher?" Croc asks.

"Look, our lives are at stake," Chet pleads.

"You're not the only ones," Croc says, lifting his shirt and revealing the bandage red with blood. He moves to a first aid bag he has for dressings.

"Let me," Chet says, following him.

Genuinely caring, Chet pulls on blue gloves like a surgeon then redresses the wound, ensuring it is clean and the stitches are intact.

"He should have been a doctor," Bjorn offers, as he sits reading the reports and notes on the screens Croc has left up. They are the ones he used to report to Hunter.

"Let's not get ahead of ourselves, this is nursing," Croc levels. "What do you guys know you ain't told us?"

"Sadly, very little. What have you found? We might be able to help you join the dots?" Chet says.

"Are you sure? You employed us to join dots," Croc says pulling his shirt back down. "If you can join dots you know more than you're telling."

"We know something bad is going on, we thought maybe drugs," Chet offers

"It ain't drugs, it's women. Someone's trafficking women. Brutal people using killers."

Chet is shocked and instantly more worried.

"How do you smuggle women on a cruise ship?" Bjorn asks from the desk still trying to absorb information.

"You guys never knew?" Croc asks.

Chet shakes his head, thinking fast. He then turns to Bjorn. "Not this, we never expected this."

Bjorn appears, "We need to go, Chet." He starts to pull Chet out. "I told you this was wrong."

Croc watches the two frightened men waiting for the door to be unlocked. He takes his phone and drops it into a pack behind Chet's saddle as he lets them out.

The light is still steely blue, the day has yet to start. Bedi gets down from the high cab first, then helps the older Hunter down. They both scour everywhere for any signs of being followed. He gives the driver his promised second one-hundred-dollar-bill which makes it his best night's work for some time. Hunter takes his bag and closes the door. As soon as the truck has gone, Hunter and Bedi start to walk towards a local spur road to hail one of the taxis driving in to start work in the city. When settled, they call Kieron Philips on the ship which must have docked. They arrange to meet inside the walled citadel by the obelisk. Hunter tells him the shuttle bus from the ship will drop him right by the gate.

Although Hunter knows where his favourite old city café is, he would not be able to describe how to get there. Certainly, someone new to Dubrovnik, who would find the city daunting, would have no chance of finding it.

The obelisk just inside Pile Gate is easy for all to find and used by tourists as a meeting place. As Bedi waits, Hunter goes to a nearby money changer to exchange a large amount of dollars into Croatian Kuna at a poor rate. Although most places take any currency, government-run areas will not take other money and that includes the ticket for walking the walls. If they get in trouble, locals will need to be bought in Kuna.

Kieron is amazed the moment he steps from the ship's shuttle bus, which could not get closer to the walled city. He is a huge fan of 'Game of Thrones' and has to pinch himself as to the fully formed state of the historic citadel he saw in many episodes on television, so much that he thought must have been an enhanced visual effects creation. It is real and alive. His brain flashes between imaging today's tourists flooding in and the crowds in period dress walking through the gate chanting. Pile Gate is iconic, and he spools through his memory of the series to when he must have seen this. Like a supper-quiz, he hears the answer from another table. Someone reveals it was when Joffrey was attacked by a crowd. He remembers the steps, the shape, the turn, the arch. He walks down the steps and through the Arch himself. He has been through a lot in his military career, things TV shows have been made of, but never visited a film set so intact.

The other side of the gate opens to a stone-built city. He has seen a few walled cities but in this one, the buildings are all intact historical examples that feel like they should have magical qualities. The main street is drawing him in. Like every other guest, he is tempted to walk down it, but he must stay at the obelisk. He sees Bedriška and Hunter on the other side. He shakes hands with Hunter and hugs Bedi hard. He looks more emotional than usual.

"Are you OK?" she says to him.

"Just happy."

"To be alive?"

"No, I'm a big fan of the show."

"Get over it," she says usurped.

Her sharp attitude shows Kieron that Bedi is back to normal after her double slaying last night. If she had three dragons, in this city she would be invincible.

He follows them down a narrow street, then up stone steps. Eventually, they come to a path which crosses theirs, and they turn left. They are walking along under the wall. As they approach an arch, Kieron has to stop.

"What now?" Bedi asks, looking back impatient.

"This is a brothel."

That makes Hunter stop. He and Bedi walk back to look into the space which is obviously not a brothel. It is an art collection or a museum.

"This is Littlefinger's brothel," Kieron says.

A well-dressed man inside nods to agree, he must get it a dozen times a day. The man walks towards them and looks up at them.

"Come in. This is the Ethnographical Museum, based in this 16th Century Granary. True, the exteriors were used as the entrance to Littlefinger's brothel. It is where Tyrion Lannister meets Oberyn Martell in series four."

"First episode," Kieron says.

"Not brothel now," Bedi says, walking away.

Kieron thanks the man and catches them up, attending to each alcove and alleyway for more excitement. They climb upstairs to a small garden café. It is idyllic, just a few tables and chairs directly under the outer defensive wall. It is quiet, and the owner is pleased to serve them.

"We can talk, I don't think we've been picked up," Hunter suggests. "Then you can scour the main tourist sites."

"You have to love cruising, this is fabulous," Kieron says.

"Until you've done Dubrovnik ten times in the East Med' season," Hunter says. Getting serious, he reports, "Croc is our night watchman. Dwight will have started by the time we have lunch. Let's hope we haven't added to the headcount before he gets in."

"We do good work," Bedi insists, congratulating themselves.

"It's been quite a headcount in collateral damage," Kieron says.

"Good," Bedi replies.

"But we still haven't connected the chocolate bars in the laundry to the sex trade," Kieron says.

Their first-morning coffee arrives, plus a vodka for Bedi and a beer for Hunter.

"I suppose you guys didn't get any sleep?" Kieron asks, looking at their breakfast.

"It was tough," Hunter replies.

"здоровье!" [za zda-ró-vye] *(good health)* she toasts.

"Sit-rep is not good." Kieron starts. After Albania, I suggested Dwight ask the cruise operators if all ships might refuse new staff here in Dubrovnik and in Zadar, but he's getting zero help from Frank Pincer."

"What? After women saved from hell?" Bedi says annoyed.

"No, he was expecting new staff in Albania. He hates running these ships and is missing staff. He suggests his new employees would have had good jobs and have been illegally abducted against their will," he continues. "So, what we did was the illegal act of abduction."

"Wow." Hunter gasps, letting it all sink in.

"Not wow. He needs me to visit," Bedi says, incredibly angry.

"Not only are we not contracted or getting paid, we're also in the wrong," Hunter muses aloud.

"Interpol must tell him?" Bedi asks.

"It's complicated. He's telling them his staff were abducted. In short, the assassins are after us and maybe Interpol are after us!" Bedi turns to the waiter lingering away at his service table. "Vodka!"

66 GAME OF SHAME

Jenny E walks into the diner and sits at the counter in front of Stan, who is cooking at the grill. He has seen her but is focussed on his job.

"I'm not happy, Stan."

"People s'posed to be happy, Miss Jenny?"

Mary sees the journalist, "Jenny. Nice, you come to eat breakfast at Wild Mary's when you can afford anywhere in Miami."

Mary passes her the menu.

"Have you added something new?" Jenny asks sarcastically.

"No."

She pushes the menu away.

"I guess the crew are not in next door yet, Mary?"

"Depends whether you mean sleeping on his desk."

"I thought Dwight might have been working late."

"It ain't Dwight. Croc fell asleep at the screen playing one of them games. Fast asleep."

"No one's playing any game."

Jenny slides a printout of a news story towards Mary. Cruise stories are always big news in Miami.

"Printed it for you, save you looking it up. It's from an early morning press release by Interpol."

"You up early?" Mary questions.

"Hunter convinced me nothing was going on. First, the Cruise Island Daily story, which I never had, then I had to take this off the wire."

Mary speed dials on her mobile.

"Yo. It's your mother."

"Hi ma," Hunter says.

"You told me 'you on holiday'."

Hunter knows that something is wrong, he recognises Mary's quite simple but perfect attempt at code.

"Tell me."

Mary turns away from her phone and faces Jenny.

"Jenny, he said not to interrupt him on the beach."

"He never said that. Are you really talking to him?" Jenny wants the phone.

"Is it bad?" Hunter asks.

"Press release early hours of the morning from Interpol. Jenny here, she furious you told her nothin'. You want me to read it out?"

"No. I can guess. Did she miss it?"

"No, she was up early."

"Good. Get Dwight to send it. Buy us some time."

Mary looks at Jenny who is holding out her hand for the phone.

"They don't need you to read it out," Jenny says. "Coz they already know. Let me speak to them."

"Order breakfast, you'll have something before you finished eating," Mary says firmly to Jenny.

"He said that?"

"No, I said that."

"Stan, I'll have the veggie special that's not on your menu."

"Comin' right up, Miss Jenny."

"Shame. Shame. Shame," the crowd chant.

"What is this?" Bedriška asks, confused as they walk down a long set of steps so long that Rocky could have trained on.

"Probably the most famous scene in the whole TV show. The conniving Queen, Cersei was punished here. She was made to walk naked down these steps and through the streets," Kieron explains.

"If only life was sorted out so simply," Hunter says.

The three continue down the ancient stone steps amongst tourists, some re-enacting the scene and recording it on their mobile phones. It sets Kieron thinking.

"The show's not simple, the twists and turns for power never stop. What you expect to happen doesn't. Maybe we're not looking in the right place."

"Go on," Hunter encourages.

Bedi is focussed on the dramatics of people shaming women, she is not impressed by the scale of the act.

"Who would have access and power to organise a crime ring within a group of ships?"

"They make her walk naked and take this abuse?" Bedi asks.

"More, far more abuse. The walk went right through the town."

Kieron points, trying to show her the direction, but Bedi is transfixed. Seeing her distaste, he adds, "Cersei gets revenge."

"Did she make mess?"

"A big mess, she blew this whole town up."

"Sometimes necessary."

Bedi powers away. Almost at the bottom of the steps, two men strongly berate a woman who is trying to walk down but looks distraught. They throw nasty insults right into her face. It is an ugly scene. Bedi gets hold of both men by the scruff of the neck, one in each powerful hand. The chanting turns to a mixture of screams and cheers as she powerfully drives them both backwards. Both men fast become her puppets. Their concentration is so focussed on moving their feet and trying to stay upright they look fools. It would be a pointless response to fight back against her rage.

"Weak man! Weak man!" she continually shouts in each of their faces.

The crowds cheer the powerful woman and shout at the two men, turning the tables.

"Shame, shame, shame."

The two men fill with fear. The crowd verbally attack them allowing Bedi to throw them away.

"Shame, shame, shame."

Hunter looks across to Kieron.

"Is she alright?"

"As long as you don't insult a woman, you should be safe," Kieron says.

67 WALLS

The ancient walls of Dubrovnik are wonderfully computerised so that you can only walk around it once with your ticket. Wherever you get on, they know that is where you must get off. Tourism has escalated since the HBO adaptation of George R. R. Martin's fantasy novel 'A Song of Ice and Fire'. Income and taxes to the city have secured a buoyant future. Like Petra and Venice, it must rank as a top place to visit, but it is, without doubt, the easiest to get to by land or by cruise ship. Ships that cannot get to berth can easily tender into the small piers inside the old city. From high on the walls, you can see historic buildings all around and why Dubrovnik is an amazing answer to any film.

"We need to give something for Jenny to report, and it can't just be the history of Dubrovnik. Interpol made it worse by releasing that story over-night," Hunter shares, standing on the wall looking at the city and sea beyond.

"That doesn't make sense. Why would Interpol release half a story, with so much unsolved?" Kieron asks.

"Release nothing, is rule of secret," Bedi says.

"You think they had spies back then?" Hunter asks.

"They did in the show."

"Of course they did," Bedi says.

Hunter calls Mary.

"Mummy?"

"You can stop that before you get home."

"Give Jenny the phone."

The restaurant is beginning to get busy for early breakfast. Jenny is still sitting at the counter and takes the phone handset,

"Did Interpol release that story. I don't think so. Follow the source."

"Why are you not mentioned?"

"That's a good question. Someone wants us to look like we're the bad guys."

Jenny goes to ask another question, but all too late.

"He hung up on me."

Mary takes the handset back, but Jenny is thinking. She has always known there is a story here.

"I'm going to set up an office over there," she says.

"I'll bring the phone over if you get a call," Mary says sarcastically. "You let me know if you need anything."

Jenny moves to the small booth by the connecting doors, next to the window.

Dwight wheels into the diner.

"Sorry I'm late, ma!"

"Don't you start that as well," Mary shouts at him.

"I hear you started it. I like it. It is a compliment to you."

"It means I'm old!"

He looks at Jenny with an open greeting.

"I hear I've got a new member of staff. Come in and grab a desk."

They pass through the connecting double doors and see that Croc is fast asleep at his desk.

"Morning boss," he says, jumping to life. He stops when he sees Jenny is with him.

"Don't worry Croc, she's a new probationary member of the CSCI team."

We gotta trace where that press release came from."

"An Albanian press company," Jenny says, pleased she got that far.

"I like you already," Dwight says.

"Tirana Press Outlet, based in between the law faculty in Blloku and the Grand Park started by a bundle of students who did not grow up under Soviet rule," Croc says to outbid her.

"That's what we do here, Jenny" Dwight shouts. "Let's work together. Think. In Dubrovnik, Zadar and Kotor in Montenegro. They got a bottleneck of women ready to deliver. We stop them, ships lose staff, clubs lose girls, and it costs them money in hotels."

"That is a great story," Jenny says.

"No, it's a trap. Find the source," Dwight finishes.

The three CSCI agents stand by the Minčeta Tower on the walls in the midday sunshine and clear blue skies. It is the highest point in Dubrovnik and has the best views everywhere, but they are reading the story

Jenny wrote from the Interpol press release. Kieron leans against the tall round stone building, looking out, thinking.

"More commentary?" Bedi asks Kieron.

"This wasn't part of the city; this was the House of the Undying."

"Women in Sarande hotel were not dying," Bedi says with a heavy tone.

Both men look at her.

"I explain. Women on way to new job on ship. They excited. They not know they to be sold for sex work," Bedi explains. "Even they will think we stole them."

"And we killed two men," Hunter growls.

"I kill all men who sell women."

"But, no one can prove they were being sold. That's why Interpol say they were abducted by rouge investigators," Kieron considers.

"We are not seen as the heroes, but could be the bad guys here," Hunter says.

"Why are we being set up?" Kieron asks.

"This is how they work; we have to fight. I know," she says in anger.

"We double down. Make it worse. Annoy everyone. Completely stop the supply of women and see who comes after us," Hunter says.

"They all will. Everyone," Bedi admits. "Let's drink."

68 BAD NEWS TRAVELS

Dubrovnik is so condensed within the ancient walls it can be a short day. The city can be explored, and the walls walked with time for a refreshment stop, and still it is possible to be back onboard mid-afternoon. Already the crowds are thinning out as guests return to their respective ship for a late lunch on board where it is free. The team still have a full two hours before the gangway is up and their ship starts to sail the extremely easy journey up the rather protected Adriatic Sea. Dwight informs them that the Magi Myrrh did not take on any new staff in Dubrovnik due to Interpol becoming involved. That might mean they are checking every guest on board. Almost certainly staff would have been from the same 'ship's crew agency' as in Albania, which he confirmed is now closed and is under investigation. It does not mean they know who the organising gang is, no one does.

It does mean the ship is short of staff, and while their guests were in the old city, senior staff on board and in Miami put some simple measures into place. At breakfast, lunch and dinner, paper napkins are to be used rather than cloth ones that would need to be washed. Guests will be asked to keep their pool towels and re-use them unless they are soiled. These measures alone take a strain off the laundry. Then trays have been removed from the buffet. This will bring complaints, but other ships within the parent company groups have adopted 'no-trays' permanently, and other cruise lines have also moved over to no-trays. No-tray ships have found a drastic reduction in food waste and the buffet runs quicker as guests dither less. Just taking the trays out has had a positive effect on the workload throughout the buffet, from production to clean-up and waste.

Venice will see the ship serviced by an Italian agency and new crew are likely to be joining there. The management's focus is on bringing all three ships up to full staff in Venice and even that is now under the watchful eye of Interpol's i-checkit. The cruises of these three ships may have changed drastically but the effect on guests should be minimal. However, Frank Pincer has not changed; he sees these smaller older ships as an inconvenient demotion. These ships were under the command of the junior executives Chet and Bjorn. However, them having been released from employment means there is only person he shouts at.

"Dwight, to be clear," he screams down the phone, "you are doing a lot of damage to our ships without permission or contract. I'll prove you abducted my new employees."

"Hey, Frank. Always good to hear from you. Glad you appreciate any way we can work together. I see Interpol is doing good for you, must be their new i-checkit system."

The call ends abruptly, and Dwight does one of his frustrated spins in his chair.

"Chet and Bjorn came here," Croc remembers.

"What?" Dwight exclaims.

"I recorded everything."

Dwight is speechless for a second. Jenny is shocked too.

"But on my phone, and I dropped my phone in their cycle bag as a trace. Before they left."

"They've got it?" Dwight despairs.

Croc gestures, so what, he draws the others to his screen.

"So, I followed them on 'where's my phone'. Basic. Even Jenny could do that."

Dwight puts a finger up and stops the bickering.

"I got the whole chat back," Croc says.

"What else happened?"

From the very last shuttle bus, Bedi rushes to the ship, hand in hand with Kieron. They were so late that after everyone on their bus has boarded, the security person in charge confirms a full ship and closes the computer. The gangway is disconnected landside, and from the stairwell above the embarkation deck they watch it being pulled up. The watertight door will be closed next.

On land, Hunter sits with another beer, half watching the cruise ship in the bay turn and leave. That is the one which had been tendering all day to the small boat pier just a hundred yards away from him. The other half of him is studying the proposed news story as directed by him and Dwight. In it, Jenny states clearly that the cruise company acted as soon as it suspected wrongdoing. Then in detail, she even covers the girlie clubs and local newspaper articles on local police activity. It is the next section that causes concern and makes him put the phone to ear.

Kieron sits with a beer on the rear sun deck away from the sail-away party where Bedi has gone to watch. His phone rings.
"Where's Prisha?"
"In the laundry?"
"She has not made contact for ten hours now."
Bedi comes back and she is attended by a waiter.
"A cocktail madam?"
"No, large vodka, I don't need sugar."
"Madam, could I interest you in the drinks package?" the waiter adds trying hard to meet his up-selling target.

"No, I don't drink enough," she says. She looks at him, daring a rebuttal to her comment. He turns and leaves, giving the usual polite smile.

She draws a chair close to Kieron who looks concerned.

"Prisha's failed to contact anyone overnight, and there's a concern because the atmosphere between her and Oona had changed."

"Croc should be on this?"

"He knows she never left the ship today."

"How he know?"

"When he was with Chet and Bjorn, he set up a phantom member of staff's computer account at cruise HQ. Last night he got key information that allowed him to get into all systems."

"Chet and Bjorn?" she accuses.

"It's complicated."

"Oh," Bedi says, lifting the delivered drink. She knocks it back,

"I go."

"No, Oona knows you. I'll go."

Kieron leaves Bedi reading Jenny's dramatised version of the local mafia hit on Interpol agents when the singing at the sail-away is disrupted by obvious gasps, screams and anger. Bedi is up like lightening and moves to the pool on the next deck. Failing to see the problem on the pool deck level, she goes up to the deck above. She sees a waitress being berated by quite a crowd for tipping a tray of drinks over several guests. Though working hard to recover the mess it has turned nasty. Bedi notices Albert and Gwen weaving away and reports to Dwight as she moves down.

Kieron is below decks. He is used to far more dangerous missions and has had to play different characters. The more decks he goes down, the noisier the sound echoes even though there are fewer people seen doing anything. He enters an unmanned supervisor's office and finds a set of green overalls and a hard hat, but he needs a lanyard and card. He searches everywhere but it is not the kind of thing people part with. He makes a note to self that he needs to collect old cruise cards, anyone's, any date. The hat and over-dressed greens are enough. He knows walking around in them means no one will question him.

He climbs the stairs to i95 and heads for the laundry, to find Prisha.

"What's on your sheet?" Oona shouts at him as he enters, looking around. Any maintenance person would have a worksheet. The area's supervisor would know what they are charged with doing and would sign off the work when completed. Oona is confident; she runs a tight ship. Kieron cannot see Prisha and he knows she was due to work. Carrying his hard hat, he walks straight at Oona, occasionally glancing around. It is obvious the laundry is short-staffed; Oona is working unaided at the folding machine.

"Me come to see Prisha, she never get time off."

Oona looks up at him surprised at his request.

"She's gone. Got off in Dubrovnik, never came back. Two of them. She's left me without staff. I am not pleased."

Kieron now knows something is wrong. He deliberately puts down his hat, looks stunned, jilted, and confused and slowly leaves. He reports back.
"Oona says Prisha's left the ship."

69 BALL OF CONFUSION

Hunter is trying to compute an awful lot.

"Dwight. There's no value in taking Prisha's off here in Dubrovnik. She's on that ship somewhere and they can't attempt to sell her until they hit land."

"I'll go along with that. Gwen and Albert have just upped disruption on the ship."

"They need to be pulled in, we gotta connect some wild dots. Tonight."

"Copy that."

"Now, do I wait for the MS Gold tomorrow? I'm liking the ships less and less."

"Agreed. I've got a plane standing by for you just in case you said that."

Kieron walks along the corridor with the Captain below decks.

"I'm getting very mixed messages about the assistance I gave you yesterday," the Captain says.

"Alleged assistance in something we allegedly did, to thwart a matter we both know was pretty nasty," Kieron says.

"Allegedly nasty. I was sticking my neck out, but, I'm now being replaced in Venice."

Bedriška has forced her way into the security office. The two red-faced security guards who failed to stop her from getting in, stand behind her. She is in front of an even more unhappy, kitted-up Maxwell Silver, head of security. She is not getting the help that she is requesting. Maxwell stands firm, it is his ship.

"I should be told when someone like yourself boards my ship."

"There is no one like me."

"You do not crash into my office," Maxwell Silver almost spits at Bedi in the heat of his anger.

"I here undercover, as guest. I just follow orders," she says.

"That's always a get-out-of-jail-free card."

"You have email now. I know."

"I don't believe emails. I await proper orders."

"From your mother? I tell you I am on board; you study deck camera for waitress. Easy."

"You will be escorted back to a passenger deck."

"That will not happen, men will die," she says.

Maxwell looks at her in total disagreement. He nods to his guards. One reaches to her, she snaps out quicker, retains his wrist as he is rammed forward under Maxwell's nose. She kicks the other in the knee and he collapses. On the desk below Maxwell, the guard screams as she twists his wrist against the joint.

Maxwell pushes the camera on his chest jacket to start. It is part of their training to start the camera. The cameras permanently record but will be set to keep the last minute or two and record until stopped.

"If you resist you will be arrested."

"More men will die."

Kieron and the Captain turn into the security office. Bedriška releases the guard. Maxwell is quite shocked. He and his team stand to a different attention.

Kieron assesses the kit they wear as he would in any situation. He might have to deal with the two men, if they can get up. The kit has changed, maybe since the heist and the serial murders that CSCI solved. They are now wearing yellow high-visibility jackets with a few trinkets that are made to look security like. But there is nothing threatening; no extendable baton, no cuffs, although he is sure he can see cable ties.

"It's probably a good idea to keep these men ill-equipped, Captain, because without training, any piece of kit could be taken and used against them," Kieron offers.

"You record death on nice camera," says Bedriška.

The chest camera of one guard is flashing red as he stands. Kieron smiles at him then leans in and to switch his camera off. The room is the same as he remembers; screens and recorders. There is access to an office behind, which will be Maxwell's office. Then to the left a retaining or interview room.

"I need to see some deck footage," the Captain asks.

"Yes, sir." Maxwell agrees.

"He know which," Bedriška says.

As the Captain, Kieron, and Maxwell study the cameras together, the two officers in the high visibility jackets watch over their shoulders. Bedi stands at the back, the only one showing her conflict training. She watches everyone, every reaction, as well as the screen. The moment it is found, freeze-framed, reversed, and analysed, it is clear the waitress and her tray are pushed by Gwen. Gwen cleverly slips away as if pushed by Albert and they weave in different directions.

"As we thought, your waitress was set up," Kieron shares.

"Why?" the Captain asks.

"We don't know. It's an escalation from putting chocolate in the dryers, which may be due to our presence," Kieron explains.

"But why?" the Captain asks, looking at Maxwell. "What do you have on them?"

"I'll pull her in and question her," Maxwell says.

Bedi is smiling, which annoys him.

"In crowd. One person can trigger riot," she says.

The Captain is nodding as he takes all this in.

"Should I tell head office?" Maxwell asks.

"No," Bedi says.

"No," the Captain confirms. It is his call, but he can see these two agents may be playing out a game. Unless Gwen and Albert are their team as well, they have uncovered something else wrong on his ship. He is now looking at them to explain themselves.

"Problem: one, maybe two of your staff may have been abducted within the ship."

"How so?" the Captain demands.

"No. I would know if staff were missing," Maxwell insists.

"Actually, one of them is another agent of ours, working in the laundry."

"What? Maxwell asks angrily. He is being shown to know less and less.

"She was trying to find the organiser planted on the ship. They wanted her to get off in Venice to work in the City, but maybe she was made. Maybe she made the organiser."

"Her name?" Maxwell insists.

"Prisha Nah. Can you check to see if you're two staff down from Dubrovnik?"

"The headcount is correct."

"Sure?" The Captain asks.

"I know it is, Sir," Maxwell says, containing his anger at being made to look like he doesn't know what is going on. He has been working on his screen. "Yes. Onboard. Look."

"How long has this been going on?" the Captain asks.

"Head office pulled us in over a week ago. What we would like, if Maxwell can help us, is to pull in Oona Mee, the laundry supervisor. She has been losing staff. Ask if she has staff missing. If so, why did she not report them to you? We need her held and her phone confiscated for about ten minutes, that's all."

The Captain nods in agreement, then looks at Maxwell.

"Maxwell, I'll get Dwight in our operations centre to call you," Kieron says offering his hand. The two men shake.

"That would be nice."

The Captain leaves. Kieron leaves a gap then follows him, unknown, while Bedi lingers.

Outside the office, Kieron is about ten steps behind the Captain. He texts Dwight. 'Ring burner now'.

A phone rings but it is back in the office.

"Sir," Kieron calls and the Captain turns and follows him back. Kieron moves back into the office fast. Bedi has Maxwell pinned against the wall. His phone is ringing. The Captain enters knowing something is happening but has no idea what.

"You two. Arrest him," Kieron says, demanding the two officers in yellow high visibility jackets arrest their superior. There is confusion and no one moves. Maxwell laughs.

"You thought it would be that easy?" Maxwell says.

Kieron is studying the two security guards, but they are genuinely confused. The phone on Maxwell is still ringing.

Kieron efficiently cable-ties Maxwell, with no care for his pain. Hands and legs.

"We don't do that on this ship," the Captain says.

Bedi looks up at him. Not that she cares, this man has been trafficking women. She takes the ringing phone from his jacket. Kieron passes it to the Captain.

"Hello."

There is the slightest of pauses.

"Get off the ship now, you've been made."

"Who is this? This is the Captain?"

Kieron holds his hand out.

"That's our office, sir. Testing Maxwell. Gradually, we are collecting the organisation's phones; they pinpoint us to the next one."

The Captain looks at Maxwell with a mixture of surprise and disdain. Kieron talks into the phone.

"Glad it's you, Dwight. Would have been embarrassing if it was his mother. This is Maxwell Silver's phone. One down. One nearer."

"Keep alert. The team could be bigger than we think," Dwight says.

70 DOWN AND OUT

Kieron is with the Captain on the Bridge. They look out to the Adriatic Sea with the sun dropping to their left.

"Female crew missing, they could be dying. We do what we have to find them," Kieron says firmly.

"What's the connection between sex trafficking and the chocolate bars in the laundry, blocked sewage, late excursions?"

"It's hard to consider there isn't one, maybe we'll know more after we've interrogated Maxwell Silver, sir."

"And Oona?"

"We have a female operative for that."

"I saw her, God help Oona," the Captain says. "You can't use violence."

"I hear you, sir. That was a clear order and you've no need to come down and check on us."

The Captain looks at Kieron concerned.

"How many of you are there on my ship?" The Captain asks but he gets no answer.

The small cell is a cabin with a table bolted to the ground and a chair either side. There are no other furnishings. Maxwell knows the room well but has never been a prisoner, never sat the wrong side of the table with his hands and feet cable-tied. He has already taken a dislike to Bedriška and she has a deep hatred for anyone who exploits women, which she is trying to contain.

"Who you work for?" she demands.

He shakes his head with an annoying negative smirk.

"I will find."

"Not from me."

Bedriška leans over and into his face; she has no fear.

"I will. Even if it the last thing you ever say."

He spits at her. She does not even flinch.

"No, you can't do anything. Let me go," he demands. He stands so he can look down on her, "We did nothing wrong. They got better employment and wages than they ever could have earned. What else can they do except lie on their backs?"

Bedriška rises, smashing her head up under his chin with force. He falls back, blood oozing from his mouth. He has bitten through his tongue.

"You wouldn't dare do that if I wasn't tied," he says through a mouthful of blood.

Bedriška opens the door,

"Hey. Someone. Come with knife."

A guard enters hesitantly and looks at her.

"Cut ties," she demands.

He does as he is told and leaves as indicated. Maxwell stands,

"Dominatrix eh?"

She knocks him down faster and harder. His anger has increased. He looks at her with more hatred.

"Trouble is, you're not my kind of woman. I like the feminine type," he says, crawling around the floor.

Bedriška knows his game, she knows he is angling to get ready to stand, with a chair. He rises, swinging it full blast at her. She steps inside the arc of the chair, grabs his head, and smashes it hard down on the table. His face explodes. She reaches over his body and grabs the back of his pants. She leg-sweeps him up, while lifting him, then letting go she spins him so his back drops across the edge of the table. In new pain, he drops to the floor, door side of the table. She snatches the hand nearest to her and cable ties it to a table leg, pulling the end hard until it bites into his skin. He tries to hit her with his other hand, but she catches it, snaps the wrist as she steps over him and pulls it in viciously, to cable-tie him prone between table legs.

"Stupid amateur," she says to him. She gets a text message and leaves him, bleeding and in pain.

Kieron enters the laundry again in his green workers' clothes. Oona, as always, on the ball in her area, sees him approach. One man in an engineering jumpsuit looking for the hard hat he left behind is far less threatening than two security guards in high visibility jackets. Oona snatches his hat and throws it at him.

"Stupid."

He springs at her while the hat is in the air. He pins both her arms. She has no chance of destroying her phone in a washing machine which might even challenge young Croc.

"Two down!" he shouts.

Bedriška is in far quicker than the two overweight security guards. Oona is cable tied, and in just those few movements Bedriška has searched every one of Oona's pockets. She learned to do that at an early age. If only she could be a child again. Holding Oona's two mobile phones, she remembers running through the streets of St Petersburg, playing football. The gag was simple, the ball was deliberately kicked to the tourist. It didn't matter if there was one, or two, or more. They would always kick the ball back, always take the next pass in fun. They would always be encouraged to kick it at the jumpers making goalposts that had not been there just moments before. Then as they score, everyone would hug and cheer. Then all the children would run off, kicking the ball, vanishing. The tourists had been totally financially raped during the hugs. Well-rehearsed life skills that will never leave her. Bedi now has two burner phones, Oona's and Maxwell's.

Bedriška goes to her cabin and follows exact instructions from Croc. This is his territory. Two more phones to build into his interwoven map of cellphones and the calls between them.

71 SEPARATE CABINS

Oona is full of fear; she has never been in trouble before. Like all who bask in the glory of power whilst ruling, she is shocked when faced with the conviction of failure. She waddles to the door, her legs bound by three cable-ties, one on each leg; the third one in the middle is the short length of her allowed stride. Her hands are bound before her. She tries the cabin door again, but she knows it is locked. She hears the neighbouring cabin door slam closed.

"I think he's dead," Kieron deliberately says as he passes.

She hears the words meant for her and waddles to the rear wall frightened. Every inch away from the door helps. She thinks she hears a groan from next door.

"Maxwell?" she whispers.

Hearing nothing, she pushes her ear into the sidewall between the two cabins.

"Maxwell?"

Eventually, she thinks she can just hear a gasp for air below her. She slides down the wall and sits on the floor next to it.

"Maxwell?"

A low grunt is all she can hear. She turns her head and looks at the wall as if she could see through it.

"Max? Max? What do we do?"

Oona thinks she hears another grunt, then nothing.

In the main security area, Kieron sits at Maxwell's desk. Bedriška walks in and stands against the wall, observing. Also present are the two security officers they both met earlier plus two more; one is female.

"I don't think Oona is capable of moving two struggling women far. I want every cabin opened either side of theirs, and the nearest ones to the laundry. I don't care who you upset," Kieron says.

"Sir?" they all question and do not move. They are not used to such orders.

Kieron stands, "Go!"

Kieron turns to Bedi, "The one thing of cash value here is women. They won't have killed either of them."

She nods.

"But. My daughter was kidnapped onboard once and put in an airtight trunk. If they are, they could die and the clock's ticking!"

"I did not know about your daughter," Bedi says to him.

"There's a lot we don't know about each other. One thing we do know, sadly, history repeats itself."

"I beat shit from Maxwell, he not talk. I show Oona? Frighten her. She will talk."

"Let me check Dwight's thoughts," Kieron says.

The operations centre feels tense. The step-up in violence on ship has reflected on them. Croc sits close to Dwight. Kieron's face is in the corner of a screen.

"Oona's burner only goes to Maxwell, he's in charge. All other calls are domestic. They go home to Malaysia. I have details of her family if you want leverage," Croc says.

Dwight studies Croc surprised at his natural ability.

"You watch a lot of spy movies?"

"Never had a TV. Nor the data to watch on my phone."

"Exceptional work, Croc. We may never use it, but your instincts are perfect," Kieron says.

"Maxwell's burner has dialled a few people," Croc continues. "There are the contacts in Albania we've already taken down, so those are confirmed. He has also called the other two ships. Then he has contacts at all the ports, that is a lot of work."

"Maybe best that is given to Interpol?" Kieron adds. "Let them do the work, try and get some brownie points."

"And here's the big one. A regular number in Miami. A Burner, no details, it is off," Croc reveals.

"That's why I'm back here," Hunter announces from behind them. He had crept in unheard. Croc turns sharply, Dwight turns smiling.

"Welcome home, big man," Dwight says with a heavy fist bump.

"I've told Kieron not to go easy on those two in the cells, to find Prisha," Hunter says.

"Good. Now tell them to find a name here in Miami, because this job has pissed me off!" Dwight says angrily.

"You tell him. I'm going home to see Elaine.

72 HOW FAR

Oona is wrenched up by Bedriška and smashed into the cabin wall.

"Where is Prisha?" Bedi asks.

"Ask Maxwell, he knows."

"You ask him. If you can."

Bedi rips her shoulder from the joint, swinging her into the empty door frame as they leave the cabin, then pushing her hard into the next cabin door frame. She looks like she has been in the wars before she can even open her eyes and see the state of the unconscious Maxwell.

"Ask him!"

She throws her down and she lands on top of the lifeless body. She retracts in fear.

"He can't talk!"

"I know, we cut half his tongue out. Look," Bedi says showing her his blood-filled mouth from where he bit his tongue.

"He needs doctor," Oona says.

"You no live in same nice world you did hours ago."

"You can't do this, we have rights," Oona screams.

"Same rights as women you sold? No! You play big girl's game; now, big girl's rules, my rules," Bedriška drills into her face.

"I know who you are, I have seen your faces."

"You will be dead in sea," Bedriška says, slapping her with a wide swipe straight into the soft tissue of her cheek.

Oona falls onto the lifeless Maxwell in total shock.

"Max?" she asks, but he has no response.

"You waste time," Bedi says, dragging Oona up by the neck and pulling her in close to her own face.

"You can die now."

Oona can see danger in Bedriška's eyes, a danger she has never encountered.

"OK. OK. What do you want to know?"

"Where are women?"

"Laundry stock room."

Oona is ripped away and thrown back into her own cabin cell next door.

"Divert team to laundry stock room and send medics," Bedi says to the female officer behind her ready to use her radio.

"Is Maxwell dead?" Oona asks, through her hurting face.

"Don't know, don't care."

Bedriška moves in close to Oona's face.

"What care you give women? None. Tell me or I kill you. Who run other ships?"

"I don't know anything about other ships, no one, never had contact but Maxwell and Micky."

"Then you useless." Bedi locks the door.

Kieron is outside the cabin, "Albert's just bought a drink in the pool bar, let's go to him, the others will look after Prisha."

They are both off.

Midnight on deck is a mixture of dress. Some still very formal, some with jackets off and shirts open, some who never dressed because it is a pool bar on a hot summer evening. Kieron and Bedriška have moved into order drinks, one each side of Albert and Gwen who sit on stools at the pool bar. Bedi nods in acknowledgement from their meeting on tour in Seville. Albert sees the blood on her, and he turns, suspicious. Two security guards' fast approach the pool bar. Albert snatches his phone; his arm goes back behind his head as he intends to throw it out to sea. Bedriška was expecting the move and saw it way too early for it to succeed. She snaps out and makes contact with the triggered arm and snaps it back further than the human skeleton was ever meant to go. The phone drops to the bar. She collects it, the guard takes Albert, another gets hold of Gwen and they are marched away quickly.

The bar fronts the elevator shaft block. Just as they arrive at the doors, some guests on the other side take their cameras out. They are kept away by other security, and social media loses out. Contained in a lift going down Albert and Gwen are searched thoroughly, cruise cards taken, and cable ties added. Kieron and Bedi leave at the deck of Albert's cabin to go and search it. The doors close and Gwen and Albert go down further with the full force of security.

Kieron turns their cabin over. Drawers, under the bed, under bedside cabinets. Bedriška watches a security guard open their safe. There is money and paperwork which she scans. She passes the money back to the guards,

"Find out if this real money. Spend it, have party."

"But," the security guard says.

"Bag."

An evidence bag is held out, Bedriška bags the paperwork.

"And here," Kieron says, calling them over. "Bag. Everything is written down. Like a diary."

"Stupid," Bedi says.

Hunter is eating one of Mary's biggest burgers, "This is heaven."

Mary smiles, "See, they can do all them fancy meals but nothing like good old home cooking."

"Damn right Mary. You get a brown envelope?"

"Got me one. Just one. I like this game."

"I never counted it. Family, right?"

"Family," she says hugging the big man. "And we wanna see more of your lovely wife in here."

"She's great. Was pleased to see me home, not pleased I left so quick."

"Croc," Dwight starts. "Another burner for you, online as before. They've pulled in Albert and Gwen."

Croc jogs across to another chair and slides to his own desk,

"I need to get me some of those wheels for in here."

"Trust me you don't want to be on wheels."

"Sorry Dwight. My bad."

Hunter is feeling very relaxed, feet up on the desk.

"Wanna know what a five-hour flight did for thinking?"

"Go on."

"I'm thinking we cleaned out ship number one on the circuit. Unless Gwen and Albert's phone adds unexpected links, the MS Magi Myrrh's done."

"Good, and?"

"They now, bring on the reserves," Hunter says slowly.

Dwight is nodding his head, slowly catching on.

"Just like in the field. Bring in the second wave or pull someone off the bench."

"That's why they use three ships," Hunter says.

"They always get to supply the market," Croc says. "And the crime is never on the ship."

There is a silence. Both Dwight and Hunter look at Croc. His remark sums up the cleverness of the whole sex trafficking operation.

"If our takedown was clean, the organisation may never have reported their failure upwards. They expect failures, which is why there are three ships. Our phone number in Miami may not know the extent of problems in the Mediterranean other than what's in public domain from Jenny's report," Hunter explains.

"Copy that," Dwight says.

"Two phones lead back home here. We have him in our crosshairs. But we're undermanned. We need a team for this."

"Big Dog?" Dwight suggests.

"There's just one problem," Croc says, swinging around.

"Go on," Hunter probes.

"Well as I'm working hard. Maybe I could get paid?"

"You live here," Dwight says.

"Not the point. I'm working hard through the night every night."

"Do you have something for us, Croc?" Hunter asks.

"Well, I do. And I'm thinking it's not good news," he pauses.

Hunter stands towering above the seated Croc.

"Albert and Gwen call a burner in Miami too, that's the number that called the Albanian press agency. Connection. Bingo!"

Croc opens a window on the computer screen with boxes on the left-hand side of his screen like a small family tree.

"Maxwell Silver calls a different burner in Miami."

"Two different Miami numbers? Could be the same person," Dwight suggests.

"No, they follow totally different towers."

"I was expecting one number, one person," Dwight says.

"I wasn't," Hunter grins.

73 SEA ORGANS

9am Zadar, Croatia –

The three agents; Kieron, Bedi, and a relaxed and smart Prisha lean over the rail on the promenade deck looking out and taking photos with their phones like the wealth of other guests around them. Just two deck levels down and to the left of the car park are the row of excursion coaches waiting, parked in marked bays on Zadar's new cruise terminal, but they are of little interest. Surrounding the gangway is a fleet of local police cars and Interpol vehicles with flashing lights and more than enough manpower to take them as well as the prisoners being handed over.

Bedi and Kieron ensure they have coverage of the arrest with their smartphones. Only too often have they got this far for it to go wrong, or someone suggest it never happened. It is important they also cover all the surrounding area; someone from the gang might be watching for them. As well as the recordings of the arrest, they study every face they can see.

Kieron steps back and begins to send the recordings for Dwight or Croc to deal with. No doubt Jenny will want to use them.

"Will I be the first to get it online?" he announces to the crowd around him playfully.

"No. I got it up on Doris Visits cruise chats and already have over five hundred views," a woman boasts.

"You get all that, Croc?" Hunter says so Miami can hear.

"Roger that."

"I'd love you to face-scan everyone, but you can't do another all-nighter."

"It's already three in the morning here. I might as well, and Dwight can take the day shift again."

"That face recognition," Bedi says.

"In China they have billions of faces recorded," Kieron says.

"They got yours?" she asks.

"I've never been there."

"I should go back to work," Prisha says.

"Are you serious? It's over," Kieron says.

"I got promoted to laundry supervisor."

"No, you come with us," Bedriška suggests.

"It could be very dangerous, you'll be alone," Kieron reminds her.

"Being around you guys can be dangerous too, and I didn't get that fridge loan for nothing. They need a new organiser in the laundry. It might lead to something," she says.

"Maxwell's down and out. How will the villains contact you?"

"Let's see how good they are. I'm safe in the laundry," she says confidently.

"Are you?" Bedi asks.

Prisha nods. The three are quiet. Nothing is ever guaranteed especially on this job, and they all know it.

The shuttle bus drops Bedi and Kieron between the water's edge and a huge city wall. It is another Citadel, but not as impressive as Dubrovnik. They have left the ship for good, Prisha is by herself. Neither have Seaman's discharge books, and they only have small handbags like other tourists. They walk from the small sheltered marina and enter at the very ornate Land Gate, passing under the winged Lion of St Mark, the ancient emblem of the Republic of Venice and a smaller St Chrysogonus, Zadar's patron saint riding a horse. The gate is meant to impress visitors; the inner side is quite plain.

They deliberately thread their way left, not keeping a direct route, to test if they are followed. They return up some steps and through an arch to a square with four wells. They move across that square, then drop down about six steps and into a much livelier square next to Saint Simeon's church. Kieron and Bedriška stand as if talking, but they each have a 180-degree view to check once again if they are being followed. Bedi is the only one saying something,

"Market only open in morning, I need clean underwear."

They head straight across the square. The market sits between where they are and the main gate. They could have chosen to do this first, but the circuit was essential. They relax a little and enjoy the vibrant colour of the fruit and vegetables, colours not found in mass-produced food.

Bedriška is turning over knickers. Kieron is looking past her to cover her back. He doesn't want them to get hit here. The woman who owns the stall is focussed on a sale. She pulls some sexy knickers from a back pile and offers them for him to see, but he ignores her gestures. Bedriška is amused and makes more of an effort to show them to him. He agrees without looking.

"Georgie will love these," she teases.

"George, buy for lady," the stall owner says.

"Yes George," Bedriška mocks.

"They are very nice, just get what you need," he smiles.

Bedi takes several pants and bras. The woman is trying to up-sell more garments to 'George', knowing the embarrassment or keenness of the man is normally the weak link.

"Yes, go for it," he says.

"I need some money, George," Bedi says.

He digs into his pocket.

"Good job Hunter gave me all his local currency. He must have known he was going home."

They move on and pass local women sitting along a wall crocheting. As they walk on, they are harassed as if their purchasing ability has been relayed down the row of vendors before them. Bedi buys denim jeans and a top and they leave the market where they have made far too much of an impression.

They cut up through the square, past the bell tower and ninth century round church and walk past the ruins to the coast. Here is where the famous windpipes play in the breeze. The Sea Organ is a set of stone crafted pipes built into the promenade steps and sea walls that play different musical notes as the wind rushes through them.

Sure, that they are not being followed, they round the tip and the water's edge path begins to return to the city. Before the bridge across the water into the main part of Zadar and the entrance to the new city is a small jetty. Here they take the rowboat ferry to the mainland at the other side of the water.

"How much more romantic can I get?" Kieron offers.

He takes her hand as they climb out.

"It would be good for us to change clothes," he says, thinking of their cover.

"Good shops here and Croatian Kuna no good in Venice. I need retail therapy."

"Retail therapy?"

"You said I need therapy. I make you more modern."

"Thank you. I will make a full report on your progress."

74 RELEASE SOMETHING

1400hrs–Miami.   1900hrs-Zadar.

As the team left in Zadar get ready for an evening off, Miami has finished lunch and they are trying to work out a plan. Tomorrow is Venice and it feels right to escalate matters, not that they have an option. Jenny is late to the table and is enjoying her new role close to the CSCI team. She must provide output for her network and keep a cameraman busy, but she feels this is the big story, and being mercenary she doesn't mind which way it goes.

"The sex trafficking story is remarkably quiet this morning; I could have used what we have as an exclusive," she bugs them.

"You could run something today, but it'll work better tomorrow," Hunter says.

"What will that be?" Jenny probes.

"Thursday. Thursday always follows Wednesday."

"You know what I mean."

"An exclusive and no one will work out how you got it. I haven't yet."

Jenny looks at him and knows a plan is being hatched. She expects to have tomorrow's story as an exclusive. "This seems sudden."

"We're sitting targets, with others on the onslaught. I don't like that. Tomorrow it is," Hunter says. "You both got passports?"

They both nod.

"Carry them. Do you get jet lag?"

Neither indicates they do but Hunter has them more puzzled.

"Get some sleep," he finishes as he begins to share the setup.

Outside, Dennis has an idea as they stride to his van, "Venice?"

"It has to be, but what has he got up his sleeve?"

"We don't need to know 'til tomorrow; we'll be the only ones there."

With Jenny gone the team can try and put things in place that will work. Hunter is drawing boxes and working out the time zone effect on his plan. Dwight has called Prisha. Speaking with her is easy now she is in charge.

"Hi, Dwight," she says cheerfully to her handler.

"You well?"

"Very. I am training staff who have come up from maintenance. All male. No one has contacted me."

"You have nothing to trade if you only have men. I have Hunter for you."

"Good afternoon Prisha."

"Well, it is evening here Mr Hunter."

"Did you get the chance to see Zadar."

"I have seen it many times, sir."

"Prisha, I'm the last person you call sir. Do you have any uniforms in the laundry?"

"We always have uniforms in the laundry, Mr Witowski, sir."

"Are you worried about something?"

"I am a little worried about being by myself."

"Stop worrying. And call me Hunter. I want you to find the highest grade uniform your size, take it and two others, large. Be ready to leave the ship early tomorrow morning in Venice."

Hunter ends the call and looks at Dwight concerned, "She's worried."

"She'll be fine."

"Can you remember your first solo mission?" Hunter asks.

"I don't wanna remember any of my missions," Dwight says.

Croc and Hunter follow Dwight through to the diner. Mary is serving the few late lunch customers and Stan is cooking to a rhythm only he can hear, but as always, he is the happiest man in the room.

"Stan, three big boys' plates," Dwight shouts. Dwight certainly is quite a frame. Whether he was thinner before he was put in the chair, no one knows. No one is going to ask. Like the rest of the team, their service career is relatively unknown.

"If we start to hit road bumps, we're a little light. I want you to bring in that pal of yours, Big Dog. I like the sound of him," Hunter says.

"Oh no. No way."

"Oh yes. We use locals all the time when out in the field."

"He doesn't work in fields. Trust me, you ain't never worked with anyone like him."

Dwight laughs as the food is put down.

"Tell him, Stan, you met him," Croc says.

"I ain't telling him nothing. Big Dog ain't so big. Mary pinned him to that wall."

"I tamed 'im and took all his stash. He's no different from gang leaders all over the world, Croc," Dwight adds.

"If you're so confident, Dwight, why you got the Uzi under your chair with the trigger on a chord?" Hunter jokes.

"Coz it can't blow my legs off, and it ain't for him. It's for the real problem."

"You sure the real problem's here in Miami? Who?" Croc pleads, annoyed that he is one step behind.

Hunter pushes his plate away. Dwight's starts to eat. Mary returns to bug them.

"When am I going to get another one of those envelopes in the post? In case your credit starts to run out."

"I'm sure it's not Mary."

"Sure is. You guys are on VIP rate."

Hunter puts his hand inside his jacket and pulls out an envelope which already has Mary written on it. She smiles.

"There's gonna be times when I ain't gonna be able to do that," Hunter says. She is still drilling through him with a wanting look that edges towards her boy Croc.

"What?" Hunter asks.

"Guess what I'm gonna ask?" Croc says.

Hunter stops him,

"Soon as you bring all your ID in, we'll open you a bank account."

Croc stands.

"Finish your food," Hunter says. "Then find Big Dog. Tell him there's an envelope for him."

"He gets one before me?"

"Croc, I'm going home for an hour."

"Give Elaine my wishes," Croc says.

75 THERAPY

1930 hrs – Zadar.

Hotel rooms are the same most places in the world. The room they have in Zadar city on the mainland is no exception. However, it is a hotel room and not a cruise cabin so Bedi is excited. She opens bag after bag of clothes enthusiastically; not just hers, but new outfits for Kieron. It looks like they could be staying a week, but it is one special night off duty, as long as an assassin doesn't find them. She is as keen to see Kieron looking different as she is to dress up herself for a night out.

After spending time pampering and preparing for dinner they both know the event will be special. This is not just a ship formal night where you dress, eat, then go back to sleep. This is an adventure. They stroll together along the waterfront looking at each of the restaurants, having made the promise that they will not make their final choice until the walk back.

Sitting outside in the warm air, on a table that presents them to the water, they both enjoy the magic of a menu with the words fresh and catch of the day.

"I thought you would want to go to the staging hotel where we think the women are kept," he tests.

"No. I learn it not easy. They don't want rescue from impressive ship job, they go to great big dream. I understand to have dream. But."

"And I don't think we could get away with a messy message again."

"I know."

The waiter stands over them.

"I want steak, rare, I want to see blood," she says.

"Grilled jumbo shrimps with garlic, please."

The waiter bows and leaves. They toast their wine glasses.

"Promise me, the women getting on ship tomorrow are not a concern for you."

"Not yet."

"And the women getting off, when they do, are an Interpol problem. We're after key organisation members and their cell phones to wedge the wound open wider," Kieron gently insists.

"You need to work on man-wife relationship, no?"

Kieron looks puzzled.

"We talk work tomorrow," she says.

"Do you like this wine?" he asks.

"No. I want large vodka. You drink that shit."

"Very romantic."

"Put vodka in wine glass, that romantic.

Kieron turns to the waiter,

"Can you bring a bottle of vodka."

Within seconds the waiter is there, and he pours a generous measure of vodka.

"No, fill. And ice," she says.

Kieron has a chair against the door with a cup and saucer on. He has empty bottles from the minibar balanced at each window. He starts to undress, having no problems being naked in bed with Bedi; it feels like they have been doing it forever. He folds his clothes and places them on the chair. The room is lit by one bedside light until the en-suite door opens and Bedi comes out in the garment from the market. Something so simple, so minimal, does wonders for her perfect figure.

She kisses him, "Don't." She stops and asserts control. "Tonight, be my friend. Maybe, I do something to help me. Maybe. I trust you are friend."

Kieron and Bedriška lay in each other's arms, post-coital. Both are very thoughtful.

"Georgie was my first romance," she says. "We not expect it. Georgie never been with woman. I just happen."

"I feel guilty."

"Maybe I ask you to feel guilty again in the morning."

"Let's not," he says softly.

"I have complicated past. You have been friend. Georgie has been friend."

"Bjorn said something to Hunter. He wanted Hunter and me to be the couple."

"What Bjorn say?"

"Sexuality is a scale from heterosexual to homosexual with no need for rigidity."

"It no help with my head. You can't see mess in my head. Don't try."

76 BIG DOG

Dog is impatiently propping up the wall in the shadows of a downtown apartment block with his hood up. He is watching Hunter and Croc fail to get in. Hunter is the one who looks out of place. Croc is trying to make an app on his cell be more accurate.

"This is the building," Croc says.

"That the best you can do?" Hunter punishes.

"Soul bro, you sayin' me stride da-way 'cross town and yer no idea wag-we-gwan?"

"The battery on my real cell is dead."

"There's gotta be sixty apartments in there," Hunter assesses.

Big Dog wags his head at the failure. Three young women leave, and Hunter mounts the steps and holds the door open for them and himself.

"Wha gwan sister, yah know da new gay-ass at?" Dog asks.

"Fifteen."

"Shukrun."

Big Dog walks up the steps and enters as Hunter keeps the door open.

"Fuck da tech shit. They in number 15."

Croc enters last, "I did get us this far."

"No point getting da pants down if yer can't raid da pussy. Just sayin' bro."

They stand outside door fifteen and Hunter knocks.

"Open up Chet, it's Hunter."

Big Dog kicks the door in. The other two look at him.

"What?" Dog asks.

Chet peers from the bedroom scared,

"Is the door broken?" he panics.

"To be honest it wasn't doing much," Croc offers.

"It's our safety barrier."

Dog lifts the door up,

"Sure?"

"You lied to us," Hunter starts.

"We were in trouble. Big trouble. They'll kill us."

"Who?" Hunter demands.

"That was what you were supposed to find out," Chet defends.

"Then you should have told us that."

"We couldn't contract you for something that wasn't a crime. We invented a bogus crime knowing you'd see the real one. Obvious, duh!"

Big Dog is looking around the apartment. Croc is looking to retrieve his phone from the bicycle pouch.

"Where's my cell?"

"On the table, we had no idea whose it was."

"And you never thought it was dropped so you could be followed? How have you survived this long?" Hunter asks.

"Yeah?" Big Dog mumbles, picking up a garish cycle helmet.

"You put the plants on each ship?" Hunter asks.

"Free cruise and spending money, that cost us nothing. It doesn't even come off our budget; it's marketing."

"I wanna get me one-a-dem cruises," Big Dog says.

"Me too," Croc adds.

"What dey do?" Dog asks.

"Each couple cause enough trouble, at regular intervals for it to be a recurring problem. Then we could allocate a budget to cure it." Chet insists.

"Trouble! Yer lookin' at the Dog. I mess a place up real good. At regular intervals."

"We thought it was rather a good plan."

"Rather!" Big Dog mocks his accent and choice of posh words. "Rather! Why didn't it work den?"

Chet has no answer.

"All you had to do was tell us what we were really looking for, the truth," Hunter explains.

"We didn't know, we still don't know," Chet whimpers.

"All we knew was something was wrong. Staff, mainly female, started leaving all three ships too often," Bjorn says standing in the doorway with a fresh French stick of bread. "Something was terribly wrong. Could have been gambling, it could have been drugs, truth told. What we didn't like was: we got promoted to run those ships. Now it seems not because we were thought worthy, but because someone thought we were stupid. They got that wrong."

"Yeah? Sound like yer is," Dog grins. "Dumb ass."

"You were being used, so you used us," Hunter says.

"You were meant to solve it, you were very well paid," Bjorn smiles, insisting he is right.

"You know Bjorn, I don't like you. A taxi driver put a gun in my face, and I have a baby on the way. The other two in the team had professionals try to take them out. They're still in danger. What's that price?"

"We're not working there now, we can't change the contract," Chet says.

"You took too long," Bjorn scolds.

"One more word from you and you'll be wearing my fist. Did you not hear me say I didn't like your arrogance?" Hunter repeats, walking towards Bjorn who backs off into the hall.

"Strikes me, whoever was trying to take our guys out, will try and hit you," Croc levels at Chet and Bjorn.

"We know. We feel it," Chet says.

"Our team dodged the bullets because it's what they do. You guys won't stand a chance."

"S'over," Dog says, relaxing in a chair. "You should share out your jewels."

"Can't you protect us?" Chet asks.

"That's not our contract, and we don't know who's trying to hit on you. Plus, I ain't armed," Hunter says.

"Ha," Big Dog breathes out as he stands abruptly. He opens his coat and drops his hood. "I carry 'nough to share."

"Dog. Zip up, man." Croc says.

Hunter sees the firepower that he expected was there. He turns to the executives.

"Look, you need to run through every detail with us, because somewhere, you'll know something. Something you've been too stupid to use."

"Nah man, dese guys is super dumb," Dog says.

"What made them choose you two?" Croc asks.

Chet is embarrassed and Bjorn annoyed. They look at each other as if there is more they are hiding. Hunter grabs the bread from Bjorn and tosses it across the room.

"We had debts," Chet admits frightened.

"Debts?"

"Gambling, playing."

"And you didn't think to tell us; just threw us into danger."

"We're in danger. We can't stay here. They'll kill us."

Hunter walks towards the door, he has had enough. He stops by Dog and leans in.

"Find out who they were gambling with, then wrap them up and take them back to the unit," Hunter waves his arms in despair and leaves in a temper. His evening is over.

77 DOTS AND TIES

0900hrs-Venice

Day thirteen of the cruise and the MS Magi Myrrh is berthed in Venice early, where it will have an overnight stay as the guests change-over once again. Prisha has three large folding uniform bags with three suits and hats inside. It makes for a bulky and suspicious carriage off the ship. If asked, she has her story ready; 'she is the laundry supervisor and is going to a facility on land'. She is not stopped, and she walks straight down the gangway and makes for the red T1 tram.

The automated tram moves people from the cruise basin into Piazzale Roma, which is the bus and taxi transport centre. The two are close and walking - even with her load - may have been possible but the tram is quicker and makes it simple.

After the tram, she walks swiftly over the bridge and along the canal where Venice and its glory become a feast for the eye, not least the church just beyond the modern Venezia Santa Lucia Train Station. She passes hotel after hotel, all with waterside alfresco dining areas across the narrow front walkway. It is not long before she turns in as directed to the Hotel Antiche Figure. She wonders how the wooden counter and dark wood ceiling of this 15th-century palace go with the floor. That is not her concern; Miami is asleep, so she can rest for now even though it is unlikely she will relax.

1000hrs – Zadar.

Bedi has been waiting for Kieron to wake up.

"Thank you," she says, and she slides out of bed. "I got breakfast."

"I am glad to have been the chosen therapist," he says, a little miffed, and hardly moving.

"I'm not sure you helped. But it was an experience."

"Should we find a chemist?"

"Why, you have disease?" She asks him.

"No. Risk of pregnancy."

Bedi throws a bowl of cereal all over him. Her face changes.

Mid-afternoon, a stream of guests is returning to the MS Magi Gold, watched by a small contingent of Interpol agents and police. It is a token force following yesterday's arrests on the first ship. Waiting at the bottom of the gangway, Kieron and Bedi form a far more convincing husband and wife team than previously. They are given their cruise cards and embark. In the cabin, they dump their bags and leave to explore the new ship. They have no idea what they are looking for, but they will know when they find it. After walking the length of the promenade deck, they pass a pub-like bar then into the atrium. They stop at photography.

"These guys never know what they capture by accident. But it's too much work to check every picture," Kieron says, remembering the work done to place each guest on a timeline to catch the serial killer on his last assignment.

They pass a lounge bar and arrive at the theatre where the water-tight doors are firmly closed. Kieron turns to Bedi,

"Why are they locked?"

"Tonight's act will be rehearsing," she explains. "Last day of holiday, it will be big act."

"Is there another way in?"

"Deck below, corridor to offices under theatre seats. We go past entertainments' office; it will be empty."

"Why?"

"Sail away party, then rest and dress for evening. Entertainers rest when spa works. Always problem for me and Georgie."

Kieron takes the stairs and Bedi follows. The lower large flood doors are also closed but not locked. They are heavy but Bedi pulls them open with ease and lets him through. He enters to hear a heated row going on. They follow the cacophony to the entertainment office where the door is open.

"What's going on?" he asks, finding a couple in a full-blown argument.

"Who are you?" A confident female demands. She snatches papers from a black-suited round man with a moustache. Kieron steps forward,

"Head Office Security, checking all grades for problems that have got out of hand. This is out of hand."

Kieron takes the papers out of her hands without any resistance. They are pages of musical dots.

"You know I'm tonight's act."

Kieron nods.

"I stayed after rehearsal and followed him in here."

Kieron can see he is the musical director from his badge. He looks at him for his story.

"I needed copies," he defends.

"There is no need for extra copies. He is stealing my parts. They cost me thousands, and years of getting it wrong."

"Some would say you still get it wrong," the musical director insults.

"Stop," Bedi demands. "Apologise."

The Musical Director says nothing.

"Apologise now."

The MD says nothing.

"What instrument you play?"

"Piano," the MD replies.

Bedi kicks him in his knee and he collapses to the ground.

"Apologise."

"Sorry."

"If you not on-stage tonight, and playing your best, I will find you."

"Where is your staff badge?" he demands still on the floor. Her reply is to kick his other leg.

"Why would he steal copies?" Kieron asks.

"Sadly, it's a widespread practice. MD's steal parts, then they can sell them to new acts. To dancers and singers who think they can make it solo."

"Don't do this. It's theft," Kieron says to the MD. Then he turns to the singer. "Are you pressing charges?"

She shakes her head, no.

"Then we are finished here. We will make no report."

"Report mean end of contract," Bedi points out to the Musician.

"We weren't here, you have no idea who we are, but rest assured we can be back," Kieron says, walking past them.

The two agents continue their search around the stage, down the rear stairs and outside into the crew area behind the stage.

Late afternoon in Venice, Prisha wakes, feeling like a princess in her Venetian four-poster bed. She tries to comprehend how such wealth has always existed when her family all lived in a room half the size of this room. Her orders from CSCI, her new employer, are not to stray too far from her hotel, so she will comply, as tempting as Venice is. Guests from her ship the MS Magi Myrrh will be exploring Venice tonight on their overnight stop. She looks over at the three uniforms she has hanging on the closet doors. She has no idea what the plan is, but she will no doubt be told when it is time.

Feeling energised and rested after a few ridiculous days of work under Oona, this is such a release. She looks at the palatial bathroom and opens the shower. This is going to be her next luxury. Then, she will try and find a terrace, eat, and watch Venice as the sun goes down over these strange buildings.

1005hrs - Miami

Hunter is at home with Elaine, reading Kieron and Bedi's last report confirming them as tourists in Zadar. He looks at his watch and knows their ship will soon be leaving Zadar for Venice.

Croc should have gone home after his night shift, but the beds and sofas are full. Yesterday should have been an easy day but it ended up with a late-night pow-wow with Dog drilling into Chet and Bjorn. Dog does not do reports, so Croc spent hours taking care of that. They are all asleep now in the expanding domestic area behind the screens.

Dwight is in enjoying his breakfast at the screens in the operations room. His shift has just started, and he checks everything from the day before then the overnight report,

"Ain't smelling as fresh in here now it's a hotel."

"Not a lot to see there," Croc says, seeing Dwight studying his report.

"That's when I go back and read between the lines."

"Still not much there."

"I know, it's all about to happen, right?"

"What? When? Today? What's the plan?"

It is nearly time for the MS Magi Gold to sail in the Adriatic Sea, and little has come in from the pair other than a text to say they boarded the ship. It is heading for Venice, a day behind the MS Magi Myrrh. Tomorrow they will berth together. Hunter spent the night with his wife in uptown Miami, worried about the hornets' nest they are about to poke. He and Elaine have a nursery to decorate and start the day on an extensive shopping trip.

A burner phone starts to ring, Croc instinctively moves to the line of cell phones with labels and brief notes. This one is Maxwell's, head of security on the Myrrh staying in Venice. A second ring. He looks to Dwight who nods. A third ring. Croc's hand hovers over it.

"What do I say?"

It stops ringing.

"Too late," Croc admits in defeat.

"Could be a code. Three rings probably means ring me back," Dwight suggests. "Bonus; an unexpected breakthrough."

"That simple? Do I ring it back?"

"No. But we need to use the code wisely and fast. On your connections, there is a cell phone on both the other two ships."

"Two on each ship!" Croc says, knowing he is not going to get much sleep, that's if he could, Chet is in his bed.

"Let's hit the Gold in Zadar, we have two agents on board. Ring those cells. Three rings, stop. Then call again. An emergency call, brief, panic them to get off the ship now!"

"Why?"

"Say, Interpol is boarding the ship and looking for you. Get off fast," Dwight says.

"I mean, why are we doing this?"

"We have a chance to clean the Magi Gold out before it sails."

"We should wait for Hunter."

"No time, it sails soon."

"But if it goes wrong, and they realise Kieron and Bedi are with CSCI, they'll kill them."

"No, I'll warn them," Dwight defends.

"And how do we catch anyone if they just run off the ship?" Croc pokes.

"Interpol is there. They do that. Kieron and Bedi should get facial images."

"I want the bandits cell phones, not pictures of them. And that puts our agents in danger," Croc insists. "This is not thought through."

Big Dog has woken and has crept around behind Croc and is listening.

1630 hrs - berthed in Zadar

Kieron is on his cell phone but visually fixed on a door held closed with tape. On the outside of the door is a fire hose. He opens the door and looks behind it. A security guard finds them.

"Who are you?"

"We sail in about fifteen minutes," Kieron says into his cell and hangs up to talk to the guard.

"Heavy hose on the outside of this door could make it swing open at any time and take someone out. Huge safety risk. Nothing holding it closed except tape. You should notice that on your rounds. Get it mended."

Kieron walks on. The guard follows them.

"Hey. Excuse me. Sir, can I ask who you are?"

"You asked."

Kieron and Bedi walk down towards the laundry and they find the laundry storeroom and open it. There are no humans imprisoned in there, but there are cable ties around pieces of shelving at the height where women may have been held. He turns to the security officer,

"Put your camera on. And pass me an evidence bag."

The officer does as directed; he switches his camera on and takes out a transparent plastic evidence bag. Cameras permanently record but only store footage when requested. Kieron wants this stored. He cuts the cable ties and drops them in the evidence bag without touching them.

"What are they?" the guard asks.

"This was a prison."

The security guard looks totally puzzled. Kieron looks at his watch.

"You have no idea who we are or why we're here?" Kieron asks checking his watch again. "Just as you have no idea what's been going on, on your ship."

The security guard indicates no. Kieron knows he is a safe companion and he picks up his mobile.

"OK Dwight, mission agreed, go for it. I'll be at the gangway in five."

"Follow us," Bedi says to the puzzled guard.

78 GET OUT

1150 - Miami   1650 – Zada.

In the dark operations room, time is once again irrelevant, though it is late morning there, afternoon in Zadar. Big Dog is watching with interest; he may wear a hood and walk with an offbeat dance step, but he is smart. A ring tone distracts them: one, then a second ring. Dwight looks across to Croc,

"Wait."

There is a third ring and it stops. Each second seems a lifetime. Croc stares at the phone.

"The call is from the MS Gold. Should I ring back?" he checks.

"Man said wait," Dog agrees. He is way cooler.

Maxwell's burner rings and Croc's hand darts out. Dog is quicker to stop him,

"Wait, bro!"

One ring set, two, three. Dwight nods, Dog takes his hand away.

"Go, bro,"

Croc answers and reads from the rehearsed sheet.

"You've been made. Get off the ship, now. Interpol is about to swarm the ship. Get off. You only have a few minutes." Croc hangs up.

"That was very posh," Dwight says wheeling away.

"Yeah. Yer def the whitest man here, coconut," Dog mocks.

"You're forgetting those two," Croc says pointing to Chet and Bjorn sleeping in the growing dormitory at the back.

"Serious? They no count."

"What's a coconut?"

"Dark outside, white inside."

Dwight sends to Kieron and Bedi, 'message delivered'. He then updates Hunter.

Kieron looks out at the badly disguised Interpol officers posted at various places around the dock, looking obvious. If you weren't looking for them, you might never notice them. A few last guests climb the gangway. There is always an officer at the bottom visually checking cruise cards before going up to computerised check-in. The female officer is doing that greeting process with a smile. A male officer is by the refreshment table, just in front of her, delivering wisecracks as well as welcome messages. Everything looks far too normal.

A fast boat noisily speeds up to the rear of the ship with an expert 180-degree parking manoeuvre. Kieron goes for his phone,

"It's a water escape. Fast boat."

He is still waiting for someone to leave the ship, but there is no sign of anyone. He looks down the gangway against the stream of returning guests. All Kieron can do is video everyone and watch the gangway.

Interpol officers run from the cover of the buildings towards the fast motorboat. It triggers the two officers at the bottom of the gangway; the wise-cracking officer and the female officer checking cards. Kieron was right to video them; they are now sprinting the length of the ship to the aft. They and the Interpol officers are in a race to get to the fast boat first and justice won't win this one.

"Dwight, I see two, one male and one female, headed for a fast boat. They will be gone within a minute. Interpol needs water and air cover. I have pictures but no chance of their cell phones."

Kieron Philips rushes down the gangway, past cruisers who complain at being roughly disturbed. Bedi is closing fast. Even if they can get there quickly, nothing will stop the boat. They need a fast boat, but all the boats are outside the secure area and they are trapped inside.

Kieron stands on the bank looking out. Cell phone to ear,

"A blue Princess 58, number 543 I think, but can't read letters, maybe DCS," he relays, but he feels helpless. "I wouldn't mind betting that boat's been used for trafficking and drug smuggling. It is well tooled up."

Bedi is by the fence shouting to a boat to aid them, and within seconds she is joined by a uniformed police officer. With officers waving, it throws more weight, though the boat owner is less likely to get paid by the police. Eventually, the new boat arcs around and several police and Interpol officers clamber on. Kieron and Bedriška realise it will never catch the bigger boat with the throaty engines. They remain on the side and watch as it powers in the same direction.

"Not our job now," she says.

"Correct."

"Or do you mean there are no women on board?"

"Correct."

Zadar, more than most places in the world, is made for someone in a fast boat to disappear. Like Stockholm, it offers a network of islands. Opposite are the two biggest islands, separated by a water channel and joined by the Ždrelac bridge. If the two criminals have not changed boats by now, they will do soon. There is little chance of finding them. The agents walk slowly back towards the ship, realising they have an audience.

"Anything you need on the ship? We're getting out," Kieron asks, seeing new orders.

"My new clothes. Your new clothes."

Prisha sits on the roof terrace of the Hotel Carlton next door to her historic hotel. She is looking at both the menu and the very distracting list of carnival events. It is like the daily newspaper on the cruise ship, full of options from the Venice Carnival to Valentine's day. She would have ordered her dinner in a blaze of autopilot had the waiter not spent so much time being helpful.

Her cocktail arrives and he is keen to ensure she has a good evening.

"I see you are mesmerised by the façade of the church of Santa Maria di Nazareth opposite."

"I am."

"You must look inside. The art is from one of our Venetian artists, Tiepolo. It is Beautiful."

"I will."

He leaves and she looks down to the water taxis and the rippling reflections. She then concentrates on her drink, because she knows very well that she will have no time to see it on this trip. She refers to her cell to read her preliminary orders again. They ask if she feels up to their demands. She smiles, sips her cocktail, and knows she is determined to make everything work despite the risks. She will not fail. Prisha wants to continue working for CSCI.

79 SLEEPOVER

2000hrs-Miami   0100hrs-Croatia

It is 1 am in Europe and the time of the night when the bars on the ship are closed to all except those in the disco which stays open till one, two or three - minutes past midnight. That is the joke on all ships using a well-timed pause. Few cruisers can stay up dancing after a hectic day. Cruising is a full day. The DJ can often get to bed early because the disco is empty, which is good because during the day he is the sports' host.

Bedriška and Kieron Philips are extremely comfortable flying at 35,000 feet as the only passengers in a private jet. The big plan needs them back in Miami and they are flying nine hours but turning the clocks back as they cross datelines. Now, it is 8 pm in Florida.

"You been in one of these before?" he asks.

"Yes. Not good memory. You?"

"The military version, no decorations, no seats."

They land in Miami just after 3am, and as Bedi does not have a residence there she will either get a hotel or stay with Kieron. The latter seems natural now. The taxi drops the two weary travellers off with the new bags that Bedi managed to rescue from the ship. They have little time but fall onto the bed, exhausted.

1150hrs-Miami – pre-lunch

Wild Mary walks into the operations room and instantly notices the higher body count, "What going on?"

"Not now Mary, I need to sleep," Croc says wearily.

Mary walks over to his bed, heaves the mattress up. Chet spins out and bounces on the floor, "Hey!"

"I'll give you hey, sleeping in my boy Croc's bed."

Dwight wheels round, "Mary, you just reminded me it's lunchtime. I'm gonna join you next door. The only place a man can get some privacy."

Dwight wags his head for Dog to follow.

"Oh, you're back, are you?" Mary says to Dog.

"Hi, Ma."

She looks at him wondering where he fits in.

Dog and Dwight settle at the table.

"I think we should get a safe fitted," Dwight says.

"Why, yer heavy?"

Mary pulls Croc out and sits him down. He lays his head on the table.

"I was thinking of somewhere for you to hang your coat up."

"Me good."

Hunter enters and sits with them. Greetings exchanged and with a wave to Stan, his order is in.

"Are the two clowns next door?" he asks.

"Mary just woke 'em up, they'll be ages in the bathroom."

Hunter turns to Big Dog, "Who they owe money to?"

"Nasty guys we don't need in Miami."

"Who?" Dwight asks.

"Albo mafia."

"How do they owe money to Albanians?" Hunter asks.

"Clubs, man. Dangerous. Cocktails at da front, gambling, and drugs at da back. Draw you in, shit you out. Start you low, take you high. Stake card games where you win, get yous confident, think yer the man, and bang, lose big time," Dog explains.

"But why these idiots?" Hunter asks.

"Cocaine idiots," Croc adds without raising his head.

"For sure. Dey work, dey got cash, cruise boys were set-up man."

"Easy to set up for the trafficking," Dwight adds.

"For sure."

"How much they in for?" Hunter asks.

"We ain't inside no albo mob. But size don't matter, they got'em, ain't no way out."

"Croc, you have a passport?"

"No man, I ain't never been out of Miami. But I got you my ID."

"Dog, you got one?"

"Got three, all work. Never been stopped."

"He ain't gonna get a cruise before me" Croc panics. "I'll get a passport."

"The fastest we can get you a passport is three weeks, and we need you to fly tonight," Dwight explains.

"I can get him a passport in hours," Dog says.

"Why does that not surprise me?" Hunter grins.

"And if you're gonna fly with him, we need that gun-safe for your jacket," Dwight repeats.

"Dwight, call Jenny in for this evening with her man and a small travel camera. Both need passports and she needs them on an employment letter for the whole crew. Venice and back. Dog, sort some passports. Croc, we're going for a walk; you OK outside in daylight?" Hunter asks him.

80 CROC'S BUSY ID

Miami mid-afternoon

Having walked two blocks towards the main road, Hunter opens the outer door to the bank on the corner and Croc goes in first. Isaiah Success, the security guard, takes over holding it, and greets them. A few weeks ago, they were in and he remembers Hunter.

"Thank you, Isaiah, this is my new guy, Croc."

"Hey Croc."

There is a slap, then a bump of the hands to show each other they are local.

"Good move Mr Witowski, swapping out the fashion disaster for a local boy."

"Oh, I've still got Mr Philips."

"I hope someone new is dressing him."

Croc coughs, restraining his laughter, then turns to look at the huge retro wooden bank.

"This looks like an old railway station, but it can't be old. Miami ain't that old," Croc says.

He follows Hunter to the window nearest to the office door, and the big wooden door opens.

"Mr Ron Stone. I brought someone special to meet you."

The manager, Mr Stone, shakes hands with Croc who is blown away.

"Name's Croc, Sir."

"Nice to meet you, Croc."

"I never knew it was so easy to walk into a bank, I'd've become a bank robber."

Mr Stone looks at Croc with worry.

"Just joking, man."

"Mr Dwight Ritter rang to say you were coming back."

"Yeah. Dwight runs our place."

"I should meet him sometime So, Mr Witowski, how can we help? Or is it you, Croc?"

Croc hesitates. Hunter nods.

"I wanna open a bank account, please."

"Our pleasure. Come through Croc. Now, I'd like to know your full name."

"Me too," Croc says.

"Ha. Ha. Funny. Ron Stone stops when he notices that no one else is laughing.

Hunter looks down at Croc, who produces his ID card. The bank manager looks at it,

"I'll get the forms, Winston Crockett. Good strong name; after 'the King of the Wild Frontier' no doubt."

"Er, I dunno about that, but certainly not my dad, no one knows who he was."

The manager nods, "well, your mother chose a great name."

"No one knows who she was either."

The manager gets the forms.

"I need a small deposit to open the account," the manager starts, then hesitates. "And some ID."

Croc looks worried, he starts to go through his pockets, but he only has chump change and his Miami State ID card. Hunter produces an envelope and a staff letter. The manager looks at the envelope.

"It's under the limit," Hunter says to relax him.

The manager nods, thanking him for knowing the restrictions, and he passes it to the teller who opens the envelope and puts it on the counting machine. Croc is mesmerised by it all.

"And I need an address just here."

Croc looks up at Mr Stone, defeated again, then to Hunter.

"You want to use my address at Coral Gables or the diner?"

"The diner. That's kinda like my real home."

Croc hasn't spoken since he saw the huge wad of cash. He and Hunter walk the two blocks from the bank to their unit in the almost closed commercial park. The change in a neighbourhood within such a short walk from the main road to a forgotten commercial champion of yesterday is a sad reflection on the speed society discards yesterday's fashions and styles.

"I ain't never had a bank account. It ain't just for you to hide money, is it?"

"No, it's yours and you earned it. This whole case has been about cell phones. You've been amazing. We'll get you put you on the payroll. Where did you learn to hack like that?"

"I used to work part-time at a small place down on 33rd, unlocking phones."

They turn the corner and the car park is a little busier. A van and a limo are amongst the few usual customer cars. They walk into the diner and Big Dog is waiting for them, grinning. He drops the passport on the counter. Croc opens it and cannot believe it.

"I gotta bank account and a passport!"

Mary is smiling; he is special to her. She looks at the receipt that he is proud of.

"How much? Don't you go getting any lofty ideas, Winston Crockett."

"Winston!" Izzy screams in laughter.

He ignores her, moving next door into the operations room.

"Waz-up? Smell like a perfume shop in here?" Croc quips.

Izzy enters behind Croc and smells him as a joke.

"Ain't us," a large-set workman says brandishing an electric drill like you might a gun. She puts it on the top of a large safe and she and her partner rock the heavy metal cabinet over the holes. It is tilted up with a large bolt hanging down which is lined up and screwed into the floor, then the one at the other corner is found. The nuts are tightened with the drill and it is bolted in.

Chet and Bjorn are washed and presentable but not in suits. They approach Hunter.

"Did you find out who is behind all this?" Chet worries.

Hunter smiles a look which might say 'of course I did' but he's not going to tell.

"Please, you have to search them out and kill them before they kill us," Bjorn demands.

"Not what we do," Hunter insists.

"It is, it was why we hired you."

"You hired us for a crime on a ship, Miami-Dade police deal with land-based crimes."

"But..." Bjorn stutters.

"You guys have suits with you?"

Sheepishly, they both indicate yes..

"Passports?"

They nod.

"Letters of employment, company passes?"

"Yes, why?" asks Chet.

Hunter turns to Dwight, "Where's Jenny?"

"Due any minute."

"I saw the limo outside," Hunter relays. "Plane?"

"On the runway."

"Let's go," Hunter demands and watches them leave through the CSCI door. Chet and Bjorn are last, but Big Dog lets the door swing and they must open it again.

From the doorway, Dwight watches them load the limo, "I don't like those two smart executives. I've no second thoughts about using them as bait. They would watch us be killed to save their asses."

81 SAFE IN

Kieron Philips and Bedriška arrive at the CSCI unit and enter through the front as the workers who fitted the safe are leaving. They are seeing the new operations centre for the first time.

"Wow!" Kieron says.

"You never see this?" Bedi asks him.

"No, when we took over the unit, we flooded it –"

"Why?"

"He did it," Kieron says, pointing at Hunter.

"Which is my desk?" she asks.

"You want a desk?" Hunter asks.

"Sure."

"Take the one at the end," Dwight says, offering his hand. "Dwight Ritter." Bedi does a lazy hi-five slap.

"Dwight, you good point man."

"Thanks, Bedriška. I've always got your back."

She sits at her desk; Dwight helps her with a login and shows her what is available.

"How you lose your legs?"

"Tripwire in a house. We were sent in on bad intel, the house was a minefield."

"Shit!"

She looks at the screen with him.

Hunter looks around in surprise. "You've never told me that much about yourself!"

"You ever ask him?" Bedi challenges.

"No, he never asked me," Dwight says, concentrating on Bedi and the screen.

"Why it smell like prostitute parlour?"

"The two young executives who hired us are staying here. Do you need to bunk as well?" Dwight offers.

"No, I sleep with Kieron. Show me cell phone connections."

She looks with interest at the connections between the cell phones while Hunter pulls Kieron into the diner for a coffee.

"The shit is back here in Miami," she says.

"We know."

Kieron walks through into the diner where Mary is always a huge presence.

"You gonna hug yer ma," Wild Mary asks of Kieron, her arms open wide. The greeting is affectionate on both sides.

"Steady, lover boy. Mary, he's dangerous with women," Hunter mocks, sitting down.

"Long time since I had a dangerous man."

Hunter sits next to Kieron at the bar.

"Bedi's great, but is she unstable?" Hunter asks.

"I'll pass on your good wishes," Kieron says.

Bedi marches in to join them and she sits next to Kieron. She leans in.

"We forgot chemist."

82 FOUR-POSTER BED

0600hrs-Venice

It is hard to imagine the effect of the travel on Croc, or for that matter on Big Dog. Neither has ever left the neighbourhood despite Dog's boasting. The downside of this high-end luxury private plane means Croc will have no idea what a normal passenger airliner looks or feels like. Even going through the airport is different. Sadly, for them, they must stay sober, the free bar is closed. The trip back they are all hoping might be a different story, though they fear other plans are already forming for Miami.

Chet and Bjorn are enjoying the luxury but will not allow themselves to admit any wrongdoing. Jenny-E and her cameraman know they will be rushed to find time to edit and upload reports. They will fly back on the same plane and Miami will wake up to the press coup she is about to film because the rest of the world will rebroadcast it.

Croc, Dog, Chet, and Bjorn rush from the airport to the Venice train. The short journey ends at a station almost on the water's edge. They follow Jenny to the bank. It is still dark and reflections paint pictures on the still water.

Croc is amazed, "What is this, Atlantis?"

"No, Venice, but called the Queen of Atlantis," Jenny explains.

"I thought Venice was a beach," Dog quips.

Croc takes a picture, "Macey gotta see this."

Jenny leans down to one of the few night-shift Gondoliers.

"I need to get to the other side."

He is keen for them all to get in.

"In dat?" Big Dog asks.

"Yes," Jenny nods, wondering what the problem is.

"Me neither," Croc supports.

"Da water?" Dog questions. He looks along to the bridge. "See you on the other side."

Dog walks off followed by Croc, while Jenny and her cameraman step into the boat, helped by the two executives. They are paddled across.

In her bright white officer's uniform, Prisha waits for them inside reception checking her watch regularly. She knows the second ship is due to dock early, at around 7 am. The earlier the better, but time is tight.

When they arrive, there is no time for niceties. Croc salutes her. She hurries all six upstairs to the room.

"Wow. Do we get to sleep here?" Croc asks in amazement when he sees the room. "I ain't never seen anyt'ing like dis."

"You don't get to sleep here, put these on," Prisha says.

"You 'ave any other colours?" Dog asks.

"No, it's an officer's uniform. Wear it."

Croc and Dog dress.

"Cruise cards," Prisha says, handing them cards. "They're all out of date, won't get you on the ship, but will get you past customs. Customs guards never know what they are looking at," she stops to inspect them and straighten things up. "You look very good."

Big Dog pushes her hand away.

"I'm good, bitch."

"You don't ever call me that again," she says as hard as nails.

Prisha finishes her inspection of them, then checks her watch.

"Follow me. They need to think we got off the ship and work for the company."

Prisha looks to Dennis, cameraman for approval. He nods to the plan.

"Jenny comes to us, asking for a quote. She will be shouting loud for the two executives," she continues.

Jenny nods; this is her area of expertise and takes over, "When one press runs in, the rest follow, especially when they see me getting an interview," Jenny explains. "Interview done, we duck the local press and go to the second position on the roof. My exclusive."

Be warned, the press gets boisterous and annoying, we must take it. Chet, you've got your script memorised?"

"I wrote it."

"Doesn't mean you can remember it."

"I'm OK."

"And I can step in," Bjorn says.

"Finally," Prisha says. "Back at the room, change out of the uniform and head for the station separately. We all meet as a group at the airport. If you are not there, we don't wait."

Dwight has tipped off the local press and TV crews in Venice that there is to be a statement by one of the ship's senior executives about the sex trafficking. He has their interest because they will want to sell their clips and have their faces go international. Journalists love to group and talk, friends until the story breaks, then they'll fight to get that extra special clip. Jenny's piece will be edited on the plane and sent to WBX25, then a similar version to Cruise News Miami.

The CSCI team congregate inside the secure area, within meters off the gangway. Dennis has his camera ready on the bridge, looking back at the ship. He has taken a good platform on the structure that elevates him so he will be just above the other journalists when Prisha and her team arrive. The flaw in the plan is that the congregating journalists are between the gate and Dennis so they might get there first. Jenny must remain the other side so as not reveal she is a journalist. When she does show that she is chasing an interview, she will have to run around the main group and get to Dennis and Prisha first. Big Dog and Croc must flank Prisha so that the journalists don't swamp her, Bjorn, and Chet on the way to Dennis.

Prisha has dared to take her team very close to the gangway before the early risers use it. It is still being guarded by the lower rank night-shift security officers who are wondering who they are. Security can see the team has company uniforms and know there is a second ship in dock, the MS Magi Gold, but it has only just come alongside. Prisha dares to go closer, then sees them look back to see if the MS Gold has its gangway down. They know they can't be from there. Now is the time to start performing, as they get louder and gesticulate, she sees the officer call in on his radio. She has seconds before more senior officers arrive, Prisha is off.

Prisha looks up at the ship's bridge and can see they have taken an interest. Each ship has its own variation of trim to the standard uniform and she knows they have recognised it is theirs. They all know it is time to move and fast. The young executives, Chet Dean and Bjorn Ironside are beside themselves with nerves, Dog wants to steam out and get going but Croc has learned to wait. Every minute feels like an hour but the plan was for Jenny to make the move on seeing Prisha's signal.

Jenny shouts, "Hey, when are we getting an announcement?"

The other journalists turn, the chat is over. They see the officers who left the ship are approaching the safe perimeter gate fast. Prisha's team leave the area and turn left, straight through the journalists and Jenny runs at the side. She must plant one line, and it goes in as Dog stops everyone and quietens them as if Prisha is to speak.

"Hey! You are ship Executives. I need a quote!" Jenny shouts with perfect timing. She does not wait for an answer, but runs to the bridge where Dennis, her cameraman, waits.

"Please," says Croc, to stall them while Jenny moves. "We will make an announcement from the bridge, so the ships are in the background."

The team are off and stop by Jenny who holds the perfect position in front of Dennis with the ships behind.

"Bjorn Ironside, you are the executive in charge of the Magi fleet, can you tell us what is going on?"

Prisha is first to reply, "Due to increased measures by Interpol to stop the illegal movement of people, the gangs of sex traffickers have found it harder to move people. It seems they targeted three ships two weeks ago to try them as their new method of carriage."

The other press shout questions and Prisha addresses the group as well as Jenny.

"The Three Kings class was hit by the gang and the unusual crew movement was immediately noticed by these two clever young executives Chet Dean and

Bjorn Ironside. They were given an unlimited budget to stamp it out, and they are here in Venice to explain how they did that and how cruise guests remained unaffected by anything that might have been going on."

She holds the microphone under Chet's chin and pretends she is listening, a knack all journalists have, to cover them thinking about their next move.

"We are here in Croatia and Italy because an overview of the three ships showed that new crew were being picked up on the Adriatic coast, then left at the huge holiday ports in the Mediterranean," Chet starts.

"We noticed a sudden high turnover of staff, almost one hundred percent of whom were women, joining and leaving. So, we had to work with Interpol first in Puerto Banus, then Barcelona to track where those women were taken. We were sure they were not expecting to become sex workers, but they ended up working in the basements of sex clubs. Our company wanted to protect these women. Our ships would cooperate to stop this crime," Bjorn explains. His hard manner worked well for that section.

Chet steps in, "We've immediately started a programme of education on the ships to inform staff of the possible employment hustles. Later today, there will be a fuller company announcement in Miami, where all the executives, assistants, and staff, who have supported us throughout this investigation, will wholeheartedly come out and stand together shoulder to shoulder as one. Every single member of staff from this company will show they are against all forms of modern slavery and will do everything they can to see it stopped," Bjorn steps back.

Prisha steps forward to close, "Thank you for your time. As Miami wakes in five hours' time, please expect a much fuller press release."

The party breaks up, ignoring all the questions that are fired at each of them. Big Dog holds the press back with a smile as the others escape.

Croc hustles Chet and Bjorn away and then into the front of a nearby hotel, through and straight out of a side door as planned. Then the route that was researched by Prisha last night and agreed by Dwight.

Dog's got to find his own route now he has gone off-book as a decoy to help the others.

Prisha is on the roof first, Jenny and Dennis are not far behind. They square up to see the ships.

"Prisha, you were actually abducted on a ship. Tell us what happened?"

While Prisha gives Jenny the icing on the cake, back at the hotel room, Chet and Bjorn are refusing to go back to Miami as Croc hurries to change. Dog arrives ripping the uniform off as he enters. He wants to make the plane and has no interest in the two executives. The damage is done in Venice, and whatever the plan in Miami, that is where it will get nasty and they will be needed.

83 CLOCK IS TICKING

In the air 1100hrs Venice time   0600hrs Miami time

The flight time to Miami and good internet are all Jenny cares about. She knows that her story will be live in Miami within thirty minutes. No one has the coverage she has which will include the abduction of a crew member. She can imagine the executive cell phones buzzing between the early risers, the gymgoers, and those who like to sleep but will be woken. Every member of the company will be turning on their television to discover that later today they will have to be on stage denouncing modern slavery on their ships. The only way for them to play this is as CSCI have invited them to, as heroes. They will be looking to wear their best suit and maybe a trip to the barber or hairdresser on the way to work. A statement, maybe several statements will need to be issued because the press is already hounding each of them and collecting outside their building. Not only that, it appears that somehow all their personal numbers have appeared on their company page of the corporate website.

Frank Pincer and Marty Kaye are charged with finding a venue that is available. Diane, their executive assistant is charged with the press validation. No one will escape duties.

In the air and Miami time 0630am

Jenny is smiling big time because she will be the queen of this story. She owns it. She has filmed a new clip from the inside the private jet showing the importance of this breaking news. She adds a teaser revealing that the Head of Security and the Laundry Supervisor from the MS Magi Myrrh had been recruited by the heinous criminal organisation. That on-ship senior crew were forced to ensure the purchased women that travelled the trade route were and delivered to the correct ports. They are now in custody at Interpol.

In the diner, breakfast has started. Stan is cooking, Izzy is serving, and Mary is on the phone. Each time she puts it down, it rings again. She turns it over on the counter, off the hook.

At a table by the window, Hunter and Kieron have thoughtful half-smiles. Bedi is not eating.

"Bedi, eat," Kieron suggests.

She is watching an old man with a beard, tweed jacket and a trilby hat leaning his bicycle against the glass.

"Who this?"

Hunter looks, "Sigmund."

Sigmund walks in and takes his bicycle clips off,

"You must be Commander Kieron Philips? Cavalry?"

Sigmund offers his hand with just the slightest hint of a bow.

"No one's used that title in a while."

"Sigmund Pervoye Henkel, professor, criminal psychology."

Offended at the exclusion, Bedriška stands sharply,

"Bedriška Kossoff, Fifth Directorate KGB," she says, ensuring she is not ignored. Now she is the centre of attention.

"Oh my. The political, artistic and religious office?" Sigmund says knowingly.

"I was sexual dissension office. We used psychiatrists."

"Yes, I know," he says.

"Waste of time."

Sigmund takes the invitation to sit next to her, but is excited that she could be a fantastic study for him.

"Easy part done, professor," Hunter says.

"Have faith, my idea to engage the help of a magician worked. Now, your special talent. Fear is the key. Induce fear, the culprit will fall."

"Sure, we know that, and as they fall, make them reveal the key players," Kieron says.

"Police use it, standard technique, no?" Sigmund asks.

"You not understand. We different from police," Bedi adds.

"How different can it be?" Sigmund asks.

None of the three chooses to answer. They know the Miami press conference must be the other half to success; the missing half that is to reveal the 'puppet master'. They chew slowly and thoughtfully. Macey and Izzy approach. Macey lays out the deck plans of a cruise ship. One deck then the next. Before Hunter can ask what they are for, she lays a new plan on top. It is the plan of a slave ship from the 1750's.

"It's a story for Jenny. Between 250 and 600 slaves were crammed into these tiny slave ships. Which is why, on a ship this big, the traffickers never thought a dozen or so slaves would be noticed. But our team did, straight away."

"I like it, work it up, I'll ask her to let you run with it," Hunter says.

Macey and Izzy leave, excited that they have been appreciated.

"Breakfast Sigmund?"

Sigmund's eyes open wide.

"Stan!"

"I hear you, Mr Witowski, sir."

"I was going to ask you to call Dwight in for me, but another breakfast would be great."

Stan laughs and calls Dwight.

Bedriška slides her plate towards Sigmund, "I will not eat."

Sigmund slides it back, "You need well-energised brains today."

The rest of their team in the plane are still 2 hours 15 mins away.

Frank Prince and Marty Price walk into the senior CEO's office with urgency.

"Sir, yet another piece about slavery and ships and bigging up the press conference."

The CEO looks at his watch.

"Sir, the venue we had earmarked is nowhere near big enough," Frank continues.

"How big do we need?" the CEO asks.

"We already have TV stations calling, asking if they can set up, run microphones. Those we advertise with are demanding good positions," Marty adds.

"How many people do you think? Hundreds?"

"At least."

"Thousands?"

"Big. The venue needs a service road for TV crews and satellite links. Then you have cruise bloggers and influencers as well as the printed press. Camera teams need space to work, we need a place that can hold a thousand," Frank computes.

"Then we need a holding-press-release now pushing the press conference to later due to the high demand and need for a change of venue."

"It has to be today, sir," Marty urges.

"Sure."

"And we need to give them time to edit ready for the evening news. That's peak audience, we need that."

"Frank. I like the way you're handling this. Work with someone from marketing because no one knows the details better than you."

"The James L Knight centre is close; it holds 4600 and is totally equipped?"

"I love that idea."

"I think fifteen-thirty is as late as we dare go, sir."

"Done. Internal memo first. I want everyone there, no exception."

Chet and Bjorn will not be there, they have decided not to fly home. They have stayed in Venice and avoided the second part of Hunter's plan which might have put them at risk. They feel safe in Italy. The sun is out, and they are on a roof terrace drinking cocktails. Although their money is running out fast, Bjorn thinks he has a book to write and he has always fancied being an author. He needs blood to be spilt and a juicy ending, but he does not need to be there to see it.

84 KGB

Miami-0800hrs. The rest of the team land in 2 hours.

"Frank! So nice to hear from you," Dwight says, as he puts the phone in his lap, speeds to the others in the diner and calls the two girls.

"Macey! Call Jenny she can break that the conference got bumped, but she's only got 15 minutes on the others so don't try to tell her your ship size idea on slavery until she's finished. Then come over and tell us all about you being followed."

"Dwight, where are we?" Hunter interrupts.

"I've given details to Interpol. They're listening now. Television and social media are so important they are listening big time. You gotta love bloggers. Frank has already got them on the invitation list. I got Croc looking for every blogger he can find. The venue's big enough."

"In the conference centre, we need to know where Interpol agents and police stage themselves. Maybe even suggest these areas," Kieron says.

"That's gonna be hard. It's a public place."

Stan wonders in with Sigmund's breakfast, "You want study people, put camera on your own face. It been a cartoon reacting to all this. You eat up, Mr Popeye." Stan laughs as he turns and shuffles away. "Popeye! He even got the God-damn beard."

"Clock's ticking Izzy," Hunter says.

"Mary, I'll be back later," Izzy says as she goes to the ops room.

"Plan," Dwight starts to break the moment. "The most important thing, Croc's certain the main burner phone they call is back here in Miami."

"Will the company's staff all stand shoulder to shoulder on the stage?" Hunter asks.

"They have too. We got them tied in a knot. But none of them is a showman. They employ showmen. I offered our plan for Jenny to host it. They resisted. I convinced them she's the face of this story that everyone believes. They agreed. We're on."

"Brilliant!" Hunter says.

"And if the phone doesn't ring, we go to plan B," Kieron says.

"Jenny announces we know who it is. In front of the world's television and press that's gotta spook them. They run, corralled into our space backstage, then frighten enough to talk," Dwight says.

"Frighten? We beat to death until they talk," Bedi says.

"No," the professor says. "I think fear will work."

"It not ethics class professor," she says. "We need gang-boss as well as cruise-idiot."

"It's got holes," Kieron says.

"I'll say," Hunter agrees.

"It needs work," Dwight adds.

"It needs Jenny's plane to get back and her through immigration early enough," Izzy says.

85 ALL IN THE AIR

In the Air - Miami time 0900hrs. 1 hour to land.

From having been sprawled around the Jet, relaxing during their premium flight, they all sit strapped in for landing. They are at the same table, except Dennis the cameraman who is asleep on a chair. Orders have come in which they need to work through. Big Dog makes notes on the stage diagram of the James L Knight building. He finds every exit from the stage and into the auditorium; he needs two guys at each,

"Two, four, six, eight, ten, twelve," Dog mumbles, then stops circling two people at every exit.

Prisha leans over, "There are also exits at the rear of the dressing rooms. You will need thirty people."

"Five-O will be on us in seconds," Croc says.

"Not if I add a protest outside," Dog says.

"Protest about what?" Jenny asks from her seat on the other side of the plane.

"Anything, nothing, it a protest."

"How about David Beckham trying to have Overland knocked down to build his stadium," she suggests.

"For sure sister. That one easy. Hunter need to splash long money to numb pain, and he has a riot," he says. "Ma crew gonna want hard meditation and broccoli tonight."

"How about a week each for them in Barcelona, we pay you there, and everyone brings their own money back," Prisha says.

"My crew can't fly."

"You got yourself and Croc a passport," Prisha provokes.

"If da work," Dog says, revealing that he has concerns.

"What! You said they're tried and tested," Croc shouts.

Dog shrugs, "I'll get a team. I don't need to be there."

Dog uses his aeroplane phone to his crew.

Croc is on his, "Kieron, why we holding this at the JLK stadium? They have the MS Cross Keys in port. The ship theatre holds 1025, fewer doors around the stage and the police stay outside the dock. Seems to me it would be a huge promotion for the executives because it sells the brand. More importantly from what I can see, there's only three gangways off the ship."

Croc is met with silence. He either said something wrong, or it was a clever idea.

"Oh Hunter," Croc adds. "Big Dog bought these passports at the local Mall. Don't rely on seeing us."

Hunter, Dwight, Bedi and Kieron are all in the tech area. They have left Sigmund outside being instructed by Stan on how to cook burgers.

"I guessed. That's why Jenny has a letter saying you're her three-man crew. Fold the letter in her passport and she goes through first. The immigration officer will remove the letter but look at it. He'll ask what it is. She explains she just broke the cruise sex-trafficking story. They will know it, they'll recognise her. Now she's a rock star, she introduces her crew. Then you follow her through, the path having been greased." Hunter reveals.

In the plane, Jenny has started to take a real interest in her immigration prospects with the other two. She leans over Croc's shoulder and speaks into his phone. "Thanks, we might all get detained," she says angrily.

The air hostess pulls the curtain and addresses them.

"Buckle up please, we're making our final approach. We'll be in Miami early."

Events jump along at speed, and Frank Pincer is pacing the room with Dwight on speaker.

"It wasn't a request Frank. It's gotta be done," Hunter replies.

"The ship is taking on six thousand new guests all afternoon. Then lifeboat drill uses the theatre. It sails at seventeen thirty hours."

"I don't see a problem," Dwight adds.

"That brand is not connected to the King Class ships. Holding the conference on any ship will automatically connect it."

"Be a grown-up Frank, this is all good; you're heroes all across the brand. Take it down the hall to your CEO," Kieron adds. "Your ship is sitting there on Dodge Island."

With the call ended the three men look at each other for the next problem to solve.

"Next problem," Bedi says. "If Jenny get arrested or delay at immigration, who run show?"

"Frank won't run it our way or to our timetable," Kieron ponders.

"You do it Kieron, you're the star they love on ships," Hunter offers.

"No, no, no. Cruise Ship Crime Investigators are not going to be revealed as the champions of this until we know everything is solved. I shouldn't be anywhere near it. The press would be all over me. Keep to the plan; CSCI steps in only when the final rogue executive reveals themselves."

"Without Jenny, we're lost," Hunter says.

"I go on in her place," Dwight says.

"What?"

"Who's gonna stop me. And, it's about time I was on a mission again. I know what to do and I'll hit every beat. It's my time."

86   LIST WHAT WE DON'T HAVE

The team are collecting coffee back in the Wild Mary's Diner. Watching them, it strikes Hunter how little he knows about any of them, and how much good Mary and Stan do. It appears Stan has a new friend in Sigmund. Hunter turns to Macey's painting of Dwight that she has on her easel. It is incredible and he had never noticed her talent. He would lay a heavy wager that her paints and materials, as well as her college fees, are paid for by Mary.

"How did you three meet?" Sigmund asks the students.

"We all had a birthday party here when we were eight years old," Izzy explains.

"Got the same birthday; came back every year after," Macey explains.

Hunter chuckles. Life can be so simple. "OK. Izzy, Macey, step up girls! You're gonna be boarding a ship."

Both are in shock.

"What are we doing?" Izzy asks him, creeping closer, Macey says nothing.

"You'll be our liaison. Eat, enjoy the ship, but be at the end of the phone when we need you," Hunter explains. "We need a point on the ship and it's you two."

"Yeah we do," Kieron adds. "Learn your way around, especially the theatre, so you can help the team hit the ground running as they arrive."

"Introduce yourself at reception and suggest they give you a pager; we want that pager number," Kieron adds.

Dwight picks up on that and is already dialling, "Frank, I need a direct dial number into the hotel manager on the ship. I have my pen hovering."

The team is working well, but there is still only a loose plan. Kieron knows these two girls will be daunted by the size of the huge ship.

"Show confidence. Be natural," Sigmund suggests.

"Find the production manager normally based in the entertainment office under the stairs in the theatre. Introduce yourselves and have him show you the stage, and all the crafty ways in and out," Kieron adds. He looks to get a nod from Dwight who will have all that pre-setup. Sigmund is agreeing.

"I don't care if you are at the back, painting. We need eyes on the ground," Hunter says. "Take your kit. And your pictures."

"I might get to stay the week," she chances.

Dwight puts his cell down, "Your taxi will be outside in two minutes," he says completing their shock.

Sigmund watches every move as Macey folds her large folder closed, her work inside. The roll of paper drops into the plastic drum with a strap and is slung over her back. She collapses the easel which also goes over her back like an archer's quiver, but her face is vacant. Bedi notices they've both lost their normally confident expressions and she steps in and high five them,

"First time! Love the ship."

Hunter slides to sit with Dwight, a whole mission is being thrown together. Any lack of confidence is because they have no certain method and no known to the team.

"You sure you want to do this, Dwight?" Hunter checks, he is worried he might just blow the stage show. It is not something that sits in his armoury.

"Even if she comes back, I'm going on that stage. I know this game better than Jenny does. I'll read it as it changes; and it will."

"What can you do Sigmund?" Kieron asks.

"I have to be back at college, but fascinating, fascinating," he whispers, not wishing to be part of the field action.

Hunter agrees with both Sigmund and Dwight. Sigmund will be an anchor they drag around. Dwight will understand the moves they might make.

They all become distracted as Prisha approaches the table. A small cheer starts as one of their team arrives back. It is short because the others are not with her.

"Where're the others?" Kieron asks her.

"I came in through 'foreign nationals'. They had a different channel and my cell went dead," she says.

"Sigmund, your star pupils arrived," Hunter says looking to Bedi at the door.

"He's gone," she says.

"Prisha, join us, we're solving problems. I'll get Sigmund later."

"I'm surprised we've not heard from Jenny or Croc. We need Big Dog's team," Kieron muses.

"How big is that team? Cash is tight. I'm spending like we work for the government," Dwight reports, texting Croc for a status report.

"Where's it gone?" Hunter asks him.

"Private jets?" Dwight reports. "You want me to go on?"

"And a cold investment in Mumbai," Kieron accuses.

Prisha freezes with embarrassment,

"Sorry I did not know this was a cause for concern."

"Not your problem Prisha. It's just that Hunter didn't run it by the rest of us."

"It is a sound investment. Please, you must come over and see it."

"To India? Not sure we have the money to travel anywhere unless we pull this sting off."

Dwight attends a bleeped in message.

"They got through immigration," Dwight reports.

"We have our double stage act," Hunter offers.

"I have an idea, how we can make the Mumbai venture very profitable," Prisha states, not wishing the subject to end badly.

"I don't plan on getting involved in running a refrigeration business, no matter where it is or what the profit is," Kieron states.

"I was thinking sixteen-million-dollars profit."

"Stop sex trafficking come first," Bedi snaps.

"I agree, stamp it out, then chase some money," Kieron adds.

"I too agree but please listen," Prisha says indignantly.

The others give her the floor.

"We will fight for the refrigeration contract with the shipping company; repairs and service when in Mumbai. The money is put into a freezer; our company removes the freezer from the ship for repair."

"I like that. A million steps to be sorted, but I like it," Hunter says.

"And as money is in India, where you to invest that?" Bedi asks.

"First we need to discharge the key bad apple from the cruise company, connect it to Miami so we are not all hit targets, then put in our invoice and get paid," Kieron argues.

"It's no different from ferreting a terrorist out," Hunter defends.

"Except you are in front of the world's stage," Dwight reminds them.

"It worth gamble," Bedi suggests.

Macey and Izzy's taxi draws into Dodge Island. Neither of them has ever been in there before or seen a cruise ship close-up.

"Holy mother, do you see the size of these? How do they float?" Izzy asks.

The taxi stops and lets them out. The account has been settled by the ever-efficient Dwight.

As instructed, both women walk through customs showing their passes. Macey, however, begins to be more and more embarrassed as she gets closer. She is in her denim painting dungarees. Her hair is up with brushes poked into it, and she has a portable easel on her back which could be a gun. They walk to the far gangway, gangway 3, where some camera crews are having equipment checked and loaded. On presenting ID they are given cruise passes to the ship and walk on. A cruise ship makes the biggest impression on someone who has never travelled, and neither of them has. Macey was never stopped, looked at or questioned. They are both bamboozled, lost already and they haven't moved away from the entrance.

"Can I help?" one of the young dancers asks them, who, like all the staff are there to assist. Her name, 'Teri' and 'dancer' are on her badge, but neither Izzy nor Macey have noticed that yet.

"Guess we gotta find the theatre first," Macey says.

"That I know, follow me," Teri says, running them up two floors.

"Wow," Izzy says, following. However, Macey is not listening. Macey has gone into her own world because at every half-turn of the stairs, the wall displays art.

On deck seven, the promenade deck, the dancer points them to the theatre past the burger bar and casino. She smiles and turns to leave.

Izzy grabs her wrist, "Hey. Wait a moment. We need a tour guide."

Teri smiles, "Where do you want to see?"

Izzy links her arm like she could save her from going overboard. Macey joins Izzy's other arm and they hang on to each other.

"Theatre, then the Production Manager."

"Are you two an act?"

"Not yet," says Macey.

"This is it," Teri says taking them in.

They gaze down at the most enormous auditorium either of them has seen. Camera crews and journalists are already setting-up in their chosen positions, dwarfed by row after row of red theatre chairs. They cling onto each other.

"Fuck!" Izzy whispers.

"Holy fuck!" Macey agrees.

"It's like a proper Broadway theatre."

"Bigger than many," Teri adds.

"We have to control what happens in here?" Izzy panics.

"You two are in this show?" Teri asks. "What is it?"

"Just helping," Izzy smiles.

"Enjoy," Teri says leaving.

Macey is already ringing back to base,

"Dwight, this is one huge mother. Camera crews and press are already here. I think I should have dressed up a bit."

At the office, Macey's picture of the auditorium comes through and the guys start to study the number of journalists and camera crews already setting-up.

"We need a huge screen at the end, like huge," Croc says.

"Now find your targets."

Now without Teri, the two girls turn out of the theatre. She rings back to base.

"We lost our guide, you need to help us out guys; this is scary," Izzy is heard to say.

"At every lift area, there's a ship's map on the wall. The map always faces the way the ship faces. The theatre is at the front, level seven, so you can always get back. Look at the carpets. Red carpets front elevators, yellow carpets midship, green carpets rear elevators," Hunter says very automatically.

"Like stoplights," Izzy shouts.

Prisha leans in, she knows how they feel. She went from living with her whole family in one room to life on a ship.

"Walk up and down that promenade deck three or four times and you will have it, trust me. The rest of the ship is not important," Prisha interjects.

"After that, go and eat in the buffet and you can study the ship map," Kieron adds. It is like a barrage of three or four people telling them how to drive.

"We don't have a map!" Macey panics.

"Plus," Izzy adds through the cell, "Big Dog and his crew need to smarten up a bit to get on here."

"No, that's exactly what we don't want them to do," Hunter adds with a smile.

87 MS CROSS KEYS

Macey and Izzy get a message that Big Dog is thirty minutes away. They are stuck, hypnotised by the atrium. The ornate brass and glass stairs snake around and down. Well-positioned mirrors make it look like they go forever. Hanging down as a centrepiece is a large three-dimensional hexagon with internal strip lights that offer a mesmerising optical illusion of eternal depth.

"It's like the biggest shopping mall I ever seen," Izzy says.

"The cleanest," Macey offers.

At the bottom, a man in black tie plays the piano. A lady in an evening dress plays the harp.

"Fuck, I only thought they were played in heaven," Izzy says."

"Dog ain't gonna get on. Don't care what Hunter thinks," Macey says in a daze. "I wanna go down and paint that."

"Later, we gotta work," Izzy says, drawn by a glittering shop behind her. "Macey, look at these diamonds, girl!"

Macey looks at the glittering window.

"They're gonna think we're casing the joint especially with your kit on your back," Izzy says, making Macey feel guilty.

Macey pulls Izzy away from the sparkling windows and the draw of the centre.

They rely on each other more and more, hand in hand, and deeply affected by scale they pass a smart lounge bar. Macey stops. She has stepped into an art gallery in the corridor of the ship.

"Oh. Now, who's slowing us down?" Izzy says.

"Look. On a ship!"

"I ain't blind."

Macey wanders slowly, looking at the hung paintings from the walls.

"Wake up girl, we got to find the back, then do it all again." Izzy pulls her, noticing they are being watched by a man with a beard straight out of a period film. He is quaint, wears an avant-garde jacket and a bow tie. He was talking to the girl at the gallery desk, but now he shows genuine interest in Macey.

"Macey, we've got to move, he's clocked us."

The man steps forward.

"Hello, you paint?" the man says in a soft French accent.

Macey shakes her head in fear.

"But you are carrying your easel and a roll. You must paint."

"She does," Izzy says. "It ain't a gun."

"A far more deadly weapon. Please, let me look. I get off the ship within the hour and I would hate not to have seen your work, maybe I can help."

"I ain't got anything," Macey defends.

He opens his eyes wide.

"If you carry that kit, chances are you have a dream, or you are hiding a gun."

They need to prove their innocence so Izzy roles the drum around and Macey opens the lid.

"No gun," Macey says.

"I want to see, and your folder."

"Get on with it, Mace, things to do girl," Izzy encourages her.

Macey unties the protective loops and slowly opens it. The first picture is one of Dwight lit by the computer screen.

"This is not my favourite version."

"No?"

"My favourite, the final one, is hung in our gallery, nothing like this. This was the first try, I got the light better."

"Where is your gallery?"

Izzy chuckles, Macey is embarrassed.

"Wild Mary's, just off the i95 downtown," Izzy says.

"I never heard of this gallery."

Izzy giggles, "It's wild."

"It's a diner, but I have a solo exhibition," Macey says.

The man persists in wanting to turn the folder.

"May I?" he asks turning to the next study. He gasps. It is the painting of the women, their arms rising, screaming in fear.

"This is not the best one either?" he suggests.

"No."

"That's in your gallery?"

"Wild Mary's," Izzy adds for her.

"You are incredibly talented. Your gallery must be busy."

"People come to eat. Never sold a painting."

"This is women imprisoned, screaming," Macey feels she needs to explain.

"It needs no explanation. Art should comfort the disturbed, and disturb those who are not," he says. "That's from an incredibly old quote referring to newspapers and often used in religious text. 'Comfort the afflicted and afflict the comfortable'. Banksy and Cruz and many others have said this about art. This is what your work does. Disturbs, afflicts."

Izzy is confused. Macey's face lights up.

"It is a shame you're on holiday and I am on a working visit to Miami, I would have loved to have seen more of your work."

"Actually, I'm-"

"Can I buy your practice picture of the gentleman, lit by blue light. How's five hundred dollars? And I'd like to see the definitive version."

"We'll get to talk to you," Izzy says taking his business card.

Macey hands him the picture of Dwight in front of the screen and holds her hand out for the money. He pays her from a huge wad.

C.S.C.I.

CRUISE SHIP LAUNDRY WARS

Izzy looks at the card. It has just one word on it, Clément.

"Clement? Is that English?" Izzy asks.

"French. Kle-Mawn. C'est bien."

Izzy nods and pulls Macey away.

"Wait!"

Macey stops. "We don't give receipts."

"How many of these are there in total?"

"Three," Macey says.

"This was the first?"

Macey nods. He hands her a beautiful pen and points to some way under the paint on the paper.

"Please sign this. Underneath write first draft, 1/3."

Macey writes, Izzy now pulls her away successfully.

"What just happened?" Macey asks.

"It was a dream. You'll wake up."

"I sold a painting!"

Jenny, Dog, and Croc walk towards the theatre. They each have their cruise card on one lanyard around their neck, but a second one has another pass: 'PRESS. ACCESS ALL AREAS'. Dennis slides past them and goes into the auditorium. His demands on the venue are totally different and first up he looks for his other WBX25 camera team. They shake hands and he starts to exchange stories.

Jenny walks down to the stage to feel the size, "Don't get excited. I'm not starting yet," she announces out to the 'audience'.

The journalists in the auditorium all know her and give a supportive laugh. She looks down and sees Dwight in the auditorium. She jumps down and joins him, "How do you get on stage?"

He smiles knowing there is always a way.

Dog stands with Croc at the back of the stalls in the theatre. He is amazed,

"Dis is real?" he asks Croc.

"Real!" Croc replies. "Dis is where posh people go in their furs."

Dog nods slowly. "Yeah. Cruela De Vil and all her crew, and dey killed puppies."

"Those two agents do crazy shit like this all the time." Croc says, turning to Dog.

"Agents?"

Croc nods.

"TV cameras are watching everything that moves," Dwight says as he approaches.

"Let's go. If you're doing a crime, and you don't wanna do time, look for all your ways out first."

Dwight leads them out of the theatre then onto the promenade deck, the side away from the island and looking out to sea. He is looking for a door, with 'Crew Only' on it. Dog is there first, door handle cracked open and he slips in.

Dog sees various curtains, technical equipment, and theatre sets. He turns back and opens the door and beckons the others in. They pass but his head remains out of the door, looking side to side on the promenade deck. Then he ducks inside.

The three look around backstage and Dog walks to the back. He is inquisitive about every exit. He drops down the stairs and sees the dressing rooms. He goes past them, out of the stage area onto the steel crew stairs. He notices exits left and right and checks the right. A door goes into the bulkhead; another goes out to the promenade deck. He looks at the outside and that is marked crew only. He lets the door swing closed and walks back into the theatre noticing ladders up to overhead footways.

"So?" Croc asks.

"Lots of doors, but 'less the dude can swim like Flipper, he need some 'science'."

"We get the rogue to run," Dwight says. "You chase him."

"He gunna know the ship better than us," Dog suggests.

"Sure will," Croc admits.

"We make him run out the back and corner him in the dressing rooms," Dwight says.

They follow him to the back of the stage.

"And keep the press out there," Dwight adds, ensuring the whole deal is firmly engraved in their heads.

"We keep everyone out, even the Captain?" Croc asks.

"Everyone. While me and Jenny drive the show on."

"OK. We can eat," Big Dog says.

They go around to the 'crew only' out to the promenade deck. They re-enter by the guest door and call an elevator.

"There might be more than one runner," Croc says.

Hunter and Kieron are in the buffet with Izzy and Macey who have plates piled high with food. Macey is not eating but sketching the obscene piles of food on her handy size pad. They all feel heads turn and know Big Dog has walked in with Croc and Dwight.

"You imagine this at a food bank?" Croc says. "They wouldn't need to stampede or fight," Dwight says.

"It a food bank for posh people," Big Dog says joining the queue. "They're stampeding. They just smell better."

"Back stairs?" Kieron asks, as the others sit down with them.

"Back stairs," Dog says. "The press won't get near you in der dressing room."

"Us," Hunter says.

"Us?" Dog asks.

"You're playing, you and a couple of threatening boys. I need the mark to believe you're there to execute."

"We need tools for dat, bro."

"Under my chair, is the spare, that awaits you there," Dwight rhymes.

"You ain't no rapper, Dwight."

"I thought that was good."

88 THE SHOW

The presentation of two ships from two ages, and the deck plan showing the stowage of a 1788 slave ship next to the huge cruise ship, finishes. The full auditorium of journalists, camera crews, bloggers and influencers wait, struck dumb in silence by the dramatic opening. At the rear of the stalls is a row of white-suited officers who stand out, as do the hooded crew at the stairs to the stage, each side and centre. Under their hoods, the crew prepare to jump on whatever unfolds. All they have been told is that it will be obvious. Half will climb the stairs and ensure whoever it is that runs is corralled backstage into a dressing room. The other half will stop anyone from following.

"Good afternoon. I'm Jenny-E. I chased and broke this story for WBX25. To put it simply, with up to a thousand crew on many ships, it is not surprising that some will look for land-based employment. Some will look to live in European countries or in the American ports where cruise ships stop. This is not new, but we can show through years of this successful cruise industry those incidences are quite rare," Jenny says, taking centre stage as the directors and staff walk in and create five rehearsed raked rows spanning the width of the stage. Lights come on theatrically. They are a strong show of everyone who works at the company. They look like the 'guest choir' on a cruise. Dennis, Jenny's hand-held cameraman, is on stage and films close-ups of them.

When they are settled, Dwight wheels on from the other side holding his microphone. The attention changes.

"But listen up, Jenny-E with good investigative reporting discovered a major problem, along with two directors who are not here because they are in hiding in fear for their lives," he says. "And someone in here, not only let it happen, but they are the person who is behind this whole buying and selling of vulnerable women."

"You mean that person is here?" Jenny asks, playing her part.

"Not only here, but get your cameras ready to zoom, we are going to reveal which staff member let the company down. Let the cruise industry down. Let everything Miami stands for down."

Dwight and Jenny turn to the directors and staff, all shocked and surprised at the unexpected change in the show. The long moment is tense. But, no one is running scared, no one is flinching. Jenny and Dwight look desperately for a crack in the armoury, but there is nothing.

"I've just been told in my earphone that the spotlight operator has found them, are you ready Jenny?" Dwight asks.

"I am. But first, remember their families and relatives watching back home. Friends that thought they knew them so well?" she continues.

The staff start to look at each other, wondering who it is, but no one moves.

"Jenny, if it was me, I would run. That is if my legs worked! Many of the enslaved women will never recover from their injuries. If it were me I would wanna get out of being probably the most embarrassing thing ever on television."

No one moves. Dwight tries harder, "Sick. I feel sick. But more than that, I'm angry, Jenny."

No one moves.

In the wings, out of audience view, Hunter looks at Kieron worried, "It's not working buddy; we might be finished."

Kieron crunches his face, he still has hope, "You've been a sniper, waited for hours, gun pointed, never deviating from the target area. Knowing, the mark will appear."

"Or not," Hunter says. "We're not in the field buddy, we are live on TV and it's becoming a joke. These people won't wait."

Hunter gives Dwight the nod.

"We are going cut the lights so they can go backstage and give themselves up privately, if not the spotlight will be on them. Cut the house lights, dim the stage lights."

The lights go down. No one moves.

"Now," Hunter shouts as they both pull on balaclavas and charge in making noise to induce fear.

"Oorah!"

It is repeated by Big Dog's crew who run taking that as the signal. It becomes a fearful battle cry.

Dwight turns and faces the staff of the cruise company, "Hold your positions," he demands. "We know who to take down!"

Kieron and Hunter run through them manhandling each director making a lot of noise. The women start to scream.

Dog's men push up aggressively. One executive bursts away from the Oorah of the army veterans. They are immediately taken down and a black blanket thrown over their head and pulled tight. Dog's men are fast and efficient and follow orders to the letter. The lights come up.

"Watch for another runner," Kieron shouts and he and Hunter turn their attentions to the shocked executives, knowing his team know where to take their suspect.

Live on TV but masked, Dog's men stop the press and handheld cameras get on stage to follow the violent story.

Jenny takes over again, though shocked by the event. Her cameraman Dennis pans from faces of the executives to Jenny.

"Interpol has a new system called i-checkit, which is being brought in for international travel. They are trying to stop the trafficking of women, and children," she adds. She knows the press has been shocked and she needs to try and make what has happened justifiable, even though some stations will edit only the violence and the negative.

"Do you know how many children are trafficked each year, sold into things too nasty to mention, so people ignore the facts," Dwight says, picking up on Jenny's point. He hopes no one asks him how many because he doesn't have a clue.

"One bad apple in a company can cause so much abuse to humanity. This as an example of what is happening in too many places. It is commendable what these brave people have done to stamp it out," she says, opening her arm in a sweep to the executives who are still locked in shock. The senior executives begin to thaw out and a few glances are exchanged to ask each other if they should take over and stop it.

"Our team followed the women removed from the ship to a club in Barcelona and with the help of Interpol raided the club."

"What's the name of the club?" a journalist shouts out.

Jenny breathes in, her mind is blank. "Dwight," she says asking him to deal with the question.

"I don't want to give any names during the investigation, but the Italian press covered it the day after the MS Magi Myrrh was berthed in Barcelona. You should note how amazingly quickly these executives jumped on the problem."

This must continue until the information about the real traffickers in Miami is obtained from the captured executive.

89 BACK STAGE

With covered faces, Dog's men are making a frightening cacophony around the prisoner still wrapped in a blanket. With no vision and pushed back and forth from man to man it is a torture.

"Must be Christmas; got me a pig in a blanket," one shouts though it is lost in the noise.

Despite being clogged together by the funnelling effect of the stairs down the corridor, Hunter and Kieron get down. Even though they are masked, the foot soldiers know who they are and let them through.

A rear door opens, and Interpol agents bully their way in, badges up. That was not part of the plan. They can only save more women from this heinous gang if they can find out who they are. To fail now would leave the gang on the streets and everyone is at risk. Not just the women but each one of them. The diner would be at risk; Macey would as Croc, Mary, Izzy and each of the CSCI team. Hunter's wife Elaine would be at risk again like she was when taken on the heist they worked on. Mafia gangs send messages, huge messages; they are all forms of death. The team have gone silent.

"We will take it from here," an agent says with a big grin. Hunter can't let that happen; the risk is too great.

"Who are you?"

With a nod, they are pushed into the other dressing room. The Interpol agents smash the smoked safety glass pane in the door out towards Dog's men and guns come out. The guns are pushed up and one goes off. The prisoner jumps. Dog's men all pull guns of varied make, shape and size all aimed at the agents. There is a stand-off as the door is locked.

"It's over," Hunter says to the prisoner.

"No, no," the captive says, but it is inaudible.

There is no turning back, the show has been half played out.

"We have orders to kill you. Orders direct from Albania. Your body is going down to the waste processing deck, churned up, dumped out at sea."

"No."

Hunter listens hard. The noise around is loud, the prisoner has no voice and he is sure he is missing things.

"Why. Albania says kill."

"I was promised protection."

"Who by?"

"Lulzim."

Hunter forces a smile. He is mentally exhausted. He knows he can't let Interpol take over. Lulzim and the others will survive. He needs more than just a name, but he has broken so many laws. Then he has a brainwave.

"We're inside an international area, the police can't touch us," he whispers to Kieron.

"I'm sure they'll try, and Interpol can. If not, the press will finish us off. We need this solved before we're the ones captured, and what we have is not enough. We have a scapegoat."

Hunter leans down to the prisoner, "I will give you one phone call, come with me. There's no service down here."

90   EVERYTHING TO LOSE

The executives on stage are still there, standing on parade. The only difference between them and the press is that they have worked out who was taken away.

Kieron arrives on stage, still hooded. He needs Dwight and Jenny to order silence which they do surprisingly fast. All are keen to see what happens next.

Hunter steers the group up the stairs and onto the stage. He kicks the back of the rogue's leg midway up so they drop to their knees. Dog's men keep a noise around them. They have no way of knowing where they are.

Hunter bends down to whisper to the prisoner.

"Phone has a signal here."

Bedi has appeared next to him on stage, her face covered as is his. She bends to Hunter's ear. "Go now."

"I'm nearly there," he says weakly.

Bedi is forceful.

"This is woman. Go."

A sense of realisation hits him. In the struggle, he never considered gender, just a crime. His mind reboots looking into Bedi's eyes. A woman was not part of the plan.

"We need to know who is handling her," he whispers to Bedriška.

"Go."

Bedi waves Jenny in. Bedi bends down to the prisoner, and Jenny does the same with the microphone.

"OK. Who you think save you?"

"Lulzim," the covered woman says.

Dwight must keep the crowd quiet as they gasp hearing it is a woman. The noise of Dog's men held the sound barrier. Now the auditorium is silent, in shock, wanting to know more.

"He boss of sex trafficking?" Bedi asks, flicking her head so the others leave. Dog and his men go, Kieron and Hunter are next. Bedi and Jenny are left.

"You ring Lulzim. Where is he?" Bedi asks.

"The Ghetto Club off Ocean Drive," the woman whispers.

"He runs sex trafficking, not you?"

"Yes, yes," she pleads.

"You arrange sex trafficking for him?"

"Yes, yes. Please don't kill me."

Bedi gets in close to her.

"I got news for you. Lulzim not big enough to save you. Who his boss? You ring him. Who is big man at top of sex traffic?"

"Sali's the top man, Sali Rustemiki, he runs the trafficking."

"He not happy with you. No women."

"Tell him, I tried to keep it going. I have three women for Barcelona. Promise," the woman cries.

In the wings, Hunter and Kieron are disrobing from their black coveralls. Hunter waves to Jenny to pull the cover from her. She walks in and pulls the black blanket off.

"It's Diane Mond," Hunter says. "I wouldn't have had her in a sweepstake."

Diana Mond looks out at the audience then back at the directors behind her, all looking down at her ashamed. She is whimpering; the audience is silent.

"Please bring the ship security and ship medics."

Kieron and Hunter look like civilians leaving through the heavy steel 'crew only' side door as the

Interpol agents arrive on stage brandishing their badges. All of Dog's crew are long gone.

Kieron and Hunter walk swiftly down the promenade deck. They look across Dodge Island at the enormous cruise industry as they walk.

"Could you imagine if all those ships were used for just a few trafficked women each?" Kieron asks.

"We don't have to now," Hunter says.

They turn in at the elevator area at the back of the auditorium and hear Di Mond in mid-speech.

"I'm sorry Mr Pincer. Sorry to Chet and Bjorn. They didn't deserve this, but I had no choice. I owed money."

The two CSCI agents creep into the back of the auditorium and watch. The press fire questions at her and she is mesmerised and confused by them powering forward and all the flashes going off in her face.

"We might have solved it, but we might not survive the press," Kieron says, worried as they walk along the deck.

"We went too far for the public. It happens every day in combat, but they don't see it," Hunter says with some anger.

"We saved a lot of women even if we can't save ourselves," Kieron says.

"Sali said you could pay off your debt to him using your ships for trafficking?" they hear Dwight asks Diane who is still on her knees as the medics arrive.

"Yes," she says.

They turn and leave.

"Tell me, was this a successful mission for CSCI?" they hear Jenny ask over the theatre's booming sound system. There is a gasp from the audience. Kieron and Hunter turn back into the theatre and stand behind the stalls.

They watch as Bedriška pulls off her own disguising, headcover.

"I was expecting man. To find woman selling other women for sex is big shock. I was abused woman. I feel sick to my stomach every time I sleep, this whole gang needed to be stopped. Interpol and Miami police finish arrest."

On stage, Dwight continues. "I want to introduce you to the new female agent at Cruise Ship Crime Investigators, Prisha Nah. Come up Prisha. Prisha was undercover in ship and got taken by this gang in the Adriatic. Both these women put their lives at risk."

Kieron turns to Hunter, "Our female investigators are both very special."

"I hope that's what it says in the press," Hunter says as they leave.

"I think we'll be ok now."

"And Dwight got his mission," Hunter agrees with a fist bump as they walk down the gangway.

"We just need to fill the freezer," Kieron says.

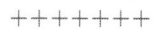

+++++++

Stuart St Paul's book hard hitting book FREIGHT, also an ICON PICTURES movie played on Netflix, is on sex trafficking in England. It won him many prizes from BEST DIRECTOR in the USA to an Excellence in Filmmaking special award in Mexico.

NEXT – CRUISE SHIP ART THEFT

a taster of the next book

1 – DEAD CITY

Miami-1030hrs

The Cruise Ship Crime Investigators' office, next to Wild Mary's Diner in Charlotte City, has contributed no beneficial effect to the complex. They are the only active unit in the otherwise dead, ex-commercial hub. Upturned shopping trolleys have replaced parked cars. If it were a disguise they were after, they have it. The days of Charlotte 'dead' City attempting to entice vendors in any shape or form are over. The blacked-out windows of their unit, with the initials CSCI in a different shade of charcoal is very artistic and they can thank Macey for that. The US Letter sheet stuck to their door saying 'go next door' is not the work of the artist Macey. That is the work of Wild Mary.

Wild Mary's is the all-day diner next door, where Wild Mary, a forceful African American woman, calls the shots and Stan does the cooking in his lazy-jazzed style. The trilby hat he always wears looks as old as him. His laughter is infectious, her's is not. Though technically a part of Charlotte City, Wild Mary's can deny association because it is on the corner facing out to the main road. Its rear wall, cupboards and toilets may adjoin the sidewall of the CSCI unit, but they have their own parking out front. Wild Mary's could use either, but never gets that busy.

Macey, like the other two students whom Mary has quasi adopted, not only works there, eats there, and studies there, but is also kept in line and on the straight and narrow by Wild Mary, a force to be reckoned with.

Cruise Ship Crime Investigators moving next door has changed each one of their lives in a major way. It started when one of the two CSCI team put a nail into the adjoining wall and burst a pipe, unknowingly flooding Mary's store cupboard and adjacent toilets. Mary took a large hammer and demolished the wall until she found the pipe and could fix it. The wall has never been put back. The door to her cupboard goes through to the major control centre which now has state-of-the-art computer power run by Dwight. He is a large African American man who lost his legs and shortly after, his wife, Ruby. An ex-military man, he is now an incredibly good, though self-taught, computer data analyst and researcher. He works with the IT student Croc from Wild Mary's next door. Young Croc was a top hacker until Mary had to bail him out of police custody then get him a lawyer. Stan's assistant burger-flipper is now an important member of an advanced investigators' unit which deals with international cruise crime. Croc can get into anything, from phones to company systems and he loves the unofficial job at CSCI.

The cupboard door between the restaurant and the Crime Investigation centre is always closed unless something is going on, and for days the intercom between the two units has been silent. Dwight has been chasing money billed as extras for what they call the 'laundry wars' job. That certainly was not as trivial as it sounds, and it would have got nasty and maybe closed them down if it hadn't been for their new female investigators saving the day. Bedriška a firmly spoken Russian, and Prisha a small and polite Indian, were both key players in the eventual outcome. Today, the same as yesterday, the only two in CSCI HQ are Dwight and 'Croc the tech'. Stan is cleaning his grill following the breakfast rush, after which, he does his own brunch. The few customers who have long since finished their meals would sit there all day if Wild Mary let them.

Macey is in her painting-dungarees, hair in a bun, brushes pushed into it at every angle possible. She sits at her easel, making beauty out of the deep decaying urban car park. Balloons are sketched as foreground earpieces. Macey's paintings have to say something, she is harsh, political, and she sees things others don't. Her painted images of the Wild Mary's Diner have adorned the walls for years. But despite it being her own private gallery, she has only sold one.

Mary is taking 'happy birthday' balloons down from all over the restaurant.

"I went to all this trouble and none of you seemed impressed," Mary mutters, though everyone can hear.

"We not kids anymore, birthdays ain't important," Macey explains.

"Let me tell you, birthdays are good for you," Stan says, breaking his quiet.

"Why would that be, Stan?" Mary demands.

"The more you have, the longer you live."

Macey laughs, Mary is not impressed. She has more than a handful of balloons.

"You gonna help, or just paint them, girl," Wild Mary barks at her.

Macey ignores her. Her attempt to paint a happy birthday scene of balloons against the backdrop of upturned trolleys is laid on a table next to her and she drops another sheet down and sits back waiting for inspiration.

For her, CSCI has stretched her artistic horizons and given her the confidence to show Mary her nastier images. The balloons seem too nice for her current mindset. She has always enjoyed painting images that play with light, and her incredible portrait of Dwight has her thinking of portraits. He is very well captured, deep in thought and lit by the computer. His face is full of different emotions and concerns. It is her current prized work, and it hangs above the jukebox. That painting is sold. Dwight bought it and as he has no time to enjoy it in his apartment, he has loaned it back to Wild Mary's 'Gallery'.

"Maybe a drifter at the window looking in and the grill foreground," Macey suggests.

"That mean I'm in it, Mace?" Stan asks.

"You ain't in nothing, Stan," Mary barks.

The military banter sometimes spars with the dry humour of Downtown Miami when the investigators are in.

"You ain't in nothing but trouble," Mary adds privately to him.

"What?" Stan whispers.

"You never worried?"

"'Bout what, Mary?"

"We now got an investigator business next door. One day they gonna find out way too much about us. Things long forgotten."

"What's them, Mary?"

"You ain't funny, Stan. Ain't funny."

Stan is left, genuinely puzzled.

Mary studies her order book, determined not to look up. Stan has annoyed her.

"Someone order a takeaway?" Macey shouts.

"Ain't no one ever ordered no 'take-away' from here. We don't sell food-to-go, never have done, never will do. Someone want a takeaway, they can just eat their food at their own home!" Mary blurts out.

"That's kind of how it works," Macey says with sarcasm.

"You been learning that English subtext stuff from Mr Commander Kieron, 'I'm British' Philips?"

"Definitely ain't one of them 'Deliver-to-you vans' pulled up outside. And it sure ain't come to collect no takeaway."

"They got lost," Mary says, refusing to take an interest. Mary pops a sinking balloon. Stan jumps.

"Me thought he was shooting."

"Only one ever gonna shoot you is me. Now get rid of the rubbish," she says, pushing him the limp balloons.

"Someone has to do the ordering; someone needs to work in this place." Mary bends further, head hidden over her order book.

"We need tomatoes, Mary," he says.

"Stan, I'm concentrating," Mary says not wanting his input. Working out her vegetable order is the only time she wears her glasses. It is the time her anger is focussed on suppliers who, far too often seem unable to find green tomatoes. Fried green tomatoes is her signature dish. Stan flips a steak on the clean grill.

"They sure got lost," Macey suggests, walking to the window. "That limo ain't the kind that gets hired for a posh kid's ball. That's super classy. Spells money."

"They come in here, I'll serve them the same seven-dollar breakfast," Wild Mary says.

"Don't think you'll need to worry. No suited-up man ever eaten in here," Macey jokes.

"What you implying girl? More English subtext?"

"Looks like they is developers. 'bout time someone knocked this place down and built something useful."

"What's more useful than a diner serving good food?"

"Let me see, shopping mall, bowling, cinema. They'd have to re-locate us," Macey says, turning to Wild Mary. "You want me to carry on?"

"They ain't knocking my diner down, are they Stan?" Mary asks, refusing to look up.

"Whatever you say, Mary, but not every dude gonna do what you tell 'em," Stan says with his usual rhythm and head nodding. He looks out of the window and frowns. "Reckon he's mafia, and he's packing."

"He ain't got a gun under that suit, look at the cut," Macey says.

"Well the driver be packing," Stan says. "They mean business, girl."

The names are all made up and no link or likeness is meant for any living person.
This is except for the wonderful comedy magic entertainer Manuel Martinez, who gave us his blessing and permission.

CAST, SHIPS AND ROUTE

The KING CLASS of ships

MS Magi Myrrh   built 1991
MS Magi Gold   built 1992
MS Magi Frankincense   built 1993

CRUISE ITINERARY

1. Lisbon
2. Cadiz
3. At sea
4. Malaga
5. at sea
6. Barcelona
7. Ajaccio, Spain
8. Naples
9. at sea
10. Sarande, Albania – Tender pier
11. Dubrovnik, Croatia
12. Zadar, Croatia
13. Venice, Italy – over night
14. Venice

All these ports can be seen on the Doris Visits YouTube channel. Just type Doris Visits then the port. Doris Visits Lisbon etc.

CAST LIST

St Vincent
Commander Kieron Philips
Georgie
Bedriška Kossoff (5th Directorate KGB – artistic affairs)
Ryan (gardener) and team.
Sylvia Cardinal (estate agent)
Nun, sister

Miami
Hunter Witowski
Izzy – Journalism student
Croc (Winston Crocket) – IT student
Macey – art student
Jenny-E – TV News reporter with WBX25
Cameraman (normally Dennis)
Wild Mary
Stan
Ron Stone - Bank Manager
Isaiah Success – Bank Guard

CRUISE SHIP LAUNDRY WARS

Big Dog (and crew)
Sigmund Pervoye Henkel

MIAMI – CRUISE HQ – The employers
Bjorn Ironside – Executive
Chet Dean – Executive
Diana Mond – Executive assistant
Frank Pincer – Senior Executive
Marty Kaye – Senior Executive

PAST SHIP
Jacob Augusto - Head of Security on old ship
TJ - Fork Lift driver – old ship

MS Magi Myrrh
Captain Martyn Fox – Myrrh
Maxwell Silver – Head of Security
Paul Lopkey – returning entertainer
Gwen and Bert Randolph small time criminals & secret shoppers from.
Micky – Laundry Manager
Oona Mee – Laundry Supervisor
Prisha Nah (brother Bukka Nah)
James Morrison - Hotel Manager (Myrrh)
Elizabeth Archer – Human Resources
Manuel Martinez – Comedy Magician
Gerry – Company singer
Mercy Longgrain – guest, seen him before.

Barcelona
Dolors Lopez - Nurse (female) Hospital hit squad
Raimon Russi - Nurse (male) Hospital hit squad

Corsica
Jean-Marc Bozzretti - Corsica Hitman 1
Corsica Hitman 2
Corsica Hitman 3

Naples
Cab Driver, Naples Hitman

THE TEAM

Stuart St Paul's first published works were all screenplays. He is an award-winning director and movie screenwriter having worked on his own projects for Universal Pictures and Icon and been a team member on projects for all the majors from HBO to the BBC, who trained him back in 1973.

As well as major movies like Bond, Aliens, Sherlock Holmes (both) and Robin Hood Prince of Thieves, Stuart created the plane crash for Emmerdale and remained an advisor for 26 years.

He lives in North London with his wife Jean Heard who he met in the theatre in 1978.

His daughter Laura Aikman and son-in-law Matt Kennard (actors), as well as his son Luke Aikman, his wife Dawn and granddaughter Heidi and grandson Dexter all live nearby.

Jean Heard is the main presenter for the cruise port guides on the Doris Visits YouTube channel
www.YouTube.com/DorisVisits
and the 'Doris Visits' web site
www.DorisVisits.com.

She is an actress with West End theatre credits. She performs a one-woman show on Royal Mistresses such as Nel Gwynne on many of the ships. Having played on the theatre in the Aurora when docked in New York, she has technically played Broadway (the definition of on-Broadway is a NY theatre of over 500 seats).

Both have cruised once or twice. But, no one can ever be an expert, just enjoy it.

Thanks to my Laura Aikman, for always reading my drafts and giving honest feedback. Due to work, playing Sonia in the 2019 Christmas special of Gavin and Stacey. She joined this book for a second edition. As a result, it became 30 pages lighter!

Stuart on David, "I have yet to meet David Withington. Well, we did meet after one of my guest talks on a ship; but in the hundreds that fill a ship's theatre, sadly my old memory is such that I can't remember everyone. However, as he runs the online cruise resource 'How To Cruise' he contacted me and a relationship was formed between his site and Cruise Doris Visits. I asked him to read my first book, Cruise Ship Heist, and then the second. I did not know he was a well-respected script editor amongst his many talents.

Considering your **FIRST CRUISE**?
Check out my
HOW to CRUISE
Website & Blog   HowToCruise.co.uk

We are now great pen friends and I hope David will remain an editor of the CSCI books and a firm member or the team."

Other books by the author

Printed in Great Britain
by Amazon